THE WALL

A Psychological Thriller

I. C. COSMOS

Copyright © 2019 ICTX Enterprises LLC

All rights reserved. No part of this book may be reproduced in any form or by any electronic or mechanical means, including information storage and retrieval systems, without written permission from the author, except in the case of a reviewer, who may quote brief passages embodied in critical articles or in a review.

Trademarked names appear throughout this book. Rather than use a trademark symbol with every occurrence of a trademarked name, names are used in an editorial fashion, with no intention of infringement of the respective owner's trademark.

This is a work of fiction. The characters, names, places, and events either are the product of the author's imagination or are used fictitiously. Any similarity to real persons, living or dead, is coincidental and not intended by the author.

The publisher is not responsible for websites (or their content) that are not owned by the publisher.

ICTX Enterprises LLC
101 E McKinney St., #234, Denton, TX 76201-4255
support@ictxenterprises.com

www.iccosmos.com

First paperback edition: June 2019

ISBN-13: 978-1-7330918-0-0 (e-book)
ISBN-13: 978-1-7330918-1-7 (paperback)

Cover design by Steve, GFX-1

To C, without whom The Wall would never have happened

Prologue

I bolt upright in my bed, startled. Did I scream? I hold my breath and listen intently. Nothing moves. Protected by darkness, I slowly lean on my pillow and linger in the sweet realization that the nightmare wasn't real. I am OK.

Then reality hits.

I am not OK. My life is falling apart. Fast.

Looking in from the outside, I am still living my dream. I have a loving husband, wonderful home, thriving business, recognition, prestige. I love my job. It's not merely a job, it's my passion. Seemingly I have it all. But I don't.

I am trapped in the clutches of a predator.

Nothing prepared me for this. Nothing. No warning, no signs telling me 'run away as fast as you can and never look back.' Nothing I could see.

Because I never tangoed with evil before.

I had no idea how it grabs you, spins you, trips you, and then blames you for the faux pas. How it hustles you to get back in step. You strain yourself to give it your best, but this is not the tango you know. The rhythm is off, the steps make no sense. You feel ill at ease, want to stop, but can't. You are trapped by an uncontrollable force that doesn't let you go. It swirls and twists and turns. When you expect it the least, it throws you high in the air and disappears.

Bewildered, you hope to never dance with it again. But as soon as you've regained your balance, it rushes back and tackles you to the ground. It bends over you, you are looking at it but don't see it. Until its hellish breath scorches you.

Is it too late then?

I shiver. I am familiar with the macabre dance steps now. The pattern was there all along, hidden, invisible to the uninitiated. It plays hide and seek with me. When it's out of sight, I question its existence. "Do I worry too much?" I ask. "This can't be so bad…surely it will pass," I try to calm myself. But I've seen the writing on the wall.

The predator is real.

The trespassing is real, the brutal scratches on my new Alfa Romeo Giulia are real, and so are the attacks on me and my marriage. The false accusations are real too. They are not true but have real consequences.

The predator has poisoned my life. The toxins are spreading ferociously, leaving paralysis and devastation in their wake. I am on constant alert, desperately trying to stay ahead.

But the predator is closing in on me. My life is on the line. Time is running out.

"What doesn't kill you makes you stronger," I remind myself. But I have yet to find out how this can make me stronger.

Because right now it's killing me.

Part 1

"I say, follow your bliss and don't be afraid."

Joseph Campbell

Montreal, Canada

The outdoor patio of Café St. Lawrence
September 8

"One lovely New Zealand Marlborough," the waiter said as he put down my wine and moved to the next table, skillfully dodging a group of cheerful newcomers looking for a spot on the patio.

I took a sip of the crisp sauvignon blanc, sat back, and let the sunrays caress my face. Tiny beads formed on the cold glass and sparkled like diamonds. I couldn't remember the last time I gave myself a free Friday afternoon. Or any afternoon.

I planned to spend the whole weekend researching my new Dubai gig, but this afternoon was mine. No demanding clients. No pressing deadlines. Just joy.

The sounds of clinking glasses and happy chatter floated through the air as the patio filled with people enjoying the last days of Indian summer. I never felt so jubilant and content. And grateful.

I pulled the glossy out of my bag. The cover said it all:

Architecture's First Couple

A picture of Jack and me in the SKY Club filled the whole front cover. The caption below invited readers to discover

The Modern Magic of Jack Carter and Alexandra Demarchelier

I flipped through the pages to the section that described SKY's design as the "perfect marriage of Carter's masculine lines and Demarchelier's artistic touch."

Bliss.

I took another delightful sip of wine. Ahhh. If I could fly, this is how it would feel.

All the blood, sweat, and tears paid off. I was on the radar. Getting the SKY job and making the cover of the prestigious glossy was my ticket to the top. Clients I could only dream of a week ago were lining up to work with me. But all I could think about when I looked at the cover was the kiss.

The kiss changed everything.

The kiss divided my life into before and after. It became my lodestar, my constant companion. All it took was to lower my eyelids and the kiss would replay itself like a movie on demand and transport me to the sunny morning in the Montreal Centre a few weeks ago, when Jack and I had finally met in person:

Jack's boyish smile caresses my heart as we step into the elevator. I touch the SKY Club button and the door panels slide shut, leaving the outside world behind. My world switches to slo-mo. Jack steps towards me and takes me in his arms. His masculine touch and woody scent sweep me off my feet. I close my eyes. Our lips brush tentatively, touch, and then take firm hold. Our bodies connect, feeling eternally familiar. I let myself soar on waves of delight. Nothing else exists, only the two of us melting into one.

The elevator stops as smoothly as it took off. The door panels open, revealing a breathtaking panorama. Montreal is at our feet, spreading before us as far as the eye can see.

"Ready for the photo shoot, Alex?" Jack asks in his rich baritone. We look at each other and break into laughter, like two kids doing something they shouldn't.

"Would you like something else?" the waiter asked, interrupting my reverie.

"No. Thank you." I shook my head. The kiss still lingered on my lips. Daydreaming with real consequences...

The kiss catapulted us to heights we hadn't dared dream of. After months of emailing, video chatting, texting, and sexting, Jack and I'd entered the elevator in the lobby of the Montreal Centre as two professionals fond of each other. We'd stepped out into the SKY as a couple.

We'd flown through the photo shoot in no time, feeling like we had been together for ages. Jack's joviality put everyone at ease, and we all but forgot about the photographer as we walked through the SKY, inspecting features we'd only emailed about before, high on our passion for design,

THE WALL

awed by finding each other. Our incredible closeness left us yearning for more.

I put the glossy on the table, my heart swollen with longing. The cover unfolded and revealed the full lengths of SKY's all-glass bar with sweeping views of Old Montreal and the St. Lawrence river. Exotic plants and free-flying butterflies breathed life into the glass and steel structure. Jack and I stood next to a lush ficus tree, smiling, emanating that relaxed, in-the-right-place-at-the-right-time attitude. A large blue butterfly perched on my shoulder like an exquisite brooch. I'd never looked so confident before. It was my best picture ever. Even my unruly auburn hair had fallen in place for this photo shoot.

My phone chimed. A text from Jack.

JACK: *What are you up to, sunshine?*

ME: *Enjoying sunshine :-)*

JACK: *I want to be there with you.*

ME: *Wish you were.*

JACK: *Want to be with you forever.*

I swallowed hard. My heart wanted to gallop to Jack's arms. "Hold your horses!" my brain screamed.

A little white cloud slid in front of the sun.

I shivered.

Montreal

The outdoor patio of Café St. Lawrence

Two tall women looking like identical twins entered the patio and sat at the table next to me. The same blue jeans, white shirts, leather bags, long blonde hair. They loudly ordered IPAs and went on talking about their mass communication class as if no one else was around.

Intrigued, I looked at them from the corner of my eye. The women weren't so identical after all. One leaned back, observing the patio with soft, dreamy eyes. Her twin was sharp as a tack. Images of their living rooms appeared in front of my eyes. That's my professional quirk. My ballet dancer friend Natasha sees dance choreography every time she hears music. I see sketches of interiors every time I take a good look at someone.

The twins switched from the content of their class to a more exciting subject: the professor.

"He eyes the redhead in the first row all the time."

"Because she asks stupid questions all the time."

My phone chimed again.

JACK: *Sunshine, are you there?*

"Tell him you miss him," my heart urged. I hesitated, although I didn't want anything more than to be with Jack. I longed for the familiar closeness we had since our first emails.

I reread the emails many times, but there was nothing special about them. Just plain business talk. It wasn't in the words. It was in the inexplicable magic that had sparked between the lines and ignited attraction we both craved but had given up hoping for.

In no time we'd been connecting several times per day. Talking business, sharing our life stories, discussing our daily events. We started our days texting and we ended our days texting. With the exception of physical contact, we became closer than many a married couple.

Our friendship gave me wings. I became supercharged. Vibrant. Bursting with ideas. Happy to work even with the most difficult clients and make them laugh. I was in love and felt loved as never before.

And then the kiss jolted us out of our cyber-bubble. We both wanted more, but could our virtual paradise withstand the test of everyday reality?

The day of reckoning was coming fast. Jack and I were scheduled to attend an event hosted by Jack's firm in Dallas. I pictured the two of us giving a workshop. Jack looking sharp in his suit, entertaining the audience, making the concepts easy to grasp. I saw myself sharing my part of the story and enjoying every minute of it because I knew that afterward it will be just Jack and I. Exploring. Taking *the kiss* to the next level.

I wanted Jack. Badly. My every cell yearned for him. But...

Maybe I should skip Dallas and go to Dubai instead. My new Dubai clients would be delighted because they wanted to start their project yesterday.

Dubai or Dallas?

The waiter delivered my neighbors' beers and temporarily silenced their chatter.

When he left the dreamer-twin asked: "Is sexting a fling?"

Her slouched shoulders and anguished eyes told a story I was only too familiar with. Because it was the specter of Jack's estranged wife Vivien that held me back from pursuing our love.

Thinking about Vivien kept me awake at night. Jack had assured me that their marriage was over and they lived separate lives. Vivien's Facebook wall confirmed it. I'd scrolled as far down as I could, through more than a year's worth of Vivien's selfies, Vivien posing with friends, in restaurants, at parties. Hundreds of pictures on display for everyone to see, but not one of them of Jack. As if he didn't exist.

Yet, I hesitated. I'd learned the hard way what it's like to be cheated on and didn't want to do that to someone else.

I took a deep breath and let my fingers compose a text to Jack.

ME: *Is sexting a fling?*
JACK: *Not in our case.*
Jack replied within seconds and immediately sent another text.
JACK: *I have big news <3 :-)*
ME: *Tell me.*
JACK: *I moved out. Am divorcing Vivien.*

My heart jumped up and down in a joyful tap dance. "It's too good to be true," a little voice whispered. I dismissed it.

ME: *Oh Jack... Darling, I don't know what to say.*

It was the truth. I was speechless. The weight of the Dallas vs. Dubai decision lifted off my shoulders. Only then I allowed myself to feel how much I longed for this. How much I hoped that Jack and I got a fair chance. Just the two of us, without a third person being part of the equation. I rejoiced, on cloud nine.

"Don't get too excited! Maybe it was only that one kiss and that's all there is to it," my brain yelled, trying to bring me down to earth. My heart wasn't buying it.

I loved Jack.

I loved Jack too much to be his mistress. It was either everything or nothing.

Dubai, United Arab Emirates

TNO offices
September 12, morning

Perry Lowell dropped his Ferrari 812 at the valet station and strolled through the lavish garden to the koi pond.

"Hi guys," he called and crouched down. The water splashed as the koi lined up for their morning treat.

"Hey, no pushing Mr. Goldfinger," Perry laughed and let the koi snatch pellets from his hand.

Perry stretched and followed the pond to a lift shaded by palm trees. He winked into the hidden camera. The sleek door silently opened and just as silently closed behind him. The lift had no visible controls but recognized Perry and knew where to take him, exactly as Perry had programmed it. He soared above the majestic palms and the surrounding buildings.

Being propelled into the sky was Perry's favorite part of the morning. When he stepped into the vast space that served as his office, Perry was ready to conquer any challenge. Not even the sky was the limit.

Building our flagship tower right here in this place is one of the best things Mo and I have done together, Perry thought.

"Hey Perry, got a new project. You'll love it. Come over anytime." Mo's face grinned from Perry's message screen.

"On my way," Perry said, his curiosity piqued. Being in business with Mo was a never-ending adventure. They co-founded TNO, The New Oil, an online marketing firm, when they were still at SMU in Dallas. They had met in a class on strategic planning, two loners friendly with everyone but not belonging to any of the tight groups.

"Are you going somewhere for the holidays?" Mo had asked during a particularly useless lecture.

"I've never been to California." Perry surprised himself by sharing a fleeting idea.

"It's great."

"You want to go with me?"

"Sure, but I have to get the travel money approved," Mo replied.

Perry did a double take. Mo lived in a downtown condo and drove a Lamborghini. Everyone thought he had access to an endless flow of Dubai oil money.

"Don't worry about that. You'll be my guest," Perry offered, getting excited about the trip.

"You don't have to ask for permission?"

"No. I've earned the money myself."

"How?" Mo asked eagerly.

"Online."

"Online?"

"Yeah. Online. That's the new oil." Perry grinned.

"Will you teach me?"

"Sure." TNO was born.

Their second venture at SMU had been TNO Domotics, designing smart home automation. After graduating, Mo had moved back to Dubai and convinced Perry to join him.

Taking advantage of Dubai's entrepreneurial climate and Mo's family's connections, Mo and Perry expanded TNO Holding to a multibillion-dollar empire comprising a broad range of local and global investments. Their next target was the hotel business. Perry assumed Mo found an exciting way to enter it and couldn't wait to share the news.

Series of doors recognized Perry and opened automatically as he walked to Mo's suite. Mo jumped up from his desk as soon as he saw Perry, eyes sparkling mischievously.

"Guess what I am going to do?"

"I am putting a falcon aviary on the top of my new penthouse," Mo said without waiting for Perry's answer. "Imagine! My falcons flying above my penthouse."

"Awesome!" Perry got drawn into Mo's enthusiasm, knowing how much Mo loved his falcons. Perry was not a falconer himself, but he loved driving through the desert with Mo, the falcons flying behind them.

"Have you seen this?" Mo projected a picture of a rooftop bar and garden on the wall. Jack Carter with a stunning woman on his arm dominated the middle of the picture. A blue butterfly adorned the woman's shoulder like an exquisite brooch. Perry scrutinized the picture, mesmerized. Those eyes...

What is she doing with that jackass? Perry's face fell.

THE WALL

Mo looked at Perry and chuckled.

"Don't worry, bro. We are not going to work with Jack," he said reassuringly. "We promised that to each other, remember?"

"We will never ever work with Jack Carter or any other jackass again," Perry recited their oath. The memory took him back to Dallas. And from there back to Houston. Those eyes…

"So, since we are not working with him, why are we looking at him?" Perry regained his composure.

"We are not looking at him, we are looking at her."

"Who is she?"

"Alex Demarchelier. She designed the butterfly garden. It was supposed to be a bird garden, but the insurance company that owns the place nixed the idea. Stupid if you ask me."

"Not if you look down and see droppings in your martini."

"Yeah, right." Mo laughed. "Anyhow, Alex came up with the butterflies. And now she is going to work with us on the falcon aviary."

"Do you have more pics of the garden?" Perry asked.

"Sure. Actually, they call it the SKY Club." Mo clicked through several more pictures.

"Well done," Perry approved.

"Yes. Nothing like having your favorite drink while enjoying the panoramic view with your favorite person."

"And there is more." Mo stopped for effect. "I also hired Alex to do the kitchen in my new penthouse. Maybe the bathrooms, too. Have you seen her kitchen designs?"

"No."

"Let me show you."

"This is her Stardust." A room washed in a smoky golden glow illuminated the wall. It looked more like a glamorous meeting place than a kitchen.

"Whoa!" Perry stepped closer to study the details. Colors, textures, and fixtures took him in and tempted him to explore more and discover something he missed the first time around. Perry loved the playfulness of the design. As if all the features came together like a symphonic orchestra playing a magical concerto. Alex got his full attention.

"I know, I know. She could use more of your domotics," Mo anticipated.

"Maybe. But I love it," Perry said quietly. "Why don't you hire her to do the whole penthouse?"

"I would. But she is fully booked. It will take some shuffling to fit in our jobs as it is."

Perry took a few steps back, still studying the kitchen.

The idea of Alex being in Dubai was strangely unnerving.

Dubai

September 12, afternoon

Perry drove aimlessly through Dubai, restless but unable to pinpoint the source of his agitation. As if a blanket of thick fog covered his mind. His mood was darkening by the minute. He passed the Jumeirah Mosque and continued on to the Burj Al Arab, one of the most luxurious hotels in the world and his favorite place in Dubai.

Perry was fascinated by the ultramodern skyscrapers around the city. He admired their sparkling lightness belying the strength of steel and applauded their audacity to escape seemingly inescapable limits. But he loved the Burj Al Arab.

Being raised in the Regent Hotel in Houston, Texas, Perry felt at home in any hotel he visited. Yet, the Burj made him happy in ways he never quite understood. He dropped off his Ferrari, let his eyes rest on the magic colors of the sky-high atrium, and immediately calmed down.

He automatically scanned the conference board. Marine biology. Dentistry. Annual meeting of the DFC Bank. Nothing he would particularly want to attend, except perhaps a couple of marine biology talks.

The main business of "his" hotel in Houston, congresses had captivated Perry for as far back as he could remember. Since his early teens he'd sneak into sessions, listen to professors, doctors, judges, researchers, and engineers, and daydream about having their jobs, longing to be a neurosurgeon or an architect.

In the summer before Perry's senior year in high school, the Regent hosted its first internet marketing conference, which was a life-changing event for Perry. He didn't have to dream about being an online marketer, he could start right away. He'd connected with several speakers willing to help him, immediately applied what he'd learned in their talks, and spent every free minute online until he'd cracked the code.

Deep in thought, Perry took the elevator to the twenty-seventh floor bar. He sat down at his favorite table and squinted so that he saw nothing else but the glistening waves of the Persian Gulf.

The picture of Alex and Jack was ingrained in his memory.

The years had treated Jack well. Tall, solidly built, he retained his boyish handsomeness. And Alex... *Lexi*, Perry decided to call her. Tall, elegant. And the loving eyes... Jack and Alex looked so in tune with each other. The harmony between them, the ease of their pose, and their radiance screamed intimate closeness. But Perry's searches came up empty. Not a shred of evidence that their partnership went beyond work. Not even a rumor.

Perry pictured himself standing next to Lexi. The image became alive, Lexi turning to him and whispering something in his ear. She had to stand on her toes to get closer. Perry bending his head to listen to her, his sandy hair brushing her sun-kissed cheek, sending a wave of tingles through him.

Perry allowed himself to linger in the happy image for a few moments, then took out his phone and searched some more. Lexi was single. Jack was still married to his wife Vivien, a Dallas disaster.

What's Lexi doing with Jack Carter? he wondered. *Why is she working with the phony bastard?* Even his designs weren't his. He stole them in broad daylight. Perry and Mo had learned that the hard way. At the end of their junior year in college, they won a contest to work with Jack at his firm Carter & Co. But Jack was too busy and teamed them with his son Victor, who was fun to be with, but was nothing more than a college freshman interested in partying more than architecture. Perry and Mo spent the whole summer working on their domotics design, but in the end Carter & Co had taken over the project without giving them any credit.

Perry wanted to protect Lexi.

He took a deep breath as his mind jumped back to Houston.

"Never trust anyone, Perry. Only yourself." Deep, loving eyes cautioning him in the evening before the accident.

She didn't trust even me, Perry thought bitterly. Why? Did she try to protect him? Keep him out of the whole bloody mess?

The fact was, she couldn't protect herself. Her life had been brutally taken in a hit and run accident, a week before Perry's high school graduation, just when he'd broken through online. Perry's fingers rolled into fists.

Had *they* ordered it?

Perry gazed at the waves of the Gulf, aching for answers. *I can't run away from this anymore,* he made up his mind. *I have to go back and find her killers.*

Not wasting a minute, Perry booked a flight to Houston.

Dallas, Texas

The Art Tower
September 15

Excitement. Expectation. Exploitation. Vivien arrived at the Art Tower fueled by this high-octane trio. She had only two vodka shots while getting ready for the party, but she would have been high as the sky even if she hadn't had any.

Vivien assessed the cars in front of her, all waiting to get into the garage. She tried to pull out and bypass them, but no one let her merge into the left lane. *People have no manners anymore.* Vivien shifted impatiently in her seat, ready to rock.

It will be the event of the year. An event with a triumphant twist. Vivien giggled. Not being invited elevated the party to the most desirable category. Crashing a party was such a *thrill!* Gloriously *bad.* Vivien giggled again, cheeks pink.

Too bad the event was at the Art Tower. Vivien wrinkled her nose. All that glass and steel and brightness. How could anyone like it? All Jack's skyscrapers were like that. *Ridiculous.*

Vivien pulled into the parking garage. The gate arm at the entrance failed to rise. She drove angrily forward until the arm nearly touched the windshield of her Lexus. Nothing. She hit the horn with her fist and rolled down her window.

"What's taking so long?" Vivien hollered, her voice bouncing around the cavernous space.

Two cars drove swiftly past her through the gate to her right. Vivien wanted to back up and switch lanes but was blocked by the line of cars behind her. She hit the horn again and kept it going. A security guard sauntered towards the gate.

"Open the gate for Christ's sake!" she barked before the guard could say anything.

"What's the purpose of your visit?"

THE WALL

"I am Mrs. Carter. I don't have time for this because I am expected at the party. Open the gate."

The guard nodded and punched a few keys on his handheld device.

"OK, Mrs. Carter. Park your car and take the Sky Gondola to the fifty-third floor. Let me get your parking card. You'll need it to exit the Tower. Here." Vivien snatched the card and tossed it on the dashboard.

The gate jumped up. Taking off as if she were in a Formula One race, Vivien barely missed the guard's feet.

Sky Gondola.

Vivien rolled her eyes. Who would ever call an elevator a Sky Gondola? As if they were on a freaking mountain peak.

She circled around the garage, but all the prime parking spots were taken. A stab of displeasure briefly assailed her, but Vivien dismissed it without a thought. Nothing could dampen her excitement. She was going to bring the fabulous Alex to her knees. Vivien smirked. She was at the top of her game.

Because she *knew*. Knowing about Jack's each and every move while he stayed completely in the dark filled Vivien with orgasmic ecstasy. *Knowledge is power.*

She couldn't wait to surprise them at the party:

"Hi, so great to meet you." She'll beam and hug Alex.

Then she'll put her arm around Jack and throw in a few intimacies Alex emailed him in confidence.

"I am so sorry to hear about your fiancé. To discover him in your own bedroom with your best friend. Horrible. No woman should ever have to go through that."

Watching Alex's face fall would be priceless. Vivien giggled.

To seal her victory, Vivien would hold on to Jack and not let go of him till the party is over.

The anticipation of seeing Alex go from surprise to discomfort to intense misery filled Vivien with pleasure and pride. And she wasn't even done yet. The best part would be capitalizing on Jack's guilt. Triumphant glow animated Vivien's face. *I will play his guilt like a violin.*

A sigh escaped Vivien's plump lips as she entered the elevator. It was a glass contraption riding on the edge of the building, offering a vertical tour of the Art District. A glass bullet that shot up, blurred the lights outside, and made Vivien nauseous.

She made a quick stop in the powder room to steady herself. She was about to leave her booth when two exuberant voices entered.

"I absolutely love the butterflies." Vivien shrugged, instantly recognizing Hannah, Jack's assistant. Vivien couldn't stand Hannah. Hannah asked too many questions.

"I love the butterflies too," the other woman said in French accent. *It must be Alex.* "We wanted to have small birds flying free up there, but NorthAlliance Insurance didn't allow it. But I guess the butterflies are better, after all. They don't poop on you."

"Bird poop brings good luck."

"I should've known that before," Alex laughed. "NorthAlliance was afraid that people wouldn't sign their contracts if a bird pooped on them."

"Is that what they use the SKY Club for? Getting contracts signed?"

"Yeah. Mega deals. That was the assignment—create a place where people feel like they are on the top of the world. As in having the best of the best. Being on the cutting edge but at the same time feeling absolutely safe. Like belonging to a club where nothing bad can happen to you. That's why we put the trees there. You know, a tree as a symbol of enduring growth and strength and protection."

"Brilliant. Should have put a snake or two there too, to make the mega-dealers feel like they are in paradise."

Giggles resonated through the room.

Vivien's cheeks blushed with excitement. She knew nothing about the SKY Club, but she planned for an opportunity to spread a rumor that Alex put live snakes in someone's boardroom. No, bedroom. Bedroom was much better.

"By the way, have you met Jack's wife yet?" Hannah's sudden change of subject pinned Vivien to the toilet seat.

"No."

"You are in for a treat." Hannah lowered her voice conspiratorially.

"Oh?"

"She just hangs on Facebook the whole day. Architecture is a dirty word for her. Nobody knows why Jack stays with her."

"Really?"

Awkward silence filled the room.

"Hm...perhaps the sex is good, no?" Hannah added as an afterthought.

Both Alex and Hannah burst into laughter.

The Art Tower

Fifty-third floor powder room
September 15

Vivien envisioned emerging dramatically from the booth, putting the two gossiping women in their place and sauntering past them as if they didn't exist. But their laughter rippled through her like a poison and paralyzed her head to toe. Vivien's knees were shaking, her legs unable to move. She could not leave the booth now even if she wanted to.

The designer toilet seat disagreed. Its high esthetics notwithstanding, it cut into Vivien's thighs and gave her intense pain. She shifted, but the pain only became worse. She had no choice but to stand up. Her right leg had fallen asleep and Vivien nearly fell down.

Dark fury lifted her up.

She will make Jack pay for this.

When she heard the women exit, Vivien limped to the giant sink. Her deflated image repeated itself infinitely in the 360-degree mirrors. Vivien's dark fury did a full 360 and became a shade darker.

Her dress had been so sexy when she bought it, but now it looked baggy. Her hair had lost its bounce. Vivien raised her hands to fluff the listless strands. The mirrors reflected rolls of flesh spilling over the band of Vivien's bra, which carved a grand canyon in her back.

Something must be wrong with the mirrors, Vivien concluded. She hated this place. She had nothing to seek here. The party wasn't worth the trouble.

She stormed out of the powder room and nearly bumped into a waiter carrying a platter with champagne. She snatched a glass from the tray. *Why not?* Vivien emptied the flute in two quick gulps, the bubbles rising up her nose. A wave of fresh strength pulsed through her veins.

She signaled the waiter before he walked away, grabbed another golden flute, and emptied it as quickly as the first one.

Marty, Vivien's go-to guy at Carter & Co, emerged from the horrendous Gondola.

"Vivien! How are you, hon?" Marty gave one of his rare bright grins.

"Oh…a bit under the weather lately." Vivien raised her shoulders and let them fall down limply while putting on her best be-sorry-for-me smile.

"Well, let's get you a drink and cheer you up." Marty put his hand on Vivien's arm.

"Oh, why not?" Lower lip quivering, Vivien gave a tiny hopeful smile. And then she slowly, demurely tilted her head, beaming inside. Marty didn't disappoint. Reassured that her powers were intact, Vivien was ready for the event.

Vivien defied reality.

The Art Tower

Trinity room
September 15

"Can you imagine, Alex? Everything's super perfect. State-of-the-art. Exactly as she wanted it." Bobby Jones gesticulated to emphasize his point. Bobby and I had collaborated on a luxurious spa on Long Island a few years ago, and it was an unexpected pleasure to run into him at Jack's party. Bobby shook his head and went on with his story about a remodel for his last client, the horrendous heiress.

"We were waiting for the sofas. Ultramodern. Handmade in Italy. It had taken forever to get the design right. You wouldn't believe how many changes she'd put us through." Bobby rolled his eyes.

"So the sofas finally arrive at JFK, we bring them in, and the place looks like a dream. Fa-bu-lous. The photo shoot is scheduled, we are ready to rock 'n' roll and guess what? She strolls in," Bobby imitated tiny steps on high heels, "looks around and says 'Take it all out. This isn't me. I want the Polar Bear sofas.' Turns on her heels and marches out."

"As in Ours Polaire? The Boule sofas?" My eyebrows shot up.

"Yep. Do you believe it?"

"Well," I chuckled, not surprised. The Polar Bear sofas were rare and thus popular among the rich and famous. "Are you getting them?"

"Yep." Bobby put on a sad bulldog face.

"How much are they going for these days? Half a million apiece?"

"That was couple weeks ago, love." Bobby laughed. "Their price has skyrocketed since the word got out that the heiress is in the market. We are talking $750,000 per sofa now."

"Holy cow!"

"Well, money is no object. The problem is that these sofas are ancient. They will look ridiculous in that space and ruin everything." Bobby sighed.

"Why does she want them there?"

"Because everyone has them, she said."

"I don't have them." A vaguely familiar man in a perfectly fitting suit joined us.

"How are ya, Rich?" Bobby gave Rich a pat on the back. "You two know each other?" Bobby looked at us and concluded that we didn't.

"Alex, this is Richard Howard, Senator Richard Howard."

"Alex Demarchelier."

"Alex, pleasure." Richard bowed his head slightly. Solid handshake, friendly eye contact. The pieces fell together. Richard's wife Liz was on my list of people to meet. Excellent.

"Rich likes to champion affordable housing," Bobby explained Richard's presence at the party.

"And my wife goes for the unaffordable kind," Richard said. "Bobby, may I borrow Alex for a second? Liz is dying to meet her. She is over there." Richard waved at an elegant woman on the other side of the room.

"Sure. I'll catch up with you later, Alex. Let's do a job together again." Bobby winked.

"Sure. Looking forward to it," I said and followed Richard, who weaved through a noisy mass of people juggling their drinks and hors d'oeuvres while exchanging the latest gossip. I returned friendly smiles and waves along the way, business as usual, but I felt jittery.

This was Dallas, after all. Jack's territory. I wanted to do well here. The professional end of things went well so far, but the anticipation of my date with Jack unnerved me. The uncertainty of it all... Hannah's remarks about "Jack's wife" took me aback. I assumed that the news of Jack's divorce had reached the office by now.

"Here she is," Richard introduced me to Liz, who met us halfway. A breath of lily of the valley perfume created an oasis of comfort.

"Goodness, this party rocks. You can hardly move." Liz's raspy voice took charge. "Let's go over there." Liz pointed to an emptier area away from the buffet. I immediately liked her.

Our refuge didn't last long. The Howards' popularity drew the crowd like a magnet, and we were soon surrounded by a large group of followers. I wondered where Jack was. I scanned the room and my heart skipped a beat. Jack's CFO walked in with a mousy blonde on his arm. Vivien.

The butterflies in my stomach went into overdrive. Jack had told me Vivien wasn't attending the party!

I continued with the small talk while keeping Vivien in my peripheral vision. She was shorter and heavier than her Facebook pictures

THE WALL

suggested. And didn't move like the imperious woman Jack described to me. I expected someone who commands the attention of the whole room, but the real Vivien entered the party head down, shoulders hunched, dragging her feet ever so slightly, as if her shoes didn't fit. A huge black bag seemed to weigh her down. Strangely, I felt sorry for her.

Vivien and the CFO sat the bar. Vivien appeared more at home there, laughing and flirting. The two of them obviously enjoyed each other's company. *Are they having a fling?* I almost chuckled.

A giant cocktail landed in front of Vivien. She hugged the straw with her plump lips and polished off half of the drink in one sip. Trying not to stare, I turned my attention to the conversation.

"...we use it to understand wind forces on the top floors. You don't want toilet water sloshing out when it storms, for instance," a tall guy was explaining to Liz.

"Really? And here I thought skyscrapers are all about views. This never crossed my mind." Liz was impressed.

"Oh, yeah. You could get motion sickness up there if the design isn't right."

I allowed myself to peek at the bar again. Vivien had a fresh drink in front of her. The CFO was gone.

More people from Carter & Co joined our group. I opened my mouth to chat with Hannah, but the crowd around us parted, making room for Vivien. I froze.

Vivien elbowed her way through, a glass of red wine bobbing in her hand. She stopped in front of Hannah and looked her up and down.

"With your body, you can do better than wearing such a silly dress."

Hannah rolled her eyes and reached for her phone. Vivien giggled like she told the funniest joke ever and scanned the crowd, her gaze stopping on Richard.

"Oooh, Senator Howard. What a pleasure. So glad you came to my party," Vivien cooed and put her hand on Richard's arm. Then she pointed her glass to Liz.

"Goodness, what happened to your hair?"

Liz automatically touched her airy hairdo. Vivien smirked in triumph and then put on a bright smile. "Text me, love. I have this product... Your hair will never go limp again."

I was no longer sorry for Vivien. Liz's face turned into an impenetrable mask. Vivien swayed. I stepped forward but was too late to prevent the catastrophe.

Vivien wobbled, spilling her red wine on Richard's perfect custom-made suit.

"Jeez…" "Oh…" People stepped back, eyes wide open, hands over their mouths.

Jack appeared from nowhere, grasped Vivien's elbow and directed her out of the room.

"Don't you dare touch me." Vivien objected loudly, arms flailing, but her voice drowned in the hubbub of the party.

I fetched a napkin and tried to minimize the damage. "Let me help. Richard, Liz, I am so sorry."

"Not your fault." Liz gave it a try too but stopped after a few dabs, shaking her head. The suit's fate was sealed: "This is a write-off, Richard."

"I wish this was my biggest problem." Richard took off the ruined jacket and rolled up his shirt sleeves. "Let's have our own party, ladies." He steered Liz and me away from the crowd.

My jitters were gone.

Dallas

Vivien's bedroom
September 16

"...nobody knows why Jack stays with her."
"Really? Hm...perhaps the sex is good, no?"
"...nobody knows why Jack stays with her."
"Really? Hm...perhaps the sex is good, no?"
"...nobody knows why Jack stays with her."
"Really? Hm...perhaps the sex is good, no?"
"...nobody knows why Jack stays with her."
"Really? Hm...perhaps the sex is good, no?"
"Hm...perhaps the sex is good, no?"
"...perhaps the sex is good, no?"
"...the sex is good, no?"

The nagging repetitions disrupted Vivien's sleep. "Yes, the sex is good," she agreed, eyes still closed. "But not the sex with Jack." Vivien laughed out loud. And then bit her lip.

A trace of an unpleasant memory bounced off the wrecking ball smashing into her brain. Vivien's eyebrows knotted. What was it? Something about the horrific Gondola. There was vomit everywhere. Jack looking disgusted.

Vivien waved it away. Nothing she should concern herself with. She took three painkillers, turned around and went back to the deep sleep of the innocent.

It was midafternoon when she woke up for the second time. Her headache was gone, but she felt bored. And irritated. Jack was nowhere to be found.

She texted him to come home. No reply.
She called him. No answer.

He must have turned his phone off. Or lost it. It wouldn't be the first time. Nobody was more absentminded than Jack. Vivien snorted.

She got dressed, ready to go out on her own. Normally she limited herself to pursuing her pleasures Monday through Friday, nine to five. Evening and weekend sessions were possible only when Jack traveled. But what's the point of restricting herself? Jack wasn't worth it.

She scrolled through her contacts, selected a name and dialed. The call went to voicemail. Vivien hung up, displeased. This was her favorite PerfectPartner member, promising an evening that would wipe out the irritation caused by Jack. Vivien couldn't imagine what she would do without PerfectPartner, a service for discerning adults. She dialed another number.

"Yes?"

"I will come over in an hour, OK?"

"Not tonight. Call earlier the next time."

Vivien glared at her phone in disbelief. He hung up on her before she could protest and make him change his plans. No manners. Vivien's eyes stopped on another name and moved on. Impossible on Saturday. The senator was a busy man. She kept scrolling, not satisfied with the possibilities. She scrolled back. Why not give the senator a try? She deserved something special. Her pulse sped up in anticipation.

"Hello." Crisp voice exerting control. Excitement swept Vivien off her feet.

"Hi. What if I came along in an hour or so?"

"Hubby out of town?"

"Sort of."

"OK."

Exhilaration kicked in. Vivien shimmied. *Persistence pays.* She fixed herself a double vodka, opened the secret drawer in her dresser and inspected her tools. She didn't need much. His location was fully supplied, but Vivien wanted to be in control.

Satisfied, she headed for the garage. A gasp escaped her mouth. Her car was gone. Confused, Vivien called Jack again. No answer. She slowly remembered that Jack had driven her back home from the party yesterday. In his own car. And did not bring her car back?

Fury swept through her. She opened the garage door and looked outside, expecting to find the car in front of the house. The driveway was empty. She called and texted Jack again. No answer.

Vivien dialed Annabel, her best friend.

"Hi, could you give me a ride? Jack forgot to bring my car back." Vivien turned on her friendliest voice.

THE WALL

"Oh... I am at the Tipsy Alchemist. Sorry, Viv. Why don't you call Uber?" Vivien put the phone down without saying goodbye. *Uber?* Vivien cringed. What's the point of having friends if they don't help you when you need them?

Her ride took forever to arrive and then took even longer to get to the Art Tower. Vivien rushed to her car and sped out of the garage.

The gate didn't open.

She needed her parking card. Where did she put it? Vivien rummaged through her bag, frustration mounting. She emptied the bag on the passenger seat. No parking card.

She pressed the assistance button.

"What's the problem, ma'am?"

"I can't find my card. Open the gate for me!" Vivien ordered, barely controlling her anger.

"I can't do that, ma'am."

"Oh, for God's sake. I am Jack Carter's wife. Let me out of here!" Vivien screamed.

"I may not open the gate unless I know that the Lexus is yours, Mrs. Carter. I'll send someone down."

I'll make Jack pay for this. Vivien was beyond herself when the security officer finally came down.

Ignoring Vivien, he wrote down the license plate number, inspected the paraphernalia spread over the passenger seat, and pointed to a white card on the dashboard.

"Would this be the parking card, ma'am?"

Vivien wanted to scream.

"I'll let you out if you give me the card, ma'am."

Vivien handed him the card without saying a word.

"If I were you, I would pack the bag before driving out, ma'am." Not a muscle moved in his face.

Vivien gave him a second look. Massive shoulders. Chest that would stop a bullet. Square jaw. Hard lips. Anticipation nearly lifted Vivien off her seat. *Is he a Partner?* He nodded slightly. Really? She will have to find out. But not now.

"Thank you. What's your name?"

"You're welcome, Mrs. Carter. Anthony."

Vivien arrived at her destination more than an hour late. She entered the exclusive code provided by PerfectPartner, but the door didn't open.

She tried again and again. The door remained shut. Vivien called the senator. No answer. This has never happened before. But the senator was an important man, there must have been some kind of emergency.

Vivien drove back home in agitated haze.

Jack wasn't there. Why was he so mean to her? And what's all the talk about divorcing her? He couldn't have been serious. Vivien hated to be alone. *Life is so unfair.* Vivien was suffering all on her own while Jack could sext with the slut anytime.

PerfectPartner should have a sexting site. Mmm…a sexting site! The perfect resource! Vivien giggled. She made herself a double vodka and dialed Jack again. No answer. *How dare he.*

An idea rose in Vivien's mind. She turned on her computer and studied Jack's calendar. She smirked. A plan was formed. She'd make Jack pay.

Big.

As always, Vivien defied reality.

Dallas

The Joule Hotel
September 17

I basked in the afterglow of our lovemaking, relishing every second. The best Sunday morning ever. Jack was everything I longed for. My soulmate. The big love that makes the earth move. I wished the weekend would never end.

Jack must have been reading my mind because he kissed my shoulder and asked, "Darling, I was thinking…what if I stay in Montreal with you for a while. Will you have me?"

I was delighted. Of course I'd have him. I wanted to be with Jack forever. But why did he look so sheepish?

"Why wouldn't I have you?" I smiled and caressed Jack's chest, hoping for a playful answer, more kisses and a never-ending weekend bliss.

"Um…because of my entanglement."

Talking about the elephant in the room.

When I'd seen Jack leaving the party with Vivien, I'd assumed our first date was over. Talking business with the Howards kept the disappointment at bay, and by the time they dropped me off at the Joule, I had new friends and an assignment to redesign Richard's Dallas office.

I went to my room bracing myself for a weekend in Dallas on my own, but as soon as I got in, Jack texted that he was on his way up. In no time he was at the door, hugging a bottle of iced champagne, smiling his boyish smile.

"Jack. Are you OK?" I asked.

"I am now."

"And how is…"

"Let this be only about us," he said.

Jack put the bubbly down and took me in his arms. His masculine touch and woody scent triggered alluring deja vu. I closed my eyes. Our lips touched, exploring hungrily. Our bodies connected as if we were together for an eternity. Nothing else existed, just the two of us, touching, feeling, melting into one, soaring on waves of bliss.

"You are my Dream Girl," Jack whispered in my ear afterwards.

I was in seventh heaven.

Jack poured our bubbly and we sipped it slowly as Friday turned to Saturday, luxuriating in our closeness, chatting about the people who were at the party, kissing, exchanging business rumors. I had to search for images of the Polar Bear sofas because Jack had never heard of them, and, as it turned out, didn't need to hear about them again. "Seven hundred fifty thousand dollars per chair? No way!"

Saturday unfolded like a fairytale about us, love, and Dallas. After dinner we'd bought a gigantic Taschen book on penthouses in the Joule's book shop and ended up designing the downtown condo we were planning to buy. Sunday had started on the same bright note.

Until Jack brought his entanglement with Vivien into play.

She called and texted Jack several times since the party, but he turned the sound on his phone off and didn't respond. The agony of loving Jack so deeply and not knowing what was going on between him and Vivien was suffocating me. I needed clarity.

"Well...you are untangling, yes?" I asked softly, looking into Jack's eyes. I needed to hear that the lawyers are negotiating the terms, haggling over silverware, whatever... But Jack's eyes filled with uncertainty and fear. He looked away without saying a word.

My heart tumbled, the silence tormenting me.

"I want to be with you," Jack said finally. "You're my Dream Girl, but it's difficult. For Viv." Jack went on saying how abandoned Viv felt because people go on with their lives and leave her behind. Viv's sister Lauren became a famous actress and moved to L.A., her brother Ted married into a super-rich family and moved to Houston. Jack was all Viv had left, and he too was leaving her. Viv had been so depressed, she had taken some meds, which made her ill at the party.

"I want to give Viv some time to adjust and find her way," Jack said. "I want a peaceful divorce. No dramas. And I want that we have a clean start, darling." Jack looked at me hopefully, his eyes begging for approval.

I took a deep breath. I didn't like this. I thought Vivien lived her own life already and her despicable behavior had a lot to do with alcohol. Her famous sister moved back to Dallas couple years ago. And I was taken aback by the intimacy implied by calling Vivien Viv. But the last thing I wanted was a war with Vivien.

I nodded, more in capitulation than in agreement. Jack visibly relaxed and we went on as if nothing happened, made plans, laughed, booked him on the same flight to Montreal I was on. But an invisible veil of apprehension crept between us.

Vivien entered our relationship.

Houston, Texas

Perry's suite
September 18, early afternoon

Perry studied the dramatic city views from his hotel suite, dispirited. It was his first time back in Houston since she died. He grew up here, but now it felt like a foreign territory. He didn't know what to expect. Or where to begin.

His business operations were complex, yet crystal clear. He was in charge. This was different. He needed answers he had no authority to demand.

Perry took a deep breath and called the valet to get his car. He'll start with Dave, the man who had taken Perry under his wing and raised him as his own when Perry and his mom lived in the Regent. The man who encouraged Perry to pursue his budding business ventures. Who stood by Perry when the accident happened.

Yet, Dave seemed hesitant to meet, Perry reflected as he got in the car. And didn't at all sound like the Dave Perry knew.

Perry's grip on the steering wheel tightened when he entered Dave's neighborhood. *This can't be right.*

"Your destination is on the right," a cheery navigation girl announced. Perry rubbed his chin and double checked the address. It was correct. He got out of the car and walked towards the building.

Concerned, Perry found Dave's apartment. He surveyed the peeling door, failed to locate a bell and knocked. If there was a response, Perry missed it. He tried harder.

"It's open," a cavernous voice directed from inside.

A waft of decay invaded Perry's nostrils. Dave sat slouched on a shabby couch placed in the middle of the dark room. Perry sat next to him, lost for words.

"I will not tell you that you look great, Dave," Perry finally said, his voice barely audible.

"That's my boy."

THE WALL

A tiny spark lit behind Dave's eyes. *Hope?* Perry held on to it.

"I didn't know... I would have... I am sorry I didn't keep in touch," Perry admitted, staring at the floor. The few emails he and Dave exchanged over the years didn't count.

"You kept in touch, son, I didn't tell you what was going on. And you had your life to live."

"What happened?"

Dave put his head down and rubbed his forehead. Not a word came out. Perry waited, motionless.

"I had this headache that would never stop. I thought it was just stress. You know the hotel. Always something. So I was popping painkillers as if they were going out of business. But then the double vision got me. I couldn't do anything."

Perry nodded, encouraging Dave to go on.

"The doc sent me to all kinds of specialists. They had no idea what was going on until someone figured out it's chordoma."

"Chordoma?" Perry wished he could wave a magic wand and make this chordoma monster go away, whatever it was.

"It's a rare type of cancer of the skull."

Perry's heart sagged. "I am sorry, Dave. I am so sorry. What's...what's..."

"The prognosis?"

Perry nodded.

"Not good." Dave shrugged. "And not that bad either. But I don't have the fight in me anymore. I fought like a lion when they removed the first tumor. They got it all out. I've got screws and bolts in my skull, but so what? I thought I'll be A-OK. But then the bastard came back. I fought that one too. And now they discovered a third one. This one's in my spine. I just can't go through it all over again."

"Dave, what's the toughest part of it? You know, the stuff you don't want to fight."

Dave put his head in his hands.

"The system. I can't fight the system anymore."

"What system?" Perry asked, not following.

"Oh, you know. Insurance, banks."

"I'll help you with that."

Dave shook his head slowly, as if protecting the hardware that kept his skull together.

"You don't understand, Perry. I've exhausted all my possibilities." He smiled a tranquil smile of a man who had come to terms with his fate.

"Besides, you are here to talk about Sylvia."

"We'll get to that." Perry jumped up and looked around the apartment. "But we have to get you out of this place first."

Dave put his hands up. "Stop Perry, it makes no sense."

"It makes perfect sense." Perry was unstoppable. "You took care of me and now I'll take care of you."

Perry started to make a list of actions. It was certainly not a mistake to revisit Houston. In fact, he had come back just in time.

"You can stay with me until we get everything sorted out. I have an extra bedroom in my suite. It makes no sense to put it to waste. Let's have surf 'n turf and a bottle of Château Margaux, shall we?" Perry lured Dave with his favorite dinner.

Dave gave in. "Why not? Nothing wrong with going out in style."

Houston

Perry's suite
September 18, evening

Dave swirled the 2009 Margaux and slowly inhaled its seductive aroma. He smiled at Perry. "Dark berries, spice, cherry." He took a small sip and closed his eyes. "Perfection. Sensual silkiness…majestic power…purity and richness. Superbly balanced. This is the best one I've ever had." Dave raised his glass.

This was the Dave Perry remembered.

"To you, Dave." Perry's eyes sparkled with gratitude.

They ate their dinner in Perry's suite, overlooking Houston's bourgeoning skyline.

"Things are surely changing here," Perry remarked.

"Yeah, there is a new skyscraper every time you look."

Perry studied the skyline, wondering what Mom would think about all this. How would she look?

Dave leaned forward. "You miss her a lot, don't you?"

Perry nodded, barely holding back his tears.

"OK, enough of entertaining me. I bet you want to hear about Sylvia."

"I want to find who killed her." Perry looked into Dave's eyes.

"I knew you would come back eventually." Dave nodded. "We are in for a challenge, son."

"I know we don't have the evidence. But just your gut feeling—do you think the Lowells did it?" Perry was hanging on Dave's words. This question was burning a hole through his heart.

Dave took his time to answer.

"I don't know whether they were behind the hit and run. But even if they didn't kill her physically, they surely did it in other ways. In a way they killed both of us."

"What do you mean?" Perry asked, puzzled.

"I loved your mom. I wanted to marry her."

Perry's eyebrows shot up. She never told him that.

"But Sylvia did not want to have a serious relationship. She told me that she came to Houston to find your dad. She'd do anything to make it possible for you to grow up with your real father."

"I don't get it. You were like my real dad all these years, Dave."

"I didn't get it either. I understood it at first. She hoped to find him and get together with him. I got that. But as the years went by, it became clear that it was not going to happen. She found him, but he was married and had two little girls. Didn't respond to any of her letters." Dave looked down, the pain still fresh after all these years.

"Sylvia told me she loved me but couldn't marry me, couldn't do it unless…" Dave stopped mid-sentence. "But I never gave up hope that someday we'd be together. Not until that day," Dave finished gently.

"I am sorry, Dave. I had no idea."

"You see, the Lowells killed her freedom. They took her life away."

Perry's mind went back to the evening before the accident.

"This is important, Perry." Mom had handed him a large envelope, seriousness clouding her face. "Open this only if something happens to me."

"Nothing'll happen to you." Perry wanted to make her laugh, uneasy about her somberness.

"You never know. Never trust anyone, Perry. Only yourself." She hugged Perry and went to her bedroom.

As instructed, Perry opened the envelope the next day. It contained a note confirming Mom's lunch meeting with Senator Win Lowell at the Cafe & Bar across from the Regent. DNA proof that the senator was Perry's biological father. And Mom's diary, in which she recorded how she and Win Lowell fell in love, how he disappeared, how she tried to reconnect with him, how she collected his DNA sample. She had included everything she had learned about the Lowells over the years and a few words of advice: "No matter what you do with the Lowells, always keep in mind that they are dangerous. The Lowells stop at nothing."

Overcome by sadness, Perry pondered Mom's last words to him. "Never trust…" *I surely lived up to it*, Perry suddenly realized. He never trusted anyone, except Dave and Mo. And his mom. Perry trusted her blindly, but should he still live by her 'Never trust anyone' motto?

Perry gazed at the skyline, thinking about what could have been if Mom hadn't rushed to the fatal appointment with his dad all on her own.

"You know what's so strange, Dave?" Perry said.

"Yes, I know. If it weren't for Sylvia's accident, you would have never become Perry Lowell, the mysterious young billionaire for whom not even the sky is the limit."

"I never thought about it this way before," Perry said pensively.

"You always would have been successful, Perry." Dave chuckled, remembering Perry's first business ventures. "You were crushing it before you were ten. Do you remember your concession stand?"

Perry remembered the stand well. Living in the hotel, he had explored every nook and cranny and knew what was happening on every floor. It didn't take him long to notice that people attending conferences were looking for something to grab quickly in the pauses between sessions, but no refreshments were served on their floors.

So Perry filled a large water dispenser with ice-cold lemonade, put it on a borrowed room service cart, and waited for the thirsty audiences as they spilled out from the lecture rooms. The lemonade sold out in no time. Perry added a second lemonade dispenser and diversified to cookies and apples, supplied by his kitchen network. By the time Dave found out about it, the stand became a signature feature of the venue. Not having the heart to shut down Perry's operation, Dave had found a way to legalize it.

"Which group gave us so much trouble? The diet people?" Dave asked.

"The eating disorders people." Perry grinned.

"That's right, you ordered extra brownies for them." Dave laughed, relishing talking about the good old times.

"And ice cream bars. They were crazy about ice cream."

"And your mama went crazy when she learned that you skipped a week of school when they had their congress."

"These people were giving me six point nine times more profit than any other group. They took the stand by storm as soon as the doors opened. I couldn't miss their business. And school was almost over by then," Perry justified himself.

"Alright, alright." Dave put his hands up. "I am just saying you were entrepreneurial from the get-go."

"But I would have never reached this level. I would have been happy with much less if Mom was alive. I would have never gone to Dallas, I would have never met Mo." And I would have a girlfriend and maybe a family, Perry thought sadly. I would have a life.

"Then Mo wouldn't have become a young billionaire prince either."

Perry took a moment to contemplate this. Dave was right, Mo's fortune was linked with the accident as much as Perry's own. *But Mo lives to the fullest and I...* Perry took a deep breath.

"OK, I see that. But Mo has a life," Perry said.

"You have a life, too."

How can I have a life if my dad had something to do with killing my mom? Because of me... The accident had pushed Perry into a bitter cocktail of grief and outrage spiked with nagging what-ifs. It had driven him from Houston to Dallas to Dubai. But there wasn't a place far enough to escape the cruel finality of what happened.

"Dave, I'll have no life unless I find who killed her."

United Arab Emirates

Dubai International Airport
October 4

"How is he?" Perry connected with Houston as soon as his plane touched down.

"He is recovering too fast." Shaun, Dave's nurse, gave a hearty laugh. "Lewis demands that if things go on like this, you'll have to double our salary. We were hired to take care of a patient, not a general."

"I knew you and Lewis were perfect for the job." Perry laughed, relieved that Dave was recovering so well.

Perry and Dave had followed their reunion dinner with a good night's sleep and after that hadn't wasted a minute to consult Dave's doctors, schedule his surgery, rent a penthouse, and hire Shaun and Lewis, Dave's nurses and companions.

Reconnecting with Dave launched Perry into the health care universe. He was impressed by the expertise and unrelenting commitment of Dave's team of doctors. But he was appalled by the health care system. Doctors wasting valuable time fighting an avalanche of paperwork instead of doing their real work. Patients running in circles and wasting hours on arranging even simple procedures. And, the icing on the cake, insurance companies throwing sand into the machine with abandon.

Rarely seeing a problem without wanting to solve it, Perry considered opening a specialized chordoma clinic where doctors can be doctors and patients get their treatment without having to fight the draconian system. He still kept this venture in mind, but discussing it with Dave and his nurses opened Perry's horizons.

"Sounds great." Shaun scratched his jaw. "Every little helps, man. But it's not gonna solve the problem."

"Yeah. The whole system needs overhaul, but in this country…" Lewis sighed.

"Our politicians use health care to get votes, but they don't really care," Dave added.

Perry listened to their heartfelt litany and let it all play in his mind, not saying much. Little by little, like a submarine rising from the depth of the ocean, a plan emerged. Unexpected, amazing, yet totally resonating with Perry's heart.

"OK. I'll do it," Perry said, determination boosting his voice.

"You'll do what?" Dave asked.

"Go into politics. Fight for a better health care system." It made perfect sense to Perry. He achieved more than he ever dreamed of with his business ventures. Now was the time to give back.

"Wow!"

"You get our votes," Lewis had promised, giving Perry a fist bump.

Never doing anything halfway, Perry had spent the flight from Houston planning his transition from a businessman to a politician. As much as committing to politics surprised him, Perry didn't doubt his decision for a second. The inner peace that filled him when the idea came up told Perry that he was on the right track. The questions that brought Perry back to Houston were far from answered, but he didn't mind. He found an answer to a question he hadn't asked: his calling.

Amazing how quickly life can change, Perry mused. But as he worked on his strategy, Perry realized that he had been preparing himself for this move for the last two years already. He had appointed high-level managers to several businesses and delegated more and more responsibilities to them as if he had known that a next chapter of his life loomed on the horizon.

Assured that all was well in Houston, Perry walked through the Dubai airport a new man. The reclusive billionaire was gone, taken over by a rebel with a cause. Giving back, improving the lives of many was the right thing to do.

Eager to take care of his business in Dubai and go back to Houston, Perry rushed towards the airport exit, scrolling through his texts, having no eye for anything going on around him.

~~~

Alex walked to her gate, just a few feet away from Perry. Excited about Dubai and about her new business plans in Dallas, she was texting with Jack and had no eye for anything going on around her.

Neither one of them looked up.

The same place

The same time

Time flies. I couldn't believe I was flying back to Dallas already. The five days in Dubai went by like a dream. So much done in such a short time! Mo's aviary morphed from a vague idea to a solid design of an oasis in the air. His kitchen and bathroom weren't far behind. I was astonished. We had been working nonstop, but still.

I didn't see much of Dubai, but I didn't mind. Doing a project with Mo opened a whole new world to me. Mo lived his life like a marvelous adventure that had to be experienced to the fullest, every second a cherished gift loaded with promise. Working with him was a magic mix of play and laughter and creativity. And hard work. Demanding and effortless at the same time. I loved the ease of it, the results, the satisfaction. I wished I could always generate so much energy on a job.

"How do you stay so positive all the time? How do you do it, Mo?" I asked after a particularly annoying problem nearly sent us back to square one.

"I don't do it. I am like that." Mo beamed.

"Do you ever get angry? You know, red hot furious?"

"Hm." Mo had to think about that. "Yes. But you know, when something bad happens, it's my chance to improve life. I grab it and dance with it."

I wished I met people like Mo earlier in my life.

"Besides, if everything was perfect, life would be boring," Mo added.

Life certainly wasn't boring with him around. And I couldn't wait to meet Mo's partner Perry, who was the brain behind their domotics. I used to subcontract home automation for clients who wanted it, but working with Mo taught me that it can be much more than turning on the oven from your phone.

Like projecting live videos of Mo's beloved falcons on the walls of his living room and bathroom and making it look as if Mo was flying with them.

It inspired me to focus on designs that use state-of-the-art technology to seamlessly merge the inside and the outside. My mind was bursting with ideas.

What should I call this line of business? Inside-Outside was used by too many people already. Inside-Outside in French? Dedans Dehors, DD? Dedans Dehors Domotics, 3D? That existed already. DDD Dallas? Too much. *DD will do for now*, I decided.

A text interrupted my brainstorming.

JACK: *Want to kiss you all over, my Dream Girl.*

ME: *Can't wait.*

Our virtual bubble was back, like in the old days. And in several hours Jack and I would be together, looking for our own place in Dallas. Maybe we could look at houses too, not just condos. A place where we could test the DD concept. Still high on working with Mo, I started to sketch ideas.

My phone chimed again.

JACK: *Love you to the moon and back.*

Happy tears filled my eyes. My life finally came together.

Dallas

The Art Tower
October 5

Jack woke up disoriented, not knowing where he was. It took him several confusing seconds to realize that the siren sounding in his ears wasn't a siren but his phone.

He checked the number. Unknown. At 5:38 a.m.?

"Yes?"

"What took you so long? You've got to help me, you've got to take me, Jack!" Vivien sobbed. "It's Ted. Oh my God, it's my brother." More sobs.

"Vivien, what's going on?"

"It's Ted. There's been a terrible accident. Victor just called me."

"Is Victor OK?" Jack's voice caught. Ever since his twins were born, his heart skipped a beat when an unexpected phone call came in. It made no difference that Victor and Jen were in their twenties now. Jack's fear that something bad happened to them was as strong as ever. Especially Victor had Jack worried more often than not.

"For God's sake, pay attention, Jack!" Vivien shouted. "This has nothing to do with Victor. It's Ted. You've got to drive me to Houston. It's an emergency. We are a family." Vivien's sobs took over.

"What happened, Vivien?"

"I can't drive. I would kill myself. It's just too much. I am shaking so hard I can hardly hold the phone. You've got to drive me."

"Why don't you fly? You can catch a flight from Love Field every hour."

"You don't understand," Vivien squealed. "I need my car. Families help each other."

"Victor can pick you up in Houston."

"He can't. He is there. Jack you've got to help me. I know you are mad at me. But you've got to help me. I need you. Do it for me this one time."

Soft sobs played on Jack's heartstrings. *Vivien needs me.* Jack flipped into rescue mode. His brain shut off. Nothing else existed but his mission.

"I'll pick you up in fifteen."

Halfway to Vivien's house, Jack remembered that Alex was flying in from Dubai later in the morning. A pang of regret jolted him. Jack pulled to the curb. What should he do?

"This is a family emergency!" Vivien's indoctrination instructed him before he could change his mind about Houston. Jack sent a quick text to Alex, messaged his secretary to arrange a limo for her from DFW, and resumed his mission.

Vivien stood in the driveway, the doors of her Lexus opened, the engine running. "Where have you been? Hurry up. We have to go."

"Get in then. Have you got any luggage?" Jack asked. He assumed that he will take Vivien to Houston in his car, turn around and be back in the Joule with Alex in the afternoon.

But Vivien had a different plan.

"I need my car!"

"And I need mine. I am driving you."

"You don't understand. We have no time to repack everything. I never ask you for anything. I need my car!" Vivien threw herself on the side of the Lexus, heartbreaking sobs shaking her body.

Jack wanted to get back to his car and drive away. But he couldn't leave Vivien alone in this state. He would never forgive himself if she drove herself and got into an accident.

I can fly back, Jack concluded and stepped into the Lexus.

Vivien settled in the passenger seat, all her attention devoted to her phone. As if Jack wasn't there. Merciless coldness filled the car.

Jack's heart sank. He wanted to send a long email to Alex but dictating it in front of Vivien was out of the question. He'd phone Alex as soon as he found out what's going on. Jack longed to have Alex next to him. He would give anything to hear her golden bells of laughter and feel her warmth.

When they passed Richland, Jack glanced at Vivien and saw her with the shocking clarity of a man who at a reunion runs into the homecoming queen and for the first time sees her without a dose of youth hormones. A perpetually angry, bitter, shameless woman sat next to him. Jack shuddered. *What happened to us?*

Jack's mind slipped back to the first time he saw Vivien. A bundle of energy, all arms and legs and smiles. Vivien was never classically beautiful, but her insatiable desire to grab life by the horns and live every second to the fullest made her irresistible. Joie de Viv, Jack used to call her.

Jack had met Vivien at her dad's birthday party. Fred Gibson, Vivien's dad, had hired Jack that morning and asked him to come along in the afternoon for a little birthday get together: "We are all family at Gibson Construction." It was Jack's first real job and the invitation meant the world to him.

The Gibsons' residence was bursting with people when Jack arrived, but Vivien connected with him right away. She brought Jack a cold beer and when she found out that this was his first day on the job, she hooked his arm and introduced him to everyone as if he were her best friend. Jack was smitten. He got the job and the boss's daughter, all in one day.

Vivien spent that night with Jack but played hard to get in the following weeks. Until she showed up at Jack's apartment in the middle of the night, disheveled, shaken, her eye swollen. Between sobs she told Jack that her ex-boyfriend abused her. Jack coddled her and took her in for the night. Vivien never left. A few months later she was pregnant. Jack was delighted.

They got married, but the promise of the deep connection Jack felt when they first met never became reality. Their marriage went from bad to worse and they nearly broke up when Jack left Gibson Construction for Russo & Russo, a renowned architectural firm downtown. Jack didn't understand it. It was no secret that his ambition went beyond Gibson Construction. Jack had dreamed about designing skyscrapers since he was a boy and Vivien embraced his dream with a verve that surprised even him. She collected pictures of famous skyscrapers and couldn't stop talking about all the things they'd do and the places they'd visit when Jack made it. All that stopped when Jack joined Russo & Russo.

"You betrayed Daddy," Vivien accused Jack. "I'll never forgive you."

And she didn't. The twins and Jack's huge raise kept them together, but no matter how hard Jack tried to please Vivien, the closeness he longed for never came.

I don't know her. She kept me at a distance since day one. She never told me who her ex-boyfriend was and why she refused to call the police so adamantly. I was married to the woman almost twenty-nine years but don't know who she is.

Jack took a deep breath and focused on the road. They were entering Houston.

"You've got to stay on the 45 to Galveston," Vivien ordered.

"Galveston? Why Galveston?" Jack asked, surprised.

"Oh, for God's sake. Why do you have to be so difficult? We have to go to Galveston." Vivien's outrage put Jack on the defensive and he obliged, following the 45 in silence.

Vivien entered a destination in her phone and barked the directions at Jack, competing with the navigation audio. Dread took over him when they arrived: Luxury Beach Condominiums.

"What's going on?" Jack asked.

"If Muhammad won't go to the mountain, the mountain must come to Muhammad?"

"What?" Jack's face wrinkled in disbelief. He grasped what happened but wasn't yet able to admit it to himself.

"Well," Vivien whined, "you wouldn't talk with me in Dallas, so I had to do something?" The rising inflection at the end of her sentences unnerved Jack. He'd smile when the young guys at the office talked liked that, but Vivien's uptalk was unbearable.

"I love you. I want to save our marriage. I have a right to talk with you about us?"

Seething, Jack wanted to open the passenger door, drag Vivien out of the car, and drive back to Dallas.

But she had a point. As much as Jack despised his wife, he wouldn't deny her the right to talk about their marriage.

Dallas/Fort Worth International Airport

The same day

"Cabin crew prepare for landing."

The plane was approaching DFW, but I was not ready to land from my trip yet. In spite of my best intentions, I didn't sleep for a second. My mind refused to shut down and kept replaying my Dubai experiences until I capitulated and used the flight to jot down all the new concepts and images. I could barely keep up with the flow; before I got one idea down, three new ones were already competing for my attention. I was exhausted from recording this "download," yet too wired up to sleep. I couldn't wait to see Jack and share everything with him.

Touch down.

I turned on my phone the moment the wheels hit the runway. A text from Jack was already waiting for me.

JACK: *Darling, I will not be able to pick you up at DFW. Have to go to Houston. Emergency in Vivien's family. I sent a limo to take you to the Joule. Will try to be back ASAP.*

I stared at the message, speechless. Emergency in Vivien's family? I checked my inbox. No email from Jack. I bit my lip. The disappointment crash-landed me in Texas. My excitement was gone, exhaustion took over.

A colossal jet lag finally slowed down my overworked mind but couldn't stop the somberness that took over me. I kept checking my phone on the way to the hotel, but Jack disappeared from the radar. Why didn't he tell me what's going on? Even the Joule's playful art collection couldn't cheer me up.

What if something happened to him? A stab of fear jolted me up. I grabbed my phone and texted him again: *Jack, are you OK?*

Deafening silence. Our safe cyber-bubble burst.

My mouth was as dry as the Sahara.

Dallas

The Joule Hotel
Still October 5

The king-size bed lured me to get under the covers until the nightmare passed, but I resisted and took a long shower instead. I needed to get on Dallas time ASAP to be sharp for the upcoming meetings with my new clients.

To stay awake, I decided to go on the Dallas Historical District Walk Jack and I had planned for the afternoon. I got a fresh fruit juice in the little health bar downstairs and walked on, secretly hoping that Jack would catch up with me, everything would be explained, we would run back to the Joule, make love, and laugh about the silliness of the last hours.

But Jack didn't show up. I made it to the Majestic Theatre, constantly checking my phone. New messages rolled in, none of them from Jack. The walk couldn't hold my attention. On edge and hungry, I put Dallas's history on hold and strolled over to Savor in Klyde Warren Park.

Dark clouds rolled in from the south, reflecting my mood. I checked the weather radar on my phone and remembered the app Jack signed us on so that we never lose touch with each other. I'd never used it before but found the icon and clicked on it. A map popped up. Jack was on the beach in Galveston.

Stab.

On autopilot, I searched the address. Luxurious Beach Condos for Rent.

STAB.

Tears sprang into my eyes. I studied the map. The condos were not far from a hospital. That could explain the emergency Jack talked about. Maybe I was overreacting.

A message popped up: "Jack Carter updated his profile picture," Facebook was telling me.

THE WALL

Jack never used his Facebook account. Puzzled, I clicked on the message.

STAB.

Jack's new profile picture was a selfie of him and Vivien with rolling waves in the background. It had to be taken recently because Jack was wearing the cashmere sweater I had given him before leaving for Dubai.

His cover picture was also updated: Jack, Vivien, and their twins playing on a beach when the twins were little. Jack's latest post announced that Jack Carter checked in Luxurious Beach Condos in Galveston with Vivien Carter. "When everything you ever longed for is right in front of you," Jack shared.

My hands shaking, I clicked Vivien's name. Her new profile and cover pictures were exactly the same as Jack's. She too checked in the Luxurious Beach Condos. Her comment completed the story: "All you need is love <3"

But Facebook wasn't done yet. It told me that Vivien Carter added thirty-seven new photos to the album Our Blessed Life Together. All of them were of Jack and Vivien, starting with their wedding picture.

I sat motionlessly at my table, watching a little boy playing with his Frenchie but not really seeing anything. Something shifted in me and dislodged a major force that was ripping me up from inside. A boiling torrent that swallowed my life, crushed it, and swept it away like worthless debris.

What made Vivien so irresistible?

I scrolled through her Facebook wall looking for answers. Picture after picture of Vivien eating and drinking. Occasionally accompanied by two or three other women, laughing, raising her glass, but mostly alone.

The pics were almost identical, as if derived from one master template. Vivien's wide-open mouth in the focus point, displaying perfectly whitened teeth. Mousy blonde hair. A wide neck that swallowed the lower part of her face, making her look jawless. No style. T-shirts and baggy shorts or even baggier jeans. The only variation came from the T-shirts. She didn't wear the same T-shirt twice. And didn't visit the same establishment twice. Strange. Just as the huge black crocodile bag that looked so out of place in Jack's party. Why was is so prominent in every picture? I zoomed in on it. It looked fake as hell.

I was drawn to the pictures as if they had the power to cease my torment. Yet, the more I examined Vivien, the less I understood what Jack saw in her. *What happened?* Jack couldn't stand Vivien for years, but now she was "everything he ever longed for"? It didn't make sense.

Jack's silence crushed me. *Why is he humiliating me like this?* If he chose Vivien, so be it. As much as it hurt, I didn't want to be with a man who didn't want to be with me. Yet, wasn't our love worth at least a final goodbye? My mind buzzed with questions without answers, but one thing was absolutely clear: I wasn't good enough. As always.

I was losing the battle with my tears. *How stupid can I get?* Fooling myself that I was Jack's Dream Girl... I grabbed my phone, ready to book a flight back to Montreal. And put the phone down just as quickly.

I will not run away.

Hell no! I had clients in Dallas. And I didn't need Jack to go on with my plans. Nothing was stopping me from buying a house here and using it as my home, office, and showroom. I reached for my phone again and found the nearest car rental. Then I dried my tears, ordered a sandwich, and dove into the real estate pages.

Dubai

TNO offices
October 6

"Hey bro." Mo was all smiles. "You missed Miss Oh la la."

"I thought she was going to stay a couple of days longer." Perry wasn't hiding his disappointment.

"She had to go back to Dallas. Urgent business."

"Hm. So what's the verdict?"

"I told you, you should have been here. Tour de force on heels."

Perry raised a quizzical eyebrow.

"She started sort of slow. Lots of questions." A huge grin filled Mo's face. "But man, once she got going, I could hardly keep up with her."

"You? No way." Perry playfully punched Mo's shoulder.

"Yeah, I guess I've met my match."

"Hey, you are married already."

"Design-wise."

A wave of longing swept over Perry. He wished he hadn't missed Lexi. He wanted to show her Dubai. And take her to the Burj Al Arab.

"Alex will be in touch with you. Has a ton of ideas to discuss."

"Like what?"

"She will be using our domotics products for her clients. Wants to work closely with us to make sure she gets the maximum effect out of all your inventions."

Perry laughed, pleased.

"I guess I could catch up with her in Dallas."

"Going back soon?"

"To Houston. I am thinking about moving back, Mo."

"Oh, really?" Mo looked suddenly serious. He cocked his head and studied Perry closely. A wide grin filled his face.

"Is it a girl?"

"What?"

"I guess not." Mo looked serious again. "Does it have something to do with your mom?" he asked quietly.

"And dad." They were silent for a few moments. Then Perry shared Dave's story with Mo.

"I want to do something about this, Mo. I want to go into politics."

"That's fantastic." Mo beamed. "Perry for President!" They both burst into laughter.

"I mean it, Perry. If you want to go into politics, why not go for the top job?"

"Because you get nothing done."

"But all our companies would get unfair advantages," Mo teased.

They joked back and forth, while Perry wondered what Lexi would think about his new career. She was on his mind more than he was willing to admit.

Dallas

The Joule Hotel
October 6

I woke up in the darkness, feverish, mouth parched. Three a.m. I slept almost five hours. Not bad. I took a sip of water and slipped back under the covers.

Jack is in Galveston with Vivien. It was so much easier to handle a broken heart during the day than in the darkness of the night. My phone chimed.

JACK: *Vivien and I are evaluating our marriage. I will try to come back tomorrow.*

ME: *Is that the family emergency?*

I asked without much thinking.

JACK: *It looks like it.*

No *I miss you*s. No *I love you*s. No *emoticons*. The coldness confirmed Jack's Facebook posts: Vivien was in, I was out.

ME: *It looks like the two of you are back together. Good luck.*

I tossed and turned, desperately seeking answers, miserable. In the end it all boiled down to one thing: Jack, the love of my life, left me for his estranged wife. Or used me to get his wife back.

Any which way, I let myself believe that I was Jack's Dream Girl, and he betrayed me. Just like Rogier, my previous boyfriend. I shivered as the memory of that afternoon filled my mind.

I had come home early because my last client had to leave town and rescheduled her appointment. I stopped at my favorite caterer and bought oysters, salad, and freshly made pasta for dinner, hoping to surprise Rogier with an unexpected treat in the middle of the week. We hardly ever saw each other because we were both working long hours, and our relationship was in dire need of revival. I rushed home smiling, looking forward to a romantic evening.

The smile on my face froze as soon as I opened the door to my condo. The sounds coming from the bedroom told me that the romance was in full swing already, *sans moi*. I recognized the velvety voice immediately: Stella Chandon, the owner of the hottest antique shop in Montreal. It had been in her family for generations, but Stella turned it into an institution.

Of all the emotions that had flooded me at that moment, the feeling of utter worthlessness was the most difficult one to shake off. It lingered like a dark, suffocating cloud over my post-Rogier life. I felt adequate only at work.

"I know exactly what you mean," Jack had commiserated when I shared the story with him. "Vivien makes me feel like that all the time."

And now she was everything Jack had ever longed for.

"At least you can't be accused of breaking up their marriage," a little voice chirped in. The irony of it made me laugh.

Still, I needed some answers. Why was Jack so loving until the last minute before my flight took off from Dubai? Were all his texts and emails false? What brought him back to Vivien?

Seeing petite, sultry Stella and big Rogier radiating like a power plant wiped out all my questions: they were great together. But Jack and Vivien?

Obviously, even rude, tasteless, drunk Vivien was more desirable than I...

Oh God, how can I survive this?

By 5:00 a.m. I gave up on sleep.

I took a hot and cold shower, put on a killer makeup and focused on work. I reviewed my notes on Megs Aldridge, my first Dallas client, and refined the questions I wanted to ask her. Sufficiently prepared for our meeting, I went on with collecting information about the house I'd discovered during my exploration of Dallas neighborhoods yesterday afternoon.

The house had originally belonged to a philanthropist and used to be a meeting place for artists, politicians, and anyone who was someone in Dallas. It was the perfect place for DD, my Inside-Outside project. I didn't want to make myself too excited yet, but I systematically researched the neighboring houses and wrote down prices, square footage, number of bedrooms, bathrooms, extras, lot sizes, and other useful details.

By the time I left for my appointment with Megs, I had the whole area mapped and memorized, ready to negotiate with the real estate agent I was going to meet later that day.

If I made it that far.

Dallas

In front of the Joule

The world spun around me and I leaned on the valet's station to steady myself. Sweat dripped down my back.

"Are you OK?" The valet jumped out of my rental car, his face filled with concern.

"I am fine," I said.

My head throbbed, knees wobbled, hands shook. Whether it was the heartbreak or the jet lag, as soon as I left the comfort of the Joule, I felt like I'd been in a head-on collision with an eighteen-wheeler. Luckily the hectic downtown traffic demanded my full attention and didn't leave any room for brooding.

Megs greeted me with her signature lopsided smile.

"I get absolutely bored with my places. And I get bored with redoing them all the time," she confessed.

"When did you redo this house?" I asked on autopilot.

"Not even two years ago. It looked so serene then. So Zen. But the colors just aren't it. It's all so...so...what's the word...? Static." Megs threw her arms in the air and let them drop in her lap with a sigh.

"So, you are looking for a dynamic, exciting place," I summed up the obvious, "a place you can change quickly, without actually changing much?"

Megs cocked her head.

"That's it. I always want to have my cake and eat it too."

"Don't we all?" I laughed.

My hairdresser had said to me once that she is more a psychologist than a hairdresser. Designers aren't much different. But now I was going to do something a psychologist would never do: give Megs her magic cake.

I was opening my mouth to propose a new solution for Megs's decorating blues when a thought flashed through my mind: *Vivien couldn't do this if her life depended on it.* Huh? *Vivien couldn't do this if her life depended on it.*

That's right. Vivien, who'd never held a real job, couldn't give Megs her dream interior, but I can. That cheered me up.

"OK. Megs, have you heard of domotics?"

"Domotics? Never heard of it." Megs shook her head. Anticipation propelled her to her feet. "Am I going to be the first one to have it?" Her eyes sparkled like fireworks.

I chuckled. "First among your friends, I guess. Otherwise you would have heard about it. No?"

"Right. So how does it work? Tell me everything."

I explained she could set the mood in the room from her phone and change the colors at her whim with a touch of a button.

High on excitement, Megs added a full-blown spa to the project. And then a professional kitchen separated by a glass wall from an airy event-kitchen with a forty-foot buffet island.

I left Megs in high spirits, ready to tackle my next project: the DD house.

Dallas

DD
October 6, afternoon

The house dominated the tranquil cul-de-sac. It stood proudly on the top of a lovely knoll shaded by live oaks and drew potential suitors' eyes as if the houses to its left and right didn't exist. It was the biggest and the most mysterious of the three residences on the cul-de-sac. It was also the most neglected one.

I pulled up to the curb and took the house in. I was drawn to it even more than the first time I saw it. *This is it!* Neglected, but a perfect candidate for my DD project. *Can I get it?* Yearning was taking over me.

I'd found the house by accident. None of the houses I'd selected while eating my sandwich at the Savor lived up to my expectations. Disappointed, I just drove around aimlessly, taking everything in, getting a feel for the neighborhood. I nearly missed the cul-de-sac, but the house flashed in my peripheral vision and seduced me to drive to it.

From afar it looked majestic and out of reach. Closer inspection told a different story. The For Sale sign leaned against a broken entry gate. The overgrown front yard screamed for care. Intrigued, I searched the listing on my phone.

It was sheer curiosity. Just like leafing through Vogue, knowing perfectly well that you are not going to spend $250K on the pearl-studded gown.

The listing popped up and made my heart beat faster. Not believing that I could buy a house like this, I verified the price on another site, making sure I got the zeros right. I did, which meant that something had to be seriously wrong with the place. It had been on the market 186 days. 186 days in a crazy seller's market, where you could list a house at seven thirty in the morning and have it under contract before noon. Puzzled, I had scheduled a viewing.

The real estate agent was late, which gave me an excuse to check my phone. Not a sign of Jack. As if the months of our friendship never happened. Feeling like a part of me was amputated, I took a deep breath and tried to convince myself that things could be worse. They could, but tell it to the amputated part. I was feeling unbearable phantom pain.

Flustered, I got out of my car and walked towards the house. A large SUV entered the winding driveway and stopped with a screech.

"I am sorry I am late. The traffic is terrible." A perky brunette tried to manage her bag, scarf, and a coat as she ran to the door.

"Are you Alex? I am Joyce," she introduced herself. "Have you been waiting here long?" she continued, looking at me anxiously.

"No, just a few minutes." I smiled.

"OK. Let's go. Shall we?" More at ease, Joyce scanned me from head to toe, undoubtedly assessing whether I was a genuine buyer.

I didn't blame her. The house had been shown more than hundred times.

Joyce fiddled with the keys and went straight to business:

"The residence belonged to Betsy Vandyck. She was a Dallas philanthropist and lived here until her last day. She was 104."

The secret was out.

Dallas

DD

Smart strategy. Many people didn't want to buy a house in which someone died recently. If I were one of them, Joyce would have saved us the trouble of viewing the house.

I looked around without saying anything. I knew the whole history of Betsy's house, including Betsy's passing away peacefully in her sleep.

Betsy had bequeathed the property to Futures, a Dallas charity helping orphans. Futures had put the house on the market within days. The relatively low price had attracted a lot of viewers but no buyers. I wasn't surprised. My heart sank when we walked in. The once proud house had been brought to its knees, the decay and disrepair sending even the most adventurous bargain hunters running.

Betsy's gift became a financial burden draining Futures' cash reserves. They needed to sell. Understandably, Joyce wasn't disclosing any of this, but thanks to my sleepless night I had plenty of time to do my homework.

The house needed a tremendous amount of work, but the disrepair didn't turn me off. Underneath it I sensed a spirited house with a huge potential.

I saw past the peeling paint, mildewed floors, hopelessly outdated kitchen, and shabby bathrooms. I didn't worry about the overgrown garden and the empty, partially collapsed pool. I gasped when I inspected the pool but not for the reasons Joyce feared. I wasn't shocked by the necessary repair work but by a realization how easy it would have been for a 104-year-old to slip and fall into the deep concrete ruin. Luckily, Betsy managed to avoid this hazard.

Nonetheless, I wondered what happened. It must have been heartbreaking for a woman like Betsy to witness the deterioration of her once gorgeous house. Why didn't anyone help her? Why was she so alone at the end of her life?

I strolled back into the house and took in its solid bones.

"Are you my DD?" I asked silently.

The house answered. In an instant I envisioned the final product. A totally open plan, glass walls, lush plants, outside flowing in and inside reaching out.

"...replaced with any type of swimming pool you want. Or removed completely." Joyce's pitch brought me back.

I nodded. "OK. How much time do you have, Joyce?"

"Now?"

"Yes."

"As much as you need."

"I need to go through every room and make a few calculations. OK?"

"Absolutely." Joyce held her breath. She wanted to get this dud off her hands.

"If I were to make a cash offer, when could we close?"

"Within a week. If your offer is accepted."

Joyce played her role, but I was optimistic. Futures needed to sell, and I was going to make a fair offer. I knew quite a few cutthroat dealmakers who would consider me stupid and push Futures to selling the house for a pittance. Not me. Making the other party bleed comes back to you like a boomerang.

I went from room to room, envisioning the face lift, estimating restoration costs. Bringing this house back to life would be a major operation.

My phone chimed.

JACK: *Love you, Alex.*

Tears sprang to my eyes. I blinked them back and took a deep breath to steady myself. *Why was he playing with me like this?* Keeping me in the dark and then texting as if nothing had happened? UNACCEPTABLE.

If that's how Jack wanted to run things, he had no place in my life, I concluded resolutely, suppressing the avalanche of emotions threatening to swallow me. I knew I'd have to wrestle with this in the darkness of the night, but I wanted to get on with my work on the house. Jack's turning the knife in the wounds wasn't helping.

ME: *Jack, I'll not play this game with you. Obviously, you've got everything you ever longed for. Enjoy!*

Jack's Facebook post was burned into my mind.

JACK: *I long for you.*

I couldn't believe he was doing this. I longed for us to be together too, but being Jack's plaything wasn't an option.

THE WALL

ME: *Count me out. I'll not have an affair with a man who is happy with his wife.*

JACK: *Alex, I love you. What's got into you?*

ME: *Your Facebook posts. Couldn't have been any clearer. Wishing you the best of luck.*

JACK: *What are you talking about?*

ME: *I have no time for this, Jack. Goodbye.*

I swallowed hard. Did he really think I'll put up with this BS? And stay with him while he is with Vivien? Outraged and hurting, I forced myself to breathe deeply until I stopped shaking inside.

Then I ran through the house renovation numbers again, checking everything item by item, making sure I didn't miss anything big. Satisfied, I went back to the living room.

Joyce got off her phone and looked at me expectantly.

"Here's my offer." I showed her the number.

"That's low. For the house prices in this area," Joyce added quickly when she saw my eyebrows shoot up. We were in business.

"My offer is based on facts and fair market price estimates," I said. We sat down on Betsy's chintz sofa and went through my offer item by item.

"Let me call the seller." Joyce stepped out and got on her phone. She was back in no time.

"Well, they want five thousand more." We both laughed. It was a symbolic move. Faces were saved. Everyone won.

"That's fine if I can come here starting tomorrow and get all my measurements before the closing."

Joyce got on the phone again, a bright smile animating her excited face.

"Done. Provided you will have dinner with me and my aunt Evelyn tonight. She is the president of Futures."

"Deal."

We hugged. Joyce couldn't stop talking.

"You have no idea what this means to me. I thought I would never sell the house. I didn't want to take it on, but Evelyn asked me." Joyce rolled her eyes. "No one crosses Evelyn O'Neill."

I smiled. "Tell me more about Evelyn, Joyce."

Operation Dallas was on.

Dallas

Vivien's bedroom
October 20

Vivien scrolled rapidly through Jack's emails, agitated. Nothing! She nearly punched the screen. She went furiously through the emails once more. Not one from Alex. Only business associates.

Vivien hated all these people. They adored Jack. Such stupidity. Jack just wasn't up to par. Vivien put up with him only because it was convenient until someone better came along. But all these people were gaga about Jack because he was Mr. Big Shot Architect. *Ridiculous.*

If she hadn't hacked Jack's emails, Vivien would have never found out how famous he had become. *How was I supposed to know?* she asked, incredulous. It didn't make any sense. Jack bored her to death with his stupid buildings. And, in her book, famous people were rich. But Jack never made enough money to give her the life she deserved.

Vivien scowled. She opened the emails one by one and closely inspected them. Alex could be hiding behind an innocent contact. Vivien had nearly missed what was going on between the two of them because she had assumed that Alex was a man. She had barely scanned Alex's first emails, totally uninteresting gibberish followed by more stupid gibberish. Even their discussions about philosophy, art history, music, wine, whiskey, and traveling did not trigger Vivien's attention. So boring. Besides, Jack chatted like this with other guys all the time. Vivien dismissed their emails as boy talk.

Until she came across an unexpected XO in one of Alex's emails.

Puzzled, Vivien searched "Alex Demarchelier." The results punched her right between the eyes. Alexandra Demarchelier, Canadian interior designer, born in France, was virtually delivered to Vivien's bedroom as a smiling, self-assured, slender, fashionable woman. A pang of envy nearly knocked Vivien over. She despised these radiant, glamorous types. They got everything handed to them.

THE WALL

Glued to her laptop, Vivien had searched her way through photos of exquisite interiors, lists of achievements, interviews. Hypnotized by her discovery, she had gone from picture to picture, site to site, gorging on morsels of Alex, unable to detach herself from the screen.

Vivien wasn't opposed to a dalliance or two. For years, the twins had been her insurance that Jack wouldn't leave her. But Jen and Victor lost their value on their eighteenth birthday. Vivien needed a new insurance. A mistress was exactly what she was looking for. She'd spied on Jack with a vengeance but never caught him cheating. Until Alex came along.

Any mistress would generate enough guilt to tie Jack to Vivien forever. A mistress like Alex was golden. The risk of a high-stakes public exposure of their affair gave Vivien the upper hand. Jack had too much to lose.

When Jack didn't return home after Galveston, Vivien *had* to rein him in. *Wait until I am done with you*, she smirked. *You'll have no choice but stay with me*. And Alex's life will be ruined. Bliss.

But Alex disappeared. *She can't do this*, Vivien pounded her fist on a cushion. She needed Alex in Jack's life. Vivien expected high drama on Alex's part after Galveston. Barrage, outrage, accusations. Threats of exposing Jack, threats of leaving him. But nothing like that happened. Only silence.

Vivien hated silence. Silence unnerved her. If someone shouts, you can shout back. But if they are silent, you can't outsilence them. You can't win against people who are not fighting you. To win, you have to drag them into the arena. Vivien snorted.

Jack must have got a brand-new email account, which hasn't been yet discovered by my equipment, Vivien reasoned. An unquenchable thirst for control propelled her forward. Nostrils flared, she restarted her search apps. These were not just some stupid apps you find on the web. No, Vivien used exclusively top technology, and it served her well. But not today. The search came up empty. Livid, Vivien shot a message to her supplier and ordered him to send her updated software immediately. She hated to be out of touch.

And she decided not to wait for the new software. This was an emergency. She *had* to track down Alex. *Now*. She activated another app that transported her directly into Alex's email account, unseen. Vivien was strictly forbidden to use this app for her private business, but she didn't care. *No one will ever find out*.

Cheeks glowing with anticipation, Vivien scrolled through the content of Alex's inbox. A sharp hiss flew from her lips. The slut was redoing Megs Aldridge's house. How dare she!

Rage shook Vivien to the core. She had tried for years to forge a friendship with Megs. Never got even close. There was only one remedy for this condition: a crystal-clear elixir delivered from Russia with love.

Lunchtime wasn't on the horizon yet, but Vivien fixed herself a double vodka, blindly believing in its medicinal quality. And then another one, to ensure a complete recovery. Then she treated herself to a large piece of syrupy pecan pie, to sooth her sugar-starved brain. The pie tasted so good, she had to have another one. *God knows I deserve it*, she pardoned herself. Besides, she hadn't had any breakfast yet.

Strengthened, Vivien went back to Alex's emails. She scanned, read, caught a scent and tracked it deeper and deeper. Her irritation about not finding any communication between Alex and Jack was replaced by triumph.

Persistence pays.

Vivien had struck gold.

Montreal

Alex's condo
October 20, afternoon

"Hey, Lexi, how are you?" Perry grinned at me from my laptop. We relied on video conferencing and texts to get our work done, as our busy schedules had made it impossible to meet in person so far.

"Where are you? Is this a new place?" Perry went on. His intense scrutiny of my background brought a smile to my face. Perry must be the nicest guy in the world. And no one ever called me Lexi before.

"No, it's my old condo in Montreal."

"You are in Montreal? Until when?"

"Just a few days. I'll be back in Dallas next week."

"So we will miss each other again. I am in Dallas now, until tomorrow."

"Oh no. I am sorry. I didn't know."

"You couldn't have. It was a quick decision."

"Are you going to see Richard?" I asked, excited.

"Not yet, but it's in the works. Made the first contact." Perry winked.

Perry had talked so passionately about his political ambitions that I became an avid supporter and engaged Liz Howard to help Perry establish informal contact with Richard.

"Great. I am sure the senator will give you some pointers on conquering the political arena."

"He has surely fought his battles. Anyhow, what brought you to Montreal?"

"The opening of the Montreal Centre."

Perry's face tightened.

"Will Jack Carter be there?"

"I suppose so," I said, wondering why Perry asked.

"Don't let him talk you into something you don't want," Perry advised. "Jack doesn't always stick to agreements."

You can say that again. I felt tears surging up, so I segued to Megs's job. I wished I could cry my heart out and share the Jack-disaster with someone, but this wasn't the right place. Perry looked at me quizzically, tempting me to spill the beans, but I fetched my list of outstanding issues in Megs's project and hammered through them one by one.

Although we resolved all the technical challenges, Perry still wanted to visit Megs's place to tune things up on the spot.

"Do you think Megs will meet with me on such short notice?" he asked.

"Let me text her."

Megs replied within seconds: *Any time. Looking forward to it :-)*

"Awesome. Enjoy the opening, Lexi. I love the SKY Club."

"Thanks. Have fun in Dallas." I gave Perry a big smile, signed off and put my head in my hands. The agony of Jack's deception wore me down. A sob escaped my lips. *How am I going to survive this?*

Jack'd emailed me that he didn't know about the Facebook posts until I told him about them, that Vivien must have posted them, that she'd tricked him into driving her to Galveston. Yet, even if that happened, he could have driven back immediately. Or at least told me what was going on. No matter what Vivien had done, Jack didn't have to leave me in the dark and break the trust between us. I refused to be played like this.

I was miserable to be back in my old condo alone. What do you do with all the love that has nowhere to go? I saw Jack everywhere. Jack sitting on the sofa next to me, sipping cognac from a large snifter. Jack making scrambled eggs and whistling to himself. Jack taking a shower. His toothpaste and aftershave were still in the bathroom.

Jack loved this condo. He had said that he did his best work in years here. He had looked so happy sitting at my desk when I videoed with him from Dubai. A few days before he went to Galveston. I froze.

Was Vivien here with him?

Montreal

Alex's condo

I started to search for evidence that Vivien had been in my condo, but my phone rang before I could find anything. A quick look at the number made me wince. Parental disapproval was the last thing I needed right now.

"Hello Papa, how are you?"

"Maman wants to speak with you." Ugh. Mother must be super furious. I knew I was in trouble when Dad initiated the call for her.

Mom grabbed the phone. "You've embarrassed me in front of my friends." I didn't know where she was heading, but contempt dominated her voice.

"Don't you have anything to say for yourself?" she went on when I didn't respond.

"I don't know what's upset you so much."

"You don't know? I had coffee with Marie today and she showed me your picture on that rag. I was so embarrassed I didn't know where to look."

It was the third time Mom had complained about the glossy cover. As far as she was concerned, everything was wrong about it: my dress, my hair, my shoes, the terrible butterfly, the way I stand, and of course my decision to throw away a respectable career in philosophy to become an interior designer.

"Marie of course didn't say how vulgar it is, but I know what she was thinking."

"What did she say?" I asked.

"Don't get smart with me. We are not speaking about Marie. We are speaking about how you humiliated me. After everything I have done for you. All my sacrifices. Marie's daughter is getting a PhD in history and you are showing off on covers of cheap rags."

I gasped. Mom's words hurt like hell. Another rejection. I expected that Mom would dismiss my Montreal Centre success just as she dismissed all my previous successes, but this time she crossed the line.

"Maman, you don't have to like what I do, and I don't have to like how you treat me. You went too far this time," I said, fully aware that disagreeing with Mom would sentence me to weeks of verbal assaults.

"Alex, Maman is upset because you are throwing your life away." Dad took over the phone. "You could still go back to school and get your degree in philosophy. That would make us all happy."

"It wouldn't make me happy, Papa," I said, not expecting any understanding from my parents. We had gone through this hundreds of times.

"Your selfishness has no limits," Mother screamed in the background. I had had enough.

"I will not participate in this argument. Have a good evening," I said, and hung up. Although I no longer tried to please my parents, their disapproval still hit me hard.

I tried to convince myself that Mom's rejection had more to do with her than with me. After all, dissatisfaction ruled her life. Nothing was ever good enough for her. Her family and friends were bad, and so were the politicians, the journalists, the weather, my dad, and I.

But maybe she was right about me. Maybe no matter how hard I tried I'll never have a family that loves me and stands behind me. I'll never have the big, passionate love. I just wasn't good enough.

It was getting darker and the lights started to turn on outside. This used to be my favorite hour. When Jack was here, we would have a drink in front of the glass wall, feeling the pulse of the city, enjoying the bright lights turning on one by one...

The space felt deflated now. I sat on the sofa in the darkness, contemplating how I would go on with my loveless life.

Sell the condo!

It never crossed my mind to move out after Rogier's dalliance. I completely redesigned the bedroom and the living room, but that was it. Getting over Jack would be much more difficult. Redesigning wouldn't erase the memories reminding me of what could have been.

Selling the condo was the way to go. I no longer cared whether Vivien was here or not. I decided to put the place on the market immediately and move on. I jumped off the sofa feeling much better. I checked my watch. I had ten minutes to get ready for the Montreal Centre opening.

My phone chimed as I rushed to the bathroom.

MEGS: *Perry was just here. He is MARVELOUS. And thinks the world of you.*

ME: *OK! Are you satisfied with the design proposal?*

MEGS: *Absolutely love it!*

My heart fluttered with joy. And then it dawned on me: I was taking the relationship with Jack too seriously. Maybe it wasn't meant to last a lifetime. Maybe it was just a morale boost to help me back on my feet after Rogier, and I made too much out of it.

I'd been in seventh heaven because such a famous architect as Jack loved my work and loved me. He had swept me off my feet and I'd assumed that our connection was the source of my happiness.

To my surprise, although I missed Jack terribly, the wings our love gave me didn't disappear with him. Jack was gone, but the key to the source of joy stayed with me.

Montreal

The Montreal Centre
October 20

The enormous lobby of the Montreal Centre glistened and sparkled with excitement. Montreal's crème de la crème came out in full force and celebrated the newest addition to the city's skyline with an abundance of bubbly and baubles.

The mayor was finishing her speech, but the festivities took off way before she pronounced the skyscraper opened.

"Great job, Jack. You've done it again," a guy Jack couldn't place said.

"Thanks." Jack smiled automatically and patted the guy's upper arm as if they were the best of friends. It was easier than saying, "Sorry, I can't recall your name."

That's the problem with being even a minor celebrity, Jack thought. Tons of people know you, and although you don't know them, they expect to be treated as your buddies. Jack didn't mind. He loved being in the spotlight and the opening of "his" Montreal Centre was the perfect occasion for it.

Jack was surrounded by a group of colleagues and fans, but the only person with whom he wanted to be was Alex. He saw her work the room and mingle with the movers and shakers. Radiant, self-assured, friendly, and above it all.

He wanted her. He wanted her back. If he had to describe hell, the last weeks would be it. He was suffocating without Alex's love, without her laughter, her text messages. He still could not comprehend that he lost Alex because he went to Galveston with Vivien. No, because Vivien tricked him into driving her to Galveston. And because Vivien hacked his Facebook account.

"It's not about your going to Galveston, Jack. It's about keeping me in the dark about it. You seem committed to Vivien. And she is your wife. I will not be part of it," Alex explained in one of her rare emails.

Jack longed to be with Alex but being there for Vivien when she needed him was as natural for him as breathing. He didn't know

THE WALL

anything else. He had taken care of Vivien since the moment she had knocked on his door after her ex-boyfriend had beaten her up. Helping Vivien went without saying. Helping Vivien didn't mean he didn't love Alex. If only Alex could understand that.

Alex's cold distance was worse than a kick where it hurts. He wanted the gentle, tender Alex. He wanted her fingers caressing his hair, her lips to kiss his ear and whisper, "Jack, my wonderful darling, let me show you how much I love you."

Jack had to do something. He extracted himself from the crowd and went to Alex.

"Let's go somewhere quiet and have a drink," he proposed.

Dallas

Vivien's bedroom
October 20

Vivien's life revolved around stories. She spent days chasing tales to tell and would leave no stone unturned when she caught a scent of something juicy. If a secret was in play, Vivien was unstoppable. Nothing could quench her insatiable thirst for revealing delicious disgrace.

She would dig and dig, until she unearthed the naked truth. And what she did not unearth, she made up. When Vivien adopted a story, reality ceased to exist. Vivien's interpretation became the truth.

Mining for raw secrets and polishing them to perfection like precious stones filled Vivien's days with exhilaration. But what would be the value of these jewels if they remained in obscurity? Vivien had an unstoppable urge to shine light on her stones and let them sparkle. Privacy was not her policy. The truth must be told, and exposing someone's dark secrets was the best there was.

Over the years Vivien perfected the art of telling her stories. She never posed as the original source of her shocking revelations. She would say she heard it from a friend or via, via. And she rarely told the whole story at once. She would release one tidbit at a time, keeping people in suspense for days, sometimes for weeks.

Some people suspected that Vivien's information came from the Lowells because Vivien's brother Ted was married to Senator Lowell's sister. Vivien neither confirmed nor corrected these assumptions. She kept her sources sealed and cultivated her image of being "well connected," which opened many a door for her.

Dishing out juicy secrets bolstered Vivien's friendships and was the backbone of her alliance with Evelyn O'Neill. Being in Evelyn's circle was as vital for Vivien as oxygen. It conveyed that Vivien *belonged*. Rubbing shoulders with Evelyn was the second best thing to having Evelyn's life,

THE WALL

which Vivien would kill for. Land and real estate money married to oil money...

Vivien spent hours dreaming about being so rich that everyone *had* to follow her orders, and no one, especially her husband and friends, dared disobey. Everything done for her. Exactly as she wanted. Vivien *knew* what to do with such wealth... She would use it so much better than Evelyn...

It wasn't fair that some people got so much and didn't know what to do with it. Or didn't deserve it. Like Alex. Vivien scowled. Alex got everything delivered on a silver platter. People like Megs literally opened their doors for her.

Well, Vivien got *that* under control. Hacking Alex's email account was one of Vivien's best decisions, and she was richly rewarded for it: Alex's inbox was a goldmine.

Just finding out about Alex's new Dallas house gave Vivien enough ammunition to put pressure on Jack for months. Vivien giggled as images of squirming Jack rolled before her eyes. But even this jewel paled in comparison with the access Vivien gained to Alex's contacts. If her life depended on it, Vivien couldn't stop herself from using the "forbidden" app to exploit their emails.

She already dispatched the app to peek into the inboxes of Megs Aldridge and a few others. Such abundance. It would take her *days* to sift through all their emails and put them to work. Vivien was salivating in anticipation of digging deeper, but put that on hold, inextricably drawn into the pursuit of her priciest catch:

Perry Lowell.

A less experienced person would have easily missed this diamond in the rough and dismissed Perry as a mere supplier of computerized gizmos. But Vivien knew better. She followed her instincts, sought, and found.

Perry was so much more than a provider of fancy light effects for Megs Aldridge's house. Perry was a tycoon. Rich beyond imagination. Rich and stealthy. Vivien had to push her equipment to the limits to merely scratch the surface of Perry's story. Even the forbidden app bounced off Perry's emails like hail off a tin roof.

Rich and mysterious alone would've sent Vivien on a hot, feverish pursuit. But Perry's full name catapulted her to orgasmic heights.

Perry Winston Lowell.

It couldn't be a coincidence. Perry had to be somehow connected to Senator Win Lowell aka Perry Winston Lowell II. And the connection had to be a dark one. Otherwise Perry's name would have been Perry Winston Lowell III. Vivien's cheeks glowed with fire. She had discovered a secret worth a fortune.

Vivien cranked up her apps and went to work. She was determined to get to the bottom of Perry's mystery even if she had to break the internet. She jumped from website to website in a mad search for dates, places, names. She was hardly breathing when a box popped up and blocked the screen.

Spending too much time online?

the headline challenged. Vivien snorted and automatically moved her mouse to the upper right corner of the popup to get rid of it. She didn't need any tips on avoiding internet addiction.

She clicked and clicked, but the box didn't move. The little x that should make the annoyance disappear wasn't there. Vivien angrily scanned the box. And gave it a second look. It wasn't what she thought it was.

Spending too much time online?

Then you are in the right place to:
    * Turn your passion into profits
    * Make money while you sleep
    * Do what you love
    * Live the lifestyle of the rich and famous

The buttons below the message offered Vivien two ways to proceed:

'NO, I don't want to be rich' vs. **'YES, I want my money'**

Without hesitation Vivien clicked the right button. And immediately liked what she saw. *Instant results.* None of the nonsense about "no pain, no gain," having to "pay your dues," and "working your way to the top."

No sir. Vivien'll get everything she needed to become an online entrepreneur on a FREE webinar. And as a bonus she'll get a FREE e-book with

THE WALL

* 5 proven ways to start an online business within minutes
* 7 rock-solid lead generation strategies
* 3 ninja hacks to earn money in the next 24 hours
* and much, much more…

Vivien never heard of lead generation before, but that didn't stop her from submitting her email address and hitting the gold "I am in" button. She would *never* turn down anything that was FREE.

As instructed, Vivien confirmed her email and downloaded the e-book. Her heart beat faster as the big descending arrow indicated that the book was in Vivien's possession. Her gateway to passion and profits. Vivien felt light and giddy. As if millions of golden flakes fluttered into her body and caressed each and every one of her cells.

So *this* was how perfect happiness felt, Vivien marveled. She celebrated her new discovery with a quick shot of vodka. She'd open the book later, but first things first.

It was time to confront Jack about Alex's new house in Dallas. Vivien congratulated herself once again on her audacity. She would have never found out about the house had she not infiltrated Alex's emails. Jack must have purchased the house with Alex. Or for Alex. *Behind my back.*

She'd make Jack pay for this.

Montreal

The Montreal Centre Bar
October 20

"Alex why do you make such a big deal out of this? Vivien just needed to talk. Look, this is really difficult. I don't want my kids to see me as a bad guy."

Why was he saying this? His kids adored him.

"Did you speak with them about you and Vivien?" I asked.

"No."

"Why not?"

"Vivien did not want us to tell them."

Vivien did not want US to tell them.

If my heart started to melt a moment ago, there was no evidence of it now. Vivien whistled, and Jack jumped.

"Well, obviously Vivien runs your life, Jack. I will not be part of it."

Jack's phone lit up. He glanced at it, frowned, and read the message again.

"You didn't buy a house in Dallas, did you?" Jack laughed.

"What's so funny about it?"

"You did?" Jack peered at me, puzzled.

"Yes."

"Why?"

"Because I wanted to." I looked him straight in the eye.

"Vivien says half of the house is hers."

Now it was my turn to laugh. It was my first heartfelt laugh since Dubai. It bubbled out of me with abandon and burst the shackles of rejection. I stood up, ready to go. I was getting out of this Vivien madness.

I looked down at Jack and shared my final judgment with him:

"Vivien is full of shit."

I turned around and walked away without looking back.

THE WALL

~~~

Jack sat in the booth, dumbstruck. Alex's laugh rang in his ears. The golden bells he loved so dearly were as genuine as they were outraged.

"Vivien is full of shit."

He shook his head and laughed.

And looked at the text from Vivien again:

"I am not stupid. I know that your girlfriend bought a house in Dallas. Half of the house is mine and my lawyer will make sure that I get the other half too."

Vivien's claim of ownership was so patently false that even Jack couldn't give her the benefit of the doubt.

Yes, Vivien is full of shit and always was. A huge load slid off Jack's shoulders. He laughed again and waved a waitress over.

"Do you have the twenty-one-year-old Balvenie?" he asked jovially.

"Portwood? Sure."

"Great, make it a double."

The waitress floated away on her eight-inch heels. Jack wondered how she could walk on those contraptions. Didn't Rem Koolhaas design a line of killer shoes? No, it was his nephew, also an architect. Jack remembered the story now: Rem's nephew designed a marvelously unique pair of shoes to get his girlfriend back. Jack chuckled.

I'll design something for Alex, he pledged. But first things first.

Feeling like he had got a new lease on life, Jack took out his notebook and sketched his strategy.

Vivien's days as Mrs. Carter were numbered.

Dallas

DD
December 8

"The plumbers will be here tomorrow," Ken said as we inspected the guest bathrooms, which were stripped to the studs.

Remodeling DD was a great opportunity to work with different contractors and test their skills before I sent them to my clients. Ken came out as a winner, head and shoulders above everyone else. Experienced, thinking on his feet, flexible. Most importantly, I could count on his guys to deliver high quality. Even the most spectacular designs in the world would be doomed if craftsmen like plumbers, tilers, painters, and electricians didn't do their job right.

"Do they have the trim?" I asked. It was one of my nonnegotiable rules to insist on having shower heads, body sprays, handles, and all their accessories delivered *before* the plumbers started. This was the best strategy to avoid rework, I had learned the hard way.

"Yeah." Ken smiled, knowing me well by now. "They've got the hardware, all the valves and whatnot, and most of the trim. Except the rain heads, but they've got the specs."

"That's OK. And please make sure the tile guys have seen the trim before they start. I'll be in and out a lot next week."

"Better out. Y'know how much dust these guys produce." Ken chuckled.

"I am out of here. It's all theirs now." The guest quarters, my refuge since the work on DD began, were the last to be gutted, and I had moved to the master suite several days ago.

"Talking about that, the master bathroom needs a few minor touch-ups."

"I'll send the painters next week."

"Perfect."

Ken left and DD became uncharacteristically quiet. At one point I had five crews here, working on the kitchen, the master suite, installing a

THE WALL

swimming pool and a pond, painting the exterior on the front side, and putting in glass walls and sliding panels in the back, all at the same time.

It was a heck of a job to coordinate them all, but I loved it. I fell in bed at night too exhausted to think about Jack and woke up in the morning fired up to keep the workers on their toes. Making sure that everyone knew what they were doing, that the plumbers would not turn off water when the other crews need it, rescheduling crews that fell behind or got delayed on other jobs. All that while taking care of my own clients. Too busy to think about Jack.

I slid my hand over the kitchen counter and let my eyes glide around the large living space. Each of the functional areas had a distinct character, but they transitioned seamlessly like rooms without walls. The inside of the house merged with the outside, being separated only by a series of retractable glass walls. Looking from the kitchen, it was difficult to point out where the house ended and the garden began. Exactly as I envisioned it.

Yet, something was missing. DD was a sleeping beauty. She needed people, laughter, a breath of life. A sudden wave of loneliness took the wind out of my sails and I doubted my decision to live here on my own. *If I can't stand it, I can sell DD and get a condo downtown*, I reassured myself and went to feed the koi, my new favorite activity.

"Come on boys, who wants a brunch?" The koi rushed to the edge of the pond, mouths wide open, excitedly swallowing their pellets.

I went back to the house, happy the koi were adjusting so well to their new environment but feeling sorry for myself. *The koi are my only companions.* I took a deep breath and attacked the pile of bills waiting on my desk. At least I'd managed to give DD a facelift without having to touch the home equity credit line I got just in case.

The phone jolted me from my thoughts. Hm... Take it? Let it go to voicemail?

"Hello Jack," I said, curious.

"Hi Alex. Good to hear you. Eh...uhm. Well, could we meet? I'd like to tell you something important."

"Tell me."

"I want to tell you in person. Do you have time around six?"

"No. I have a meeting at five o'clock."

"Are you at home? I can be there at four thirty. I'll be quick."

"OK. See you then." Let's get it over with, whatever it is. Make peace? Maybe stay involved professionally? I wanted closure.

I bit my lip. Three months ago I had been sipping my sauvignon blanc in the St. Lawrence Café, on cloud nine because Jack and I got a chance to be together. I checked my calendar. Exactly ninety-two days later and we were over. So much for my big love. I wondered what would happen in the next ninety-two days.

Life goes on, I cheered myself up. Perry will come at five, we'll work on the domotics, chat about his political career, maybe have a dinner? Feeling much better, I got up and turned on the music.

"Come on DD, wake up, beauty!"

Dallas

Senator Howard's office
December 8

"Just one last question," Richard Howard said.

Here we go, Perry thought, curious whether Richard would bring up the obvious. The interview went extremely well so far, both men being on the same wavelength as if they had known each other for ages.

Perry was getting far more than just pointers on entering the political arena. Richard needed a high-level consultant and offered the job to Perry. It was exactly what Perry was looking for, a springboard for his political career.

"It's about your name. Perry Winston Lowell. The same as the name of my political nemesis, Win Lowell aka Perry Winston Lowell."

"I've never met Senator Lowell," Perry replied truthfully, not disclosing the bigger part of the story for now, thankful that Richard didn't ask a more direct question. "And I intend to run for his seat one day." That settled it.

"All. Right." Richard laughed. "When can you start?"

"Tomorrow."

"A man of action. All right. Let's get the paperwork done."

The men shook hands, both eager to begin their collaboration.

Perry sent Lexi a quick text and went back to his hotel. He wished he had taken Lexi up on her offer to have a lunch together. He had opted for a later meeting because he wanted to take her out for dinner, but now couldn't wait to share the good news with her.

Having several hours to spare, he searched the real estate pages, looking for a penthouse for himself and an office space for a home automation group he was going to start in Dallas. Lexi was giving him so much business, he couldn't handle it on his own while working for Richard. He had already teamed up with several creative guys and was going to set up a joint venture with them.

Looking forward to his meeting with Lexi, Perry drove to her place much earlier than he needed to. He couldn't wait to see the renovation of Lexi's new house. She had shown him several areas on video chats, but it wasn't the same as the real thing. From what he'd glimpsed so far, the place looked great, signature Lexi. Perry was going to give it an extra boost with his state-of-the art domotics. And add home security. He was concerned about Lexi being alone in the unprotected house.

He loved to work with Lexi and her clients, especially Megs. Perry smiled when he remembered giving Megs a choice of three lighting systems, one of them slightly more expensive than the other two.

"I bet that's the one Megs will choose," Lexi predicted.

"Why?"

"Because it's the most expensive one. Megs must have a highest price homing device in her head. Or in her finger. It hadn't failed once yet. Every time I give her a choice, her perfectly manicured finger goes to the most expensive item, even if she doesn't know the prices. The other day, we were selecting hardware for her kitchen cabinets. And wouldn't you know it, she pointed to the Schaub pull at $480 per piece. It added almost $40K to the cost of the kitchen."

"A perfect client."

"Yes. Megs is magnifique."

But Perry wanted more than talking about clients. Much more.

High on anticipation, he drove slowly to Lexi's cul-de-sac. It was 4:32, far too early. A dark sedan passed him impatiently and drove up the knoll to Lexi's house. *I should have insisted on the security system.* Perry sped up, ready to protect her.

Jack Carter jumped out of the sedan, carrying a magnificent bouquet of white roses. *What's he doing here?* Lexi appeared at the door. Jack drew her to himself and kissed her.

Perry drove away, swallowing tears. He parked his car around the corner and put his face in his hands.

Oh Lexi, why?

Dallas

DD
December 8

"Let's go inside," I said, unnerved by Jack's hug and kiss.

He handed me the gorgeous roses, stepped in, and looked around. Took a few steps forward and stopped. I never saw Jack so surprised.

"Oh my God, Alex. This is fantastic..."

"Thank you." A few months ago, I would have been thrilled to get such a compliment from Jack. Now I was hurt, not allowing myself to think about what could have been.

"With whom did you work on this?"

"Oh, five different contractors. And a garden designer."

"I mean the architect."

"I didn't work with an architect. It's my design," I said, not amused that Jack attributed it to someone else.

"And the glass?"

"My design, enhanced and executed by SeeThrough Dallas. Young, very creative guys." I touched the controls to show Jack how the glass panels worked.

"Clever," he said, smiling his boyish smile.

"You came here to tell me something." I sat down and pointed to the chair across from me.

"I am divorcing Vivien. It's official. She signed the papers. I filed the petition today. The divorce will be final in sixty-one days. That's the law."

"Oh. I am sorry, Jack. I thought..."

"No." Jack shook his head. "She and I were never happy together, but we were together almost twenty-nine years. You don't just push that aside."

Twenty-nine years... I was starting school when they got married.

"We had problems from the beginning, but the twins came so quickly. I hoped we would become closer, but things got only worse. I only stayed because of the twins. They were my whole life. I'd move mountains to make Vivien happy, so that the twins grew up in a happy family."

I wasn't sure where was Jack going with this. He'd told me about his early struggles many times before, and I wasn't interested in hearing it all over again. I was about to say that when my phone chimed.

PERRY: *I can't make our appointment.*

I could hardly hide my disappointment.

"My five o'clock can't make it. Let me take care of it please." I stood up and went to the kitchen.

ME: *Sorry about that. I was looking forward to our meeting. Let's reschedule. What's a good time for you?*

PERRY: *I'll get back to you later.*

Ugh. Something was wrong.

ME: *Hope you are OK. Have a good weekend.*

Maybe Perry had a hot date. And I stupidly thought we could have a dinner together. Feeling sad, I took mineral water from the fridge, got two glasses, and went back to finish the talk with Jack.

"Let me help you with that." Jack met me halfway.

"Well, to make a long story short, I screwed up." Jack looked at me sheepishly. "I wanted to please everyone and pleased no one. Anyhow, I came to make you an offer."

I sat down, curious.

"I thought a lot about your Inside-Outside concept. It fits perfectly with the direction I want to take my firm. Would you consider becoming a vice president at Carter & Co, responsible for these activities?"

Holy cow! VP at Carter & Co! One of the most prestigious architectural firms in the world.

"I'd consider it," I said, stunned.

Not so quickly, my brain meddled. *Remember the rumors.* People in the business saying that Jack is losing it, that his creativity dried out and he was taking advantage of his young associates in order to stay in the game.

"Don't let Jack talk you into something you don't want," Perry had warned me in Montreal. "Jack doesn't always stick to agreements."

Hm. Nothing a good contract can't take care of. I stood up and let my eyes rest on the freestyle pool, which seemingly flowed over to the koi pond (but didn't). I *wanted* to be a VP at Carter & Co.

"This house is proof that you are the perfect person for the job." Jack joined me.

"What's the job description?" I asked.

"Whatever you make of it. Provided it's in line with Carter & Co's philosophy."

I nodded, tempted.

"What are your conditions?" Jack asked.

"Let me think... You caught me by surprise," I admitted. "That I would be allowed to go on with my own business, certainly in the beginning. That my designs are my intellectual property and I may reuse them. I guess the lawyers would have to resolve this. And flexible hours. I would be in the office when needed, but I don't work nine to five."

"You work twenty-four seven," Jack quipped, looking happy. "That's all fine with me. Do you accept?"

"If the legal stuff's right."

"That's a formality." Jack chuckled. We looked at each other, unsure what to do next, our familiar responses on hold.

"In that case, would you like a glass of bubbly to celebrate?" I broke through the awkwardness.

"I thought you'll never ask." We both laughed. "May I look around a bit more?"

"Sure. Here is the before." I handed Jack my before and after folder. "I don't have the after pics yet, but it'll give you an idea."

Jack opened the folder. "Oh my."

"Yeah. Let me make us some snacks with the bubbly." I was starving.

I went to the kitchen, allowing myself to feel happy. *VP!* It felt good to be friendly with Jack again. I made a few quick smoked salmon hors d'oeuvres and opened the champagne. I was going to bring it to the living room, but Jack wasn't there. I took the two flutes and went to look for him.

Jack was leaning against the wall of my office.

"You'll never be happy with anyone else. You'll not enjoy anything you do with her because it's at the cost of my suffering," a voice hissed. "You can divorce me, but you can't get rid of me." *Vivien.* "You will pay for this for the rest of your life," she added. I gasped.

Jack turned around, looking devastated.

"I am so sorry, I didn't know... I went to look for you." My heart went out to him. Jack just stood there, rubbing his forehead, slowly shaking his head.

"Let's go to the living room, Jack." I coaxed him to sit down on the sofa.

"I've done everything for her. Always been there for her. Turned down great projects and built lots of stupid buildings because they made money for her." Jack pounded the sofa with his fist. "I am sorry," he apologized.

"You can do the creative stuff now," I said.

"She and I never worked as a couple. All I was asking for was some basic decency. What did you say?"

"That you can do the creative stuff now." I smiled at him.

"It looks like I got myself a VP for just that." Jack raised his glass. "So, how did you find this house?"

I told him about driving around, almost missing it, about Betsy Vandyck, about coming in the first time with Joyce and seeing the final product in front of my eyes, knowing it would be my DD.

"Betsy must be dancing the happy dance in heaven." Jack chuckled. "I love how you drive up, see a nice traditional U-shaped house, and then you step in and are in a totally modern world. It's almost like a loft but taken to the next level."

"Yeah. I gutted the whole thing." My stomach grumbled. "Oh jeez. I am sorry. I forgot the snacks."

Jack laughed. He took our glasses to the kitchen and refilled them while we nibbled on the snacks. Jack brought in my before and after file and compared the before with the new kitchen.

"You would never believe it's the same place... So, what's next?"

"Well, the guest quarters." I waved to the left wing of the house. "The mud room, gardening is far from finished, more art and artifacts, maybe a touch of something antique, the showroom behind my office." I pointed to the other wing. "And a home security system."

"I wouldn't go too heavy on that."

"Why not?"

"This is a safe part of town, and I would hate it if some security cowboy watched me in my own house." Jack's smile would melt a stone. We took our snacks back to the sofa.

"So, what are you up to these days, Jack?"

"I have a tower proposal in Vancouver. You'll love it." Jack shifted towards me. "And I love you. I love you so much, my Dream Girl. I missed you terribly, it was hell."

My heart was melting. We hugged, hungry to reconnect, the familiarity stirring more desire. We kissed. And kissed some more. As in the old times. A spark jumped over, reigniting the magic.

Before I knew it, Jack was kneeling in front of me, opening a little velvet box.

"Alex, my Dream Girl, will you marry me?"

Part 2

"Strange, I thought, how you can be living your dreams and your nightmares at the very same time."

Ransom Riggs, Hollow City

Dallas

DD
March 10

"I now pronounce you husband and wife." Jack drew me close to him. We kissed, melting to each other.

"Now you may kiss the bride...again." The Honorable Joe Clelland, Justice of the Peace, chuckled goodheartedly, joined by our friends.

We couldn't have wished for a more beautiful day. Sparkly blue sky, sunny but not too hot, perfect for having our small, informal ceremony in the DD garden. The caterers poured champagne and I was overcome by joy seeing everyone smiling and happy.

Jack's daughter Jen, looking gorgeous, holding hands with her husband Peter. Megs Aldridge, Evelyn O'Neill, Liz Howard, without Richard because he had to be in DC, Hannah leading the Carter & Co group. Bailey and Ian, Jen and Peter's kids, giggling, running around with their lab Henry. Even the typically reserved Victor, Jen's twin brother, grinned cheerfully.

"To a lifetime filled with love." Jack raised his glass and I joined him, elated. My dream came true. Pictures from the three months since Jack had come to DD for the first time cycled through my mind. A celebration of love, joy, togetherness, sharing. The most blissful time of my life.

"Congratulations!" Jen came over and gave us a hug.

"Look at you. My little girl. You look fantastic, Jen." Jack complimented her and I seconded him. Jen and I had become close friends in the last few months, and I was delighted to witness her transformation from a shy young mom to a beautiful, determined woman. She got in tip-top shape, and, cheered on by Peter and me, published her book of modern fairy tales for children. All while doing fundraising for Evelyn O'Neill's Futures and seeking a job as a journalist.

A line of cheerful well-wishers formed behind Jen. The caterers wheeled in delicious-looking hors d'oeuvres and the party took off. Jack and I went from hug to hug, laughing, jubilant.

"I've put a platter of hors d'oeuvres in the fridge for you, Miss A," the caterer said when the party was winding down. "I've noticed you didn't have a chance to get any."

"Thank you, Dylan. That's lovely." No wonder he was in such a high demand. Dylan did our party only as a special favor for Liz.

"Calling you Miss A means that you made his list," Liz whispered in my ear when Dylan went back to the house. I laughed, wondering how he selected his clients.

When everyone left, Jack and I took our shoes off and stretched out on the comfortable patio sofa, holding hands, enjoying a glass of champagne.

The doorbell rang.

"I'll get it," I said and stood up. "Someone probably forgot something."

I walked to the front door, a smile on my face. Jack caught up with me and put his arm around my shoulders.

Vivien was the last person I expected to see. She had all but disappeared after her vicious call to Jack months ago.

"Oh hi, I just stopped by to wish you lovebirds good luck." She walked in, looking around curiously.

"I hear you love roses." Vivien shoved a fading pink bouquet into my arms. Petals with brownish edges, a few heads hanging down, an orange 'reduced' sticker screaming from the cellophane.

Before I could say anything, Vivien wrapped herself around Jack and gave him a full-body hug. She kissed him and disentangled herself.

"I'll leave you two alone now. I know you have million things to do," she chirped and walked to the door.

I relaxed, ready to throw the roses away and forget the whole episode. Vivien stopped and turned around, a triumphant smile lighting up her face.

"I'll be back," she said sweetly.

A chill ran up my spine.

Dallas

The Frog Prince Restaurant
March 15

The three women leaned conspiratorially across the table. The hustle and bustle of the restaurant dampened their voices, but they took all precautions not to allow a whisper to escape from their table.

"She told me that she could have taken Jack to the cleaners and destroyed him in the media, but she took a lesser deal to protect the children," Annabel reported.

"Vivien taking the high road?" Evelyn's eyebrows shot up. "I doubt it… She was absolutely furious when Al advised her to settle. She begged me to find her another lawyer." Evelyn rolled her eyes. "I told her 'if Al is telling you to settle, you should settle.' No one could get her a better deal than Al."

"That's absolutely right, Al gets the max for his clients." Annabel nodded knowingly.

"And he isn't afraid to go to court to get it. He settles only when he is absolutely sure he can't win."

"Yeah, you know, Janet said Al asked her not to put Vivien's calls through to him anymore. Just give her a standard answer and bill her immediately."

"Janet told you that? That's not like Al. He cares about his clients." Evelyn knitted her eyebrows. "There must have been something incriminating."

"Hm…do you remember the rumors a few years back? About Senator Lowell?" Annabel asked.

"Yes. But it was hushed up really quickly."

"And nobody could tell what really happened."

"Maybe we should ask Vivien. She loves revealing these dark secrets."

"About others. Not about herself."

"It was some kind of accident." Annabel frantically searched her memory. "Vivien's uncle was involved too, the one who disappeared, remember?" Annabel looked at Evelyn, hoping that she would fill in the blanks.

"Ralph? That was financial fraud." Evelyn snorted. "He can never come back here. Too many people lost too much money. Oh, there she is."

The women sat back in their chairs and observed Vivien who rapidly typed on her phone while walking into the restaurant. The horizontal magenta stripes on Vivien's tight pink mini-dress stretched over her imposing middle and drew attention to the quivery pudginess above her knees.

"Oh my." Fiona sucked her breath in. "Is she pregnant?"

~~~

Vivien looked around the restaurant, spotted her friends, and rushed to their table. She loved being important. Having lunch at the best table in The Frog Prince with Evelyn and Annabel made her bubble with pride.

But who was the third woman? Evelyn hadn't said anything about bringing in a stranger. And how come the woman had taken Vivien's regular place? Where was Vivien supposed to sit? With her back to the room? *Unacceptable*! Vivien *needed* to see and be seen. A burst of anger shot through her, but she kept a smile glued to her face.

"I am not late, am I?" Vivien stood by the table, hoping the intruder would stand up and walk away.

"Why don't you sit down, Vivien," Evelyn said, pointing to the dreaded fourth chair. "Do you know Fiona? She and her husband just moved in town from London."

Vivien shook her head.

"Fiona is Megs Aldridge's friend. They used to spend summers together in Southern France."

Summers in Southern France. A balloon filled with envy exploded in Vivien's chest. She sat down and turned to Fiona just in time to catch Fiona's shocked look follow the pink dress as it rode up on Vivien's thighs and revealed a vast area of cellulite. Not bothering to pull the dress down, Vivien asked, "What's your husband doing, Fiona?"

"He is in oil. And your husband?"

Vivien flinched. She didn't expect to be questioned about Jack. She ignored Fiona and studied the menu.

"So, what do *you* do, Vivien?" Fiona didn't give up.

THE WALL

Evelyn and Annabel looked at each other, smiles playing around their lips.

Vivien took it all in and replied triumphantly, "I am in internet marketing."

Evelyn drew her breath in. "You never told *us* about this... You aren't one of the scammers, are you?" Evelyn looked at Annabel and Fiona, her face filled with mock horror.

Vivien froze. Evelyn was never so rude to her before. *How dare she criticize my business?* Vivien didn't deserve this...but she didn't want to cross Evelyn, so she searched for something cheeky to say that would turn it all into a joke.

Evelyn changed the subject before Vivien could exonerate herself. "Tell us about your new house, Fiona."

Vivien hardly listened. Her friendship with Evelyn was threatened! The only friendship Vivien cared about... *This can't be happening to me...* Vivien blinked rapidly. *It's all Jack's fault.* She hated to be divorced. She never expected it would be so hard.

Vivien deeply regretted signing the divorce papers. It was a thorn in her side, a wound that festered and became deeper and deeper each day. She should have never listened to Al and Evelyn. She should have dug her heels in and postponed, postponed, postponed until Jack capitulated and came back to her. The divorce should *never* have gone through.

And as if the divorce wasn't bad enough, Jack had married Alex the first day he legally could. A decent man would have waited a year or two... *He married her right away to spite me*, Vivien seethed.

She tried to ignore it all, but the damage was too much. It rendered her powerless. Insignificant. Jack had made a laughingstock of her. Vivien's fingers tightened into hard fists. *He'll pay for this.*

Big.

Dallas

The Frog Prince

Soothed by the fantasies of sweet revenge, Vivien tuned back to the conversation. A dynamo clad in chef's outfit stopped at their table.

"Amalia, so good to have you back." Evelyn jumped up and squeezed the chef in a happy hug. "We've missed you. But your staff has done a fabulous job."

Vivien had never met Amalia before. Owner and a chef? Why would you sweat in the kitchen when you are the owner? *Stupid.* Vivien observed Amalia as if she were some repulsive exotic bug.

"So, how was the chefs' convention? Did you come back with exciting new recipes?" Evelyn never tired of trying Amalia's new creations.

"Oh, absolutely. Today we have my new version of key lime pie. I've totally deconstructed it and it's feather light."

"Interesting. By the way, do you have something delicious that's pink or orange?" Evelyn asked.

"Yes, please. I eat only pink and orange food," Fiona said. Vivien looked at her incredulously, noticing Fiona's pink and orange outfit. *I bet she takes diamonds in all colors*, Vivien sniggered. Evelyn gave her a look that would freeze the Sahara.

"Hmmm…would you like a pumpkin soup with pink Gulf shrimp?"

"Is it organic?"

"Yes. We work only with organic seasonal produce and use the most natural techniques. We are not a chemical lab." Amalia smiled. "What you see is what you get."

"So if everything is so simple, why is your menu so huge?" Vivien smirked. She had nearly knocked over her cocktail with that oversized nonsense.

Amalia stopped talking. Vivien looked around in triumph, expecting her friends to laugh. Evelyn had always laughed when Vivien said out loud what everyone thought, but no one dared to say. Not this time.

THE WALL

Evelyn didn't laugh and neither did Annabel and Fiona. They hung on Amalia's lips, curiosity written all over their faces.

"The menu is part of the Frog Prince experience, ma'am," Amalia answered cheerfully. "Each menu is individually designed and handwritten. It tells you our story and the story of our dishes."

"It's exquisite." Evelyn softly touched her menu. "Tell us your story, Amalia. I can't get enough of it."

"Once upon a time a little girl fell in love with a prince, who was beloved by the whole universe. She adored him and would do anything for him." Amalia stopped dramatically.

That's right, Vivien recalled, someone told her that Amalia's husband was a rock star. Vivien relaxed in her chair, looking forward to the happy ending.

"When the girl became a young woman, she gave her life away for the prince," Amalia continued. "She kissed the prince, but he turned into an ugly frog." Amalia paused again.

"And when I realized what a SOB he was, I left, opened my restaurant and called it the Frog Prince, as a reminder to never fall for anything superficial again. To stick with the real stuff. And that's what we do with our food."

Vivien didn't get it. Who divorces a rock star to slave in the kitchen? *Ridiculous.* The whole Frog Prince experience was overrated.

The ladies chatted on, laughed happily, and ignored Vivien as if she weren't at the table.

An ominous lump settled in Vivien's throat. But she didn't give up easily.

When the waitress came along asking, "Anyone ready for dessert?" Vivien grabbed her opportunity to get back into the game.

"I will have the key lime pie," she ordered.

Evelyn politely declined any desserts. Fiona and Annabel followed suit. It was too late for Vivien to take her order back. Feverish heat wave flushed her head to toe.

"Oh, I almost forgot, Evelyn." Fiona shook her head in horror. "I saw Megs the other day. She is going to give you a call about a fundraiser idea."

"Good. I haven't seen her in ages. How is she?"

"Great. She is absolutely thrilled about her house. Alex has done a fabulous job. I've seen it myself. Phenomenal." Fiona described the glassed-in professional kitchen, the cabinet pulls costing $480 a piece, the "mile long" buffet bar that can easily serve at least a hundred people, the miraculous living space that changes colors with Megs's moods, and the heavenly spa, which only Megs's very best friends may enter. Each ooohh and aaaahh the ladies uttered in admiration of Alex's work sent Vivien deeper into her exile of powerlessness and insignificance.

Shaken to her core, Vivien focused on a large helping of the so highly recommended key lime pie, which didn't even look like a pie. And the one helping was almost the whole thing.

"How is the pie, Vivien? It looked absolutely stunning." Evelyn inspected Vivien's plate. Her disapproving look constricted Vivien's throat like a giant boa. The pie turned to poison on her tongue. She couldn't swallow so much bitterness if her life depended on it.

Vivien put her hand in front of her mouth, grabbed her bag, knocked over her chair, and made it to the ladies just in time to dispose of her lunch in a black stone wash basin. She wondered if the basin was one of Alex's phenomenal designs and threw up again. Neither Evelyn nor Annabel came to check on her. Vivien stormed out of the restaurant without returning to their table.

Alex will pay for this.

Dallas

Vivien's bedroom
March 16

Vivien hadn't had a bite to eat since the lethal lunch. She'd never set foot into the horrendous Frog restaurant again. Just the memory of it shot reflux into Vivien's mouth. She attempted to wash it down with a swig of vodka, but the acidity had already entered her mind. *My friends deserted me.* Vivien's mouth twisted with displeasure.

"We'll go live in one hour! Don't miss it, Vivien." A message popped on her screen. Vivien let out a sigh. Another webinar she wasn't in the mood for. She expected that Evelyn or Annabel would call her after the lunch and all would be well again. But no one called. It was all Alex's fault. She had alienated Vivien's friends. Vivien couldn't remember when she felt so abandoned. Not since her ninth birthday.

Vivien had been looking forward to her birthday for weeks, but Lauren and Ted, Vivien's older siblings, had chosen this day to bully her mercilessly since the early morning. Vivien didn't want to ruin her birthday and heroically resisted them. But their attacks went on and on, not giving Vivien any choice but turning to her last resort defense: running to Mom and crying her heart out.

"Don't be such a crybaby," Mom ordered.

"Lauren said I am so ugly no one will ever marry me," Vivien wailed.

"Sticks and stones can break your bones, words can't hurt you."

Vivien screeched from the top of her lungs. She wanted revenge.

"Vivien, if you don't stop right now you will not get your birthday present."

The present stood on the table, next to the rich chocolate cake. A large box with a beautiful, blonde Barbie. Vivien calmed down and was rewarded by a large piece of the cake. She would have liked to have a second helping, but the Barbie won. Vivien grabbed the box and ran to her room.

Mesmerized by the doll's curves, Vivien lovingly caressed her silky hair. The Barbie was her most prized possession.

"You are my best friend, Barbs," Vivien whispered into the doll's tiny ear.

Lauren and Ted barged into the room.

"You are too fat to have a Barbie," Lauren exclaimed, hands on her hips.

"Too fat and too stupid," her brother clarified, grabbed Barbs and twisted off her right arm.

Lauren giggled and ripped out a thick patch of the doll's hair. Barbs crashed to the floor. Mortified, Vivien leaped to her rescue, but Ted was faster. He pushed Vivien away and crushed Barb's face with his heel.

Vivien screamed like a wounded animal.

"What's going on here?" Dad entered the battlefield, holding a cigar between his fingers.

"Vivien ruined her Barbie, Daddy," Lauren explained sweetly.

"We tried to stop her, but she attacked us," Ted offered his part of the story.

"Noooooooooooo…" Vivien squealed, tears gushing over her cheeks like Niagara Falls.

"Stop being such a crybaby," Dad said. They all left Vivien's room.

Vivien collapsed on the floor and lay there for hours, curled into a motionless ball. No one came to check on her. Finally, she stood up, lips set in a tight line. She kicked Barbs to the corner of the room.

The doll's head flew off in midair.

Vivien had gone to bed and never ever cried herself to sleep again. And no matter how hard Lauren and Ted tried, their assaults bounced off her without leaving a mark.

The next day Uncle Ralph had come by and given her a new Barbie. Vivien had climbed in his lap and glowed with pride when he called her his little bad girl. Vivien loved Uncle Ralph.

Vivien lingered in the memory and let it restore her strength. She will not let Evelyn bully her. *All the bad things people do to me have nothing to do with me.* It was all about them. She didn't need to spend thousands of dollars on therapy to get this message. She figured it out on her ninth birthday, all on her own.

If her friends looked down on her because Jack divorced her, so be it. She didn't need them. *I'll show them.* Vivien laughed. Gone were the days

THE WALL

when she merely read people's emails. Since Jack left her, Vivien upped her game and built a priceless collection of juicy secrets she'd reveal when the time was right. The market craved secrets, and Vivien was ready to supply them.

Her "friends" would regret deserting her when they no longer got the priciest stories in town…when they *became* the priciest stories in town. Vivien giggled.

And Alex would regret the day she had laid her eyes on Jack. If Vivien couldn't have the man she loved, neither would Alex.

Vivien turned on her computer, studied the calendars and smirked. A plan was formed.

Vivien's love defied reality.

Dallas

The Art Tower; Carter & Co offices
March 21

Hate at first sight.

There was no other way to describe it. Marty Watson, Carter & Co's CFO, couldn't stand me from day one. And things only got worse as time went on.

"You must be imagining it," Jack had dismissed my concerns. "Why would Marty hate you?"

That's what I asked myself: Why would Marty hate me? I'd never experienced such open animosity in my entire career. On the contrary. Getting along with people in spite of our differences was one of my strong points. Yet, Marty and I didn't get a chance to even declare our differences because the antipathy took over as soon as Jack introduced us. I extended my hand to Marty, but he refused to shake it, giving me a condescending look instead. I certainly didn't imagine *that*.

And I also didn't imagine all the errors and omissions Marty made in the budget for our new project, a multi-million remodel of an old skyscraper downtown. We weren't talking about some negligible slips of the pen. Marty's mistakes were big enough to jeopardize the part of the project I was responsible for, which featured a new retail space, inside-outside dining, waterfalls, and lavish landscaping.

I took a deep breath, deciding what to do. I went to a great length to fix the budget with Marty before this meeting—tried to make an appointment, emailed him, texted him—but Marty ignored me. So now I had to address the errors in front of everyone else. I straightened up in my chair and bit the bullet.

"Marty, could you please tell me under which section are the costs of the terraces?" I asked, in as friendly a tone as I could muster. The terraces were the key feature of the newly designed outside area. I had given Marty a detailed spreadsheet with an estimate of their costs three weeks ago, but these numbers didn't make it to his version of the budget.

Marty put down his reading glasses and glared at me as if I had committed a cardinal sin.

"Alex, don't meddle with my numbers. I don't meddle with your designs," he said dismissively. Several people snickered.

Tension filled the room. My heart was beating like crazy.

"Don't let Jack talk you into something you don't want," I recalled Perry advising me.

But I *wanted* to work on this project. It was my debut at Carter & Co, a model project for the new Inside-Outside Group I was heading. It was imperative that everything went well, but the tense, doubting faces of the people around the table weren't encouraging. Did they hate me just like Marty? This wasn't how I imagined my job at Carter & Co.

"When something bad happens, it's my chance to improve life." Mo's words came to my mind.

I must have smiled because people were looking at me quizzically, deadly quiet.

"I totally agree with you, Marty," I said. "It wouldn't cross my mind to meddle with *your* numbers. The point is, what we are talking about right now are *my* numbers." More people snickered. I had their attention now.

"No worries, Marty," I went on. "We can adjust the budget. Let's review the spreadsheet to make sure we've got it right. The terraces are our opportunity to rock downtown. Let's grasp it and run with it."

"OK!"

"Yeah!"

"Let's do it."

"I've got it right here. Let me beam it up." Charlie Bullard, our master of all things "Outside", projected the spreadsheet on the wall.

The tension left the room. We were in business.

Dallas

Vivien's bedroom
March 29

"Awesome, awesome! We are on the air! Gimme a sign you hear me!"

Vivien typed "hear you :-)".

"OK, OK. Nick and Dick here. Let's see. OK, the recording IS ON."

"Let's get rollin'! Hi everybody, wasup, wasup, wasup! I am pumped! We have so much news, it's not gonna fit in one call. Maybe we will have another call on Friday!"

Vivien loved this mastermind. She couldn't wait to hear all the news, pumped about being in a group of such awesome internet marketing entrepreneurs.

All of them shared the same mindset: use any hack you can to make as much money as you can as fast as you can.

There was nothing simpler than that. It was *so* right.

To think that she'd almost missed this opportunity. She had discovered the mastermind a week after the registration deadline, but she had known right away that this was *it*. This was her BREAKTHROUGH writ large. She *had* to get in and *nothing* would stop her. Not the missed deadline, not the fact that this was by far the most expensive training she had ever come across. She talked Nick and Dick into accepting her to the program and then got Marty on board as well.

As far as Vivien was concerned, Nick and Dick couldn't do anything wrong. No one else was as brilliant and generous as these two entrepreneurs.

Vivien became an internet marketer by accident, but she was hooked from the moment she had downloaded her first free e-book. She had attended the free webinar that came with the e-book, and in no time her inbox was bursting at the seams with marketing offers, newsletters, invitations, and reminders.

Vivien loved it. For the first time in her life she felt truly important. Out of the blue she connected with people who understood her like no one else ever before. She belonged. The promise of crushing it and becoming fabulously rich was like music to her ears.

She followed webinar after webinar, bought product after product, signed on to training after training, all promising internet marketing riches.

There was nothing like the euphoria she experienced when she bought something new. The glorious feeling of a new beginning, the anticipation of living the perfect life. Being just "three ninja tricks" from making it big or "five simple steps" from financial freedom triggered the golden flakes that danced through Vivien's body and made her forget everything else.

Yet, Vivien had rarely made it past the first step of each new program. She didn't understand what was going on. The marketing gurus preached about a lack of commitment, but that wasn't Vivien's problem. She was genuinely committed: she wanted to crush it, she wanted to proudly share screenshots of bank accounts overflowing with thousands of dollars earned in a day or two, she wanted to post pictures of herself on a tropical island, next to a luxurious car, or in front of a fabulous mansion.

Yet, the same thing kept happening again and again: filled with hope and determination to succeed, Vivien would attend the newest training or download the hottest course, but it was never what she expected. The simple steps weren't simple, the assignments required hours of work. And before she could get deeper into the newest product, there was already a newer offer that promised so much more, only to disappoint her again.

Until Nick and Dick came along. They promised "earning while learning." No one else offered that. And no one else offered newbies an opportunity to earn up to three thousand dollars per day in the first week of the program.

Vivien followed every second of Nick and Dick's training. Nick explained the larger picture, and Dick demonstrated step by step what students had to do. Everything made sense! The steps were so simple, Vivien could easily repeat them on her own. Her confidence grew by the minute, and she loved participating in the program's Facebook group, where students could help each other 24/7. Vivien soon became one of the most active members of the group.

She learned how to purchase Virtual Private Servers and create fake Facebook accounts for monetization. By the end of the first week she had one $800 day and one $1200 day. She had to split her earnings with Nick and Dick, but she didn't mind. She could easily scale up with more Facebook accounts.

Vivien was thrilled. Everything went according to the plan.

Until the unthinkable happened.

Dallas

Vivien's bedroom
Still March 29

Just when Vivien was gaining speed, Facebook clamped down on Nick and Dick's rogue advertising, nearly forcing them out of business. The enormity of the injustice shook Vivien to the bone. But Nick and Dick put the fiasco down as a minor business inconvenience and vowed to come back with an even more profitable advertising model. "You've got to see problems as opportunities."

That was six weeks ago. The webinars went on, Nick kept promising that a new killer campaign will be released next week, and next week, and next week... After the third postponement people started to get nervous about losing their investment in the program.

The Facebook group wasn't the same since. Instead of talking about hacks, people turned all their frustrations against Nick and Dick and accused them of being scammers. Marty teamed up with a couple of other students who gave up on Nick and Dick altogether and switched to a horrendously expensive internet marketing mastermind based in DC

Vivien was appalled. Sure, nobody earned their training fee of $10,000 back, but it wasn't Nick and Dick's fault. If Facebook hadn't changed its policy, they would have gotten their fee back in couple of weeks. Vivien sighed, frustration taking over her. But Nick's excitement pulled her in:

"Dick's testing the new method, and it's UNBELIEVABLE. We are PRINTING MONEY. There's no other way to put it. You throw a thousand in and two thousand come out, over and over and over again." Nick paused to let them digest the abundance. Vivien reached for her vodka bottle. Golden flakes fluttered through her.

"Stick with us another week or two and you've got yourself a money machine. In the meantime, keep creating new accounts. The more, the better."

"Let's take a little quiz. Are you creating new accounts? Type yes in the box."

"Yes, yes, yes. OK! And now type in how many accounts you have."

Vivien typed 37.

"Three, six, two, six, five, three, thirty-seven! Wow! Shout-out to Vivien. She is the winner with thirty-seven Facebook accounts."

Vivien took another gulp of vodka. She loved winning. She loved to be Nick and Dick's best student.

And she loved creating each of her thirty-seven fake Facebook accounts. She could make at least $10,000 per account. Which came to $370,000 in total. And that was just the beginning. Golden flakes tickled Vivien's heart.

With a little luck she could make $20K on some accounts before Facebook caught on and shut them down. Vivien snorted. She didn't get Facebook. What was the point of shutting down profitable accounts? She would understand it if people hated the offers. But the diet pills and anti-wrinkle creams Nick and Dick promoted were selling like crazy. OK, so the products didn't work exactly as in the before and after pictures. But who cares? People loved buying the stuff, it made them happy.

"You are not selling a cream. You are selling hope," Dick explained many times. "HOPE is HEALTHY."

Vivien shifted impatiently. If the new campaign was more Facebook resistant, her accounts would bring in more than half a million dollars! Half a million doing something she loved! Vivien giggled. Her fake personas were so much fun. They were the best cure for all the misery Jack put her through.

Every time Vivien was upset, she activated her accounts and trolled her heart out until she felt better. And when she felt good, she did the same, to feel even better. She couldn't understand why she didn't think about this before. Being free to post whatever she wanted was the best there was.

Vivien couldn't thank Nick and Dick enough. They saved her life.

"And by the way," Nick went on excitedly, "a second shout-out to Vivien for making an awesome testimonial video for us. I posted it in the group to inspire all of you to shoot something like that." Vivien burst with pride. Making the video was the easiest thing in the world. She was looking forward to the compliments she'd get from the group.

She couldn't wait and went to the group right away.

"Hey Vivien, do you know that Nick and Dick used your testimonial to recruit more people to the training? All these people paid ten grand for shit that doesn't work. Because your vid is so awesome," A guy Vivien didn't know claimed.

"What training?" Vivien had no idea what he was talking about.

"The same as our mastermind but a different group. Check this out."

Vivien followed the link. Her blood froze. Nick and Dick indeed used her video throughout their promotion. They cut it into pieces and edited it to show a bank account with $75K when she talked about how she profited from the program. *This is not my account!* Vivien glared at the slide, anger taking over.

In the meantime, more people saw the promotion and filled the group's wall with furious remarks about Nick and Dick selling a fake training program with Vivien's help.

Vivien held her breath, face glowing, fists clenched, outraged that Nick and Dick didn't include her in the deal. She deserved to get a commission on everyone who bought their program. She almost messaged Nick to demand her fair share but stopped herself in the last second. She jumped to her feet and took a gulp of vodka.

Her video sold the training! Better yet, *she* sold the training!

Why should she fight for a measly commission if she can collect the whole fee? With her experience, she could sell her own training program and get rich.

Vivien defied reality.

Dallas

DD
April 6

"Take a picture of us, will ya?" Vivien ordered Dylan, the caterer, handing him her phone without giving him as much as a look. She put her arm around Jack's waist, threw her head back and opened her mouth to show off her perfected teeth.

A pang of jealousy shot through my heart. The plain and plump Vivien was gone. The new Vivien was confident, exuberant, and at least fifteen pounds lighter.

Dylan took the picture and showed it to Vivien. She inspected it, lips curled down.

"Let's take another one," she ordered, and struck her pose again, this time making sure that Jack's arm hugged her shoulders.

"Smile Jack, I don't bite." Vivien fluffed her new platinum blonde hairdo and signaled Dylan to take the picture.

What else is she going to do? I wondered. Whatever it will be, Vivien ruined the party for me already. Again. My own party in my own house.

Just as two weeks ago when she'd crashed our party the first time, Vivien came in early and leeched on to Jack, not leaving him for a second. Every time I came to talk with Jack, she put her hand on his arm and stepped forward as if she were protecting him from me. Just as the last time, Jack didn't extract himself from her.

Hannah came over and we chatted about the downtown remodel. Vivien was still shadowing Jack as if she were his alter ego, although she was glued to her phone in the last few minutes. She put the phone down and threw Jack a triumphant smirk.

The knot that had occupied the pit of my stomach since Vivien entered the house tightened up. I excused myself and went to my office. Cued by the last party Vivien crashed, I went directly to her Facebook wall. Sure enough, the photo of Vivien and Jack that Dylan just took was on the top. Accompanied by Vivien's "state of mind": "With Jack, the love of my life."

The second photo was of me carrying dirty plates. The caption read: "our help today ;-)". Vivien tagged Jack in the pictures so that his friends got them too. I leaned on my desk, my heart pounding as if this was my last minute. The chutzpah.

How can I get Vivien out of my life? The hurt and humiliation were getting to me. Three hits in two weeks. Two crashed parties and one ruined dinner. Let alone all the phone calls at the worst moments. *How does she know when we entertain?*

Many people could have told her about the parties but the dinner? No one present at the dinner knew Vivien. Except Jack. But Jack swore he didn't invite her.

"In that case it looks like she hacked one of our computers," I'd said to Jack.

"Do you really have to be so paranoid?" Jack had dismissed me. And let Vivien get away with crashing our events.

"Just give her a break, Alex. The transition is hard on her. She is the mother of my children. Give her time." Jack had defended Vivien every time she overstepped.

As much as I sympathized with his concerns and her difficulties, Vivien's intrusions were breaking us apart. I took a deep breath to suppress the tears welling up in my eyes.

Jack and I were so great together when Vivien wasn't involved. Our love was the real thing. Partners for better and for worse. Except for Vivien.

What went wrong? This should be the happiest time of my life, but if I were totally honest with myself, I'd say our wedding day was my last happy day.

Fed up with being humiliated by Vivien, I wanted to run to the living room and kick her out. But it would make her look like a victim and me like a villain, which was exactly what she was after. I was between a rock and a hard place.

I took a few more deep breaths to temper my anger before going back to the party. I didn't see Vivien anywhere, but her huge faux crocodile bag dominated the buffet table, ruining the display. She nearly pushed several platters off the table to fit the bag in. My barely suppressed anger flared up again. I walked over to rearrange the table, but Dylan got there ahead of me.

"I've got it, Miss A." Dylan removed Vivien's bag and put it in on a chair in the corner of the room while I fixed the buffet. Two roses I used for decoration were squashed as if a cow had chewed them up and spat them back on the table. This wasn't an accident...

"Where is my bag? What have you done with my bag?" Vivien yelled. She charged towards me and stopped barely an inch from my chest. Still holding the crushed roses, I looked down to face her, resisting the urge to take a step back. The room went silent, all eyes turned on the two of us.

"Where did you last see your bag, Vivien?" I asked in a friendly voice and looked directly into her eyes.

Vivien looked away, surprised, as if not expecting to be questioned. She took a step back and bumped into Jack.

"Take it easy, Viv." Jack put his hand on Vivien's shoulder. I froze.

"She took my bag," Vivien whined.

"No, she has not, ma'am," Dylan said. "Your bag is over there." He pointed to the corner. "It was on the buffet table, ma'am. It could have got soiled there, so I moved it."

Several people chuckled.

Vivien's eyes went wide open. She gave Dylan that covetous look reserved for long lost lovers. Then she shook her head slightly as if she made a mistake. Her face turned into a hard, disdainful mask.

For a millisecond Dylan's mouth curled in a cruel satisfaction. A chill ran up my spine. Dylan's quick smile covered up their bizarre exchange, but you can't unsee what you've seen...

Not saying a word, not looking at anyone, Vivien snagged her bag from the chair. Her face turned from disdainful to demure. She walked slowly towards the front door, head down, shoulders hunched, dragging her feet ever so slightly, as if her shoes didn't fit. It was the walk designed to make people feel sorry for her. I knew better. I looked at Jack, but he looked away. My heart sank.

Something was terribly wrong.

Dallas

Senator Howard's office suite
April 10

"Did you know that your dad was going to run for president?" Dave asked.

"No." Perry straightened up in his chair.

"Our guy in Houston made some progress," Dave explained.

"Our guy" was a private investigator hired to find as much as he could about the hit and run that killed Perry's mom. The investigator specialized in cold cases, but after several false starts and frustrating dead ends, Perry almost gave up on catching the killer.

"It appears that Senator Lowell was going to announce his presidential candidacy at your Grandma Gloria's birthday party in Galveston. But the police came in before the event and questioned him about your mom's accident."

"And he dropped his presidency bid," Perry said, shocked by the implication.

"Yes. He left Galveston before the party, and he and Gloria reportedly didn't speak for years after that."

Perry drew his breath in.

"That's all we have so far. Lowell's employees are extremely tight-lipped. Nobody wants to end on the wrong side of Gloria." Dave smiled apologetically.

"Well, this is quite a breakthrough. Thanks for coming to Dallas to tell me," Perry said.

"Sure. But that's not the only reason we are here." Dave turned to Shaun and Lewis.

Still unsettled by the guy's unexpected visit, Perry braced himself for trouble, worried that they got bad news from Dave's doctors.

"We have to level. This went on too long already," Dave said. "It makes no sense to keep a penthouse in Houston when you work in Dallas and DC"

"But your doctors are in Houston."

"I have a clean bill of health," Dave said. "Had it for weeks." Shaun and Lewis nodded.

"So you guys want to move to Dallas?" Perry asked, hoping they'd move. He missed their camaraderie. And being around them would make it easier to get over Lexi. *Why did she marry the jackass?*

Dave was looking out of the window. "The main reason we are here is because we have a business proposal and we thought it would be more professional to talk about it in your office."

Perry relaxed. Business deals were easy.

"We've prepared a presentation." Shaun took a laptop out of his bag and turned it on.

"I was looking for something gainful to do and started a blog about hotels, restaurants, wines, the good life." Dave took the lead. "But I quickly realized how difficult it is to build a presence online, and how difficult it is to find a training that REALLY helps you with it."

Perry knew exactly what Dave meant.

"Now, I told Shaun and Lewis about my frustrations, and it turns out that they spent a pretty penny on all kinds of courses that promised to teach them how to create an online business but did NOT live up to it," Dave said dramatically.

"So in the last months we've inventoried the courses out there, and let me tell you, the state of affairs is abysmal." Dave paused and took a sip of water.

"Even if we leave out the obvious scams, most of the programs simply don't deliver," Dave continued. "That's why we decided to create our own online marketing academy."

Perry was intrigued. He had delegated most of his business dealings and focused on politics, but now caught himself longing to be part of the guys' start-up.

Shaun and Lewis took over the presentation. The more Perry listened, the more impressed he was with their work.

"So, in a nutshell, you want to start with a basic product and snowball it from there," Perry summed it up.

"Yes, the first product is about getting results fairly quickly," Lewis answered.

"But we are not promising the 'become a millionaire overnight' thing. We want to show people that it's possible to get a foothold in this business and make progress step by step," Shaun added.

THE WALL

"We want to become a solid player," Dave said. "We are looking for a long-term presence, something people can rely on."

"Great job," Perry said, excited. "I love it. Could I somehow partner with you?"

Shaun and Lewis exchanged surprised looks. Dave gave his I-told-you-so face.

"The thing is, you are a partner already," Lewis said. "That's why we are here. To make sure that everything is fair and square businesswise."

"What do you mean?" Perry rubbed his chin. "You guys have done all the work, I haven't done anything."

"But we've done the work on your time," Shaun explained.

"You pay us to take care of Dave," Lewis said. "We do, but it takes less and less time. Let alone we worked on this while waiting in the hospital and so on. So you've actually paid us for doing this."

"No way," Perry exclaimed. "You could've just as well played video games while waiting. If we partner, it has to be fair and square. As you said."

"And if we partner, it will make sense to move the whole show to Dallas," Perry added with a grin.

"It's a deal," Dave agreed, radiant. "OK. Enough for one day. Anyone in for a dinner?"

"Sure, where would you like to go?" Perry asked.

"I was thinking about the new place on Flora. I've read great things about it, and they are supposed to have a marvelous wine cellar."

"Done," Perry agreed, feeling happy and rejuvenated.

Life made sense again.

Dallas

Vivien's bedroom
April 16

Men are stupid.

Vivien carefully filed the sexting session, including the evidence that it was conducted from the senator's computer. She smirked. The guy was totally unprotected. Stupid. *Beyond stupid.*

Or take Jack. He thought that she was still crushed because he left her. Jack had *no right* to divorce her, but Vivien wasn't crushed. Far from it. She was having the time of her life. She was no longer the gray mouse living in the shadow of the more fortunate women. She'd never felt better or looked better. She had lost twenty-one pounds without even trying. And she was an entrepreneur in her own right, free to explore online and offline as much as she wanted to.

Explore and exploit.

A triumphant smile filled Vivien's face. She was on the verge of becoming an internet guru, and Jack and Marty financed her venture without even knowing it. Vivien laughed and took a deep swig from an oversized vodka bottle. Another advantage of not having Jack around: she didn't have to mix her alcohol with sickening fruit juice anymore.

Vivien stretched in her bed. Her bedroom became her war room. It was all she needed, and she rarely left it. She hated the house. So old and shabby. She'd assumed Jack would continue maintaining the house as he always did, but he had abandoned it as he abandoned her. Vivien tried to sell the house and get a condo downtown, but the house wouldn't bring in enough money to buy a condo in a prestigious building with a twenty-four-hour concierge... Vivien *needed* someone to welcome her when she came home.

She wished she had demanded the condo in the settlement. The festering divorce-wound shot arrows of pain through Vivien's psyche. *I was too nice*, Vivien chastened herself. But it happened so fast. Despite everything, she counted on Jack's returning to her. Jack wasn't supposed to *marry* Alex.

A picture of Alex's streamlined interior filled Vivien's mind. *It should be my house. It is my house. Alex stole it from me.* Vivien clenched her fists. *Jack must buy me the condo.* She'd tell him it's an investment for the twins. He'll do anything for the twins, Vivien frowned.

Jen was insufferable. And even Victor didn't live up to expectation. Such a disappointment. Vivien snorted. She went to great length to bring Victor back to Dallas, but he didn't take care of the house either. Just went to parties at her expense. Victor will have to go. She had no use for him anymore.

And Marty will have to go too. Marty went too far. Behaving as if he owned her. Just because he was helping her launch the training program? That didn't give him any rights. To top it off, Marty refused to participate in the Hugh Donaldson investment. Vivien fumed.

It had started so innocently. They had been at Oceans, celebrating the completion of Vivien's launch videos. Marty raised his glass to her: "You are a natural, Viv." He leaned over and kissed her on her hair. "I am sure the launch will be a great success."

"We'll crush it," Vivien agreed, irritated by Marty's kiss.

"To crushing it." Marty raised his glass again. "And to rinsing and repeating," he added nonchalantly.

Vivien wasn't amused. Rinse and repeat? Launching products was too much work even if you are a natural. She didn't want to go through *that* again.

"Let's wait and see what happens," she said. "By the way, I came across something worth considering." She took a sip of her drink and put her hand on Marty's arm to get his full attention. "Hugh Donaldson's investment plan."

"No way."

"What do you mean?" Vivien winced, taken aback by Marty's swift refusal. She had counted on getting a fat commission for signing him up.

"Donaldson is a crook. Nobody in my mastermind would touch him with a ten-foot pole." Marty had cut the conversation short and switched to babbling about moving to Crooks Island and the fab lifestyle they'd have there.

My mastermind. Vivien hated it when Marty acted like he knew it all. Just because he got involved with some DC scammers. Vivien would have loved to be in that mastermind too, but they weren't accepting new people anymore. *So unfair.* Marty claimed that he recovered his $50K membership fee in ten days and planned on retiring to the island in a few months. And he'd counted on her to join him. *Ridiculous.*

Well, she needed Marty only a few more weeks. She'd get rid of him after the launch. Vivien smirked.

Men are stupid.

Vivien's alarm buzzed. Half an hour to the download. Her mouth twisted. Where should she go? I'll stay right here, she decided. Why should she go through all the trouble for one download? Vivien fetched her bag and pulled out her small laptop. Her Little Fella. Like a loyal dog, Little Fella went where Vivien went. She was forbidden to leave it out of sight, and she was forbidden to use it in her house. *Ridiculous.* Vivien was sick and tired of all this nonsense.

She'd use the shortcut Marty had given her, which would make it look like she signed on to Little Fella in Arizona. No one would ever find out. And if they did, she'd make up a story to get off the hook. Excited, cheeks glowing, Vivien employed the hack. In less than half an hour she'd get the download, which would give her full access. She giggled.

"You can do whatever you want, as long as you get away with it," Daddy used to say. That's what it was all about. Getting away with murder.

Ahhh. The thrill. The unforgettable feeling. There was nothing like it. Daddy was so right.

Waiting for the download, Vivien went through her photos, selected three of them and altered them. The photos turned out so well, she wanted to send them out immediately. But timing was everything and she'd wait for the perfect moment. She giggled when she imagined her targets opening their email and seeing the photos. Surprise, shock, fear. *Priceless.*

She hopped over to Alex's calendar. It was easy since she abandoned the precautions required for the forbidden app. Why should she remove the app from Alex's computer after every session? Such a waste of time. She was checking Alex's emails more often than her own. Besides, no one would ever find out.

Vivien stepped on reality's toes.

Dallas

Alex's neighborhood
April 20

The mild Dallas winter did wonders for my shape. Running never felt this good. The lightness and effortless rhythm made me feel powerful. I easily scaled the hill that marked the halfway of my five-mile run. As I turned to run back, a color palette for my latest design emerged in front of my eyes.

Yes! I had struggled with the colors ever since I'd got the assignment. All my previous ideas were either too flat or bordering on kitschy. But this was it. These colors will achieve the scintillating effect my clients, Trey and Carl, were looking for. Their desire was to create an impression of living on a cloud. I couldn't wait to assemble the full palette and take it over to their condo in the W Residences.

Trey was uncompromisingly selective, and I smiled in anticipation of scrutinizing the palette with him and coming up with something even more exciting. I played with the colors in my mind, looking for specific combinations that would emphasize the character of each area of the condo. I got most of it sorted out on my run, except Trey's office. The space had to accommodate several computers so that Trey, a hotshot software designer, could reach them blindly without any obstructions. The sound system had to be perfect, and the colors just right to foster Trey's concentration and creativity.

"I grab the code from the cosmos," Trey had laughed during our first meeting. "I need a place where I can get into a trance."

This called for a sight and sound system Trey could adjust in accordance with his mood without thinking much about it. Maybe part of it could automatically reflect the light, the weather, or the music he plays.

I was excited about working out my ideas later in the afternoon. But first I was going to drive to Mesquite and get more water lilies for the DD pond. And maybe a few koi. And I'd stop at Jimmy's on the way back and get one of their signature Italian sandwiches and freshly made pasta for a dinner with my friend Nicole, who was coming to town to run in a half marathon.

Nicole and I had studied philosophy together in Montreal and had become disenchanted with it at the same time. When I switched to interior design, Nicole opted for business administration and eventually became an investment banker in Geneva. I was looking forward to spending the weekend with her and catching up on the latest news.

Jack had just left for Vancouver, so I had some extra time to fit in all the chores. I flinched. Married only a few weeks but already happy when Jack was gone. I missed Jack when he traveled, yet I secretly cherished being on my own. Jack's business trips gave me a chance to get my work done without having to deal with the chaos Jack brought to my life. And the reunions were like falling in love all over again. I smiled.

Ready for the day ahead of me, I sprinted up the small hill to DD and ran to the kitchen, thirsty for the mango *agua fresca* I'd made in the morning.

A loud gasp escaped my lips. I was stunned as if struck by lightning.

Dallas

DD
April 20

Vivien sat at the kitchen counter, drinking coffee and flipping through my mail.

"I made myself a coffee, hope you don't mind," she said with a smirk.

I did mind, but Vivien went on before I had a chance to say so.

"Jack let me in when he was leaving for the airport. In case you wondered." Vivien looked at me victoriously.

My stomach somersaulted. I just stared at her, speechless...

"Jack forgot some pictures of the kids when they were young. So I stopped by to bring them over." Vivien slid a yellowish envelope towards me. "I didn't want to leave the pictures here just like that. I waited for you to make sure you got them."

"You could have given them to Jack." I slowly came to my senses.

Vivien opened her mouth to say something, but this time I jumped in.

"Thank you for bringing the pictures. And now please leave."

"I didn't finish my coffee yet," she replied, taking a sip.

"Leave. Now!" I pointed to the door, sick and tired of her games. A day didn't go by without Vivien making a mark on it. "And do not come back unless I invite you," I added, staring Vivien down until she looked away.

She sauntered to the entry hall, head up in defiance.

I bolted the door behind her and ran through the house making sure all doors were locked. My heart was beating as if it wanted to jump out of my chest.

How could have Jack done this to me? I took out my phone. I almost clicked Jack's number when I realized that I forgot to check the garage door. I ran through the house and flipped the garage lights on. And gasped again.

My brand-new Alfa Romeo Giulia had nasty scratches on the driver's side. I traced one scratch with my finger, hoping against hope that it was just a paint that could be washed off. It wasn't. I walked over to the passenger side. The same deep, brutal scratches spanned the whole length of the car.

I leaned against the garage wall. Fury raged through me, seeking an outlet. It would have been so easy to blame it all on Vivien, but things were not that simple.

Because it was Jack who allowed this to happen. *My Jack.*

Feeling defeated, I took pictures of the Giulia. What would Vivien do next? How could I stop the never-ending flow of intrusions in our life?

One thing was certain. I was getting a top-notch home security system. I no longer cared that Jack didn't like it. I wasn't going to spend my days worrying about who was visiting the house when I wasn't here.

I went back to the kitchen and fired a text to Jack, too angry to call him: *Brilliant to let your ex-wife in when I was running. Look what happened to the Giulia when Vivien had the run of the house.*

I attached the pictures I just took and sent the text.

Jack called before I had a chance to put my phone down.

"I didn't let Vivien in the house."

"Then one of you is lying."

"I am not."

"Jack, Vivien was sitting at the kitchen counter when I came back from my run. Drinking coffee she'd made for herself. She told me you let her in on your way to DFW."

The image of Jack letting Vivien in sent my stomach on another series of somersaults.

"Alex, I would've never done that."

"So how did she get in?"

"Did you check all doors?"

"Yes. Everything was locked."

Jack's end of the line went deadly quiet.

"This has to stop, Jack," I said much sharper than intended. "I don't ever want to see Vivien in my house again."

"Alex, the divorce is hard on her. Give her some time." Jack countered with his standard response. I winced. How many times will I have to hear this?

"Give her more time so that she can do more damage?" Anger was getting the better of me.

"Vivien would never damage the Giulia. Maybe it got scratched yesterday and you didn't notice it."

I drew my breath in. Jack *had* to defend Vivien at all costs.

"Blaming the victim, Jack?"

"Don't make so much out of this, Alex." Jack sounded exasperated. "I'll talk with Vivien."

"Yeah. Knowing her she'll tell you that she has never been in the house. Or that I let her in, scratched the Giulia myself, and blamed it on her. Any which way, this has to stop, Jack. I am getting a home security system, so that the next time your ex-wife can't handle the divorce, I'll have the evidence on video." My voice was rising to levels I was not familiar with. I'd never yelled at Jack like this before.

I hung up and stared mindlessly at the kitchen counter.

My phone chimed.

JACK: *Vivien said she was not in the house today.*

Of course not... I stared at the counter some more, feeling hopeless.

And then I saw it.

Dallas

DD

The coffee cup with Vivien's lipstick and fingerprints, and the envelope I never touched finally caught my attention. I snapped several pictures of both items, making sure that the time stamp was turned on. The screaming pink lipstick showed nicely in the pics. Vintage Vivien. Nothing I would ever wear.

On impulse, I put on the surgical gloves I bought for work around the house but always forgot to use. I carefully emptied the coffee cup and put it into a Ziploc bag. Then I picked up the envelope and slid it into a large freezer bag. The color of the envelope got my attention. It looked yellowish at first, but pissy green was more like it. Yikes. Vivien's colors were as far from mine as her worldview. I walked over to my office and deposited both bags in the safe.

It was a silly action because the cup and the envelope merely showed that Vivien was in the house this morning. It wasn't a sufficient proof that she damaged the car. But something was telling me to hold on these items. And securing the evidence made me feel more in control.

I sat down and texted Jack back: *Believe whatever you want to believe. I have solid evidence that Vivien was in the house today.*

Then I called the security service I did business with, hoping that referring several clients to them in the last few months would expedite my DD job.

"I'll check who's available. Can you hold for a sec?" the agent asked. Soft waltz filled my ears. "Thanks for waiting. Andy can come over at eleven thirty. Is that OK?"

"Perfect."

I took a quick shower, trying to figure out how Vivien could have got in the house if Jack didn't let her in. The garage was my best bet. She could have sneaked in when Jack was pulling out.

I went to the garage and hit the open button. The door panels shook a bit and slowly rolled up. One could easily crawl underneath them and

THE WALL

hide behind the Giulia without the driver who was backing out noticing anything. I inspected the area around the garage. Several branches of the lovely Mexican heather at the corner of the garage were broken. Someone trampled over them. My anger took over self-righteously: *How dare she.*

"Mrs. Carter?"

I jumped.

A large man studied me and the broken branches.

"Hi, I am Andy from FS, Forever Secure. I am sorry I scared you." We both laughed.

Andy inspected the house, listened to my requirements, and started installing the equipment. Two more people stopped by after lunch. They brought extra parts and helped Andy to finish the job.

In the middle of it all Jack texted me from Vancouver: *Please don't file a police report.*

Filing a police report didn't even cross my mind, but Jack's text made me consider it. Too busy helping Andy with positioning and testing the security cameras, I didn't answer Jack right away. It took him only a few minutes to text again.

JACK: *Alex, I'll get the Giulia fixed or get you a new one. Please do not file a report.*

Hm. Why was it so important that I didn't call the police? Besides, fixing the Giulia went without saying. I texted Jack as much. Not amused, I went back to testing the cameras.

It was late afternoon when I finally got to the color palette for the W condo. But my mind wasn't on it.

Was it a mistake to marry Jack?

Dallas

The Kay Bailey Hutchison Convention Center
April 21

Time was running out. I circled around the parking lot, quickly losing my hope that we'd find an empty spot. Nicole shifted in the seat next to me and checked her watch for the umpteenth time. Her flight had been delayed by more than four hours, which left us only twenty minutes to spare before the registration for her half marathon race closed.

Just like me, Nicole used to run to keep her weight down. But her father's sudden death had changed everything. A man in the prime of his life, an active mountain climber, Nicole's dad had bent over in terrible pain during a business meeting and was gone before the ambulance arrived.

"They told us it was abdominal aortic aneurysm. Nothing could have been done." Nicole had called me when it happened, out of her mind with grief. "There wasn't one sign to warn us, Alex. He was absolutely healthy."

Nicole stopped smoking shortly after the funeral, and long-distance running became her way to cope with "life's cruel unpredictability," as she put it.

Maybe I should run more to deal with Vivien and her cruel unpredictability, I thought. Or was it cruel predictability? I shuddered.

Just when I decided to pull in front of the Convention Center and wait in the car while Nicole registered for her race, we passed an empty spot.

"We have to find Exhibit Hall A." Nicole jumped out.

We rushed to the entrance and found a red arrow directing us to the half marathon registration. Nicole visibly relaxed.

"Are you running together?" the girl behind the stand asked.

"No, I am not running." I stepped aside.

"Why not? Do you run?"

"Yes, but only five miles."

"Then you can run in this race." The girl smiled, unrelenting.

"Yes, why don't you run, Alex?" Nicole chipped in.

"It's for charity, for the children's hospital," the girl went on. "And you have four hours to finish the race. That's a lot for 13.1 miles."

"You can do it even if you just walk."

"That's right. Many people just walk."

"Why not, Alex?" Nicole challenged me.

Why not, indeed? I'll be at the race with Nicole anyhow.

"You can sign up right here," the girl pointed to the next stand.

I moved over and started to fill the forms.

"What predicted time should I put in?" I asked.

"Three hours? That's what I started with," Nicole suggested. "It's just for the start corral. You can run at whatever pace you want."

"Done." I submitted the form and paid.

"OK. The receipt was emailed to you. You need it to get your bib."

"Do you have a running belt?" Nicole asked.

"No. Why?"

"For your gel."

"Gel?"

"Energy gel." Nicole laughed. "You can't run a half marathon without refueling. I have enough gels for both of us. Let's get you a belt."

We bought the belt, strolled over to Reunion Park and walked the quarter of a mile leading to the finish line. Nicole wanted to run the race in less than two hours and didn't leave anything to a chance.

We sat down under an oak tree and I downloaded an elevation map of the race.

"A big climb around the ninth mile," I reported. "Two climbs, actually."

"Yikes." Nicole seemed worried. "The ninth mile is the most difficult for me."

"You got this." I gave her our pre-exam hug. "You'll fly tomorrow."

I stood up.

"Let's get something to eat. And let's remember this tree and meet here after the race OK?"

"You haven't changed a bit, Alex. Got everything under control, as always." Nicole laughed goodheartedly and returned my hug.

I wished. Jack hadn't texted since yesterday.

But being with Nicole softened the pain of his siding with Vivien.

Dallas

Vivien's bedroom
The same time

"I am a single mother of two. When I started in this business, I had nothing. ABSOLUTELY NOTHING. Just debts. Let me tell you, I was dead broke. The kids haven't had ice cream in ages. At one point the city turned our water off because I couldn't pay the bills."

Vivien was telling her from-rags-to-riches story, the opening of her launch webinar. Passionately in her role, she *was* the young mother abandoned by her husband, desperately trying to make ends meet but getting deeper and deeper in debt. Vivien projected the despair onto her audience and let them feel it to the bone, never mind that she was never left behind penniless and the city of Dallas had never turned off water in her spacious house.

"I was working days and nights, but nothing worked. I hit rock bottom," Vivien shared heroically. "Everyone was crushing it but me. Almost ready to give up, I tried this one last thing. I was so exhausted I took a nap, and when I woke up I had 3K in MY ACCOUNT. The rest is history." Vivien pulled the audience of out their despair and brought them into a land of abundance, using photoshopped bank accounts and pictures of cars she had never driven, boats she had never sailed, and places she had never visited.

"I had to figure out everything on my own, but you don't have to go through that misery. Because I HAVE DONE IT FOR YOU." Vivien planted the hook. "I don't want you to struggle like me. That's why I am doing this training. Hang around to the end and I'll give you everything you need. Nobody else is teaching this." Vivien let that sink in for a moment.

"Internet marketing saved my life. If I can do it, you can do it. Does it make sense?" She asked the audience. "Type '1' in the comments if it makes sense."

THE WALL

Ones scrolled in the comment section of Vivien's screen. The audience was spread all over the world, participants sitting behind their computers, invisible to Vivien, but she could see them in front of her, thousands of people hanging on her words. Golden flakes waltzed through her body.

"One, one, one, one, one," Vivien read out loud. "OK! Let's go on and let me tell you what this is all about."

Vivien didn't bother with explaining her method. *Don't sell them what they need, sell them what they want.* She jumped directly into the benefits, painting a vivid picture of the dream life waiting at the end of her training.

The sentences came to Vivien easily as they were planted in her mind by the best gurus, ready-made, ripe to persuade buyers to open their wallets. Trained by years of storytelling, Vivien effortlessly sped up, slowed down, raised her voice, paused dramatically, convincing the audience that they must get this training, that their life would be irreparably damaged if they didn't.

"This is your chance to make it big, guys. Follow my method because you'll be printing money." Vivien was ready to close.

"This is an exclusive training, only twenty people will be selected. I can't take on more because I couldn't give you the quality you deserve. Sign up for your acceptance interview NOW."

An "I WANT IN" button popped on the screen. Vivien reiterated the benefits of her training and reminded attendees of the 45-day, 100% satisfaction or money back guarantee, no questions asked. *People need to feel secure.*

"I have never done this for this price. If I ever do it again, the price will double. GRAB YOUR SPOT NOW!" Vivien went for the kill.

Her phone lit up. The first person signed up. And the second and third. Vivien read their names out loud to encourage others. She didn't have to do that. The enrollments were coming in faster than Vivien could read them.

Marty gave her the thumbs-up. "You did it, Viv!"

Vivien poured them vodka shots and watched Marty's calendar fill with requests for interviews.

"Oh my gosh, Viv, we will have to get someone to do the interviews with me."

"Whatever." Vivien didn't care as long as the money came in. The point of the interview wasn't to select the best twenty people, as they were told, but to collect their payments. $12,000 per person. Anyone who could pay it was accepted.

"This is phenomenal, Viv!"

Vivien had never seen Marty so excited. Not even when he talked about retiring on his stupid island.

"We've got almost eighty people already. And everyone who didn't attend the webi live will get the replays, which will bring more people in."

"It doesn't mean anything unless they pay," Vivien replied coldly.

"They will, Viv, they will. Oh man, this is just phenomenal," Marty repeated, jumped up and paced around the room. "I bet we'll get at least hundred paying people. That's almost a million dollars, after paying commissions."

Vivien refilled their shot glasses.

"Let's wait and see. You have to close them first," Vivien reminded Marty of his next job.

"That's no problem." Marty raised his glass.

Vivien gave him a demure smile. Marty responded with a kiss. *I have to get him out of the house ASAP,* Vivien decided. Blame it on a headache. *Never reward people before they've finished the job.* Besides, she was getting excited about the numbers and puppy love didn't cut it. She wanted the real thing.

She wished the money was in already. In her book, a hundred paying people translated to $1.2 million. She didn't have the slightest intention of paying the affiliates who promoted the training. Why should she? She did all the work. She'd tell them that their clients didn't like the program and she had to return their fees under the 100% satisfaction or money back guarantee. She had no intention of returning any fees either.

Once students paid, to get access to the training website, they'd have to sign an agreement that made their fee nonrefundable. People would be so excited to start the training, they'd click on "agree" without reading the terms. Vivien giggled. Nick and Dick were the best teachers ever.

"To rinse and repeat." Marty refilled their glasses again.

Vivien raised hers without saying anything. Rinse and repeat was the last thing on her mind. Hugh Donaldson was right. "Why should you work for your money if your money can work for you?" She'd get in his program as soon as the next investment round opened.

Serving others to earn her money was never Vivien's idea of a good time. She got sidetracked by Alex who considered slaving at work

THE WALL

glamorous. But Vivien persevered and was back to her senses. She'd max her profits from the training and let Hugh turn her million into ten million. And the ten million into one hundred million. She closed her eyes and let the golden flakes take over her.

Now I can do whatever I want. Vivien giggled, knowing exactly what to do next.

Vivien lived her reality.

Dallas

In front of the Omni Hotel
April 22

"Good luck." We hugged and gave each other the thumbs-up sign. Nicole winked and jogged to her starting corral. The area in front of the Omni buzzed with pre-race energy as thousands of runners of all shapes and ages lined up for the start. I headed towards the corner of Lamar and Market to join the crowd expecting to finish in three hours.

The morning was uncharacteristically gray and humid. I looked up to check out the clouds, hoping it wouldn't rain. The observation deck of the Reunion Tower was partially hidden in low-hanging fog. My corral was almost full already. I squeezed in through a small opening in the railing and found a place behind a woman who had "13.1" tattooed on her left shoulder and "Running for Life" one the right one.

Most of the runners waited for the start in small groups, chatting, stretching, setting up their watches, and taking selfies. They looked like running 13.1 miles was the most natural thing to do. A sudden wave of loneliness left me feeling out of place, incompetent. I wondered whether my somberness had something to do with the gloomy weather. Or was it Jack's need to protect Vivien at any cost? Why did he defend her all the time? What made her so special?

My abdomen tensed. I fiddled with my watch, regretting letting Nicole talk me into signing up for this. "One minute to start." The announcer's voice vitalized the crowd. I swallowed hard.

The starting gunshot went off. Rock 'n' roll blasted from the speakers, yet the mass of people in front of me hardly moved. It took another twenty minutes of hard rock and encouragements from the announcer before my corral finally made it to the start line.

I took off, fired by the excitement all around me, but most people merely jogged or just walked. I weaved through them for at least half a mile before the field opened up and I could get into rhythm.

THE WALL

The miles went by surprisingly easily. My troubles with Jack became less biting with every step I took. When the course turned down Elm Street, I felt like I was running on a cloud and started to dream about finishing in under two hours. I ran up the ramp to the bridge across the Trinity River feeling strong, but hit a wall when the freeway turned into Singleton Boulevard.

My lungs burned, my legs felt like lead. Many people were taking it easy by this point, taking selfies, video chatting, turning the race into a social event. Maybe that's the way to do it, I thought. *Why do I take everything so seriously?* My body wanted to stop too, but something deep in me wouldn't allow it. I forced myself to keep running. My "under two hours" fantasies crashed to the pavement, I just wanted to get it over with and finish.

Then I remembered the gel Nicole gave me. I retrieved the small packet and ripped the top open. The honey-like liquid caressed my throat and I visualized it sliding down to my battered quads. Gradually I picked up my tempo again and cruised along on a runners high.

Shortly after the eighth mile sign, I reached for my second shot of the liquid gold to fuel up for the nasty hill that was ahead. I was ready to tear the top of the packet when someone pushed me from behind and knocked the gel out of my hand. Outrage rushed through me as my arms flailed around to regain balance.

"Need the fuel to finish the race," my shocked quads shouted.

I turned sideways, trying to spot the gel. My eyes landed on a burly man dressed all in black. He was closing in on me, jaw set. There wasn't one drop of sweat on his face. *The pusher?* I stepped out of his way, but he mirrored my move. Two strong hands pushed me with full force and sent me flying.

My right knee hit the pavement, but I managed to soften the blow with my arms. "This was not an accident," warning sirens blared in my head.

I lifted my hands from the street. Tiny beads of blood were oozing from the fresh abrasions on my palms. "Get up!" the sirens screamed. A heavy boot kicked my ribs before I could scramble to my feet.

Definitely not an accident!

I hit the ground again. Sharp pain shot through my left elbow, followed by a blow to my hip.

My race is over.

Everything slowed down. Two petite feet in flip-flops stopped in front of me, toes adorned with rhinestones and tattoos of butterflies.

"Oh my gosh. Are you OK?" The owner of the toes helped me to my feet.

"Yes. Thank you." I managed a tiny smile.

Demoralized and utterly humiliated, I took a few painful steps, trying to piece together what happened. *Why?* I was just a nameless soldier in an army of recreational runners. It made no sense.

Why did this happened when I was running so well? Had I kept my pace, I could have finished in under two hours. Tears ran down my cheeks.

And then anger kicked in. *I'll not let anyone steal this race away from me!* My quads took the lead and propelled me across the pavement. Everything else faded out. All I heard was my breath rushing out of my mouth as if I were diving. I stopped checking my watch. I ran as I'd never run before.

I scaled the hill, passing people left and right, and moved on through Bishop Arts and back across the Trinity giving it my all, fearless, in flow.

The Reunion Tower drew me like a magnet. I sped up at the end of the bridge and picked up even more momentum running down to the park. The finish line was only a couple hundred yards away. I crossed it with my arms above my head, smiling and crying at the same time.

I stopped my watch. Ah... 1:56:26. Sweet!

It was all worth the trouble.

Dallas

Reunion Park
April 22

Elated, I grabbed two bottles of water from the refreshment station and jogged to our tree, assuming Nicole was already waiting there. But she wasn't. The high I was on ebbed and exhaustion caught up with me. I sat down on the grass, took a few sips of my water and used the rest to rinse the blood from my hands and forearms.

Cleaned up, the scrapes turned out merely superficial. I gingerly rotated my left elbow. It was tender but nothing to worry about. I ran through my stretching routine, trying to work the pain out of my muscles, hardly making a dent. I couldn't wait to get back home and soak in the Jacuzzi.

I stood up and scanned the grounds looking for Nicole. *Where is she?* I walked away from our tree and spotted her crossing the finish line. I ran to her, ignoring the sourness that took over my body. She was barely standing up, her face crumbled with pain.

"You are OK Nicole, you are OK, here, have some water." Almost collapsing under her weight, I leaned against a pallet of bottled water.

"I had a monstrous side pain." Nicole was gasping for air. "I had to walk for a while." Crying now, frustrated. "This one was for Daddy. He loved Dallas." She punched the water bottles with her fist.

"He'd be proud of you, Nicole."

"Oh man, I wanted it so much." I could feel she was coming back. She slowly let go of me and stood on her own. Took a sip of water, brushed away her tears. We grabbed two bananas and walked back to our tree.

As we sat down Nicole noticed my cuts.

"Oh my God," she gasped, "what happened?"

I told her. Nicole jumped up. "That's terrible. We've got to tell them."

"It will not change anything."

"Not if you let it go. Come on." She pulled me up, looking for someone who would listen to her.

"Oh my God, and here I worry about my time. You were so lucky he didn't push you under the tram."

"There was no tram," I said, but Nicole was already talking to one of the organizers.

"He pushed her three times!" The Swiss investment banker took charge. "It's unacceptable. You've got to do something about it."

"Well, at this point we can file an incident report."

I shook my head. A report would not soothe my bruises. I'd rather go home and get in the Jacuzzi, but Nicole insisted.

"You can't allow such things happen."

Describing the incident brought back the fears I'd pushed away during the run. The joy of finishing my first half a marathon in less than two hours was gone. *What if this wasn't a random attack?* But besides Nicole, no one knew I was running today. Not even Jack.

"Could it be the same person?" Nicole interrupted my thoughts.

"What?"

"The scratches on your car and the pusher."

That's exactly what I couldn't get out of my mind. *Vivien?* Too outlandish. *Don't blame everything on her*, I scolded myself. But if not Vivien, who?

"Nah, it's just a coincidence," I said lightly, but my stomach was doing its somersaults routine.

Yet, *could* Vivien be behind this? "Yes," my gut was telling me. "You have no evidence," my brain countered. How could she have known about the race?

We reached the Giulia and I retrieved my phone from the glove compartment. It buzzed with messages. Jack had called and texted several times. I clicked on the last text.

JACK: *Are you OK? PLEASE call me.*

The picture attached to the text loaded. A photo of me lying on the street filled the screen. A foot wearing a heavy black boot got caught in the upper right corner, running away from me. I froze. *How did Jack get this?* Then I saw it. Vivien texted it to him.

VIVIEN: *It looks like your wife had a nasty fall at the Dallas marathon. Is she OK?*

Vivien's smirk popped in front of my eyes.

She knew. A chill ran up my spine. Did she take the picture? "This is not a coincidence," the sirens in my mind blared.

"Are you OK?" Nicole was observing me closely, a deep furrow bisecting her brow.

"Yeah," I reassured her. "Let's go and get in the bubble bath."

I wanted to sit down and tell Nicole everything. But I was too ashamed that I got myself into such a mess.

Dallas

DD
May 8

"And last but not least, how do we name this baby?" I asked.

Finding a unique name for our Inside-Outside venture was the last item on our agenda. We were almost ready to officially launch I-O, and I held the founding meeting at DD because I wanted to treat the team to dinner afterwards.

"Yes, we must come up with a name and secure the domains ASAP." Charlie Bullard, who had become my right hand on the project, looked around the table.

"We have several potentials so far." Charlie rummaged through the pile of papers in front of him. "But this is a brainstorming session, so come up with as many names as you can."

"I like DeDe Design," Jack said.

It was one of my old ideas, but it didn't fit with the business we had in mind now. I was looking for something sharper.

"I am not too late, am I?"

I turned around. Vivien was leaning on the partially open glass panels, smiling expectantly. *How long had she been there?* I wondered. We were so absorbed by the project, no one notice d her. Crashing another dinner, no doubt. This time I was prepared. I knew Vivien was trying to draw me out and create a scene in front of others, but I wasn't going to give her the pleasure.

"Hello, Vivien, how are you?" I stood up and gave her a smile. "Late for what?" I asked innocently.

"For the dinner, of course. Jack invited me." Vivien beamed.

"I see. Let me check the calendar." I reached for my phone. "Oh, here it is. You are not too late but too early," I said softly.

"I can wait, that's no problem." Vivien cocked her hip and put a hand on it.

THE WALL

"Actually, the dinner Jack invited you to is two weeks from now. But no worries, you can have dinner with us today too, if you want to."

Vivien looked like I had thrown a bucket of icy water over her head. This wasn't the response she expected. I got her with her own weapon: a fake story. There was no dinner planned in two weeks. She looked at Jack, but he was writing something in his notebook and didn't look up.

"No. I would never intrude like that." Vivien blinked her eyes, put on her demure face, turned around and walked away, head down, shoulders hunched, dragging her feet ever so slightly.

I looked at Jack. He still didn't look up. The momentary triumph of seeing Vivien leaving the house dissipated as quickly as it came. *What's wrong with Jack?* He hadn't been himself since he came back from Vancouver. Seemed preoccupied, distant, unfriendly. Told me it was insane to even consider that Vivien was somehow involved in the half marathon attack.

"Viv saw the picture on Facebook and sent it to me because she was concerned about you," Jack had said, eyes full of longing I couldn't place. "Why can't you be friendlier to her?"

What if the longing was for Vivien? What if Jack had invited her to today's dinner as she said?

Is Jack going back to Vivien?

Dallas

DD
Later in the evening

"That was a mean thing to do," Jack said.

"What was mean?" I reran the meeting in my mind. Nobody seemed upset or offended. We got a lot done, regained the momentum after Vivien's interruption, and came up with several good names for Inside-Outside. The patio reverberated with enthusiasm, great ideas, laughter. And everyone loved the dinner.

"Insulting Vivien."

Insulting? I looked at Jack. He seemed deadly serious. I didn't know what to say.

"You didn't have to embarrass her like that."

"Embarrass her? I offered her dinner."

"You made her feel like a fool when you told her she got the date wrong. She texted me several times this evening. She is really hurting."

"I can't believe you are buying this, Jack. The woman comes in uninvited, interrupts a work meeting, I give her an excuse, offer her dinner, and I am the mean person?" My voice was rising dangerously. If we go on like this, I'll become a nagging wife like my mom. I shuddered.

"Alex, try to see it from her point of view, it's hard on her."

"It's hard on all of us. She is way out of line."

"It could be worse. She is not as bad as she could be," Jack said.

"So you want me to reward Vivien because she isn't ruining our life as much as she could?" I snapped. The double standard! Vivien gets rewarded for not being as bad as she could be, and I get punished for not being the saint Jack expects.

That did it. I couldn't take this anymore. The woman was destroying our life, but all Jack cared about was pacifying her. Did he expect me to do the same?

"Jack, if you care so much about Vivien, go back to her."

"Alex..."

"I mean it, Jack. I am done with this. Everything revolves around Vivien. As if our life doesn't count. Just go back to her and leave me out of it."

Jack seemed lost. "I am trying to build a blended family. I don't want to cut anyone out."

"You are cutting me out."

"Alex, I love you." Jack looked at me as if I got it all wrong.

"Then get the woman out of our life!" I screamed from the top of my lungs. She might be the mother of his children, but it doesn't give her the license to kill our life.

Jack shrugged.

I ran outside and walked aimlessly around our neighborhood, hurting through and through, trying to make sense of it all. Without much success. What happened? We had such wonderful time together before we got married…

What am I doing wrong?

I remembered Jack's face when he came to DD to tell me that he filed for divorce. The boyish happiness… And then the devastation when Vivien called and claimed that he'll never be happy with anyone else, that he'd pay for divorcing her for the rest of his life.

Vivien hurt Jack so much, and yet he kept defending her and protecting her. *Why?* I couldn't understand it. He was risking our marriage to make her feel better. Obviously he didn't care about us. And about me. He never protected me as he protected her. He excused her and blamed me.

Anger and humiliation pulsed through me like toxic twins. Why did he marry me if he didn't give a fig about me? I felt like I was being eaten alive.

What can I do?

The warmly lit up houses on my path glowed with the promise of love, coziness, connectedness. *We had that.* I sobbed, heartbroken. How can we get it back?

Without noticing it, I walked a full circle back to DD. It looked just as inviting as the other houses. A bastion of the good life. But that's not what was happening behind the closed doors.

Jack sat in the living room, watching the talking heads on TV and drinking whiskey.

"Alex, let's get over this. We've got so much going for us. I love you so much." He looked exhausted. It hurt seeing him like this. I longed to hug him, kiss him, comfort him. As I'd hugged and kissed him before, smoothing over Vivien's attempts to break us up. But merely brushing the hurt aside would not fix our problems. Not this time.

"Maybe you love me," I said quietly. "Yet, you don't seem to care about us, about me." Jack's sigh failed to stop me. "I am not a Vivien worshiper. I am not out to hurt her, but I am not going to dedicate my life to satisfying her whims. I married you, Jack." I was looking directly in his eyes. "Not you and Vivien. If you want to get over this, you have to get over Vivien. I will not stay in a marriage dominated by her."

Jack stood up and threw his hands in the air. "I can't make you happy. No matter what I do, I can't make you happy." Anger and bitterness laced his words. This wasn't the Jack I fell in love with. His aloofness felt like a frozen hand crushing my heart. We had been so close, even when we were continents apart. Now we stood next to each other, yet so far away.

"I am going to bed," he said coldly. "I have an early start tomorrow. Someone has to put bread on the table."

"That was uncalled for," I replied, but Jack was going up already.

I sat in from of the TV, stunned. I saw the talking heads opening their mouth but didn't hear a word. *What's going on?* How did our beautiful connection turn into such ugliness?

Someone has to put bread on the table? Was Jack talking to me or to Vivien? What did he mean by that? I contributed more to this household than he did. He lived in my house, I paid all my expenses. Maybe that's what was bugging him. That I didn't need him to provide for me.

Could that be it? I didn't expect such silliness from Jack. Didn't he tell me endless times how frustrating it was to be with Vivien who never worked and spent all their money before Jack even earned it?

We had to talk this through, but Jack was going to DC early tomorrow morning. I went up, not wanting Jack leaving on such a bad note.

Jack was on his side of the bed, as far from the center as he could be, sleeping. I slipped in and stuck to my side.

The honeymoon was over.

Dallas

DD
May 9

*L*ife *sucks.*

I dragged myself out of bed, feeling tired, dispirited, defeated. Heavy and broken. *What should I do?*

If I stopped objecting to Vivien's intrusions, Jack and I could go on for a while, but I'd get destroyed in the process. If I stuck to my guns, we'd clash in a big way. Any which way, our marriage was doomed. And with it all my hopes and dreams. I bit my lip.

What's wrong with me? I asked myself without expecting an answer. I automatically put on my running gear and stretched. *What's the point of running if my life is in shambles?* I sighed. *What's the point of anything?*

My minor in philosophy should have provided me with a rich menu of options, but it stayed suspiciously silent. *Nothing makes sense*, I concluded morosely, and got out of the house.

It was a gorgeous spring morning. Warm but not too hot yet. Just right for running. I listened to the birdsong symphony and let my eyes roam over the perfectly manicured front yards along the way. One step after the other, simple repetitive movements.

Somewhere deep down I still hoped that our love was stronger than Vivien. I knew I wouldn't quit unless I was a hundred percent sure that the wonderful connection Jack and I had was irreparably broken. I wished I could delete the misery and go back to the happy times. *What should I do?*

Don't try to solve it all at once.

Hm. I considered that for a moment. The tension Vivien provoked was so debilitating, I wanted to get rid of it with one stroke. Once and for all. But maybe Jack was right saying that a situation like this needed more time.

Why don't I do what I always do? Focus on my goals, chop problems into doable chunks, stay with facts, manage what's manageable, keep going.

If nothing else, this approach would give me something to do instead of endlessly replaying in my mind everything that went wrong. I finished my run in a much better mood. There. That's the point of running. I smiled. Who needs philosophy?

I showered while finishing a list of additional Inside-Outside action items. Charlie called me immediately after I sent it off.

"Hey Alex, did you buy any domains with the company names we were considering yesterday?"

"No."

"Well, they are all unavailable. I was just checking it out, but all the names we came up with are taken. There are no active websites behind them, so I thought maybe you reserved them just in case."

"No. Can you find out who owns them?"

"Looking into it right now. Oh, it's Vivien Gibson. Maybe Jack asked her to buy them?"

"I'll ask him, Charlie. Thanks for telling me."

"Alrighty then. By the way, that was a great dinner yesterday. Everyone loved it."

"Thanks. Good to hear that."

I sat back and almost laughed. Luckily, our hearts weren't set on any of these names. But still, how did she find out about them? Did Jack tell her? I texted Charlie and asked him to email me the screenshots of the domains' ownership.

Then I emailed Vivien and told her that the dinner we talked about yesterday is off and reminded her that she is not welcome on my property unless I personally invite her. This covered me should I ever have to take a legal action to stop her trespassing. Which I hoped would not be the case.

Charlie's screenshots arrived accompanied by a simple question:

"Is Vivien going to work on our project? I've heard she is doing marketing for Carter & Co."

What? I read the email three times, not believing what I saw.

"No. There are a lot of rumors out there, Charlie. Please take them with a grain of salt," I replied and sat back. Now what?

It was 11:45 and I was getting late for my lunch with Liz Howard. Not even noon yet and Vivien had claimed my day already. I grabbed my phone to call Jack. And stopped myself. Interrupting Jack in a meeting and nagging about his ex's latest peccadilloes will not improve our chances of staying together. The domain-gate would have to wait.

THE WALL

Not calling Jack was a small act of control, but I felt better already. I wanted our life back.

Dallas

Love Field Airport
May 9

"Where is Don?" Vivien asked coldly. She was working on her third glass of champagne, suddenly reluctant to get on the plane.

She had booked the training because Don Diamont was a phenomenon famed for taking businesses to the next level and making their owners fabulously rich. Don had thousands of followers, but only a select few had the good fortune of getting a private session with him. The two-hour $30,000 air consultation was Don's cheapest event.

"Where is Don?" Vivien repeated when the assistant didn't answer her.

"It's Dan," the assistant said impatiently. "Dan will meet you on board. Please follow me."

Obnoxious punk. Vivien rolled her eyes and finished her champagne. She couldn't stand the assistant from the moment he greeted her and Marty at the airport. The ridiculous bleached hair, the I-am-super-important smirk. So full of himself.

"Fasten your seat belts, guys. Dan will be with you shortly."

The small plane took off. Vivien clutched the armrests, nauseous. She hated flying.

"Ms. Gibson, Mr. Watson, welcome on board." A pudgy, balding guy dressed in a rumpled shirt and pants held by golden suspenders joined them.

"Who are you?" Vivien asked, annoyed. First the assistant and then this.

"I am Dan."

"And where is Don?"

"Don?"

"Don Diamont."

"Why do you ask?"

"Because I booked a 30K air consult with Don."

"Ms. Gibson, you booked a consult with me."

Dan's smug smile infuriated Vivien. "I can't believe this. You scammed me." She jumped up.

"I have certainly not."

How dare he. Vivien scrolled furiously through her photos. There. A screenshot of the ad. She shoved the phone in Dan's face.

"And what's this?" Vivien hissed.

"My ad. Air consult with Dan."

"May I?" Marty looked at the ad. "He is right, Viv."

"But." A wave of nausea forced her to sit down.

"Obviously it's a mistake," Marty concluded. "What can we do now?" He turned to Dan.

"You are stuck with us for the next two hours, so we might as well work on your business."

"I want my money back," Vivien demanded.

"That's impossible Ms. Gibson. You've signed a waiver to that effect. Now, let's use your time wisely and get the job done. If you aren't satisfied with the results, I'll give you a discount. I never do that, but this is a special case."

Vivien sulked in silence. *Marty must handle this.*

"Hon, bring us some water," Dan asked the assistant and opened his laptop.

"Here we are. Internet marketing, 1.3 million revenue." Dan nodded approvingly. "So, what's your secret sauce, Ms. Gibson?"

Why doesn't he just give me a fix for making more money? Vivien thought, not in the mood to answer stupid questions. Filling out their ridiculous questionnaire had taken enough time already. "Let him in on the secret, Marty," she barked and closed her eyes. The flight was killing her.

Marty obliged.

"So you sold 1.3 million worth of a product you don't have." Small beads of sweat covered Dan's forehead.

"Well, it's an information product, we'll create it live on the webinars," Marty explained.

No way! Vivien frowned. *Marty has to go!* She wasn't going to create any content. That's why she hired this moron. And paid him $30K. Actually, Jack's firm paid the $30K, and because Vivien convinced Marty to reimburse her for his half, she was $15K richer. *Men are stupid.*

"OK, that's possible, but you don't have a POC yet."

Vivien shifted impatiently. *The moron doesn't know the first thing about business.* "POC?" she asked sweetly, turning on her southern charm.

"Proof. Of. Concept." Dan didn't hide his irritation.

"That's why we hired you." Vivien batted her eyelashes.

"I am a business consultant, not a fucking savior."

"Exactly, we are consulting you to take the business to the next level."

"That's impossible if you…"

"Nothing is impossible," Vivien asserted. "Just do it." Their eyes engaged in an air battle, lightning jumping back and forth.

Dan rubbed his chin. "Hon, get me Nick on the phone," he yelled.

Nick? Vivien cocked her head.

"Give me a minute." Dan walked to the front of the plane. Vivien followed him and listened to the conversation, unseen by Dan. *Definitely Nick of Nick and Dick.* She smirked and went back to her seat.

"OK. I have someone who is willing to take your students over." Dan came back. "They want 5K for every student they take on."

Vivien laughed. "You got to be kidding. You are cutting my business in half, not taking it to the next level."

"That's—"

"I am not selling MY students. But tell you what. I am willing to hire Nick and Dick as teachers." Vivien made it sound as if she was doing them a great favor. Dumping the students on Nick and Dick was fine with her, but she wasn't going to pay for it.

Dan had to fix this with Nick and Dick. That was the least he could do for his outrageous fee.

"Nick and Dick have the whole curriculum recorded," she said. "They don't have to do anything live. Just provide the videos."

"We could consider licensing," Dan offered.

"Well, Nick and Dick's reputation has been compromised lately," Marty said. "Licensing is not the way to go."

"And Nick and Dick don't have any POC to speak of, bless their heart," Vivien drawled, giving Dan her brightest smile.

Dan didn't say a word.

"Well, perhaps some means of compensation for Nick and Dick's materials could be found if we could get more students into the program," Marty proposed.

"Oh, I can mobilize an army of affiliates to sell the training." Dan's eyes lit up.

"Deal. We'll get you the replay of Vivien's launch webinar. It's phenomenal."

"OK, OK. Do you have a hot Facebook account, Vivien?" Dan asked.

"Sure." Thirty-seven of them. She giggled.

"Well, I have a diet offer that's absolutely crushing it. Shoot a video of yourself making an ad, getting it out there, and making sales. It'll be our POC. OK?"

What's his problem with POC? Vivien didn't get it. You photoshop the whole thing, say that it works for you and that the students are doing it at their own risk. No student will ever ask for proof. But she could try the diet product. Why not? She had several templates for diet pills ads provided by Nick and Dick. She'd use them to put her thirty-seven Facebook accounts to work.

"Sure," Vivien agreed.

"Hon, get us more champagne will ya?" Dan ordered, beaming.

He and Marty bonded and chatted about their college years. *So silly.* Vivien took a gulp of the champagne and let the bubbles tickle her nose. Daddy was so right.

"Education is for the stupid," he used to say. "All you need to know is how to get people to do what you want."

Vivien defied reality.

Dallas

Deep Ellum's Rooftop Heaven
May 9

Liz was on the patio of our favorite Deep Ellum restaurant, chatting with the waiter. As I neared the table, her face lit up in brilliant smile. And then she cocked her head while studying me intently.

"Alex, what's wrong?"

I took a deep breath before plunging into the misery.

"Let me guess," Liz went on before I said anything, "Vivien's giving you trouble."

I nodded and took another deep breath.

"And Jack behaves as if you are making too much of it." I nodded again.

"And you think your marriage is on the rocks." She looked at me gently.

"Liz, are you a psychic?"

"No. Just experienced. Honey, men are notoriously slow to recognize how dysfunctional they are with their ex-wives."

"Yeah. I can attest to that." Talking with Liz made the whole mess looking less grave.

"You bet. It took me and Richard two years to get his ex out of the picture."

I had no idea Liz wasn't Richard's first wife. Liz was reading my mind again:

"Most people don't know Richard was married before. Five years in hell."

"Sorry to hear that."

"His ex was a borderliner if I've ever seen one. You wouldn't believe the stuff she tried to pull off." Liz rolled her eyes. "And she told lies about us to anyone who would listen. I bet Vivien does the same."

"Probably." That would explain some of the strange looks I got at Carter & Co lately.

"What else is she up to?" Liz asked.

Her raspy voice worked like balm on my bruised soul. This time I didn't let my shame hold me back as it did with Nicole and poured my heart out, feeling the weight of it all sliding off my shoulders. At the end I was almost my old self again. Liz laughed when I described Vivien's unceremonious exit from the Inside-Outside dinner.

"Good for you, honey. You've got it under control."

"Not quite." I shook my head. "Vivien's Vivien. She does what she does. It's Jack's response to it. That's the heartbreaker."

Liz nodded, urging me to go on. I got Jack's double standard off my chest.

"You see, I do feel for Vivien. I get that this is hard on her," I added. "It's just..." My voice caught.

"Honey, don't even go there." Liz put her hand over mine. "Jack was just an ATM for Vivien. There was nothing between them."

Music to my ears.

"This takes tough love," Liz continued. "I hated Richard's ex, but I had the same doubts as you. And you know what Richard told me?" Liz paused. "He said 'it was an act of kindness' to stand by him and help him extract himself from that toxic marriage."

Hm...an act of kindness. What an eye-opener.

"How did you do it? How did you get Richard's ex out of the picture?"

"I told him what I need."

"That's it?"

"You see, in a situation like this, the natural thing is to talk about her, Vivien has done this, Vivien has done that. Or tell him what to do. Like 'don't answer Vivien's calls when we go out.' Does she call him right before dinner?"

"All the time. We've lost several dinner reservations because of her calls. It's as if she knows when we go out and calls exactly when we are leaving the house."

"And holds him on the phone for ages," Liz added. I nodded.

"OK. You've got to refocus him from Vivien to you. He can't control Vivien and it makes him feel powerless. You have to empower him to do things *for you*. The next time you go out, make it all about yourself. Text him how much you are looking forward to the dinner. Tell him how important it is to you to have this time together. If she calls, go to him, kiss him, take his phone away and remind him that this is your time.

Don't talk about her, don't mention her name. It's all about *you*. Can you see yourself doing it?"

"Yes," I surprised myself saying, "I can do that. But I don't like to be so pushy."

Liz gave me a sharp look.

"That's exactly what Vivien counts on. She takes advantage of your decency."

"And Jack's decency," I added.

"You've got it."

"Oh my God, Liz. Thank you. You are an angel."

"We are not done yet." Liz looked at me. "You have to make sure your money is safe because Vivien doesn't shy away from shady deals."

A chill ran up my spine. Jack's remark about putting bread on the table took on another meaning.

"They settled everything during their divorce," I said slowly.

Liz gave me a look I couldn't decipher. What was it? Surprise? Pity? Both?

"Yes, but they go back a long time."

"Liz, is there something else I should know?"

Liz's eyes darkened.

"No, no. It's just…make sure your money is safe. Ask a lawyer to look into it for you. Texas can be tricky."

A point well taken. "Would you recommend someone?"

Liz bit her index finger and closed her eyes briefly. "Emma. Emma Fitzgerald is exactly what you need. You'll love her. Her office is at the Trammell Crow. Tell her I sent you."

"Thanks, Liz." I took out my phone and searched on Emma. She popped up like a bright star. I clicked on her appointment calendar and secured the first available slot.

"I never liked Vivien." Liz leaned across the table. "There was always something about her, something, ugh…sinister."

"I can't thank you enough, Liz," I said quietly. "You've saved my life."

"Just returning a favor—you saved mine." She laughed easily, her eyes sparkling with joy.

"I did? How?"

"By recommending Richard to Perry."

"Oh, I didn't do much. It seems that they found each other."

Bittersweet nostalgia tightened my chest. I missed working with Perry. We hadn't done anything together since he signed up with Richard.

"Well, Perry says that your talking highly of Richard was the deciding factor."

"Really?" That was a nice surprise. "Glad it worked out."

"It's much more than that, honey. Richard is like a new man. Perry is so much more capable than anyone ever working for Richard, including me." Liz laughed.

"You worked for Richard?"

"That's how we met. I was interning for him. I wanted to go into politics but moved on to another job when we started seeing each other. And never regretted it since." Liz chuckled.

The waiter brought our favorite crawfish Caesars and we chatted easily for the rest of the lunch hour.

"Let's get together for dinner soon. The four of us," Liz suggested.

"That would be great." We hugged.

I got a new lease on life.

The Art Tower

Offices of Carter & Co
May 9

Jamie gave me the evil eye.

I was trying to make an appointment with Marty, but she couldn't find an opening. Obviously she was very protective of her boss.

Marty had rescheduled my meeting with him three times already and now had no time at all. I sat back and looked at Jamie. I could brute force this and order Marty to show up or else, but I wasn't that far yet. Besides, I wondered what had got to Jamie. She was always the picture of friendliness.

"Jamie, what's going on?" I leaned towards her.

Jamie was silent. I waited. She let out a deep sigh. "How could you do that to her?"

"Do what, Jamie?"

"How could you force Jack's ex out of her house?"

I must have looked as dumbfounded as I felt because Jamie asked, "You didn't?"

"No," I said, flabbergasted.

Jamie shook her head.

"I don't get it. She sat right here where you sit, crying, telling me that you are forcing her out of the house."

"That's nonsense. How often does she come here, Jamie?"

"Almost never? She was here only a couple times to see Marty. He wasn't in the last time, so she waited here for a while. Told me about the house and on her way out told Hannah to look for a new job because you are going to talk Jack into firing her. That you are going to get most of us fired just like you killed her marriage." Tears filled Jamie's eyes.

"Jeez." I wondered how many people heard this and believed Vivien's lies. Liz got it right.

"When did this happen, Jamie?"

"Two days ago."

"I see. Well, I don't plan on firing anyone. Never did." I looked squarely in Jamie's eyes.

"Now, let's order sandwiches for lunch tomorrow. For everyone. I am going to tell them that their job is safe."

Jamie was all smiles again.

I walked back to my office, fighting tears, feeling like a villain. Reminding myself that the accusations were false didn't help. Fury rose up in me and hit my temples. I wished that Jack had been already divorced when we met, no one could accuse me of being a homewrecker, and Vivien couldn't use the divorce to undermine my position at Carter & Co. But she would have fabricated another story to compromise me, something far more seductive than facts. I desperately wanted to take a shower and scrub it all off, but no shower in the world would wash away Vivien's viciousness.

Vivien was everywhere, poisoning everything.

Anger took over my fingers.

ME: *Stop your ex-wife from visiting Carter & Co and demotivating people.*

I typed and stopped in my tracks. Ha! That's exactly what not to do. I deleted the text and started over.

ME: *FYI. I am having a lunch with everyone tomorrow to assure them that their job is safe. There were some rumors floating around about firing people.*

JACK: *Great job!*

There was hope for us.

Dallas

Vivien's bedroom
May 29

"Create what you want to consume, or you'll be consumed by what you've created," the guru shouted.

Vivien loved it. *I have to treat myself to these webis more often,* she promised to herself. Even an accomplished businesswoman like herself needed a little boost every now and then, she concluded. Not that she'd learn anything new, but it was good to keep in touch.

Still in her pajamas, Vivien adjusted her pillows and let the guru entertain her.

"Create what you want to consume, or you'll be consumed by what you've created."

"Did you get it?"

"Type one in the comments if you got it," the guru ordered.

Vivien typed 1.

"1, 1, 1, 1, lots of 1s. Angela 1, Josh 1, Kevin 1, Stacy gives us 111. Way to go, Stacey!"

Who's Stacy? Vivien asked, upset that the guru didn't call her name. *Rude.*

"OK, let's make it clear," the guru surged on. "If you create a bad business, it will consume you. You'll be working 24/7 and make no money. Got it? If you create a bad marriage, it will eat you up alive. Got it?"

Vivien was getting bored. She opened her Little Fella and checked the balance in her overseas bank account. Golden flakes flowed through her body in delightful swirls.

"Nothing is impossible if you COMMIT," the guru screamed. He opened a blank slide and typed: I am 100% comited to…

"OK! Copy this and insert your calling where the dots are. Got it?"

"What do you mean Stacy? The spelling's wrong?" the guru asked, amused. "I am rich, I don't have to worry about spelling." He laughed.

THE WALL

"Fuck spelling, COMMIT," he thundered. "That's good, really good. I just made that up." He laughed again.

Vivien wasn't amused. Unless the guru wins her back with something spectacular, she'd not buy his product.

I don't need his stupid product, she realized. She had more than $2.4 million in the bank. Dan's affiliates came through and almost doubled the sales of her training. And the diet pills she was promoting on Facebook were selling like hot cakes. Vivien stretched luxuriantly.

"OK. So you've got your calling and you commit and then you have to CARRY IT OUT. It's your RESPONSIBILITY," the guru yelled.

Vivien stopped listening. She didn't need another sermon about "the buck stops with you." All that talk about responsibility and accountability was lost on her because it was so *negative*. It was all about what you *can't*.

You can't eat ice cream until you burst, you can't drink three margaritas too many, you can't buy clothes you don't need, you can't stretch your credit cards past the limit… Vivien smirked.

She could go on and on, but why should she? She was a *positive* person. Responsibility was for fools. Responsibility took all the excitement out of life and thus was *irresponsible*. *Negative*. Once you understood that, you didn't have to worry about what you can't.

Dissatisfied, Vivien signed off the webinar. What a waste. *So many people in this business don't deliver.* Vivien shook her head in disgust. She'd never participate in this guru's events ever again. She switched over to Facebook to share her experience with friends. A little box popped up:

Account disabled.
Your account has been disabled. If you have any questions or concerns, you can visit our FAQ page.

Vivien squinted and read the message again. *That can't be true!* Irritated, she tried to sign in to another account. Disabled. Next one. Disabled. Disabled, disabled, disabled. All thirty-seven of Vivien's Facebook accounts were disabled.

Dallas

Vivien's bedroom
An hour later

"On whose side are you?" Vivien's face contorted with fury. "You are ridiculous!"

Marty cringed.

"They can't do this to me. I am a Facebook personality," Vivien shouted.

"Vivien…"

"Don't you Vivien me. You must get my accounts back."

Marty wished he could. But he couldn't. Nobody could. The emails Vivien received from Facebook were clear. Marty highlighted the message and read it out loud.

"'Unfortunately, your account has been permanently disabled for violating Facebook's Terms. We will not reactivate it for any reason.' Nobody can fix this, Vivien," Marty tried to explain, but Vivien wouldn't see the obvious.

"Why are you so mean to me?" she lashed out.

Marty flinched. Vivien had called him at work, begging him to come over, inconsolable but not saying why. Nearly paralyzed by the fear that something life-threatening happened to her, Marty rushed to Vivien's rescue. And now she used him as a punching bag.

"I am not mean. Facebook doesn't tolerate fake accounts. It's that simple," Marty said.

"But someone in your mastermind could fix that?"

"No way."

"What do you mean? There MUST be a way!" Vivien demanded. "I'll pay for the fix if that's the problem."

All Marty saw were quivering lips and two teary eyes. He desperately wanted to help Vivien, but his hands were tied.

"You can't pay people to do this. It would get them fired."

"I don't care, just get my accounts back," Vivien shouted.

Marty would pay thousands to make Vivien happy. He would bribe anyone willing to restore her accounts, but there was no one to bribe.

Like a doctor who has the daunting task to communicate that the patient didn't make it, Marty gently turned his head left and right. He stepped closer to Vivien and put his arm around her to comfort her. She pushed him away with a force that threw him off balance. A whiff of sweat and alcohol opened Marty's eyes.

Taken aback, Marty took in the spots on Vivien's pajamas, the unkempt hair, the smudges of yesterday's makeup, the venom twisting Vivien's mouth.

"Is that it?" Vivien hissed, her eyes squirting icy fury. "After everything I have done for you?"

"Vivien…"

"You used me, you took my money, and when I need help, you abandon me."

"That's not fair." Marty raised his voice. "*I* made your videos, *I* created your ads, *I* recruited the affiliates who promoted the training, *I* found the guys who ran your campaigns and closed all the contracts with students," Marty argued, hopelessly trying to bring Vivien back to reason. But Vivien wouldn't have it.

"You would be nowhere without ME. I made you. And what do I get? You and all the other leeches you brought in are profiting from me."

"That's not true and you know it," Marty interrupted.

"It's all your fault." Vivien stabbed her finger at Marty. "I was doing fine, but you pushed me to the diet products."

"I did not. I told you you can't run diet ads on Facebook using before and after pics. I told you you were risking your accounts," Marty shouted, outraged. He dropped everything at work and ran over to help Vivien, only to be accused of something he hadn't done.

"It's all about YOU, but when I need something you are not there. You wouldn't even invest in Hugh Donaldson's product and I missed my commission," Vivien screamed.

"I told you it's a bad investment," Marty said automatically, his mind still on Vivien's accusations. And then he realized what she had said. *Commission.* Did she work for Donaldson?

"Are you promoting Donaldson's products?"

"And I'll become a top Donaldson investor, with all the privileges. When the next round opens." Vivien's face filled with triumph.

"Don't you know what you've got yourself into?" Marty exploded. "I told you Donaldson is as crooked as the Brazos. I can't get you out of this one!"

Vivien's eyes narrowed.

"You aren't any different, are you? You took advantage of me, but when I am down you leave me behind. You are just like Jack."

Blinding rage consumed Marty. He did everything for Vivien and she equated him to Jack, the man she hated beyond measure. Marty was used to walking on eggshells not to upset Vivien, but this was too much. He jutted out his chin and delivered his blow without blinking an eye.

"Just look at yourself. You are a mess. And you don't know what you are talking about. No wonder Jack left you."

Vivien's fist landed on Marty's jaw before he had a chance to duck.

"Don't you ever contact me or come near me again," she hissed. "You are finished."

Dallas

Perry's penthouse
May 30

"Have a few minutes?" Dave stuck his head into Perry's study.

"Sure. What's up?"

"The picture you got the other day helped our guy a lot," Dave reported.

It was a photograph of an old Jaguar with a smashed left front light and bumper. Perry shuddered. Was it…? The photograph came in a greenish envelope, which had been delivered to Perry's desk at work. Someone must have brought the envelope in person, as there was no address or post stamp. Only Perry's name.

"It turns out that Gloria Lowell owned exactly the same Jaguar at that time. The car had been reportedly stolen one day before the hit and run and never found. And that's not all. The car was supposedly stolen on Thursday, but they reported it on Monday, four days later," Dave said.

Perry swallowed hard. "So Grandma Gloria could have done it, got rid of the car, and then reported it stolen."

"In theory. But if she was behind this, her car would have never been involved," Dave reasoned.

"I didn't say it was planned. It could have been an accident. She was driving to the meeting with Mom and ran a red light."

Dave gave it a thought.

"Well, never say never. Anyhow, the theft was reported by Ted Gibson, your aunt's husband. He said he left the Jag in the airport parking lot on Thursday, for a family friend who never found the car there. They presumably didn't hear the car was missing until Monday because they were all in Galveston during the weekend, celebrating Gloria's birthday."

"That's what the police said, too."

"Yes, but we were concentrating on your dad then, who indeed seemed to have spent the Thursday and Friday in Galveston."

"And Grandma didn't?" Perry asked.

"We don't know whether Gloria spent the whole weekend in Galveston. But our first PI reported that Ted Gibson went to Galveston only on Friday afternoon because he threw a huge party Thursday night in the Houston house. The servants said it took them the whole weekend to restore the house to normal." Dave took a sip of water.

"And here comes the interesting part. Some of the female guests and Ralph Gibson, Ted's uncle, stayed overnight. The thing is, Ralph was reportedly the family friend who was supposed to pick up the Jag at the airport." Dave looked straight at Perry.

"Oh my God!" Perry drew his breath in. "If the car was really stolen on Thursday, Ralph would have told Ted about it immediately. They lied about it."

"Yes. Lied and got away with it. The police bought it and the insurance company paid," Dave said.

"And we didn't put two and two together then because we didn't know about the stolen car," Perry concluded.

"Correct. And if you remember the police report, nobody mentioned a Jaguar. The witnesses couldn't even agree on color. Some said dark sedan, some said white sedan."

"It happened terribly fast," Perry said, bleeding inside, praying that his mom didn't suffer.

He had been so happy on that day. He had finally made serious money online and ran to Mom's office, taking two steps at a time, excited to tell her that she no longer had to worry about money, that they could do all the things she said they would do if they were rich. He entered her office, yelling "Mom, we are rich!" but stopped when he saw Dave and a police officer standing in front of her desk. One look at Dave had told him that something horrible had happened...

Perry snapped back to reality and mulled over the new information Dave shared with him. *Ted and Ralph Gibson.* Perry's fingers rolled into fists.

"The police never connected the hit and run and the stolen Jaguar," Perry concluded. "And now someone is connecting them. I would like to know who took the photo I got. If it's a photo of Grandma's car." Perry winced.

"That's the million dollar question," Dave said quietly. "Do you realize you are probably being blackmailed?"

"It crossed my mind," Perry agreed. "But why me and why now?"

Dallas

Vivien's bedroom
May 31

It's all Alex's fault.

Killing her wouldn't be enough punishment for the misery she put Vivien through. Vivien punched her pillow, overtaken by fury even vodka wouldn't cure. She kicked and punched, but the agony was only getting worse. She wasn't herself since Marty had abandoned her.

Jack would never be so rude to me as Marty.

A wave of longing washed over Vivien. She reminisced about the golden days when Jack was just one phone call away, ready to fulfill her wishes at a minute's notice. She had to get Jack back. *I deserve a man who adores me.* Who is there 24/7/365 for her and takes care of her needs. Who comes and comforts her when she needs it. Who is always one hundred percent behind her.

I have a right to live like that.

Vivien had it all and Alex took it away from her. *Alex stole my perfect life.* Vivien squirmed in agony. Alex had to go. Vivien had a right to get a second chance with Jack. Jack was her man. Tried-and-true. Things'd be so much better between them since Vivien had become an entrepreneur in her own right. She was an asset for Carter & Co.

Vivien was determined to make the second time around even better than the first. To start with, she'd take care of business. Literally. *I'll become the face of Carter & Co,* Vivien decided. She will attend all Carter & Co events, take videos, be photographed, and post everything on social media until people have no doubt that Vivien is Carter & Co and Carter & Co is Vivien.

Being Jack's business partner will give her the prestige and recognition she deserves. And he'll get the connection he wanted so much because Vivien will never leave his side. No intruder will ever take her rightful place again.

A match made in heaven.

She closed her eyes and imagined her new life. She was thrilled about reclaiming Jack, not having the slightest doubt that she'd defeat Alex. *Anything is possible when you are positive.*

The excitement of triumphing over Alex blushed Vivien's cheeks. She jumped off the bed and paced around the room. She could hardly contain herself. Destroying Alex Demarchelier was a high priority since day one, but now it became Vivien's *mission*. Winning Jack back was the ultimate revenge.

Bursting with energy, Vivien opened a brand-new Virtual Private Server and created a new Facebook account in the name of Vivien Carter, making it look almost exactly the same as her disabled Vivien Gibson account. Almost, because Vivien Carter's new profile contained two major differences:

Family and Relationships - married to Jack Carter

Work and Education - owner at Carter & Co

Vivien created her reality.

Satisfied with her progress, Vivien took a short vodka break and moved on to the most exhilarating part of her work.

She opened Little Fella, accessed another VPS and created a new Facebook account for Alex Demarchelier, a clone of Alex's original account. Then she made Vivien Carter the clone's first friend. Vivien giggled.

Who needs thirty-seven Facebook accounts to be in business? Facebook can keep them! Vivien was getting tired of maintaining them anyhow. Sheer madness! *Freed myself from that slavery!* Vivien congratulated herself. Her new mission was so much more exciting.

She picked several Alex's friends and asked them to befriend Alex's clone. Once they'd connected, Vivien Carter would systematically like their posts. When she has enough of Alex's friends on board, the sky is the limit. Influencing bonanza.

Vivien imagined how Alex's clone would make people hate the real Alex. She spent several exhilarating hours composing posts the clone would leave behind. Some of them were so good, she had to post them immediately. Her appetite came back. Shaking with excitement, she rewarded herself with a pint of triple chocolate ice cream.

Satiated, she called her sister Lauren. Celebration was in order.

When I am done with Alex, she'll have no friends left. And Jack will beg me to take him back!

Vivien defied reality.

Dallas

DD
May 31

My phone chimed two times in a fast succession.

FS: *Camera 4 detected activity by your fence line.*

FS: *Camera 5 detected activity near your pool.*

I clicked on the link and watched a live coverage of the intrusion. Two dark figures balanced at the deep end of the pool.

"You are a killer," one of them screamed. A woman. *Is she talking to me?*

The other figure pushed the screamer into the pool. It happened so quickly I missed what exactly happened. A weak "help, help," blended with the splashes in the pool.

Without thinking I ran outside, jumped in the pool, grabbed the drowning and kicking woman and dragged her to the shallow end. She was thrashing around, definitely not helping.

"Stop! Relax!" I yelled, without any effect. She kicked and flailed her arms as if her life depended on it, her panicky moves sabotaging my rescue efforts. For a moment I thought she would take both of us down.

I came up for air, trying to keep her head above water, determined to save this trespasser, whoever she was. I kept pushing forward until my feet reached the elevated section of the pool floor. *Thank God.*

The woman kept kicking, unaware that she could stand up. I dragged her further, and finally we both collapsed on the softly descending pool steps.

We held on to each other, gasping, coughing, catching breath.

"Thank you," she said softly. I nodded and looked around. My heart was beating like crazy. Where was the second intruder? Police sirens filled the air and came to a sudden stop.

"What happened?" I asked. My answer was rushing in through the living room.

"Arrest her!" Vivien yelled at the two police officers who followed closely behind her. "She pushed my sister in the pool and tried to drown her."

"You've got to be kidding," I said and turned to the woman I rescued. *Is this Vivien's famous sister Lauren?* She seemed to be falling asleep in the pool. I put her arm around my neck. "Let's get out of here."

"Don't touch my sister," Vivien screamed at the top of her lungs. "Arrest her."

"Oh, for God's sake." I dragged Lauren out of the pool, not quite believing what was happening.

"Let go of her," the tall officer yelled while drawing his gun. Everything switched into slow motion. *The officers believe Vivien's version of the story.*

"Officer, I am Alex Demarchelier Carter. I am the owner of this house. Call in to verify it. These ladies are on my property without my permission."

"She is lying," Vivien screamed.

The shorter and stockier cop wrestled me to the ground. My cheek hit the flagstone while he handcuffed me.

"Stay down," he shouted.

"She is armed!" Vivien screeched. "She is armed!"

Fear shot through me. *What if they panic and shoot me?* I shivered. *It's all recorded on the security tapes.* I imagined Jack watching the last tape, finally seeing what Vivien's all about. But it was too late... I snapped back to reality. I had to let them know they were being recorded.

"Officer."

"Shut up!" he yelled. "You have the right to remain silent. Anything you say can and will be used against you in a court of law." I couldn't believe he was reading me my Miranda rights. He was actually arresting me. *As long as he talks, he wouldn't shoot me.* My hopes went up. He wouldn't shoot a handcuffed woman. *Don't count on it!*

"Do you understand these rights I have explained to you? Having these rights in mind, do you wish to talk to us now?"

"Yes, Officer. I want to tell you that all your actions are being recorded by security cameras."

"Is this true, Viv?" the other cop asked and laughed. "Is the camera rolling?" He mimicked my accent and laughed some more.

Viv! He called her Viv. They know each other! I gasped. A heavy hand pushed my face to the stone.

"She is lying," Vivien said. I couldn't see her, but she sounded less exuberant. I loudly jumped in.

"Your actions are recorded. Stick to the rules. Verify the house ownership. Is that clear?"

The cop that was holding me down was breathing heavily in my ear, sounding like a freight train. I couldn't see what was happening but kept talking.

"The recording is live. Do you understand? Do the right thing. Someone is watching you right now."

"Jesus. Fuck." Viv's friend exclaimed. His voice was drowned out by more sirens. There was commotion in the house. I turned around to see what was going on. That was a mistake. The cop smacked me to the ground. A cold, hard object was pressed to my right temple. I slowly identified it.

A gun.

Dallas

The outside patio of DD
May 31

*S*tay *calm. Stay calm,* I kept repeating to myself. I heard heavy boots pounding through the living room. Shouts filled the air. I didn't move.

"Ma'am, are you OK?" Friendly, deep voice. *Someone fussing over sweet Viv*, I thought.

"Mrs. Carter, are you OK?" A hand touched my right shoulder. The gun was no longer on my temple, but I still didn't move.

"Uncuff her!" The order was urgent and authoritative.

My arms slid to the ground and released the oppressive tension in my shoulders I noticed only now. The hand rested on my right arm.

"Can you stand up, Mrs. Carter?" The voice was talking to *me*. "Let me help you."

I slowly turned around and met gentle, somewhat tense dark eyes.

"You are safe now, Mrs. Carter. I am Sergeant C.J. Young. I am sorry for what happened here."

I stood up and took in the scene. My patio was crawling with police. Vivien and her sister were handcuffed. Two agents were trying to take a statement from Vivien. She sat defiantly in my pool chair, not saying a word. Her sister was slumped in another chair. Vomit covered her hoodie and pants. If this was Lauren, I hoped nobody was taking pictures. The media would have a heyday.

"Jeez." I walked over to her. "Are you OK?" No response. I turned to the sergeant.

"I think this woman needs a doctor."

He nodded. "On the way."

There was more commotion at the door. Andy from Forever Secure ran in, accompanied by a tall, elegant woman.

"Oh my God. Alex, I am so glad you are OK." Andy was out of breath, angst straining his face.

"Are you OK, Mrs. Carter?" The woman stepped forward.

THE WALL

Andy introduced her as Forever Secure's lawyer, but I missed her name.

She was like a beacon of normalcy amidst this madness. Skinny beige pants, light creamy top, high heel sandals, silky blonde hair brushing her shoulders. Her calm sophistication brought to my attention my disheveled appearance. I looked down. Water dripped from my pants. My hand automatically brushed a lock of hair from my face. Not much help, I guessed. My fingers rested on my stinging cheek. I felt humiliated. Violated. And angry.

I. Will. Not. Be. Victimized.

I took a deep breath, wanting to turn around and walk away without a word, but that would be childish.

"Are you OK, Mrs. Carter?" the lawyer repeated.

I carefully formulated my words.

"I am OK considering I was held at a gunpoint in my own house while the police who were supposed to protect me flirted with the trespasser." Sergeant Young bit his lips and looked down.

"We've got it all recorded," Andy said. "The two morons were way out of line. I can't believe what happened."

"Thank you, Andy. Excellent job." I wanted to hug him. Intense relief brought tears to my eyes. The cameras worked! *I have evidence.*

"Sergeant, I am still under arrest?"

"No ma'am."

"Thank you. In that case I'll go change. I'll be back shortly."

"Let me snap a few close-ups first," the lawyer stopped me. "It's all on the videos, but when dealing with police brutality, you can't have enough evidence."

I nodded, suddenly aware that there would be a nasty aftermath to this trespassing. Vivien would not get away with her lies this time. I'd make sure of it. I felt defeated and victorious at the same time.

I walked to my office, leaving a wet trail behind me. I didn't care. The most important thing was to secure the videos. The time of the first warning was 7:47 pm. I downloaded everything from 7:40 until now and copied the vids on the external drive I kept in my safe. Another copy went on a flash drive, which I put in the secret compartment of my antique Japanese chest.

Now I could change.

I studied my face in the mirror. It was not as bad as I thought. I cleaned it and studied it closer. Foundation and concealer will cover most of it, I concluded, relieved. And then something switched in my mind. Why should I camouflage this? If anyone cared to ask about the bruise, I'd tell them exactly what happened. *I* had nothing to hide.

Feeling better, I returned to the patio. Vivien and her sister were gone.

"It looks like they were both under the influence," Andy offered. "There was an open bottle of vodka in Vivien's car." The sergeant shot him a look and asked me to describe what happened.

I told the story in as many details as I remembered. Andy listen intently, the lawyer took notes.

"Why did you jump in the pool to rescue one of the trespassers?" the sergeant wanted to know. His question jolted me. Was I supposed to wait for the police to rescue Lauren?

I took a few seconds to recall the chain of events. "It all happened very quickly. A woman was pushed into my swimming pool and screamed for help. I jumped in to help her without thinking about it."

"Did you know who she was?"

"No. Not at the moment. Later I heard she's Vivien's sister."

"When did you realize Vivien Gibson was one of the intruders?"

"When she came to the pool area with the two officers."

"How can you be sure she didn't come in with the officers?" the sergeant inquired. The lawyer looked up from her notes.

"Sergeant, the house was completely locked before this incident. Someone must have let the officers in while I was rescuing Vivien's sister. Besides, if Vivien was not the second intruder but came in with the officers, how would she know that her sister had been pushed into the pool?"

"Perhaps a third person let the officers and Vivien Gibson in and told them what happened to Lauren."

He had a point there. If that's what happened, the pusher escaped. I shivered. *What if that person comes back?*

"If there was a third person, the security tapes will show it," I concluded and looked at the sergeant.

He asked legitimate questions but irritated me nonetheless. Why do *I* have to justify myself? *What's happening here?* Innocent are guilty until proven innocent and guilty go scot-free? The sergeant opened his mouth to say something, but a fresh surge of anger gave me an edge.

"Sergeant, let's make one thing very clear." My icy tone got his full attention. "Even if Vivien came into the house with your officers, she had no business being here. As for the officers: they were called in to handle trespassing, not to entertain Vivien's fabrications. And if a third person let them in the house, they should have never let that person go because it's the trespasser who pushed Lauren in the pool. I sincerely hope you are looking for this person."

The sergeant studied his fingers.

"Have you ever told Miss Gibson that she is not welcome on your property?" he asked.

"Verbally and in writing," I said.

"Sergeant, to our knowledge there wasn't a third person," Andy said.

"Thank God," I said, still angry.

"The intruders climbed over a solid six-foot fence, which has private property signs all over it," Andy added.

Sergeant Young unsteepled his fingers and looked up.

Dallas

The outside patio of DD

"Trespassing is a criminal offense," the sergeant said. "So here is what happens. We'll file a report. A prosecutor will review it and determine whether the evidence is sufficient to proceed with the case. If so, the intruders will be charged."

They'll never charge her, I thought. She'd lie her way out of it.

"Are you willing to testify?" A pair of gentle eyes searched my face.

"Yes." It was the last thing I wanted to do, but I was willing to go the whole nine yards to get Vivien out of our life.

"OK. My work here is finished, ma'am." The sergeant stood up. "I'll be in touch."

"Thank you." We shook hands. Solid grip. Strong eye contact. A hint of smile. I felt much better.

"You have a strong case," Andy said when the sergeant was out of earshot.

"You would think," I replied. "But Vivien is an accomplished liar."

"It will not be so easy this time, Alex," Andy said. "Did you know she is on probation?"

"No." My eyebrows shot up.

"Possession of controlled substances." Andy took in my puzzled look and smiled. "A little bird told me."

"Jeez." That's why Jack tried so hard to stop me from filing a police report after the kitchen incident. My heart sank. What else didn't Jack tell me?

"Yep. A shitload of trouble." Andy got up. "Let me check that the property is secured and all cameras are on."

It was almost 11 p.m. when I was finally alone. Still too early to call Jack, who was attending a conference in Amsterdam. Maybe I'll just text him and wish him good luck with his talk. It was a prestigious invited lecture and I didn't want to ruin it for him because of the pool drama. There'll be plenty of time to bring Jack up to speed later.

I went to my office and opened the video recorded by camera 6. Andy said there wasn't a third intruder, but I wanted to eliminate this possibility with absolute certainty. I carefully fast forwarded from 7:47 until I saw a person shrouded in a black hoodie walk along the pool towards my patio and out of the camera's range.

My hands trembled as I switched to camera 11. The person walked in the house, put down a large bag, took off the hoodie and ran a hand through her platinum blonde hair. Vivien.

I sat back and closed my eyes. My heart thumped in my chest. Got it! The irony of it. I got the damning evidence thanks to Vivien. Because if she hadn't shown up uninvited in my kitchen, I would have never installed a security system that covered every inch of my property. And I would be in deep trouble right now, trying to prove that it wasn't me who pushed Lauren into the pool. *My word against Vivien's.* I shuddered. I could never win that.

My phone rang. Jack. Do I tell or don't I tell?

"Good morning, darling." I tried to keep my voice neutral. "Good luck with your presentation."

"Oh, for God's sake, Alex! Is Viv there?" Jack asked, agitated.

"No." I swallowed hard. *How did he know?*

"Damn. I can't reach her. She must be scared to death." A frozen hand grabbed my heart.

"Jack—"

"Do you know where she is?"

Jack's words cut through me like a knife. So that's all he cared about. Vivien. Deadly calmness took over me.

"Probably at the police station."

"Why have you done it?"

I braced myself for all hell breaking loose because the police got involved.

"Vivien trespassed again."

"That's not a reason for drowning her sister."

Aah, the lie machine was spinning while I naively held back, not wanting to disturb Jack in the middle of the night.

"No. I *rescued* Lauren from the pool," I said.

"Oh, don't give me that. You don't get arrested for rescuing someone." Disdain dripped in over the airwaves.

"Maybe you should check your facts, Jack." I lowered my voice.

"I have my facts all right. They speak for themselves. I'll forward them to you."

I clicked his text.

VIVIEN: *Your wife got herself arrested. She almost drowned Lauren in your pool.*

She included a picture of me face down by the pool, handcuffed.

Vivien was taking pictures! Fury decimated my calmness.

"What else did she share with you?" I asked icily, keeping the fury in check.

"A video of the officer tackling you down," Jack said.

My mouth was as dry as parchment. A video! The chutzpah.

"That's a fraction of the facts, Jack," I said, raw inside, barely holding together. "It hurts like hell that you are buying this BS. That you'd even consider that I would drown someone." I heard my voice rising.

Then a chilling thought shook me to the core. What if *my* videos aren't enough? What if he believes *Vivien's* stories anyhow? Our marriage was hanging by a thread. Overwhelming sadness nearly choked me.

Jack sighed.

"I guess all you worry about is that if charges are pressed, Vivien's probation gets revoked," I said. "But it's not in my hands this time, Jack. It's up to the prosecutor now."

"What you are talking about?"

So I told him. My voice trembled, but I held my own. Jack kept saying "I am sorry, I am so sorry." I needed more than that. I needed clarity. I needed actions showing what Jack stood for. I said as much.

"I love you, Alex," Jack responded. "I've never loved anyone as much as I love you. You are my Dream Girl."

"I love you too," my heart replied. Our love was under siege, but it wasn't dead yet. We managed to switch to Jack's talk at the conference, but it wasn't business as usual. We were both shaken and hurt, unsure where we stood with each other.

It was past midnight when we hung up.

The image of Vivien recorded by camera 11 assaulted me from my laptop. I restarted the video. The sirens were getting closer and closer. I followed Vivien through the living room. The doorbell rang.

Vivien stopped. The doorbell rang again. Vivien disappeared from view. I switched to camera 10 and saw her open the door.

"Bruce. Oh, it's so good to see YOU." Vivien was all over the tall officer. "Come in. Come in. Something terrible is happening. Follow me."

THE WALL

I hardly breathed as I followed them from camera to camera back to the pool. Camera 8 had the best angle. It caught Vivien taking pictures when the short officer tackled me down. She looked thrilled, just as people look when they are whale watching and a big blue emerges right in front of their camera.

"She is armed!" Vivien screeched.

The officer was visibly panicking. His gun pointed to my head. "She is armed!" Vivien screeched again. I gasped. Didn't she see how she agitated him? He nearly shot me because of her antics. Didn't she get it?

Then I got it. A chill ran up my spine.

Vivien wanted the officer to shoot me.

Dallas

DD
June 1

I bolted upright in my bed, startled. Had I screamed? I held my breath and listened intently. Nothing moved. Protected by peaceful darkness, I slowly leaned on my pillow and lingered in the sweet realization that the nightmare wasn't real. I was OK.

Then reality hit.

I was not OK. My life was falling apart. Fast.

A few hours ago I still hoped for an easy fix. A police report, the videos, a heart-to-heart with Jack. But now, in the darkness of the night, the pieces of the puzzle were coming together. I glimpsed the whole picture and shuddered.

I was trapped in the clutches of a predator.

Nothing prepared me for this. Nothing. No warning, no signs telling me 'run away as fast as you can and never look back.' Nothing I could see.

Because I never tangoed with evil before.

I had no idea how it grabs you, spins you, trips you and then blames you for the faux pas. How it hustles you to get back in step. You strain yourself to give it your best, but this is not the tango you know. The rhythm is off, the steps make no sense. You feel ill at ease, want to stop, but can't: you're trapped by an uncontrollable force that doesn't let you go. It swirls and twists and turns. When you expect it the least, it throws you high in the air and disappears.

Bewildered, you hope to never dance with it again. But as soon as you've regained your balance, it rushes back and tackles you to the ground. It bends over you, you are looking at it but don't see it. Until its hellish breath scorches you.

Is it too late to stop it?

I shivered. I saw the macabre dance pattern clearly now. It was there from the beginning, hidden, invisible to the uninitiated. It played hide

THE WALL

and seek with me. When it was out of sight, I questioned its existence. "Do I worry too much?" I asked. "This can't be so bad... Surely it will pass." I tried to calm myself. But I saw the writing on the wall.

The predator was real.

The trespassing was real, the brutal scratches on my new Giulia were real, and so were the attacks on me and my marriage. The false accusations were real too. They were not true but had real consequences.

The predator poisoned my life. The toxins were spreading ferociously, leaving paralysis and devastation in their wake. I was on constant alert, desperately trying to stay ahead.

But the predator was closing in on me. My life was on the line.

"What doesn't kill you makes you stronger," I reminded myself. But I had yet to find out how this could make me stronger.

Because right now Vivien was killing me.

And the law would not protect me.

Part 3

Now you see me, now you don't.

The Art Tower

Offices of Carter & Co
June 1

Camouflaging the bruises was out of the question, even if I wanted to. The cheek was swollen, black and blue, marked by prominent scratches. I took a selfie for Forever Secure's evidence file and braced myself for a day filled with strange looks and awkward inquiries.

Jamie was the first one. "Oh my gosh, Alex! What happened?" I told her the story, leaving Vivien's name out.

"Was it Vivien?" she mouthed.

I nodded and entered Marty's inner sanctum, meaning business. I'd discovered more problems with Marty's accounting and wanted answers.

"Good morning, Marty." He didn't even look up.

"Good morning, Marty," I repeated. Nothing. I walked around his desk and put the dubious spreadsheet in front of him.

"Marty, your numbers don't add up. And if they still don't add up when I leave this office, you are in serious trouble," I said quietly.

"Really?" Marty smirked.

"Absolutely. A CFO whose numbers don't add up isn't worth a broken penny."

"What are you talking about?" Marty's eyes shifted to the spreadsheet.

"Your Inside-Outside estimate doesn't make sense."

"It makes sense to me."

"Your total is 150K off."

"It can't be. It came right out of the budgeting system." Marty opened a file and highlighted his final numbers.

"Well, let's check the budgeting system then."

"I have to ask Victor about this. He installed the program. It saves us a lot of time, y'know."

Jack's son Victor had moved from Houston to Dallas at the beginning of the year and had done a few odd jobs for Carter & Co. He found a new job in real estate, but still came in every now and then.

"I think you and I can figure it out on our own, Marty," I said. "Could you please open a new project?"

"Jamie does that," Marty said reluctantly.

I looked over his shoulder. "Just click on new. Right here." I pointed to the button.

"OK, let's enter an expense. 100K will do."

Marty gasped. The total came back as $130K. He put in a second expense of $100K. The total came to $260K. Marty and I stared at the screen and then at each other.

"That explains it," I said. "The budgeting system adds thirty percent to the expenses. Where is that money going?"

Marty retreated to his silence. *How can Jack trust this guy?*

"Was the previous system adding 30% to the expenses?"

"No."

"Did Jack agree to add the thirty percent?" I asked, running out of patience. Such incompetence. If this were my company I'd fire Marty on the spot.

"No."

"So stop using it. By the way, when did Victor install the program?"

"Not that long ago."

"When?"

"About six weeks ago," Marty admitted.

I drew my breath in. "Please correct all budgets that were generated during this time."

Marty nodded, his obnoxiousness gone.

"Now, let's make an appointment to go through the whole financial system," I said. It had been on my to-do list for weeks…

"I will be on vacation the next two weeks. I haven't had…"

"The week you are back, then," I interrupted him, not willing to entertain more delays. "In the meantime, I'll go through the basics with Jamie. Perhaps she knows where the thirty percent surcharge goes."

Marty made the appointment, looking lifeless. I felt sorry for him but wasn't done yet.

"And I want to schedule an accounting audit to make sure we don't have more bugs in the system."

Marty didn't reply.

"Thank you for helping me out," I said.

Marty gave his wordless nod. "I am sorry about your cheek," he said when I was almost out of his office.

THE WALL

"Thank you." I turned around.

A surprisingly warm look filled Marty's face.

I walked to my office, unsettled about the budgeting system but determined to get Carter & Co's finances in order. A lovely bouquet of champagne-colored roses waited for me on my desk. I looked at the card. *Love you forever and ever, my DG.*

In spite of everything, my heart filled with joy. *Maybe this is a turning point.*

Jamie knocked on my open door, her face hidden behind peonies.

"Mmmmm... You won't believe this fragrance. They just came in for you."

"Thanks. Oh my..." The message took me by surprise: *Thank you for rescuing me. Please forgive me for the disturbance. Lauren*

"I've always been a big fan of hers, you know," Jamie said.

"I felt really sorry for her yesterday." I nodded.

"Wrong place, wrong time." Jamie shook her head. "Got to run."

The whole office would soon know about the flowers. My phone chimed.

JEN: *Can we meet for lunch? It's urgent.*

ME: *Of course. Will get back to you in a minute.*

I took a deep breath. This would not be easy. I got on the Frog's website, hoping their two-person booth was still available. Most people didn't like it because it was not in the center of attention, but that made it perfect for sharing private stories. I booked it.

ME: *The Frog OK? Got us the little booth.*

JEN: *On :-)*

Dallas

The Frog Prince
June 1

"I bet Mother is furious that Aunt Lauren got all the attention." Jen didn't beat around the bush.

The news indeed reported only Lauren's arrest and didn't mention Vivien.

"She is lucky she didn't make the news," I said.

"Not from her point of view. Mother loves to be in the spotlight. Positive, negative, it doesn't matter. As long as it's about her. She would just turn it around and say that she was wrongly arrested because of you."

I was speechless.

"Alex," Jen said, breaking the silence, "I know what she is capable of." Sadness washed over her eyes and made them look a hundred years old. My heart went out to her. It takes courage to admit to yourself that your mom isn't a nice person.

"Jen, I don't know what to say." My voice caught.

"I do. You and I shouldn't be paying for what she does." Jen's melodious voice was rock solid. I didn't detect the slightest trace of bitterness or combativeness. Just determination and strength. Knowing Jen, she didn't come to this conclusion lightly.

"I agree," I said gently. "Thank you for saying this. Was it the urgent message?"

"Sort of. But I have two more. What do you want first, the good news or the bad news?"

"The good news." I needed to hear something positive.

"I got the CNN job." Jen's face radiated like a sun.

"That's wonderful!" We both jumped up to hug and nearly bumped into Evelyn O'Neill who had just come into the Frog with a woman I met at Megs Aldridge's house. Fiona, I recalled.

"Goodness, what are you two celebrating?" Evelyn gave us a huge smile.

"Jen's got her dream job," I said, my heart filled with pride.

"Yes. With CNN."

"You go girl." Evelyn hugged her.

A waitress approached our booth, eager to recite today's specials.

"We are blocking traffic." Evelyn moved on. "Let's keep in touch. Hope you'll still help me with the new fundraiser."

"Absolutely, you can count on me," Jen promised.

"Please tell me all about the job," I encouraged her after our order was placed. We'd prepared for her interview in this booth, and I was dying to hear the details.

"I will, but I have to tell you the bad news first. It's really urgent."

So much for joy. "OK."

Jen took out her phone. "Someone cloned your Facebook account. I found out because your clone made a nasty comment on my friend's post."

I let out a sigh of relief. "Oh man. I was afraid it was something worse. I'll report the account. The same thing happened to Hannah and it got resolved pretty quickly." I reached for my phone.

"Hannah?" Jen thought about it. "Well, I think I know who did it. Let me text you the link to your clone. You can see it for yourself."

Vivien? I guessed correctly. Vivien Carter was one of the clone's friends. I clicked her profile. Married to Jack Carter. Owner at Carter & Co.

"Oh jeez." I looked at Jen.

"I am sorry."

"Don't be. You said it yourself. We shouldn't be paying for this." I quickly took screenshots off both accounts and reported them. I was warning my friends about the clone when our salads arrived, accompanied by a basket of freshly baked bread.

"Ooh, this smells heavenly. Let's celebrate your new job and enjoy the rest of our lunch, OK?" I proposed.

"Yes. Just one more thing. You have to get it off your chest, Alex. I know what you are going through." Jen looked at me intently. "The worst part is that *people don't get it*. I've heard so many times, 'Oh, she didn't mean that. You are making too much of it. Moms don't do things like that'. Or they'll just point-blank tell you that it's your fault." Jen's eyes took on the sadness again.

They'll just point-blank tell you that it's your fault. In Jack's recollection, Jen had been a rebellious teenager driving her mom crazy. Was it Jack who "didn't get it"?

"Oh Jen." I put my hands over hers, wishing I could erase her pain. "That goes both ways," I said. "You have to let it out, too. Any time you need to. OK?"

"Yes." She squeezed my hand, eyes brimming with gentleness. "But today we are celebrating." She raised her water glass. "To our friendship."

"To our friendship and to your new job," I said, smiling, but shaken up by Jen's revelations.

"All Viv ever wanted was to be a good mom," Jack had said time after time. When defending Vivien, when explaining why she never worked, when pleading with me to give her a break.

Did Jack mislead me?

Dallas

The Nasher Sculpture Center
June 1

"Hey Alex, do you have a minute?" Andy's excitement resonated through my phone.

"Sure."

"Vivien has been charged. Multiple charges. Criminal trespassing is one of them. Lauren is cooperating, and they will not charge her," Andy reported. "I've just got off the phone with the prosecutor's office. The videos did it. Overwhelming evidence. We've made a compilation of the key points for you. I am texting you a link to it right now."

"Thank you so much, Andy."

A wave of blissful peace caressed my battered self. *The prosecutor went with the facts.*

I let my eyes rest on the beautiful trees and the luscious lawn sprinkled with sculptures. The Nasher was "my" oasis of serenity in the middle of Dallas. I came here after the lunch with Jen, too wound up to go back to the office. Heartened by Andy's news, I sat down and took stock.

The law enforcement people recognized what Vivien *did*, which I was immensely thankful for. Still, the law would not *protect* me from new intrusions. Because Vivien didn't live by the law. Vivien danced to her own tune, regardless of the consequences. That was the most shocking thing. Did she assume she'd get away with it all?

In hindsight, I should have stood up to her much earlier. *Why did I let her get this far?*

Because I felt sorry for her. She hadn't seen the divorce coming and I wouldn't wish that on anyone.

Because I gave Jack the benefit of the doubt when he asked me to give Vivien more time.

Because I didn't want to make a scene and look like a villain when she crashed our events.

Because, because, because... I bit my lip. These were all valid reasons, but I was still missing something.

"I know what she is capable of." Jen's hundred-year-old eyes gave me the answer.

I didn't know what Vivien was capable of.

That's it! I'd treaded lightly, not knowing that I was clearing the way for Vivien to spread her toxins. I enabled her just as Jack did! I bit my lip, astonished, ashamed that I let myself be manipulated like that. To be slowly boiled like the proverbial frog.

All this time I went about my business as if all was well. But the past twenty or so hours revealed the naked truth: I was far from OK. I finally admitted to myself how terrible I felt in the last weeks. I could barely drag myself out of bed in the morning and spent my days constantly watching my back, bracing myself for another attack from Vivien. Feeling derailed, inferior, compromised. As if a layer of fog separated me from myself.

I stood up and walked through the garden. All this time I assumed that I was merely a bystander, that it was up to Jack to keep Vivien at bay. I was wrong. From now on I'd put myself in charge. No more walking on eggshells, tolerating flimsy excuses, giving BS the benefit of the doubt.

The macabre dance was over.

Dallas

Perry's penthouse
June 7

"It's absolutely unbelievable," Dave said. "She charged people $12K for a training that doesn't exist. They can't get their money back. To top it off, she didn't pay her affiliates. Took the money and disappeared from Facebook and everywhere else."

"How did you find out about it?" Perry asked. He thought Vivien Gibson Carter was lazy, not a con artist.

"Shaun and Lewis heard it from their friend, who closed the contracts with half of her students. His commission should have been around a hundred thousand dollars, but he didn't get paid either."

"How did he get involved in this?"

"Vivien's then-boyfriend Marty Watson asked him. Marty put the whole marketing and selling machine together for Vivien, assuming she'd do the training. But she jumped ship."

"Argh," Perry grunted, lost in thoughts. "People like Vivien ruin the business. They make everyone distrust everyone else."

"Talking about distrust." Dave changed the subject. "I told you nobody working for the Lowells talks, but our guy got hold of Gloria's old butler. He is retired now but remembered the party on the night before the hit and run accident well. This is what he said." Dave consulted his phone. "Sir Ted and Sir Ralph threw a lot of these parties when Miss Gloria was gone. They always had the girls with them. But this party was a nightmare, totally wild. We didn't have enough staff to clean up because they were in Galveston for Miss Gloria's birthday. And we weren't able to replace the broken Baccarat pieces in time and Miss Gloria was livid when she came back."

"Who were the girls?" Perry asked.

"The Gibson girls. Lauren and Vivien."

Perry whistled. "Vivien?"

"Well, the butler said that your dad often joined these parties. This time he didn't and Vivien, who seemed very fond of him, threw a fit because of it. That's how the Baccarat crystal got broken. Anyhow, the butler is one hundred percent sure the Jaguar was in the garage early Friday morning. He checked it because the party was so crazy, and the Jag was Gloria's favorite car. No one else was allowed to drive it."

"Interesting. So on Friday Mom goes to meet Dad, who is in Galveston and presumably doesn't know about the meeting. Grandma's Jag is presumably stolen but is in the garage in Houston. Anyone in the house on that Friday morning could have driven the car to the Regent and hit my mom. Grandma was presumably in Galveston, but she could have come back to Houston and thus remains suspect. On Saturday Dad drops his presidential candidacy, and he and Grandma stop speaking. The Jag disappears. And now someone gave me a picture of a Jaguar which fits the description, but we can't say for sure that it was Grandma's and killed Mom."

"Whoever sent the picture will reveal more. They want you hooked."

Perry pressed his lips into a thin line, frustration taking over. He was convinced that the Lowells got away with murder, but he didn't have the facts to prove it.

Dallas

DD
June 8

Sweat ran down my forehead. I wiped it off impatiently and checked that the hole I dug out was big enough for the Texas Star Hibiscus that rested next to the koi pond, ready to be planted. The hibiscus was huge, even for Texas. I'll be soaking wet by the time I'll manage to put it in the hole and position it so that it reflects nicely in the pond.

Gardening in Texas heat wasn't a walk through a rose garden, but it helped me cope with the aftermath of Vivien's transgressions. Jack and I were both willing to repair our marriage, but the injuries ran deep this time. As if our house got damaged by an earthquake and we were trying to rebuild it, not trusting the ground it stood on.

I sensed something and looked up.

A tall man in chinos and a white shirt walked towards me. Perry!

I straightened up. What brought him here? This wasn't how I imagined our first meeting in person!

"Perry... What a surprise! Glad to meet you. Finally."

Our eyes locked. A stream of silent messages transmitted within a nanosecond.

I lifted my gloved hands. "I will not shake your hand now. Sorry...too muddy."

Perry laughed and spontaneously squeezed my naked forearms.

A wave of tingles swept through me. We were staring at each other, mesmerized.

Everything would have been different had you gone to Dubai first. The thought was as surprising as Perry's touch, but I had no chance to examine it.

Victor came out carrying a tray with Mint Juleps. "Here we go." He carefully put the tray on the garden table. "Oh, I see. You two have found each other already."

Perry slowly let go of my arms.

Now I understood. Victor had texted that he was bringing a friend from college over for drinks, but I had no idea that the friend was Perry.

"Alex, this is Perry. The guy who makes rooms talk and fridges walk. Perry, meet my stepmom Alex, as delectable and sweaty as she can be." Victor bent down and pecked me on my cheek.

"Darling, do you need help with that huge sucker?" All three of us turned towards the source of the melodious baritone.

Jack entered the garden, hugged me, kissed me, and chuckled as he removed a smudge of dirt from my forehead.

"Jack, you are home early."

"The meeting with the Dutchies went better than expected, we've got the contract signed, and I decided to get back to my girl pronto."

"That's great." Carter & Co needed the new contract.

"So what are you boys up to? Are you staying for dinner, Perry?" Jack asked.

"Yeah, why don't you stay, Perry?" Victor said, "We could order pizza."

Perry took a sip of his Mint Julep. "OK."

"Hm, I have a better idea," Jack proposed. "Do you have time to throw together something simple for us, darling?"

He looked at me expectantly, knowing that I'd love to have them all for dinner.

"OK, something simple it will be." I winked, my mind already on the dinner menu.

"Thank you for inviting me," Perry said quietly.

Our eyes locked again.

Penny for your thoughts, I wanted to say but bit my lip.

I waltzed into the kitchen, relaxed, hoping that things were going to turn for the better. Jack had a contract for a new shiny tower, I had a steady flow of new clients, and we hadn't heard from Vivien since the pool incident.

All good reasons for a little impromptu celebration. I called Alfredo's catering, my secret entertaining weapon. I could count on them to deliver the freshest produce at a minute's notice.

I took a quick shower and started my creamy champagne pasta sauce, looking forward to talking with Perry over dinner, curious if I'd find him as enchanting as Liz did. Our exchange in the garden was too short, but the mere recollection of his touch sent tingles through me. I bit my lip, puzzled...

Saved by the doorbell, I collected Alfredo's delivery and focused on finishing the dinner. I carefully unpacked the freshly shucked oysters, put them on a large serving tray filled with ice, and surveyed the remaining items, all set for last-minute preparation.

I lifted my eyes from the kitchen counter and looked outside. Jack and the "boys" were vigorously discussing something, drawing, gesticulating, laughing. It was a beautiful evening and I decided to serve the dinner al fresco. I put a bouquet of roses on our outside dining table and lit the candles. All that remained was to open the champagne and select the music.

Rachmaninov... Rachmaninov's piano concertos sounded like the perfect company for the gentle evening air.

Dallas

DD
Half an hour later

Perry puzzled me.

He didn't say much and steered away from my attempts to involve him deeper in the conversation. Yet, every time I looked up from my plate, his eyes met mine, inviting me to connect.

Jack and Victor didn't seem to notice any of this intricate force field building up between me and Perry. They chatted away while working on their generous portions of pasta and prawns.

Victor stopped mid-sentence and looked at me. "I love the sauce, Alex."

"Yes, it's absolutely delicious," Perry agreed. A happy grin replaced the deep, soul-searching looks.

"It's my favorite pasta," Jack shared while refilling our glasses. "It was the first dish Alex ever cooked for me, and I've loved it ever since."

"I loved the ambiance, too," Jack went on, "You could see all of downtown Montreal from Alex's apartment. Quite spectacular at night. But none of your fancy gizmos, though." Jack turned to Perry.

"Guess Montreal is not up to par yet." Another grin lit up Perry's face.

"Maybe not Montreal but the designer wasn't up to par," I laughed. "Although we are bringing Dallas up to speed."

"Your glamorous clients surely got the domo-bug." Perry looked into my eyes, commanding my full attention.

"And they love your team of young cyber-gods."

"Is that what they call my guys? Cyber-gods?"

"Yes." I chuckled.

Our conversation took off from there. We went from skyscrapers to foreign laborers in Dubai to the Sharia law to human rights to the US immigration laws, and a new shopping mall in Dallas.

Wafts of jasmine floated through the air as we talked through one another, sharing insights, serious one moment, laughing the next. Perry was as charming as Liz had reported, and Victor surprised me with his knowledge and dry sense of humor. Jack beamed.

We finished the pasta dish and I stood up to collect the empty plates. And there it was again: Perry's look that touched me to the core. I left the table and went to the kitchen, unnerved.

I focused on putting the last touches on our baked Alaskas, but Perry's gaze lingered in the back of my mind. I looked outside. Perry laughed, and I saw myself running my hand through his sun-bleached hair and kissing him. Shocked, I let go of the dreamy image. I had not fantasized about another man since meeting Jack.

Fantasies are just that: fantasies, I regained my footing. I rescued the desserts from the broiler, put sparklers in them, and brought them triumphantly outside.

Jack applauded and rewarded me with a jovial hug.

"Fire and ice," Perry commented.

"In perfect harmony." I looked in his eyes, not leaving space for any games.

"That's what we just talked about," Victor said.

"Harmony?"

"No. Fire and ice. Opposites. Dilemmas."

"Agonizing dilemmas," Jack added and shuddered.

"Hypothetical agonizing dilemmas," Victor specified.

"Like what?" I asked, curious where this was going.

"For instance, let's say your lover got unjustly into trouble. It would take all your money to clear his reputation. If you don't do it his life will be ruined. Would you give all your money to help him?" Perry asked.

Jack shifted in his chair uncomfortably. Perry was looking straight at me, demanding an answer.

"That's not a dilemma," I answered without wasting a second. "If you truly love someone, you help."

"OK. Now, would you still give all your money even if your lover deeply hurt you?" Perry fired his next question.

Is this hypothetical? I wondered and looked around the table. Three pairs of eyes observed me intently. I couldn't help but consider this dilemma from my own point of view. What would I do if Jack got into trouble? Did I love him enough to stay by him? I didn't know.

"It would depend on the love," I answered, troubled by my ambivalence. "If I loved him unconditionally, I'd do whatever I could, regardless of what he has done."

Perry nodded thoughtfully and went on.

"OK, so it's not your lover but your friend. You are the only person who can help. Would you give all your money, or would you watch him suffer through a ruined life?"

Jack sighed. The conversation had gone too far. I had to stop it.

"That's an intriguing mind exercise, but life isn't so black and white," I said quietly. "There are many possibilities, many alternative solutions. It would depend on the particular situation. OK, let's switch from hypotheticals to the real thing," I said lightly. "Otherwise you'll have to suffer through a ruined dessert."

Jack laughed, visibly relieved. Perry glimpsed at Victor, who was looking down, deeply in thought.

"Let me top our glasses." Jack's baritone dampened the tension.

We resumed our earlier conversation and hopped from skyscrapers to design to domotics. Perry brought up Senator Howard's housing programs, and we brainstormed about apps that would make quality design available to more than just the happy few. The evening flew by and there wasn't enough time to cover it all. Perry and I made an appointment to continue our discussion about the apps over lunch.

"You are right, Lexi," Perry told me when I walked with him to the front door. "Life isn't so black and white."

My stomach contracted into a tight ball in premonition that life would prove me wrong.

Secret Residence

June 14

"Welcome to the Clair It Up show. Our panelists this morning are Dr. Sandra Bloementhal, a clinical psychologist, and Vivien Gibson, owner of a sexting website." The audience applauded. Vivien nodded regally.

He sat back, jaw tight, watching the show like a hawk stalking prey. His rules were clear: no publicity. Vivien was getting out of hand.

"Let's start with Vivien." The perfectly put together Clair checked her notes. "You host a website that allows people to indulge in safe sexting, regardless of their marital status."

Vivien nodded. "It's a club actually."

"What motivated you to start this…this sexting club?" Clair found her words and smiled to the camera.

He tightened. The only goal of the site was to collect compromising material that could destroy lives when the time was right. It was Vivien's idea, but he put the site up for her.

"Because it saves marriages." Vivien answered as if she were the Delphi Oracle.

"Research doesn't support this," Sandra disagreed, but Vivien didn't let her finish.

"It does. Sexting saves marriages. All our members would tell you that. And it's easier than having an affair, which saves marriages too, by the way."

Sandra's eyebrows shot up. She opened her mouth to object, but Claire jumped in.

"Vivien, how do you define sexting?"

"Oh, it's just like waving a gun, honey," Vivien laughed. "It excites you, but you don't kill anyone."

The audience laughed, and Vivien waved to them.

He laughed too. Viv was crushing it.

"It's exciting but you don't kill anyone. Sandra, what are your thoughts on this?"

"You don't kill anyone, but you kill their trust," Sandra said.

"You don't have to tell them. And when you use our site, they'll never find out." Vivien turned to the audience. "www sextfree dot com. You can sign up for free."

"Research shows that sexting destroys intimacy." Sandra tried to get into the conversation, but no one listened. The audience was checking out Vivien's website on their phones.

"Research isn't reality. Myself, I am a reality gal." Vivien took control. "I go by what works. Sexting works, believe me. I can tell you from my own experience, having affairs kept my marriage going for decades."

"Are you still married, Vivien?" Clair asked innocently.

"No." The audience quieted down, all eyes on Vivien.

"So having affairs didn't work," Sandra triumphed.

"It wasn't my fault." Anger contorted Vivien's face. "I divorced my husband because he cheated on me."

The audience gasped.

He laughed out loud. Blatant, bullish Viv was the only person who could make him laugh.

The show went into commercial break. When they returned, the viewers would be taken behind the scenes of Vivien's website, Clair teased.

"OK." Clair beamed, looking like the commercial break energized her. "And now we have for you an exclusive video of a real-life sexting experience. Are you ready?"

The audience roared.

"Our protagonists are SenHowdy21 and NumberOne. They gave us permission to share their session, but their names aren't real."

He frowned.

Vivien giggled as the camera zoomed in on how SenHowdy21 desired to please NumberOne.

Blinded by fury, he hardly saw the words. Vivien was dragging Senator Howard into a sexting scandal. Without permission!

He shut the TV off.

The stupid bitch put years of my work at risk. His head was exploding with the enormity of Vivien's transgression.

He hurled the remote control across the room. It smashed into a mirror and came crashing down, followed by a swish of shattered glass.

The shards escalated his fury. He couldn't stand any disorder in his space.

THE WALL

But as always, fury, his loyal companion, sharpened his mind. Vivien was finished.

He had given her a stern warning after the pool incident. He let her squirm and beg and bailed her out only after she had sworn that she would never draw any publicity to herself again. Publicity was his biggest enemy.

All it took was one reporter trying to make a name for himself. Or herself, which was even worse. One zealous idiot that searched Vivien on the web, connected the dots, and put a bunch of sniffing dogs on *his* tracks. He couldn't afford such risks.

He had spent hours and hours knocking out websites that reported Vivien's trespassing arrest. And now she brought the whole political machinery around Senator Howard into play.

Didn't she understand? He needed her invisible. She was his secret agent in Dallas, flying under the radar until he was ready to execute his coup. He paced around the room, searching for solutions.

I don't need Vivien. She must be eliminated. His mind delivered the verdict with supreme clarity.

He puffed his chest and smirked. He'll seize power like no one ever before. He'll make the worms squirm. It will be too late when they finally realize that he controls all the strings. That they can no longer hide behind their precious rule of law. Twitching little naked worms. Exposed and powerless. That's how they'll live under his rule. If they live.

Vivien could have ruled with him. She could have had it all. She was his kindred spirit, his perfect bad girl. Fearless and ruthless. While fooling everyone into believing that she was just a silly, needy little woman.

But she didn't fool him. He knew from the beginning what the little girl with the huge sultry eyes was capable of. He had high hopes for her.

Vivien broke all the rules in the book, listened to no one but him. She was his model disciple. He wanted thousands like her, millions. Hundreds of millions of ruthless, fearless, obedient followers.

He could almost feel them. He was so close. But her carelessness put his mission at risk. She disobeyed him. She became one of the worms.

Briefly, he considered a quick kill. Pictures of Vivien's dead body floating in the Gulf of Mexico filled his mind but didn't satisfy him. Hit and run would be better. Leave her behind for everyone to see. He laughed. Poetic justice. The beauty of it pleased him. But it wasn't the way to go. A quick kill would be as foolish as Vivien's indiscretions. He stood up, his mind made up.

He would ruin Vivien financially. And that was just the beginning.

Dallas

Cafe Magnolia
Exactly the same time

I zigzagged through the elegant cafe to Perry's table. He stood up and waited for me, a happy grin playing across his face.

"Wow, what an entrance. Everyone's looking at you." Perry kissed my cheek and triggered a tsunami of tingles.

"Maybe they were looking at you," I said and returned Perry's kiss.

"No, it was you. You look absolutely terrific, Lexi."

"Thank you." Our eyes locked. "But you are the most sought-after bachelor in the world."

Since he'd signed up with Richard, Perry was frequently featured in the social pages, accompanied by stunning models and celebrities. For some reason, my heart wept a little every time I saw one of these pictures.

A tiny hint of sadness clouded Perry's eyes but disappeared as we sat down.

A waiter descended on our table. We ordered and went directly to business.

I pitched ideas for two apps, one with easy templates helping people to get the shapes, proportions, materials, and colors right when they are redesigning their space. The second one was "Instant Mood Lifter," an app that would change room colors without much ado.

"We could do the Mood Lifter in different degrees of sophistication," Perry proposed. "From changing colors only to providing the ability to display patterns and dynamic images. People could start with the basics and upgrade later on."

"I like that. Returning clients are the best."

"You know, we could also use the Mood Lifter to get people interested in more home automation," Perry went on. "Give it to them for free if they bought the more advanced stuff."

"Yes. That makes sense."

Working with Perry was so *easy*. It was such a pleasant contrast to the minefield my life had become since I married Jack. For the umpteenth time I wondered what would have happened had Perry not cancelled our first real-life meeting. Would we have explored the electric tingles further? Would that have prevented me from marrying Jack?

But Perry was more than three years younger than I...and had all the models and celebs to choose from. I waved the speculations away.

Still, I wished I hadn't restricted myself so much by marrying Jack. In spite of our attempts to fix our problems, being with Jack was like living in exile. I wanted my life back.

"Let's look at the marketing side of things." Perry dove into blogs, ads, memberships. The heavy intensity of our dinner was replaced by the passion and playfulness of a man who knew his stuff and used it to get the best results. A key to my heart.

Being used to getting clients by the word of mouth, online marketing was an exciting new challenge for me. I wanted to master it. The great news was that Perry was a partner in a small company that could help me with it. And the cyber-gods could get involved with the technical features.

"But I have to be completely honest with you, Lexi. Victor did his best the other day to resolve some grievances that go back to our college days, but I'll not do business with Carter & Co."

The words cut through me like a knife. I'd never thought I'd be embarrassed by being associated with Jack's firm.

"That's no problem. I have my own company," I said, working hard on keeping my voice leveled.

"That's good. Please keep all your intellectual property and finances totally separated from them." I nodded. Perry was the second person after Liz urging me to make my business safe. I took a deep breath. This was my moment to ask Perry about the agonizing dilemma:

"Perry, I am curious. You don't have to answer if you don't want to, but why did you bring up the love versus money dilemma?"

Our eyes met.

"Because of Victor. He is working out some rough issues with his mom."

"I see," I said, recalling Victor's troubled look.

"And you are one of her targets too, yes?" Perry said quietly.

"You could say that. Sometimes I think she has full access to my emails and calendar," I blurted out. "In fact, I am surprised she didn't crash our dinner."

Perry's brows knotted.

"Did you have your computer checked?"

"I have an anti-virus program."

"You need more than that. I'll give you some names."

"Thanks." It was nice to be taken seriously. What a contrast to Jack's calling me paranoid when I suggested the possibility of being hacked.

"Sure. Let's hope your computer is OK."

That's what I hoped too. But if Vivien didn't hack it, Jack was the culprit. I was between a rock and a hard place.

"I have a question too, Lexi. And you don't have to answer, either."

"Go ahead."

"Why did you marry him?"

Should I say, "Because I felt down, you cancelled our meeting, I felt sorry for him and hung on to old camaraderie and expired loyalties, thinking it was love?" I noticed something vulnerable in Perry's eyes and felt tears coming to mine.

"Because I loved him." My voice was barely audible.

"Loved?" Perry asked gently and took my hands in his.

I nodded, not trusting myself to speak. We sat in silence...

"You could..." Perry started to say, but his phone rattled on the table.

"Sorry, I have to take this," he said apologetically and stepped outside.

I sat back, mulling over our exchange. Perry was back in less than a minute, his face hard, impenetrable.

"I am really sorry, Lexi. I have to go. Richard's in trouble. Vivien Gibson just accused him of sexting via her website."

"Jeez. I am sorry." I wanted to wish them both good luck, but Perry was already on his way.

I sat down and composed a text to Liz.

ME: *Just heard what happened. Let me know if you need something. Anything. Giant hug & the best of luck.*

LIZ: *She is a monster.*

I took a sip of water, rattled, sorry for Richard and Liz. They were such a great couple, I couldn't believe he was involved in the sexting. But why would Vivien go after him? Was she trying to discredit Richard to help Senator Lowell, her relative and Richard's archenemy? I couldn't see how that would work, yet, anything went in today's politics.

I tried to make sense of it, and then something else came to me: Jack and I weren't Vivien's only targets. She was also after Richard and Liz, Victor, Jen, and maybe more.

This wasn't about us, it was about Vivien. If Jack and I stuck together, we could free ourselves from her.

A wave of hope cheered me up.

I drove home, enjoying the beautiful day, thinking about how to delete the doom and bring joy back to us.

With the exceptions of the dinner with Perry, Jack was somber ever since he came back from Amsterdam, but he wouldn't say why. Was it because of what Vivien did? Because she hadn't contacted him since? Or because things were so awkward between us? He said he worried about the kids, but they seemed OK, taking it all better than Jack.

Maybe we should get out of town for a while. Go somewhere we'd never been before. Deeply in thoughts, I reached for the garage door opener, ready to pull in DD. And stepped on the brake, heart pounding. The garage door was slowly going down.

Barely breathing, I went to the Forever Secure site, looking for the latest videos. The garage door started to go up. I frantically backed onto the street, expecting Vivien going after me.

Jack walked out, hugging the biggest bouquet of roses I ever saw, his boyish smile turning to concern.

"Alex, Alex...what happened?" He ran to me.

"I didn't know it was you. I thought you had a meeting this afternoon." I felt totally stupid.

"I cancelled. I wanted to handle the latest scandal together. The news people aren't talking about anything else."

"That bad?"

"Unfortunately."

I took a deep breath, still shaking.

Jack handed me the roses. "I want to give us another chance, Alex. I want to take us all on a great trip. You and me and the kids and grandkids. Go somewhere far away, exotic and exciting. Europe, India, whatever." Jack's eyes were two big question marks.

"That's what I was thinking about."

We hugged. We kissed. As in the old times.

The Art Tower

Offices of Carter & Co
July 13

The temperature app turned fire engine red: 108 degrees Fahrenheit. One half of Dallas was vacationing in Colorado, and the other half dreamed about it.

I didn't mind. The heat was much easier to take than the Canadian cold. Besides, I'd take anything as long as we didn't get any heat from Vivien. I kept my fingers crossed: so far she had laid surprisingly low this summer.

The only event was the gargantuan tantrum Vivien had thrown when she found out that Jack and I were taking the whole blended family on our dream trip to India.

"I will absolutely NOT allow this. You are NOT taking MY children and grandchildren to India." Served with an unabridged edition of all Jack's sins.

But then she had quieted down, and we hadn't heard from her since. Still, I wondered how she had found out about the trip. Both Jen and Victor swore they didn't tell her. I was puzzled but thankful that Vivien hadn't bothered us. Her lawyer kept delaying the trespassing case, but I didn't mind. If that's what kept Vivien from going after us, he could delay it indefinitely.

I clicked on my emails and sighed. My inbox needed a liposuction.

There was an urgent knock and my door burst open. I looked up.

"Alex, did you know about this?" Jamie waved a piece of paper in front of me, shock swimming in her eyes.

"What is it?" I asked, bracing myself for a disaster.

"Marty's resignation."

"Jeez." I scanned the letter.

Resigned as of this day, which was also his last day in the office because he still had two weeks of vacation. Bastard. Left like a thief in the night. Without a word of warning.

I had several meetings scheduled with Marty next week to find out what was going on with the firm. It was barely breaking even, which worried me. We should be doing better than that.

"What did he tell you?"

"Nothing. He just walked out this morning and didn't leave any instructions. I just found this in Jack's in-basket."

"Jamie, did Marty mention anything about resigning to you?"

"No." She shook her head. "Didn't say a word. Not even goodbye." Tears sprang from Jamie's huge eyes. She slid her phone from her pocket and dialed. She disconnected the call and dialed again.

"His voicemail doesn't work."

I reread Marty's letter. It couldn't have been clearer. He was gone.

"What are we going to do?" Jamie's voice caught.

That's what I was struggling with.

"I will call M&O Accountants," I said. "Maybe they'll be able to send someone until we find a new CFO."

Jamie nodded, still trying to reach Marty.

"Who was Marty's contact there, Jamie?"

"Jeff McMahon, the owner. I'll text you his number."

"Do you remember who did our last audit?"

"Stan." Jamie smiled. "Stan Nowak. He is such a good guy."

I clicked the number in Jamie's text and explained the situation.

"So Marty resigned." McMahon laughed. "The old bastard made it to his tropical island after all."

Tropical island?

"I don't know anything about that, Mr. McMahon. All I know is that we need your help."

"Huh? He didn't tell you which island?"

"No. He just left a resignation letter."

"Hm. Lemme see... Going through my emails here... No, nothing. That's what he always said. That if he ever made enough money, he'll quit this slavery and move to a tropical island. We were golfing together, y'know."

"I see."

"So you need one of our boys?"

"Yes. Stan Nowak, if possible."

"All you girls are crazy about Stan." Jovial laughter filled my ears.

"Stan did our last audit, Mr. McMahon. And we'll need a full audit again." I took my chances. Jack and Marty had dismissed my request for an audit, calling it overkill. But the situation was different now with Marty disappearing without a trace. Besides, Jack traveled so much, the daily operations of Carter & Co became increasingly my responsibility. I had to know what was going on.

"It's Jeff. Hmmmm. Lemme see, lemme see. OK, I can send Stan over on Tuesday. I can probably free him two or three days per week. That good?"

"Excellent. Thank you so much, Jeff."

"Sure. Good luck to y'all."

Jamie gave me the thumbs-up and left. My phone rang. Trey from W-condos.

"Hey Alex, I have a few questions about the color system. Is this a good time for you?"

"Yes."

We discussed a few minor adjustments to Trey's domotics and chatted about the condo and how the light played with the colors in the living room. I was thrilled both Carl and Trey liked it.

"No, *love* it, Alex," Trey said warmly.

On impulse I took Trey up on his earlier offer to answer any computer questions. Within a second the chatty Trey disappeared and a professional sharp as a blade took over. He expertly guided me through several procedures and asked more questions than I could answer.

I felt like I was taken on a sightseeing ride through a software land, going faster and faster. My head was spinning from all the screens jumping in front of me when Trey announced:

"OK kiddo, your laptop definitely needs some TLC. It looks like a brilliant brain surgeon operated on it and then forgot the scalpel inside."

"What does it mean, Trey?"

"I am not sure yet. I have to consult someone. Do I have your permission?"

"Absolutely."

"K. Will call you back in about two hours."

"Sure. And thanks Trey. I had no idea. I thought it was just a simple question."

"No problem." Trey chuckled and hung up.

I wished he'd told me more. I sat back, finally having time to text Jack about Marty and Stan and attack my emails.

Trey called by the end of the day.

"Carl nearly killed me—I forgot to invite you to our post-remodel party on Saturday. That's tomorrow. Can you come?"

"Sure."

"Cool. I want to introduce someone to you. You should definitely meet this person. And I'll give you the fix for your laptop then, it will take only a minute."

"Great."

If it took only a minute, why didn't Trey give me the fix right away?

My stomach tied up in knots.

Dallas

The W Residences
July 14

"Alex, darling, you've made it! Wonderful!"

"Oh Carl, I wouldn't miss this for the world!"

"Here is a lovely glass of bubbly for you. You know, I almost strangled Trey. He is so absentminded. He should have invited you much earlier."

"Carl, Trey can do no wrong by me, you know that." I laughed, happy to be at the party.

That was the positive effect of encountering Vivien: I felt so grateful for being with people who cared, who weren't out to destroy others. The misery Vivien inflicted upon us made happiness so much deeper and stronger. So precious, not to be taken for granted.

Carl took me around the room introducing me to his friends. There were so many of them in such a short time, no memory hack in the world could have saved me from forgetting their names. Carl's audience hung on his words as he told story after story about the horrors the previous owners had inflicted upon this place and the heroic effort it took to transform it into a "cloud living experience."

He made it sound as if we reclaimed the condo from an army of barbaric aliens. People loved it. My business cards went like hot cakes and my phone chimed with Facebook friend requests. People were telling me about the challenges of their own homes, and I found myself giving an impromptu masterclass.

I chatted, answered questions, and observed the light play on the walls. It was all I had hoped for and more, even with so many people filling the space. The whole condo looked like a dream. Big bouquets of peonies hovered in the air, platters with snacks and fruit abounded, champagne flowed in profusion.

A ray of sun hit the crystal chandelier Trey had almost vetoed, and sent hundreds of scintillating reflections throughout the living room.

People oohed and aahed, recording the magic with their phones. Mission accomplished.

On cloud nine, I was taking in the action, moved, grateful that I was part of it, happy to have a normal moment. Happy that I existed.

Carl came over and hugged me.

"Darling, this is beyond." He put his arm around me and gently steered me away from the crowd.

"Trey is upset that I am stealing all your attention. He wants to introduce you to a very special friend."

"Where is he?" I smiled, joy still reverberating through me.

"In his place. You made it too perfect. I'll never get him out of there."

"Carl, are you telling me you are underestimating yourself?" I teased him. "Just cook one of your signature dishes and Trey will be sprinting to the kitchen as if he were on fire." We both laughed and stepped into Trey's sanctuary.

Trey and his friend sharply turned away from Trey's computer screens but relaxed when they saw us.

"Alex, here you are." Trey got up and hugged me. "I thought Carl's chi-chi crowd ate you alive."

Before I could reply, Carl introduced me to Trey's friend who stood up and towered over all of us. The man had to be at least six foot eight. Athletic, dark hair, chiseled features. He reminded me of someone, but I couldn't recall whom.

"Alex, this is Collin Frey. Collin with double l. One of our oldest, dearest, and most trusted friends."

"Pleasure to meet you, Collin." I was looking straight into Collin's smoky gray eyes. Trustworthy. Just as his strong handshake.

"Alex. Pleasure to meet you too. I love your design." Deep, pleasant voice.

"Thank you."

"Trey told me a lot about you." Collin smiled. Crow's feet spread from the corners of his eyes.

My eyebrows shot up. I turned to Trey looking for explanation.

"Yes. Collin has an important project to discuss with you, Alex." Trey didn't waste time on small talk.

"OK." I nodded.

"Before I forget." Trey scooped an envelope from his desk and gave it to me. "Here is the fix for your laptop. I've printed out the instructions.

Just follow them step by step and everything will be A-OK. If you get stuck, call me. OK?"

"Thanks Trey. I really appreciate this."

"No problem. All right, Carl and I will go back to our fancy guests now. Keep the door shut, we don't want any company secrets leaking to the streets of Dallas." Trey winked and ushered Carl out.

Collin held a chair for me and then sat down, immediately looking less imposing. I put my bubbly down and pushed it to the far end of the table. I had only a few sips, but this meeting didn't look like a champagne party.

Collin leaned forward, tented his fingers, untented them, and looked at me.

"Let me start from the beginning."

I was all ears.

Collin gave me a quick run through his career and told me what our meeting was about, instantly capturing my attention. This was much bigger than I suspected. The hacking of my computer, which Collin described in detail, was only a minor event in the whole scheme of things. Still, having my suspicions confirmed was a big deal for me. *I am not paranoid after all...* I wondered what Jack would say when I tell him about it.

Collin must have read my mind because he asked me not to share our conversation with anyone, especially not with Jack. His explanation why I had to keep it secret gave me the shivers.

"Do you want me to sign a confidentiality agreement?" I asked.

"Not at this time." Collin shook his head and sketched the scope of his project: large scale financial fraud, extortion, computer crimes, voting fraud, potential multiple murders. He was concise and clear, the only thing I didn't understand was why he was telling this to me.

Yet, Trey wouldn't have introduced me to Collin unless he had a good reason, so I listened without interrupting. The picture that looked so vague at first became sharper and sharper. I sat on the edge of my chair, hanging on Collin's words. My role in his project emerged like Venus from the sea.

Collin finished, and we looked at each other for a few seconds. Then I fired my battery of questions. He patiently answered every one of them.

"We need you, Alex." Collin looked into my eyes. "You have the exposure, the experience, the equipment. You are our missing link."

I was speechless. Collin's story seemed rock solid, but I wasn't willing to decide on the spot.

"Thank you, Collin. I...I am honored." I finally broke the silence.

"Is it a yes?"

"No." I shook my head. Collin froze.

"It's almost yes."

"What do you need?"

"To meet with your team."

"Why?"

"To see whether we can trust one another."

Collin nodded.

If I take this on, it would be the most important job I ever had.

Saint Crooks, the Crooks Islands

The same time

"What do you mean the car is not available?" Marty gave his anger free rein. *Nothing* went according to his plan.

This was supposed to be a glorious exit from Dallas. Instead, Marty's flight had been half way from DFW to Miami when some idiot discovered that a dog had been mistakenly loaded onto the plane. The pilot didn't know any better than turn around and fly the dog and all his paying passengers back to Dallas so that the airline avoided negative publicity.

That reduced Marty's celebratory night in Miami to a limp room service burger. Then his early morning flight to Saint Crooks got delayed because of storms. It was midafternoon when Marty finally made his way to the car rental. The SL 550 convertible he reserved weeks ago was no longer available.

"I am sorry, we do not have an SL-Class or any other Mercedes left, Mr. Watson."

"And what do you have?" Marty snapped at the clerk.

"Audi, Porsche." The clerk studied his computer. "Corvette."

Marty hated Porsches. "Give me the Vette," he ordered, still displeased. He left Dallas to do whatever he wanted, whenever he wanted. Getting a car he didn't select wasn't a part of the deal.

But Marty started to feel much better when he put the top down and drove the Vette into town. He never had to wear a business suit again. The world was at his feet. He decided to go directly to the Vic's Bar & Grill.

He swung the Vette into a prime parking spot and strutted to the bar. Dressed in crisp white shorts and a navy polo that accentuated his dark curls adorned with a touch of silver, Marty exuded triumph. At the age of forty-eight, he'd finally made it. No more slavery for him. No sir.

Tim, Marty's favorite bartender, smoked his joint on the Vic's patio, staring aimlessly at the sea. His face broke into a huge smile when he saw Marty.

"Marty, you look like a Master of the Universe. Good to see you man. Your regular?"

"Absolutely."

Tim sprang to action, happily preparing the Vic's signature extra-large martini while chatting away.

"How long are you staying?"

"For good."

"You won in the lottery, man?" Tim laughed goodheartedly.

"Sort of. Better than lottery." Marty couldn't hide his superiority. And he didn't want to.

"Ooh la la." Tim gave a happy dance. "Really? Not going back to the big D this time?"

"Nope."

Caitlin, a waitress and occasional bartender, strolled by and gave Marty her brightest smile.

"Welcome to the island! And you know what? The happy hour starts right now!" she added with a giggle.

"At three o'clock?" Marty probed, taking Caitlin in, her exotic beauty not lost on him this time. He remembered seeing her couple times before but never paid attention to her. That's what the slavery does to you. It makes you miss the fine things in life. *But I am free now*, Marty congratulated himself.

"Sure," Caitlin singsonged. "You have something to celebrate, no?"

Tim topped the martini with a giant olive and Caitlin served it to Marty, sparks jumping between them.

"Yes, I do have something to celebrate." Marty was in the mood. "Have yourself a drink on me."

"Thank you, sir. Perhaps after work."

"It's Marty. Tim, have yourself a drink too. Hell, the next round is on me, everyone," Marty yelled and turned around on his barstool. "Just call in the orders, guys, it's all on me."

The few patrons scattered through the bar barely looked up, but Marty didn't care. He had arrived.

The Vic's was the place to celebrate and Marty treated himself to another extra-large martini. And another one. He had an early dinner and stayed on to enjoy the drink with Caitlin. By the end of the evening, Caitlin drove him to his house. And stayed.

It was nearly noon when Marty woke up the next day. Caitlin was waiting for him in his recliner, naked. The nicest fruit on the island, Marty thought victoriously.

"I am looking for a personal assistant," Marty said over brunch. "Do you know someone?"

"Yes. Me," Caitlin answered.

Marty inspected her for a few seconds and then asked: "What do you know about internet marketing?"

"ROI is the king. You've got to get good Return on Investment. At least fifty percent. One hundred percent is much better. Two hundred percent gets you somewhere."

Marty laughed.

"What else?"

"I know stuff about campaigns, cloaking, cold traffic, black hat, bitcoin. It could buy you one of the fancy mansions on the hill."

Marty laughed again. The girl made him feel good. In control. An image of Vivien jumped into his mind, but he pushed it away.

"Have you ever tried it?"

Caitlin shook her head.

She'd probably overheard some multimillionaires boasting over their mojitos at the Vic's, Marty thought and inspected her some more. She sure was a looker.

"OK. Let's give it a try," Marty decided. "You'll do exactly what I tell you and I will triple your Vic's salary. If you don't follow orders, I'll hire someone else. Got it?"

Caitlin nodded.

"By the way, I'll teach you a lot of valuable stuff. It's up to you what you do with it in your free time," Marty added nonchalantly. "Just do what I tell you and you will be fine. We are going to print money, baby."

That said, Marty went back to enjoying the fruits of his labor.

The Art Tower

Alex's office
July 16

10:29 a.m.

My chest was too small for my heart. I took a deep breath, trying to calm down.

"It's business as usual. A meeting. Just as another meeting," I kept telling myself, to no avail. My sympathetic nervous system kicked in gear, and once that horse got running, it wasn't easy to bring it back to the stables.

At ten thirty sharp I walked from my office at the Art Tower, entered the Sky Gondola and descended to the parking garage. I took in the oily, rubbery smell and walked to the Giulia, which was parked in slot #126 as agreed. But instead of getting into the Giulia, I slipped into the passenger seat of the dark van parked to its left.

Collin was behind the wheel. So far everything had gone as planned. The fight-or-flight horse was still racing in my chest, but I invested all my energy into looking as if clandestine meetings were my core business. Not a muscle moved in my face.

We drove out of the garage and got on 35 North. In total silence. That, too, was part of the plan. Collin ran a tight ship, and security was as holy to him as scrubbing was to a surgeon. No viruses in the system.

Secrecy was another of his select weapons. No one—NO ONE—knew about this project unless they absolutely had to. Collin wasn't thrilled about my insisting on meeting his team, but I wouldn't take the job otherwise.

I made a hard deal with myself: if I had the smallest doubt about working with them, I was out. The risks were too high. The tasks Collin asked me to do were deceptively simple, mostly maintaining regular email contact with several people as if they were my clients. But I was just one link in a long chain. If Collin or his guys made a mistake, I'd be at the mercy of people who had no mercy.

The van entered a relatively modern building. Collin parked it and we walked to his office. Only then he offered a brief, "Well done."

Thankfully the racehorse quieted down. I hadn't yet agreed to take the job, but I wanted it. Badly. I wanted to be on the team. The rewards were enormous. And so were the risks. Fear played worst case scenarios in front of my eyes, like when you stand at the edge of a cliff and see yourself tumbling down. I shivered. *These images aren't real, it's only a warning.* The thought kept my nerves in check.

"Ready for the War Room?" Collin asked.

"Yes."

We walked into a large meeting room. The project lived on a windowless wall. I walked from section to section, taking it all in. My confidence rose when I saw several scenarios I'd come up with myself while considering Collin's proposal. I studied the alternatives I hadn't thought about. Clever. I couldn't wait to start.

A young woman came up to me.

"We weren't sure about this one"—she pointed to a part of the wall—"but we figured we better take it into account as well."

"It could go that way," I said. "The greed-takes-it-all option."

More people came in and joined the conversation. We talked priorities, logistics, materials. Talking through each other, finishing each other's sentences. I was sold.

Collin joined us.

"You've got an impressive team," I said.

"It's a go, then?"

"Yes."

We went back to his office to handle the paperwork and planning. All the prep work I was needed for had to be completed before I left for our family trip to India.

"I knew you would do it," Collin said matter-of-factly.

"When did you know?" I was curious.

"When you pushed away the bubbly."

I laughed.

"What would you do if I hadn't said yes?"

"That wasn't an option." He was right.

"Even so, I think you should have a Plan B."

"Why?"

"Because this is a risky business. You can count on me to do my best, but you can't discount the unexpected."

"Would you have a Plan B if you were in my shoes?"

"Absolutely," I said.

Collin tented and untented his fingers, his eyes fixed on the floor. Then he looked up, his face unreadable.

"The code name of the project is TW. As in The Wall. Don't talk about TW with anyone but me."

Secrecy reigned.

I looked around and took in the surroundings.

This place definitely needed remodeling.

Dallas

DD
July 28

"Hey guys. A major storm will hit Dallas later in the afternoon." Peter studied his phone, frowning.

"You are kidding."

"There isn't a cloud in the sky."

Jen and I savored our summer rosé on the patio, watching Ian and Bailey jumping off Jack's shoulders into the deep end of the pool, giggling, competing for Jack's attention.

This was exactly what we had in mind. An easy family picnic before we all went to India. Joy, fun, good food, lots of laughter.

I hoped Vivien would not show up and ruin the day. Coming here uninvited wouldn't help her case, but Vivien being Vivien, anything could happen. It wouldn't surprise me if she created some "horrendous" emergency to interrupt our party or prevent us from traveling.

Jack and the kids got out of the pool, starving. Ian and Bailey grabbed a few snacks and chased each other around the patio, Henry, their lab, chasing after them.

"Who wants a lemonade?" The kids sprinted to the kitchen ahead of me, led by Henry. I held my breath as they barely missed the kitchen island, fantasizing about turning the hard materials into a crash-safe foamy rubber. Ian and Bailey were certainly teaching me a lesson or two about designing kids-friendly environments.

They tasted their lemonades and carried them carefully to the patio. Henry decided to stay with me, knowing that I'd give him a handful of his favorite treats.

Liz called, excited to tell me that Richard had agreed to a last-minute trip to Nepal.

"He'll be working on a housing project there, but we could get together in Kathmandu."

"Great plan."

"I hear they have some marvelous artifacts there. Can I steal you for a few hours to go on a shopping expedition?"

"I am looking forward to it already," I said. "Anything specific you want?"

"Not really. Something unique, exotic, spiritual."

"OK. I'll research the possibilities." Which was a nice opportunity to call Mo, who had a network of merchants all over the world.

"Enjoy India, honey. It's an assault on your senses. All things delightful and not so delightful. And don't be surprised if you get pinched. It happened to me several times," Liz's raspy voice warned me.

I laughed.

Excited about searching for unique Nepalese artifacts, I finished the cheese platter and salads Jen and I had prepared earlier and assembled everything on the buffet table near the patio. Arranging the buffet like a painting was my most favorite part of the job. Bailey assisted me with adding a few zinnias and dahlias from the garden, lips rolled in utmost concentration, while Henry stretched out under the table and wagged his tail from side to side. *Happiness.*

"This looks gorgeous, ladies." Jack appeared from nowhere and hugged me. "I think champagne is in order."

"Hmmmm." Peter came along. "Time to fire up the barbecue?"

"Yes."

"I'll get the bubbly," Victor chipped in.

Peter was almost finished barbecuing the last burgers when the wind picked up and a few rain drops flew in. The sky was still perfectly blue, but this was Texas. The weather could change in no time. Peter checked his phone again.

"Oh my gosh. The storm will hit us in less than half an hour."

Jack turned on the TV.

The screen filled with red and pink radar blobs. I gasped. Pink meant hail, a scourge in North Texas, where hailstones can get larger than golf balls.

"Peter, park your car in the garage."

The wind gusts intensified. It was getting darker by the minute. The broadcast showed flooding, roofs blown away, and cars damaged by fallen trees not so far to the southwest of us.

I ran to the garage and reparked the Giulia to make space for Peter's car. There were plenty of cars driving around Dallas looking like they had chickenpox, and I didn't want Peter's Beemer to become one of them.

THE WALL

When Peter and I returned to the picnic, the tree tops swirled in a violent wind gust dance. Lightning scissored the sky. Jack and Victor were securing the umbrellas. Peter and I collected the kids' toys as large raindrops splashed in the pool. We ran in and Jack closed the outside glass panels, turning our picnic area into an inside party space.

Jen refreshed the buffet table and brought out the desserts.

"Wow!" The kids tackled their brownies as we all watched the storm developing outside and on TV. At one point the hail hit, making the pool look like there were hundreds of geysers in it. The TV commentators warned people not to drive unless absolutely necessary. Three tornados touched down east of Dallas. And that was just the beginning.

The weatherman excitedly showed a series of storm cells on the radar, repeatedly saying that we were being battered by one of the worst storms in years. We had hours of violent weather ahead of us.

I was glad that everyone was safe at DD, but I couldn't get Vivien out of my mind. I wasn't fooled by her relative silence. She had it in her to hit us out of the blue, just as the storm.

The question was when.

Dallas

Vivien's bedroom
July 29

"This can't be!" But it was. It was Hugh's voice. Vivien knew it intimately. She often replayed his videos just to hear him. Hearing him calmed her down and confirmed that she belonged. She loved his voice. So strong and soothing.

And now Hugh Donaldson's voicemail ordered her to pay him two point four million dollars.

I can't pay that! Vivien wailed. It would wipe her out. She got three emails from Donaldson Investments over the past few days, informing her about the new balance. At first she thought that she made that money, but the subject of the second email shouted "Your payment of $2.4 million is due in 14 days!"

Vivien didn't understand. Hugh promised to ten-tuple her investment. Confused, she dismissed the emails as a scam. But the voicemail was clear: according to the terms of investment, she owed $2.4 million. If she didn't pay it within twelve days, her car, house and other assets will be repossessed.

Vivien frantically scrolled through her inbox. Her hands were shaking so violently, she almost dropped the phone. The Donaldson emails where nowhere in sight. She had to scroll up and down several times before finding the first one. Relieved, she forwarded it to Marty. *He'll know how to fix this,* she reassured herself. Exhausted, she collapsed at the foot of her bed and fell asleep.

The room was dark when she woke up. Discombobulated by feverish dreams, Vivien didn't know where she was. She reached for her phone. The screen lit up and jolted her into reality.

"Pay in 11 days and avoid criminal prosecution."

Vivien vomited on her white carpet, not sparing the phone. She rolled away, too spent to get up.

THE WALL

This can't be happening to me, she sobbed. It was so unfair. Every time something big was about to happen in her life, every time she was reaching the heights she yearned for, a brutish force yanked her down and pushed her into the insufferable hell of loss. The love of her life, Facebook fame, endless wealth...all ripped away from her.

She was so close this time, she had the power of big money almost at her fingertips. She could smell it, taste it, revel in it. So close...but it slipped through her fingers. "Noooooooooooo!" Vivien screamed. *No woman should ever have to go through this.*

Vivien curled into a motionless ball. Everything would be different if Daddy was still alive. Daddy would know what to do. Daddy would take care of her. Daddy would put Donaldson in his place. Vivien giggled.

"If you do something, do it big," Daddy used to say.

Vivien stopped in her tracks. YES! That's it... It was so simple... She'd solve everything with one stroke...

ONE. BIG. STROKE.

Vivien defied reality.

New Delhi, India

Chandi Chowk in Old Delhi
August 2

"Hey!" I pushed away the offensive hand and glared at the perpetrator. He was just a boy.

"What's going on?" Jack put his arm around me.

"He pinched me." On the butt!

"Don't ever do that again!" Jack scolded the boy. Without much effect I predicted, remembering Liz's story about being pinched multiple times. The crowd moved us forward and we laughed, taking in the madcap chaos of locals, tourists, hawkers, rickshaws, and electrical cables swaying haphazardly above our heads as we weaved through a mind-boggling array of saris, trinkets, gold embroidered textiles, gadgets, fried food, silver jewelry, flowers.

Kissed by wafts of incense, fumes and decay, we strolled to the Gadodia Market, where our overwhelmed senses suffered the final blow coming from rows of huge sacks filled with fire hot red peppers, silky orange turmeric, and pungent brownish masalas, mixed with piles of ginger, rice, nuts, dates, tea, and fruits I had never seen before.

"Can you imagine all the mysterious concoctions that will be cooked with this stuff?" Jack said.

"Yeah, secret sauces." I couldn't even identify some of these ingredients, let alone cook with them.

Jack laughed. We walked hand in hand to the Jama Masjid, India's largest mosque, and caught a motorized rickshaw to take us from the pandemonium of Old Delhi to the calmness of our modern hotel.

"What a great start of our trip." Jack put his arms around me. We kissed, happy as we were on our wedding day.

We had all let out a collective sigh of relief when our plane took off from DFW without incident. None of us had mentioned Vivien, but we had been all dreading a last-minute drama ruining our trip.

Now, thousands of miles away from Vivien's toxic cloud, we finally allowed the excitement of our adventure to take over. Elated, I looked at Jack.

"It was all worth it," I said.

Our love was back.

Jaipur, Rajasthan, India

The Nahargarh Fort
August 4

Jack and I were exploring the Nahargarh Fort, holding hands, enjoying every moment. We couldn't have given ourselves a better present than this trip.

The guide was taking us through suites said to be haunted, but assured us that the ghost wasn't present. A text popped up on Jack's phone. I peeked at it, surprised that Jack had a connection, but he turned away before I could see where the text came from.

"I've got to call the office immediately," Jack said.

Tell that to the mobile gods of North India. Their service was more fickle than the restless sea. We went outside, but our phones didn't have a signal. Our best bet was to return to the hotel.

We ran to the parking place and found our driver talking animatedly with a group of other drivers waiting for their tourists.

"Get us back to the hotel," Jack barked. "Fast!"

Within seconds, the driver negotiated a jumble of tourists on foot, tourists on elephants, tourists in rickshaws, potholes, and Rajasthan's most stubborn cows.

Jack's tight jaw and impenetrable eyes annihilated the boyish smile that had played on his face since we left Dallas.

"What happened?" I asked quietly.

Jack shrugged. His coldness and distance gave me the shivers. *Is the text from Vivien?*

"Jack, what's going on?" I tried again when we made it to our hotel room.

"Trouble in the financial department." Jack flared up and focused on getting his devices connected, swearing, pounding the table with his fist. Without success. He finally called the front desk, only to learn that Jaipur was experiencing a major malfunction that knocked out internet and most mobile providers. Nobody knew when it will be repaired.

"I have to return to Delhi. Can't do anything from here," Jack said.

"I'll go with you."

"No. I will work the whole time."

I looked at him, not following his argument. "But Jack, it's our trip. And I am your VP, remember? I don't mind working with you." By now I knew more about Carter & Co's finances than Jack did.

"No. Stay with the kids, Alex. I will catch up with you in a day or two." Jack tried to connect his phone again.

"Jack, the kids have their own program, they don't need me. Let's fix this together." I gave Jack a brief kiss, trying to regain the closeness we shared since Delhi.

"For God's sake, Alex." Jack stood up angrily and pushed me away. "Stop making things more difficult than they are!"

So *I* am the difficult person now. I stepped back, hurt, shocked by Jack's sudden switch from loving closeness to chilling distance. *Vivien must be involved.*

"Is Vivien part of the trouble?" I asked, looking directly at Jack.

"That's enough!" he snapped. "I have to get going now." Jack threw his toiletries and a change of clothes in his overnight bag and stormed out of the room.

No hug. No kiss. No love.

A frozen hand crushed my heart.

Houston, Texas

Gloria Lowell's mansion,
August 6

If Gloria Lowell were carved from granite, her jaw wouldn't have been set tighter. She pored over a photograph of her old Jaguar, consumed by bitterness and anger. The car's beautiful line was ruined by a fatal crash.

Gloria pressed her lips into a thin line. She hated making mistakes. And she rarely did. Gloria ruled her empire with an iron fist, forget the velvet glove. Nothing was left to chance.

Yet, more than thirty years ago, Gloria made a choice that returned to her like a deadly boomerang.

How could a decision that looked so right turn into such a colossal disaster? The mistake put her legacy under siege.

Gloria's family had come to Houston in the 1850s and had risen to prominence on the wave of the newly developing iron industry. Gloria's grandfather expanded the family holdings to gas and oil and shrewdly benefited from the boom Houston companies enjoyed during the Second World War. His only child, Gloria's father William, was born to wealth and privilege reserved only for the luckiest few.

The apple of his mother's eye, William grew up surrounded by art and artists. The boardroom held no appeal to him. The unexpected conception of Gloria thrusted him into an early marriage but didn't slow down the swirl of his bohemian lifestyle. William and his young bride left Gloria in the care of her grandparents and sailed off to Europe.

After spending half a year in Paris, the couple indulged in the charms of Marbella, Tangier, and the French Riviera. Their carefree journey ended abruptly in a fatal boating accident near Antibes, one day before Gloria's sixth birthday.

The total opposite of her father, Gloria more than filled the void William left behind. She grew up behind her grandfather's desk, the family holdings being her playground. Why play with dollhouses if you can buy hotels? Why fantasize about being a princess if you can reign over an empire made of oil, electronics, and retail giants?

Making business decisions became as natural to Gloria as breathing. By her mid-teens she completed her first takeover and on her twenty-first birthday took charge of the entire business. Disliked by women and feared by men, Gloria multiplied the family's fortune many times over and had no plans to slow down.

At seventy-four, Gloria was as strong as ever, not looking a day over fifty and feeling even younger. Her youthfulness could be attributed to many factors, but happiness wasn't one of them.

No one looking at Gloria's magnificent life would spot a hint of the bitterness she endured day in, day out. No one could ever fathom the cruel irony of having it all, yet not being able to obtain the one and only thing Gloria truly desired.

The White House.

As far back as Gloria remembered, she'd wanted to be the First Lady. Thus when Perry Winston Lowell proposed to marry her, Gloria's reason for accepting wasn't Perry's love for her, which she didn't trust, but Perry's love for politics and his keen ability to make voters love him.

Perry became a popular congressman, seen by many as a future president. But his and Gloria's road to the White House was brutally interrupted by Perry's fatal heart attack at the age of forty-two, in the arms of one of his many mistresses.

Enraged, Gloria withdrew from the public eye and succeeded in keeping the circumstances of Perry's death out of the media. Deeply mourning the loss of her dream, she retreated to what she did best: running her companies. She shrewdly leveraged the market deregulations unleashed by Reaganomics and expanded her holdings beyond wildest imagination. Yet, material wealth meant nothing to her.

Gloria had only one priority: The White House.

Being the First Lady was out of reach, but she could still become the first mother. When her only son, Perry Winston Lowell II, turned fourteen, Gloria began to groom him for his march on the White House.

Perry II generously indulged his mother's ambition but kept his options open. His utmost aspiration was to make a name for himself independently of the Lowell empire. He took to calling himself Win and established technology parks in Houston and Midland way before graduating from Harvard Business School.

Gloria approved of Win's ventures at first, but her tolerance ran out when he fell in love with Sylvia, the daughter of a Midland banker. Based on her astute judgment of marital success, Gloria firmly believed that love was the worst reason for getting married. For years she kept track of suitable girls, compiling a master list of potential brides, uncompromisingly crossing out candidates who disqualified themselves. By the time Win fell for Sylvia, only three young women had survived Gloria's scrutiny.

Sylvia wasn't one of them.

So when Sylvia excitedly wrote to Win that she was pregnant, Gloria intercepted the letter, blocked all communication between Sylvia and Win, and convinced Win that Sylvia had left him. Win was crushed, but Gloria didn't doubt he'd get over it. She couldn't allow an unwanted child to interfere with Win's road to the presidency.

Sylvia, a remarkable scholar, still had two years to go to earn her degree from Stanford. Gloria assumed that her parents would convince Sylvia to terminate the pregnancy. No harm done. No one's future ruined.

When a picture of the newborn child arrived, Gloria was jolted as if struck by lightning. It wasn't so much the shock of the child being born, as the pain that seized Gloria's heart. *I'll never hold him,* she moaned, tears filling her eyes. *My first grandchild!* Perry Winston Lowell.

Why didn't Sylvia write earlier that she kept the child? Gloria lamented. It was too late now. Win had recently married the top girl on Gloria's list and they were expecting their first child.

Win must never find out about Perry, Gloria decided, pragmatism gaining the upper hand on her uncharacteristic outbreak of emotions.

Yet, in spite or perhaps because of his unreachability, Gloria found herself more attached to little Perry than to her own children. She ensured that she was informed about Sylvia and Perry's every move.

When little Perry turned five, Sylvia moved to Houston. They lived in the Houston Regent hotel where Sylvia worked, and which Gloria owned. Gloria took pleasure in visiting the hotel and watching the boy, but she continued intercepting Sylvia's letters to Win. Win was running for the Senate, and a scandal would ruin his chances.

Sylvia almost got to Win when little Perry became a senior in high school. She managed to collect Win's DNA sample and sent the proof of paternity to him, asking Win to support little Perry's college education. Something had to be done.

Gloria sent a go-between to meet with Sylvia and negotiate a financial settlement in exchange for absolute silence. But the meeting never took place. Sylvia was killed in a hit and run accident on her way to it. To Gloria's horror, the police came to Galveston and questioned Win because someone told them that Sylvia was rushing to a meeting with him.

Telling the truth, Win easily convinced the police that he didn't know about any such meeting and was never linked with the accident. But the damage was done. Win announced that he'd not pursue any political ambitions beyond keeping his seat in the Senate.

Gloria's mission to protect Win's road to the White House collapsed under its success. The road was clear, but Win had refused to take it. It had been Gloria's biggest failure ever.

And the punishment wasn't over yet.

Houston, Texas

Gloria Lowell's mansion

The photograph of the ruined car burned in Gloria's fingers.

Always on guard to protect her family from scandals, Gloria had not challenged Ted Gibson's story about the missing Jaguar. But she had not believed it for a second. Quietly, without the family's knowing, she conducted her own investigation. Although the evidence wasn't 100% conclusive, Gloria *knew*.

It didn't matter to her that she wasn't behind the steering wheel on that fatal day. She was guilty of triggering the chain of events and got a life sentence for it. She'd be forever haunted by being responsible for the death of her grandson's mother.

I should have never intercepted Sylvia's letters and kept her pregnancy hidden from Win, Gloria admitted to herself bitterly.

She slouched in her chair, slipping into darkness.

And then a bright voice straightened her up: "Would they have kept the child?"

Maybe not, Gloria concluded. And if they had, would he have become the man he was now?

The irony of it all. Gloria almost laughed, her strength returning.

She couldn't fix the past, but she could fix the current situation. Gloria inspected the picture of the Jaguar again. Someone was trying to blackmail her. And that someone had made a capital mistake: they assumed Gloria would spare no expense to prevent a scandal.

But she no longer cared about scandals. She wanted her grandson back. Gloria's eyes lit up.

Little Perry became a billionaire before the age of twenty-eight and had moved on to politics! Win never ran with the opportunities Gloria created for him, but little Perry created his own. A chip off the old block. He even looked like Gloria's grandfather. Tall, handsome, with the slightest touch of roguishness that made him irresistibly attractive. The perfect presidential material.

And the audacity of working for his father's political archenemy! Gloria was certain that little Perry knew who his father was. If her information was correct, Perry was tracking down his mother's killer. Gloria had to find a way to connect with Perry before the blackmailers got to him.

Three people were in the Jaguar on that fatal day. Any one of them could have caused the accident. *Let's see what they'll do when all three of them are accused,* Gloria thought. But she knew that already: they would twist and squirm and then implicate one another. She knew them well. She had wanted to remove them from her life for years, and this was a perfect opportunity. Gloria dialed her lawyer.

Justice will be done.

New Delhi, India

The Taj Garden hotel
August 7

The whole financial hoopla looked to Jack like one of those incidents that scare you at first but later make for a great dinner conversation. The more often you tell the story, the more dramatic it gets, and the more you cherish the happy ending.

Jack imagined sharing this drama with his friends, making them feel the terror of losing all of their money, and when everything seemed lost, letting them off the hook, their life intact.

Jack wasn't in the habit of giving in to catastrophic scenarios. So when the first message had arrived back in Jaipur, Jack had assumed it was a mere misunderstanding:

STAN: *Jack, Carter & Co's tax installment is due, but there is no money in your accounts. What's going on?*

Alarming, yes. But nothing a phone call and a good internet connection couldn't solve. It crossed Jack's mind that this could be Vivien's way of disrupting their trip, but he couldn't imagine that she could have pulled something like this off. It must have been a mistake in the financial department. Maybe Marty paid the taxes before he left. Or the money was in another account.

Besides, millions of dollars couldn't just disappear without a trace.

Assured that it was an annoying but minor glitch, Jack had expected to catch up with Alex and the kids the next day. But due to the time difference, failed connections, and miscommunications, it had taken him more than two days to get down to the facts.

"Jack, there is almost no money left in your accounts. Everything went to your ex-wife. Some of it with your approval."

Stan dropped the bombshell with clinical calmness that didn't leave any room for doubt, but Jack still hoped that it was all a mistake.

"I didn't approve anything like that."

"I have invoices signed by you right in front of me, Jack."

"I didn't sign any invoices from Vivien. Can we block the transfers?"

"We are disputing several of them. But this went on for months. I'll email you copies of everything. If you didn't approve the transfers, I'll call in our forensic unit."

Jack winced. He hoped to resolve it without forensic investigation.

"Stan, did you speak with Marty about this?"

"No. We've tried to reach him, but he didn't respond. No one knows where he is."

"I see." Stan's answer filled Jack with new hope. "Stan, maybe Marty did it and covered his tracks by implicating Vivien."

"Right now, we can't say what's Marty's role in this. But we have clear evidence that Vivien's involved."

"I'll call her and get back to you."

"Sure. Did you get the email I've just sent you?"

"Let me check… Yeah."

Jack's hands trembled when he opened Stan's attachments. The evidence was devastating, but he couldn't believe that Vivien engineered the theft. Marty must have been behind the whole thing.

Hesitantly, Jack picked up his phone. And put it down as if it were too hot to handle.

He sighed and walked out on a patio that opened to the hotel's garden. But the regal trees and perfectly manicured flower beds failed to soothe him. If anything, their lushness brutally underscored the arid devastation of Jack's inner landscape. He went back to his room. He had no choice but to face reality, never his favorite strategy when Vivien was involved.

Jack closed his eyes and wished he could rewind time. He wished he had paid more attention and protected himself better.

But even if he had been more alert, nothing could have prepared him for this crisis because he didn't believe that Vivien was capable of doing something so vicious on such a large scale. Jack could comprehend her talking Marty into cutting her a check for a few thousand. That was more like Vivien's style. But hacking Carter & Co's bank account and stealing millions? A woman who could hardly sign on to her own computer?

For the first time in his life, Jack looked older than his age. He never worried about his looks because his lucky blend of genes, charm, and good spirits gifted him with time-defying youthfulness. Not anymore.

Dark bags rimmed his exhausted eyes. Deep nose-to-mouth grooves carved his face, emphasizing the despair of his newly hollow cheeks. His normally bouncy hair lay over his forehead, lackluster.

In spite of all the facts, Jack still couldn't believe that Vivien had done this to him. There was only one way to find out. Jack braced himself for the verbal onslaught and dialed her number.

The Taj Garden Hotel

Jack's suite

"I am on my way out, Jack," Vivien said. "Make it quick."

"I will be very quick if you return the money you took from Carter & Co."

"Why would I return it?"

"Because the money doesn't belong to you."

"Don't you try to cheat me again. You signed the invoices yourself."

"No, I did not. And there isn't an invoice for the last transfer. Two point four million dollars. Pay it back."

"I don't have the money."

"Who does?"

"Hugh Donaldson. He lost my money. He victimized me. Can't you see that?" Vivien's voice raised an octave.

As always, Jack was perplexed by Vivien's logic. "Vivien, you aren't the victim here. You stole my money!"

"How dare you accuse ME of STEALING! It's my money... YOU CHEATED ON ME... YOU CHEATED ME OUT OF THE MONEY...after everything I have done for you."

An all-consuming, white-hot rage that only Vivien could trigger swept through Jack like a brush fire, curling his fingers and striking his temples but not finding a way out. In all their previous arguments, this had been the point when Jack walked away and let Vivien win. Not now. A lifetime of suppressed anger surfaced, yearning to combat Vivien's lies.

"My forensic accountants are on the case. You took more than the two point four million. Start repaying it immediately or I'll sue you."

"You promised the money to me. You were going to help me with my new condo."

"I have not—"

"You did. And then gave MY money to the twins. I had no choice."

Each word loaded with enough venom to paralyze an army.

"Vivi—"

"Don't Vivien me." Vivien cut him off. "I could easily refill your petty piggy bank," she went on, laughing triumphantly, "but why should I?"

She has the money. A spark of hope compelled Jack to lower his weapons.

"Because you should repay what you've borrowed," he said.

She laughed.

"You don't get it, Jack, do you?"

Vivien paused, ready to go for the kill.

"I've invested in you! YOU SHOULD HAVE NEVER LEFT ME!" she yelled from the top of her lungs.

"Viv," Jack tried to edge in, but Vivien was unstoppable.

"You don't care about ME, you only care about the twins. AND THEY AREN'T EVEN YOURS."

The Taj Garden Hotel

Jack's suite

"Loser! Loser! Loser!" Vivien's laughter roared. Jack collapsed onto the oversized couch, spent. For decades his life revolved around pleasing Vivien. She never gave him the love he longed for but rescuing her was like a drug to him. Jack was besotted with Vivien's unwavering belief in his ability and willingness to pay her debts, mend the friendships she broke, bail her out of her blues, make her life happen.

Even now, being divorced and after she nearly bankrupted me, she trusts that I'll clean up the mess and let her get away with it.

Alex never gave him such a rush of omnipotence. Alex wanted him. Vivien needed him. Jack missed being indispensable. He wanted to be there for the little girl who was hiding behind Vivien's boldness. The little girl who was drowning him and at the same time counting on him to rescue her.

Part of him wanted to let Vivien off the hook and give her the money. He despised himself for this, but the urge to indulge her was too strong. Like a gambler, he hoped that the next bet would hit the jackpot: Vivien's praise.

And her reassurance that he is the father of the twins.

If I get a loan and a few extra contracts, I could make the whole thing disappear, Jack schemed, driven by his need to give the little girl what she wanted.

There is no little girl. A grown woman bankrupted me. In a flash Jack saw how the "little girl" tricked him. How she played on his heart strings and seduced him to please the woman with the sinister laughter.

Shocked, Jack shivered.

He desperately longed to be with Alex. Hold her hand, look into her eyes. Alex would have been furious about Vivien's fraud, and she would let him feel it. Jack was sure of that. But once that was out of the way, Alex wouldn't waste any time and redirect her fury into rescuing Carter & Co.

Jack put his head in his hands. He didn't understand why he'd discouraged Alex so forcefully from coming to Delhi with him. Because dismissing her requests for a financial audit made him feel like a loser? Or was it the hurt in Alex's eyes that made him push her away?

The look on her face when he left Jaipur had haunted Jack ever since. *Would she still want me when I come back?*

Tears flooded Jack's drawn face. He wanted to call Alex and ask her to join him in Delhi, but he didn't dare. He couldn't face her rejection.

Until a few days ago, Jack had considered himself a fortunate man. With a touch of pride he used to say that his fairy godmother granted him his three biggest wishes: he had become a successful architect, fathered healthy children, and found Alex, his soulmate. Now he was sick with fear of losing it all.

His whole existence came crashing down, everything he lived for came undone in a matter of days. Jack sighed.

"Life is not so black and white," he heard Alex saying. "There are always more possibilities." He needed to get in touch with her. A text was the safest way.

JACK: *Love you and miss you. Working on fixing the problem. Will get back ASAP <3*

Jack straightened up, determined to get their life back.

Dallas

WiFi Cafe
Twenty minutes later

Vivien sat down and opened Little Fella. Acute anger contorted her face. She despised being dragged all over Dallas for a few minutes of computer work.

On top of everything else, Jack had made her late and she didn't have enough time to get her favorite giant frappe before the download came in.

Her life sucked and it was all Jack's fault. She'd make him burn in hell...he hadn't seen anything yet.

Vivien checked her watch. Almost time. A message lit up on the screen. Ready. She inserted a flash drive and transferred the information exactly as instructed. Another instruction informed her that the job had to be finished in two days. A payment drop wasn't mentioned. *He hasn't paid me in two months!*

Unacceptable! Vivien stomped her feet. Who does he think he is?

She was sick and tired of this work. It was exciting at first, brought sweet cash, and gave her power. She giggled recalling all the people she hacked. Nobody ever found out who exposed their secrets.

Vivien frowned. She outgrew being anonymous. She deserved recognition. What's power good for if people don't fear you?

That's it, maybe she should put some fear in *him*. Vivien giggled. The connection was still open and Vivien seized her opportunity.

"No way," she typed instead of the required confirmation that the transaction was completed.

Her rebellion had an immediate effect: the message box disappeared.

Have it your way! Vivien put Little Fella in her oversized bag and ordered her frappe. She hadn't even had a chance to take her first sip when her phone blinked:

UNKNOWN: *It's me or rotting in jail.*

Vivien deleted the text. There were too many sick people roaming around these days.

She squeezed into her car seat, not sure what to do next. She wanted money. But Jack's bank account was empty, and Marty didn't answer her emails. Her phone blinked again:

UNKNOWN: *2days or jail*

Vivien screamed.

Thick frappe splashed all over her Lexus.

New Delhi

The Taj Garden hotel
August 8

Jack spent the whole night, a day in Dallas, raising funds for Carter & Co. He called his friends, poker buddies, business acquaintances. He asked, begged, pleaded, ready to sign his soul away to anybody who would help him to bridge the abyss Vivien blasted through his life. No one was able to bail him out on such a short notice.

But several guys suggested that Perry could help, either directly or through his impressive network of business partners. To Jack's surprise, Perry seemed to have amassed a sizable fortune in the last years and could easily come up with the money himself.

Jack used to like Perry but didn't understand his choices lately. How could a talented innovator go into politics? To Jack, becoming a politician when you were capable of creating something real reeked of betrayal.

But none of this mattered to Jack anymore. He was beyond personal preferences. Exhausted and discouraged by a night spent on unsuccessful rescue attempts, he was grasping at straws. When the sky began to lighten, he managed to reach Perry, who was in Nepal with Senator Howard.

Perry listened while Jack struggled through the story.

"OK, so you need at least two million dollars," Perry finally interrupted.

"Yes, to cover the most urgent expenses until I can sort it all out."

"And then?" Perry asked, anger creeping through his words.

"Well, I guess I will have to restructure the whole business."

"How long have you known about this fiasco?"

"Almost four days."

"What's Alex's take on this?"

The question surprised Jack. "I have not told her yet."

"You have not told her yet?" The coldness in Perry's voice chilled Jack to the bones.

"I was protecting her, Perry."

"Hm. I will see what I can do. The two million can be arranged. As for the restructuring, I need more information. I must have free access to your financial people. Call them and tell them I am involved."

Jack sat back, relieved, grateful beyond description.

"Thank you, Perry. Oh man. I don't know what to say."

"Now," Perry went on without missing a beat, "I guess you've heard the senator is dedicated to housing and other services for minorities. He has funds to build a hospital for kids here in Nepal and he is looking for an architect willing to design the hospital. Donate the design, I mean. Are you in?"

"Absolutely," Jack replied without hesitation, thrilled to be back in business. "Count me in."

"I knew I could, Jack," Perry said. "Let's see where Richard stands on this. I will get back to you within a few hours. By the way, did you say you are in Delhi now? In a hotel with a solid internet connection?"

"Yes."

"Can you stay there until we get all the paperwork sorted out?"

"Sure. How long will it take?" Jack's heart sagged. He wanted to get back to Alex immediately.

"A day or two. The senator and I will be in Kathmandu in three days. I'll try to schedule a meeting."

"Thanks again, Perry. I owe you big, man."

"I'll help you out, Jack. But keep in mind that I am doing it for Alex, not for you."

Jack swallowed his pride and thanked Perry again.

Agra, India

Evening of the same day

I was chatting, putting on a cheerful face, and swallowing tears. Taj Mahal dominated our view from the tiny rooftop restaurant. I nibbled on my vegetable stew, not hungry. This was the last chance for Jack to catch up with us before we got on a night train to Varanasi.

And a last chance for Jack and me to see the Taj Mahal together. We'd dreamed about it so many times before going on this trip, planned our day in Agra around a sunrise visit to the Taj, and now, at the moment supreme, Jack was missing in action.

I got only one response to the many texts and emails I sent Jack when we traveled from Jaipur to Udaipur, Chittaurgarh, Kota, and Agra. I'd hoped that the good internet connection in Agra would fill my inbox with messages from Jack that hadn't been downloaded during our travels, but all I got was the one text:

JACK: *Love you and miss you. Working on fixing the problem. Will get back ASAP <3*

Nothing concrete. My heart cringed. Jack cut me off. Didn't love me enough to tell me what was going on. It was hell visiting all the amazing places while being kept in the dark, not knowing whether Jack was OK.

Upset, I rested my eyes on the Taj. Magnificent. A monument to love. Lost love... That's where our love was: lost.

My mind went back to the day when we'd decided to go on this trip. Vivien's sexting-gate had taken over the news channels, given it involved Richard, a prominent US senator. Jack and I sat on the edge of the sofa, watching the talking heads competing for airtime with Dr. Sandra Bloementhal, one of the few people profiting from the scandal. Richard came on saying that he never sexted with NumberOne and that his cybersecurity team had detected an attack on his computer system, which was still under investigation.

After a long silence, Vivien issued a statement confirming that the person sexting under the name SenHowdy21 was not Senator Richard Howard. But the damage was already done.

"Ms. Gibson isn't a reliable source, to say the least," one of Richard's opponents said. He used snippets of the Clair It Up show to prove his point. I gasped when in one of the segments Vivien said that she'd had affairs during her marriage for years.

"I am so sorry." I hugged Jack, hurting for him as pain filled his face.

We'd vowed not to let Vivien get between us and destroy our marriage.

And now Vivien probably dealt us a terrible blow.

"Alex, can I use your phone to take a video?" Ian interrupted my brooding.

"Sure." I smiled. Taking videos for my domotics app kept me sane since Jack had left, and I turned it into a new game for Ian and Bailey.

Ian put the phone over the fresh cucumbers we were too afraid to eat and slowly circled over the juicy slices, zooming in and out.

"That's very good, Ian," I complimented him. Jen turned towards me, looking for explanation.

"That's for Alex's app, Mom, the Mood Lifter," Bailey explained. "We are helping Alex to make videos that enhance people's habitat."

Wow! I wondered where Bailey got the big words. Certainly not from me.

"Make people happy," Ian clarified. "Look Mom?" Jen took the phone from him, grinning proudly. A text popped up and I moved closer to see if it was from Jack, but Jen was already shaking her head, eyes filled with anguish. I put my arm around her shoulders. Bailey came over to watch the video.

"This is really good, Ian," Jen said, surprised. "Perfect for the kitchen on a hot day."

"Can we make more, Alex?" Bailey asked.

"Of course."

Jen checked her phone.

"I could surely use a mood lifter," she said. "The uncertainty is killing me."

"Tell me about it."

Jack hadn't gotten in touch with his kids since Jaipur. The one text he sent me was all we had. *You don't treat people you love like this...*

THE WALL

Something in me hardened. Deep down I still loved Jack, I still longed for us to live "happily ever after," but I couldn't be Jack's partner if he didn't treat me like one.

Hoping that going on a magic trip would return us to our pre-marriage paradise was silly. If we want to be together, we have to build something more sustainable.

"If you have built castles in the air, your work need not be lost; that is where they should be. Now put the foundations under them."

"Penny for your thoughts," Jen said.

"I just recalled what Henry David Thoreau said about castles in the air."

"Yeah, Dad is much better at building skyscrapers than relationships." We hugged. Jen had a point.

It was up to Jack how he managed his relationships. I couldn't force him to love me, I couldn't force him to treat me fairly. But I could build with him the foundations under our castle in the air.

If we are both in, we'll rebuild together…

I looked at the Taj, feeling strength returning to me.

Not all was lost yet.

New Delhi

The Taj Garden hotel
August 12

"For Alex, the love of my life."

Jack added the dedication to his last sketch, right above the entrance to the hospital. For several blissful hours he had forgot about the money nuisance and focused on the children's hospital. Guided by the images of the location Perry emailed to him, Jack submerged himself in sketching, designing, redesigning. Ideas poured from his mind as if they had been locked away there for years, impatiently waiting to be released. The architect took over, oblivious to anything else until the first impressions of the hospital were safely in his notebook.

Jack reviewed the sketches and carefully took a picture of each one of them. Satisfied with the results, he almost sent them to Perry but then decided against it. It'd be much better to go through the initial design in person and make changes on the spot if needed.

The hospital is my best work ever, Jack thought. The building was certainly not his biggest or highest, yet definitely the most inventive one.

A magic place where children can heal. He fantasized about seeing happy families leaving the hospital with healthy children. He fantasized about receiving awards for this work.

He'll ask Alex to do the interior design. Jack knew she'd love it. It was the perfect place for her Inside-Outside concept. They could spend more time in Kathmandu together while working on the hospital and make up for the days they lost because of Vivien.

The phone vibrating in his pocket interrupted Jack's musing. He reached for it quickly, hoping to hear from Alex. She and the kids should be in Pokhara, Nepal, by now. The text message was Perry's confirmation of the meeting with Richard in Kathmandu. Disappointed, Jack tried to call Alex again, to no avail.

And then a thought struck him: *if I can communicate with Perry, who is in Nepal just as Alex is, why can't I reach her?*

Fear grabbed Jack by his throat. What if Perry told Alex everything? What if Alex couldn't take Vivien anymore and left him? *Alex isn't like that*, Jack reassured himself. But the fear refused to be chased away.

Reality hit him in the face. Alex would eventually find out what happened. Knowing her, not telling her about Vivien's theft would do more damage than the financial disaster itself. Would she ever forgive him?

Jack couldn't stand the tension for another second. He planned on telling Alex everything *after* it was resolved, but he needed to connect with her immediately. He called her again.

"Jack?" Alex's voice came through as clear as if she were sitting next to him.

"I've missed you so much. I can't tell you how much I love you."

"Love you too, darling. Where are you?"

Jack's heart smiled and cried at the same time. They've got a chance. He wanted to tell her everything but didn't have the heart to tell the story over the phone. He needed to hold Alex's hand, see her reassuring look, hear her loving voice when he was explaining it all.

Jack didn't mention the hospital either, because the connection was getting shaky and he wanted to save the good news for tomorrow to sweeten the deal. But he told her he had a great surprise for her.

"Tell me," Alex asked.

"Tomorrow, when I am with you. But I'll have to kiss you all over first."

She laughed, and Jack wanted to hear her laughter forever. He put his phone down and wiped tears from his eyes, relieved beyond words.

The Taj Garden Hotel

Jack's suite
August 13

Afraid to oversleep, Jack checked the time every time he turned. It was 3:36 a.m. the last time he looked. He went to bed happy, but sleep escaped him. He was too excited about his meeting with Senator Howard and too worried that something would go wrong at the last minute.

He had pangs of guilt about not telling Alex the whole truth right away. He would give anything to rewind the last week, go back to Jaipur and share the first disturbing message from Stan with Alex immediately. It wouldn't have made Vivien less vicious, but at least they would have dealt with her together. Vivien's maliciousness stupefied Jack. *Why Viv? Why?* he asked over and over.

Unable to handle these questions, Jack's mind shut off and dragged him into a few minutes of restless sleep. Under the cover of darkness, the little girl crept in and took control of Jack's heartstrings.

What if Vivien was right? Jack sat up, startled. Yes, what if the financial settlement wasn't even close to what she deserved? Both his and her lawyer assured him that he was generous. But Jack imagined Vivien struggling, all alone, being driven to desperate measures. Not having a choice but to take what was rightly hers.

Jack shivered. He'd not be able to relax until an independent lawyer looked into the matter. And he'd not be able to sleep tonight either. He turned the light on and took his notebook from his bag, hoping that working on the hospital would lift his spirits. But his inspiration was gone. He closed his eyes, wishing that he'd wake up in Nepal, with Alex by his side.

The phone buzzed. Jack reached for it and read the message.

Change of venue. Had to fly to Lukla urgently. Will meet you there at 12:15 p.m. Richard

Jack swallowed hard. *How am I going to get to Lukla on such a short notice?* His life depended on the meeting and he wasn't going to miss it.

Not wasting a second, Jack called the airline, hands shaking, his heart trying to break through his rib cage. *Please, pick up. PLEASE.*

"Good morning. How can I help you?"

Thank God. Jack explained his situation. He heard the pleading urgency of a desperate man in his voice but didn't care.

"I absolutely must be in Lukla by 12 p.m." My life depends on it, he wanted to add, but stopped himself.

"Let's see what can be done, Mr. Carter."

Jack was hardly breathing, besieged by a debilitating tension. Please, please, please, he pleaded.

"OK, your regular flight will not get you there by twelve, but if you can catch a flight two hours earlier, you will be in Lukla at 11:30."

"OK. Can you get me on these flights?"

"Yes. There will be a surcharge for the late change."

"No problem."

The tension seized Jack once more as he waited for the confirmation that his flights were booked. He bit his nails, eyes glued to his watch. He didn't have a minute to spare to make it to the airport on time.

"Thank you for waiting, sir. You are booked on both flights. The charge will appear on your credit card. How would you like to get your ticket?"

Jack gave a sigh of relief. Luck was on his side again.

"Via email, please. And THANK you. You've saved my life!"

Jack quickly brushed his teeth, threw his toiletries into his bag, and rushed to the airport. As soon as he sat down in the taxi, he fired a confirmation text to Richard and then leaned forward, willing the car to go faster. He repeatedly dried his sweating palms on his pants, praying that the taxi would not get stuck in the traffic or get a flat tire.

Doom scenarios involving overbooked flights and malfunctioning planes bombarded Jack throughout checking-in and boarding. He tried to distract himself by searching legal sites and studying Texas divorce laws but couldn't relax until his flight to Kathmandu took off.

He made it.

Jack sat back for a few minutes and closed his eyes until his heart stopped pounding in his chest. Several new ideas for the hospital design started to form in front of his eyes, and he reached into his bag for his notebook to sketch them.

The notebook was gone.

Aboard flight DI101

August 13

Jack rummaged through his whole bag several times, but the notebook wasn't there. Then he remembered taking it out at night, when he tried to chase away the images of Vivien. He must have left the notebook on the nightstand.

Jack put his head down, upset. The notebook was his first present from Alex. One of a kind, leather-bound, handmade to order... He tried to catch up on some sleep, but his mind kept wandering back to Vivien.

Contrary to what the little girl claimed, studying the legal sites convinced Jack that the lawyers were right: his divorce settlement with Vivien was more than fair. "Erring on the side of generosity," as his lawyer said.

Why had she done this to me?

"Because you let her, Jack," Alex had said to him after the pool incident. "You let her get away with hurting you and others. You enabled her."

Jack closed his eyes and rubbed his temples in a futile attempt to squash his pounding headache. *This isn't just between Vivien and me,* Jack realized for the first time in his life, thinking about the people who'd pay for Vivien's theft. Alex, his guys at Carter & Co, his clients, Jen and Victor.

These people need me to do the right thing. Vivien just used me.

Jack straightened up, as if invisible shackles sprang open and freed him.

Why didn't I see this before? Jack thought. It was so obvious. So simple. A wave of fresh energy surged through him. He might have been slow to take care of business, but it wasn't too late to set things straight.

He couldn't wait to get back to work and recover the losses. He wanted to double the retirement fund that Stan had to deplete to keep Carter & Co afloat. And he wanted to make this all up to Alex and the kids.

Deep longing grasped Jack's heart. He wanted to hold Alex close to him.

But first things first.

Jack composed an email to Stan and authorized him to hire the forensic accountants. The next email went to his lawyers, and the last one was for the manager of the Taj Garden hotel. Jack didn't expect much of this, but he asked the hotel to mail his notebook back and charge the shipping costs to his credit card.

The emails ready to be fired off as soon as his phone connected, Jack reviewed the facts Stan discovered so far. Marty must have played a role in the fraud. Either by being careless or by knowingly helping Vivien. But Marty couldn't have helped Vivien with the last and most damaging transaction because Stan changed the authorization system. His mind sharper than in a long time, Jack scrutinized his text messages.

The plane was preparing for landing. Jack popped his ears, ready for the next leg of his journey. He knew exactly what needed to be done.

A few negotiations, a few signatures, and he would be free to live the life he longed for.

Pokhara, Nepal

The Happy Tea House
August 13

The imposing Annapurna Range was hiding behind a thick wall of clouds. Suddenly the peak of Machapuchare cut through like a shark fin knifing through water. And disappeared in the blink of an eye. *Did I see the peak or was it just another cloud?* I wondered, my eyes fixed on the cloud formation.

When I no longer expected it, the peak stabbed through again, its sharp edge glistening in the sun.

I checked my phone for the umpteenth time. Nothing. Jack's flight landed in Kathmandu forty minutes ago. I swallowed hard. We always texted each other as soon as our plane touched down.

On edge, I took a deep breath and looked around. Heavy clouds rolled over the horizon, but it was a sunny, mild day down here in Pokhara. Boys played soccer near the lake. Birds were chirping. Incense wafted through the air. Nepali prayer flags fluttered on a string tied between "my" teahouse and a wobbly dock, a home to a fleet of rowboats painted in pastel pinks, blues, and greens.

I closed my eyes and pretended that Jack was sitting next to me, sketching in his leather-bound notebook. Our forearms touched and triggered a wave of delight. We rented one of the little boats, caught up with the kids on the other side of the lake and surprised them with tea and cookies.

I opened my eyes. No Jack.

Part of me stubbornly held onto the possibility of an easy explanation. The other part trembled. A huge stone annexed the pit of my stomach, telling me that an impending disaster threatened my world. I didn't know what it was, it was hiding from me, but I glimpsed its sharp edge.

Pictures of us in Jaipur roamed around my mind like restless ghosts. I bit my lip. If only I had insisted on going to Delhi with him…

THE WALL

I peeked at my phone again. Why did Jack disappear from the radar again? Jack's secretiveness and the uncertainty of it all were killing me.

I opened my notebook and stepped into the relative safety of my Mood Lifter app. The sunset videos I'd taken last night were perfect. The dynamic of the fast-moving clouds rocked, and the mix of the cold whites and grays with the warm yellows and oranges was exactly what I was looking for.

Sunset over Lake Phewa was the coolest, most un-kitschy sunset I ever saw. The kids and I had been admiring it from the Lakeside BBQ last night when my phone had startled me.

Jack.

He sounded exhausted and kept it short, afraid that the connection would be cut off. The trouble wasn't over yet, he said, but he found a way out and booked a flight to Pokhara, with a stopover in Kathmandu.

"Jack, what is this all about?" I asked, refusing to be kept in the dark any longer.

"Difficult stuff, love, I will tell you everything when I am with you in Pokhara. Oh Alex, I can't wait to hold you."

"Darling…"

"And I have a great surprise for you." The old Jack was back at last.

"Tell me."

"Tomorrow, when I am with you. But I'll have to kiss you all over first."

We had all felt relieved after the call. Except Victor. The strained look on his face spoke volumes, but his lips remained sealed. I should've touched base with him. But I had been catching the sunset on videos, overjoyed that Jack was coming back.

I checked my phone again. Nothing.

Dammit, Jack! You have no right to keep me in the dark like this!

I shoved the lifeless phone into my bag and got up. I couldn't just sit in the garden sipping tea and doing nothing. I had to find Victor. Victor knew something I didn't want to know.

I was half running, half walking along Baidam Road. The tempting shops and their mysterious objects lost their pull. The dark rock in the pit of my stomach was taking on the dimensions of the Annapurna.

A small crowd blocked the way in front of the Trekkers. They all stared at something inside the bar, strangely quiet. I got closer and saw what drew their attention. It was CNN Breaking News.

Helicopters circled in front of a massive mountain wall. Looking for debris from a commercial airliner that crashed into that wall.

Pokhara

Trekkers Bar
August 13

The sound of the helicopters was so loud, I could barely hear the report. Not much was known yet. Pieces of information were dripping in, most of them unconfirmed. The local correspondent came into full view and stopped dramatically while pushing in her earpiece.

"Rachel, the flight number has been confirmed. It's SW122 from Kathmandu to Lukla," she reported.

It wasn't Jack's flight. A sigh of relief escaped my lips.

"Lukla is the most dangerous airport in the world," the correspondent told Rachel and the viewers.

"That was Ditya in Kathmandu," Rachel explained. "Stay tuned, we will come back with more news after the commercial break."

I leaned on the bar. My hands were shaking as I checked my phone. Nothing. But I was no longer angry with Jack. I just wanted to hug him and feel him close to me.

I turned around to walk out, chastising myself for being so paranoid. An old picture of Jack jumped at me from another giant TV screen.

"According to latest reports, Jack Carter, one of the world's most renowned architects, was on the fatal flight to Lukla this morning." Flashes of Jack's towers appeared on the screen. I tried to swallow, but my mouth was dry as a desert.

"Carter was in Nepal to design a children's hospital. He was fifty-three years old and is survived by his wife Vivien, their two children and two grandchildren." Jack's photo was replaced by a picture of Vivien, Jack, and the twins on the beach in Galveston. It was the photo Vivien used as her cover picture on Facebook.

"Carter's untimely death comes in a difficult time for his firm, which is said to face bankruptcy."

Rachel moved on to the typhoon season being exceptionally active this year. I stood in the middle of the bar, paralyzed.

Now I will never know what Jack's surprise for me was. Strange what your mind comes up with when a disaster hits. *They got the wife wrong. Maybe they got the flight wrong too.* I was grasping for hope. *Bankruptcy?* That would explain Delhi. It must be Marty's fault! That's why he had disappeared like a thief in the night. *I'll take the bankruptcy if Jack is alive.* I was negotiating with powers that don't negotiate.

Jack wasn't flying to Lukla. That was the most reasonable conclusion my mind produced.

"This cannot be true," I heard Jen saying behind me.

"Jen, I think he was on the flight." Victor's voice cut through me like a dagger. "He had a meeting in Lukla."

A deep sob escaped my mouth. I bit my lip but couldn't stop the tears from flowing. In slow motion, I saw my world hit the ground and shatter into thousands of little pieces like a delicate vase that can never be repaired.

I turned around. Jen and I hugged. She broke into heart-wrenching sobs. I held her close to me and mumbled soothing nonsense to her ear until the sobs slowed down. Victor just stood there, his eyes hijacked by guilt and fear. Jack's face filled the screen again and the news item was repeated.

Hearing the message second time froze my tears. My mind was chillingly clear. The worst thing that could happen had happened. And there was more to it.

"Victor, how did you know that Jack was flying to Lukla?"

"Mom told me."

"When?"

"This morning."

"I see." So Vivien *was* involved. And I was cut off from the family communication. Enormous pain numbed me to the last cell.

"What did she tell you?"

"That Dad is flying to Lukla for a meeting and not to believe anything he says about her and Carter & Co."

"What was the meeting about?"

"Carter & Co." Victor's voice was barely audible.

"And what did Jack tell you about Carter & Co?" I asked, but Victor couldn't take it.

"I am so sorry." He hid his face in his hands.

"I didn't know this." Jen looked at me, crushed.

"Neither did I." We hugged again.

"I have to call CNN. They were terribly misinformed. They have to pull the report immediately." Jen got on her phone. Putting on her journalist hat allowed her to escape the pain, even if just for a few moments.

"I'll try to get the airline. But where are the kids and Peter?" I asked.

"By the lake. Jen and I went to look for you when we first heard of the crash. But we didn't know yet then…" Victor sobbed.

The news item replayed again.

"Let's get out of here," I ordered.

I wished I was on the flight with Jack.

Pokhara

August 14

Two dark sedans pulled in front of our hotel. Peter directed Victor and me to the first one, while Jen and the kids slid into the second one. None of us talked. We were exhausted after spending most of the evening and night on the phone with the US Embassy, the airlines, Perry, and Jen's CNN colleagues.

The chaos surrounding the crash had given us hope that the initial reporting had been a mistake. But as the time went on, the truth emerged and hit us hard: Jack was on the passenger list of flight SW122.

Nobody could explain why.

We decided to go to Kathmandu to be as close to the sources of information as we could. Peter was like a quiet, solid rock watching over all of us, making sure that no one derailed. He'd tried to get us on a flight to Kathmandu, but all flights were fully booked. Then he'd tried to hire a van, but all vans with a driver were taken. The two cars were the only option. Not that we cared much. Grief made the lack of choices irrelevant.

Victor and I rode in silence, the tension between us palpable. I sensed that Victor wanted to tell me something but let him take his time. He fidgeted and sighed, looked outside, and then shifted towards me.

"I am sorry, Alex," he said, looking down as if he hoped to drill a hole in the car's floor and disappear through it.

"So am I." Victor looked so much like Jack. Only his sharp nose reminded me that it's not a young Jack sitting next to me.

"Yeah. I am sorry about Dad, of course. But that's not what I meant." Victor looked at me briefly, agony contorting his face.

I nodded to encourage him to go on.

"I still can't believe Mom did that." Eyes fixated on the floor mat, Victor recapped how he left a good job in Houston and moved back to Dallas to be with his mom because she felt terribly lonely and left behind. How he ran all her errands and accompanied her to her parties, dinners, and events.

How she made him feel like the best person in the world, calling him her golden boy, the one and only person who didn't abandon her. How he trusted her and thought she meant it.

How he never questioned her stories about Jack and me and believed that Jack neglected and abused her.

"I used to hate you, Alex," Victor said. "Well, not you, really, but I hated how you turned our family upside down. Mom and I were always the good guys, while Dad and Jen were in the dog house. You've changed that."

I looked at Victor, stunned. This wasn't what I expected. I braced myself for being accused of ruining Vivien's life, not for getting Jack and Jen out of the dog house.

"Dad's happy and look at Jen. But I still thought that if Dad had stayed with Mom and kept her happy, she wouldn't have done all the stupid things."

Victor lifted his head and looked at me apologetically. "I had no idea what Mom is capable of. I did not want to know, I guess."

He gave a short, bitter laugh and told me how devastated he was when without warning he went from a golden boy to an undesirable intruder. How Vivien accused Victor of being just like his dad and kicked him out of the house, while still demanding that he do her errands and help her financially.

"I never realized that Mom could be so harsh," Victor said bitterly. "Of course, I saw her being nasty to Dad. I thought that was normal. I loved Dad, he always played with us, Mom never. But Mom made me feel special. But when she changed like that I finally understood what Dad had gone through. And Jen. Mom was nasty to Jen all the time, but I always thought it was Jen's fault."

I kept nodding, too upset to say anything. I could understand why Vivien hated me or Jack but inflicting so much misery on her own children was incomprehensible.

We drove in silence for a while. Victor looked out of the window and put his hand in front of his mouth. I worried he'd get sick, but he just coughed and then resumed his story.

"I knew Mom was taking money from the firm, but I had no idea how much it was. I was aghast when Perry told me she bankrupted Carter & Co."

A gasp escaped my mouth. Now I had to look to the floor to steady myself.

The bankruptcy had loomed in the back of my mind, sending a tremor of dread through me every time it forced its way to the foreground. Without having any other information, I attributed it to Marty. Not for a second did I suspect Vivien. Which was strange, as Vivien was the first person to jump to my mind every time something bad happened.

Beyond shocked, yet inexplicably liberated, I watched the river valley pass by, my senses heightened. Everything seemed bright and vibrant. The greens of the valley seemed so much livelier than a minute ago. As if an invisible hand gave them a refreshing wash. Every detail of Victor's tortured face made a lasting imprint in my brain. The sweat drops on his forehead. The tears, the tiny mole under his right eye, his mother's sharp nose.

Finally I understood why Jack didn't want me in Delhi with him. How do you explain to your new wife that your ex-wife bankrupted you? When you are on a trip that was supposed to celebrate your blended family.

Still, I wished Jack had told me.

I straightened up. I had to find out what else Victor knew.

The Prithvi highway between Pokhara and Kathmandu

August 14

"Victor, how do you know that your mom was taking money from the firm?" I asked, surprised by the clarity and strength of my voice.

"She bragged about it."

"What did she say?"

"That men are stupid. That Dad trusts Marty and Marty trusts Dad and neither of them knows what's going on."

"That doesn't mean that she was taking money."

"Oh, she was. She submitted some invoices and Marty put them through the system without checking with Dad. She said that Dad really screwed her when they got divorced and that she was only taking what's rightfully hers."

"Did you tell Jack about this?"

Victor shook his head.

We both contemplated the heaviness of Victor's admission. Maybe Jack would have paid more attention to Marty's dealings if I weren't the only person pointing out irregularities.

"I wanted to tell him, but..." Victor stopped himself.

"It was Marty's responsibility to tell him, Victor," I said.

I was furious with Marty. At the same time, I was berating myself for not fighting harder for the financial audit. If Vivien's fraud had been discovered earlier, maybe Jack wouldn't have ended up on the fatal flight. And maybe he wouldn't have been on that flight had I gone to Delhi with him... Guilt was choking me, but I had to get to the bitter end of this.

"Victor, Marty told me you were working on some kind of accounting program," I asked, aware that I was pushing Victor.

"Accounting program?"

"Yes. Budgeting system. Marty said it saved him lots of time."

"Oh that. Mom gave me the app to help out. She got it from a friend."

"And you installed it on Carter & Co's system?"

"Yeah."

"Vivien doesn't shy away from shady deals." I heard Liz's raspy voice. Right on.

If my thinking was correct, there wouldn't be any traces of Vivien's "friendly help" on the system. I looked at Victor, but he either didn't grasp the significance of his little download or gave an Oscar winning performance. I pushed further.

"Vic, did you download more apps to the system?"

"No. Wait, yes. It was just a game. Mom gave it to me for my birthday."

Just a game. I shivered thinking what else had entered the system with these gifts. And then I recalled how difficult it was to install my color scheme program on Carter & Co's computers. The tech guys had to perform miracles to let it pass through the firewall.

Fear tightened my throat. If Vivien's apps entered the system without any hiccups, I was dealing with a professional. A dangerous professional.

"So, you downloaded the programs from a site?"

"No, Mom gave them to me on flash drives."

"I see." I nodded and changed the subject.

"By the way, how did Perry find out about the bankruptcy?"

"Dad told him, I guess. Dad asked me about Perry because Perry works for Senator Howard. I didn't know what it was all about, but Perry called me and asked me questions about Mom and Carter & Co. I was sort of defending Mom, and Perry got short with me and told me what Mom did. I thought it was a misunderstanding or something. But Perry said he was arranging a meeting for the senator and Dad in Kathmandu to fix it."

"So if the meeting was in Kathmandu, why did Jack fly to Lukla?"

"I don't know. Mom told me Perry changed the location."

I closed my eyes. That Vivien knew all this while I was kept in the dark was ripping me apart.

The driver went around several sharp turns without slowing down one bit. The car hit a hole in the pavement and swerved dangerously close to the unprotected edge of the road. Unperturbed, the driver sped up to pass a slow-going truck.

I looked out of the window, all the way down to the deep ravine, and vividly imagined the car rolling off the road and exploding. I closed my eyes and wished it would happen. Because being burned alive in a car crash seemed less of a hell than the mental inferno I was going through since Jack's face jumped at me from the giant TV in Trekkers.

Private flight from Kathmandu to Dallas

August 19

*T*he *restaurant shakes. The terrace tilts to one side and I barely catch my water glass. Where is Jack? He should have been here half an hour ago.*

I reach for my bag, but it's not there. It must have slid away. I look under the table, but the bag is gone. That can't be possible. The shoulder strap was firmly secured to the chair. I stand up and look around the terrace. The restaurant shakes again. I run outside, still looking for my bag. I zig zag between piles of debris but make it safely to the dry river bed in front of the restaurant.

Someone calls my name. I turn around. A giant wave gushes down, jumping the river banks and taking down everything in its way. Its dark body hisses, growls, and rises from the river bed like a mountain.

I want to run, but my legs don't move.

"Alex, Alex." Liz softly rubbed my shoulder. Perry squatted in from of me. I double-blinked. Had I screamed?

"I am sorry. I had a nightmare."

"Oh sweetie." Liz squeezed my shoulder. Perry put his hand over mine. Pity dripped from their eyes. I wanted to push them away and scream. Instead, I gently untangled myself from their hold and stood up. I needed to be alone.

"I am going to get water. Do you want some?" I asked. They silently shook their heads and exchanged a hopeless look.

They were desperately trying to comfort me. I would have been doing exactly the same had I been in their place. But I wasn't. I was a *victim*. Singled out. Different. No matter how much Liz and Perry touched me, I felt like there was a glass divider between us. I desperately wanted to shatter it and be one of them again.

Crushed, I headed towards the galley. The images of a giant wave taking down everything in its way lingered in front of my eyes. My life was still intact when I had this nightmare for the first time. It was not a perfect life, but I would take it back anytime. It seemed like ages ago when I naively thought that I figured out the evil tango, that Jack and I could fix our troubles with Vivien and live happily ever after.

Jack is gone. It was so final, yet so surreal.

In spite of the overwhelming evidence, when we'd arrived in Kathmandu, part of me had still hoped that Jack would be at the Embassy, everything would be explained, and we would get a chance to put our life together, for better or for worse. Jack wasn't there. But the next day brought us several hours of hope when the airline doubted that Jack boarded the flight.

That hope was gone now. The crash ripped Jack and me apart with uncompromising finality. Tears streamed down my cheeks. I dove into the lavatory. A ghost eyed me from the mirror.

I looked at my watch and leaned against the door to steady myself. We were scheduled to land in Dallas at 4:25 p.m. local time. Which meant I had about thirteen hours to put myself together.

I splashed water on my face. Where to start?

Liz waited for me with a bottle of sparkling water.

"Are you OK?"

I nodded but wondered whether I'd ever smile again.

Jack's passing officially put me in charge of Carter & Co, and I had to figure out what to do. Will I have to file for bankruptcy? What will I say to the team? What legal steps can I take? I tried to come up with a plan, but my mind kept going back to the nauseating drive from Pokhara to Kathmandu.

The narrow road, reckless drivers, trucks barely holding together, deep ravines, my images of the car tumbling down and exploding. And Victor's monotonous voice telling his shocking story.

"I still can't believe Mom did that... I knew Mom was taking money from the firm... I was aghast when Perry told me she bankrupted Carter & Co... Mom told me Perry changed the location."

"Perry, why did you move the meeting to Lukla?" I had asked as soon as we met in Kathmandu.

"I did not." Perry had looked at me quizzically. "We were driving to meet Jack in Kathmandu when we learned about the crash. We waited for him more than an hour, and then CNN reported that Jack was on the flight."

Someone was lying.

Vivien? Victor? Perry?

And someone didn't want Jack to meet Richard Howard.

Why?

Whatever the reason, they succeeded. A wave of grief threatened to split my heart wide open. The anger at Jack that traveled with me from Jaipur to Pokhara was gone, replaced by sorrow that we'll never hug each other again, never kiss, never design anything together, never again enjoy a dinner on DD's patio...

I'll forever regret not being there for Jack when he found out what Vivien had done to him. Whatever happened between them, destroying Carter & Co was not what Jack deserved. And neither was tricking Jack into booking a flight destined to take his life.

I remembered Perry's disturbing dilemma: "Would you give all your money to clear your lover's reputation even if he deeply hurt you?"

YES! I hadn't been sure I'd fight for Jack when Perry posed the dilemma, but I was now. *I'll avenge you Jack, whatever it takes.*

And the best way to do it was to rescue Carter & Co and preserve Jack's legacy. Steely calmness cleared my mind. The first step was to take control over Carter & Co's finances.

"Mom gave me the app. She got it from a friend." Victor's voice cut in again.

Who was the friend? *A hacker on the top of the game.* I gasped. Could it be? Did my quest to avenge Jack merge with the Wall?

"Are you OK?" Perry gave me a worried look.

"I think I know who is behind Jack's killing," I almost said but stopped myself just in time. "Don't talk about TW with anyone," Collin had warned me. For a good reason. Many more people were at risk, and I was determined to do my darndest to protect them from what Jack and I went through.

The Wall became my number one priority. Several scenarios unrolled in front of my eyes.

This time I felt no fear.

Part 4

"What doesn't kill you makes you stronger."

Friedrich Nietzsche

Dallas

The Art Tower, Carter & Co offices
August 20, morning

"$2.7 million in nine months." Stan frowned and handed me a file with documents showing how much Vivien had stolen from Carter & Co.

I had underestimated Vivien. I thought she was vicious but lazy. I assumed that she somehow used Marty or Victor to transfer money from Carter & Co to her own account. I expected a series of simple, traceable transactions that we could dispute and get our money back.

Stan disabused me of my naiveté.

Vivien outsmarted us all. Most of the money went to offshore accounts we couldn't touch. I opened the file Stan gave me and studied the docs in chronological order.

A couple of $5K cash advances around the time Jack filed for his divorce.

A $7,000 invoice for unspecified marketing services a few weeks after Jack and I got married, to be paid weekly. I swallowed hard. Jack's signature was in full sight.

A $30,000 credit card payment to Advantage Marketing in Mitchell, SD.

"Have we ever done anything with Advantage Marketing?" I asked Stan.

"No. Not really."

"What do you mean?"

"We have no contract with them," Stan explained. "I tried to dispute the charge, but Advantage Marketing came back and said that the payment was for their high-end training. It's a two-hour session given on a private plane flight."

"A private plane?" I looked up from the papers.

"Yes. Advantage Marketing produced records showing that the trainees were Vivien Gibson and her assistant Marty Watson."

Vivien Gibson and her assistant Marty Watson. The chutzpah. I took a deep breath and returned to the file. The dollar amounts were escalating.

The next invoice was for $150,000 submitted by VG Marketing to compensate them for "marketing services: Inside-Outside project," payable to VG's foreign account. I looked at the date: three days after the pool incident. I guessed this was the price of having Vivien arrested for trespassing my property. My stomach flip-flopped. Did Jack authorize this? His signature on the invoice was unmissable.

"Have you found a contract regarding this work?" I was reaching for straws.

"No. And we don't have the original version either." Stan explained that accounting was required to keep two versions of each invoice: a paper version with the original signatures and a digital copy thereof.

"It's clearly a breach on Marty's end," Stan concluded.

But we were not done yet. I took out the last document.

$2.4 million transfer to another foreign account. Unauthorized. This is what bankrupted us. The transfer was initiated when we flew to Delhi. Apparently, the sigh of relief we'd all let out when our plane took off from DFW had been premature. We'd been so happy then, totally unaware of the bomb ticking at the heart of our lives.

"Let's start with the transactions that have some paper trail, OK?" I looked at Stan. "Which ones have the double invoices?"

"Only the first 5K. Jamie and I have turned the office upside down but haven't found the other originals."

"I see." An idea started forming in my head.

"She submitted some invoices and Marty put them through the system without checking with Dad," Victor said.

I took the first 5K invoice and compared it with the second one. They looked identical. I lined up the invoices and held them against the window.

Stan gasped.

I added the 7K and 150K invoices. The signatures were exactly the same and in exactly the same places on all four documents. Maybe Vivien *was* lazy after all. Such carelessness. No one can produce perfectly matching signatures time after time.

"It looks like the forensic accountants have their hands full." I put the papers down.

"That's some sloppy photoshopping." Stan rubbed his chin.

"But lucrative."

"Wait a moment," Stan searched through his files. "I saw something."

"Here we go." Stan lifted up a document and lined it up with the 5K invoice. "Bingo."

"This looks like the source of it all. It's an old note allowing Vivien to get up to a 5K advance from the firm to cover the children's expenses."

"How old?" I asked.

"Seventeen years. Jack's signature matches perfectly."

"Excellent job, Stan. Thank you." I took a deep breath. "This means a lot to me."

It meant that Jack probably didn't approve any of Vivien's invoices. Vivien copied his old signature to get past Marty and the system.

"I am sorry, Alex," Stan said gently. "This must be very disturbing."

"Yes. But we are getting to the bottom of it. Now, just to make sure we've covered everything. Let's assume for a moment that Vivien didn't do it. Who else could have initiated these payments?"

"Jamie and Marty had the authorization. Jamie isn't involved. I trust her." Stan looked at me pleadingly.

"And Jack?" This question burned in me like an eternal torch. Because if Jack somehow helped Vivien to collect the money, this was not only a fraud but a Betrayal with capital B.

"No way." Stan chuckled. "He delegated it all. There wasn't even a sign-on created for him. Alex, if it looks like a duck, quacks like a duck, it's a duck." Stan said. "This is a fraud and Jack's ex is in a world of pain with what we have here."

"I don't understand how she could think that she'd get away with this."

"She probably counted on Jack never charging her."

"That's probably right," I said. You could count on Vivien to make up some heartbreaking story to get away with anything.

"Now, what can we do about the 2.4 million?" That was the most important issue.

"I tried to take steps as soon as I found out about it, but it was too late." Stan looked at me apologetically.

"The transfer is entirely different," I said hopefully. "It looks like we were hacked."

Stan shook his head.

"Jack's ex-wife admitted to him that she has done it. All of it. Including the 2.4 million."

"She admitted it?"

"Yes. Jack phoned me from Delhi and told me that she took the 2.4 million to pay off a bad investment. She claimed the money was rightfully hers."

Sure. Just like my house.

"Did Jack tell you what he was going to do about it?"

"He wanted to sue her and Marty. Jack said he never authorized her invoices."

My heart fluttered. Finally, Jack was willing to stand up to her. *I'll fight for you, Jack!* I promised.

"Well, that's what we should do then."

"We can try, but it will be difficult." Stan took a deep breath. "I am sorry," he went on. "I have to be honest with you. I am not an expert, but any legal action will be difficult if not impossible without having Jack's death certificate."

"Which will not be available for months." In an instant I glimpsed the enormity of the trouble I was in legally and financially. Without the death certificate I not only couldn't start the legal proceedings to get our money back, I also couldn't get a loan to bridge the gap.

How am I going to keep Carter & Co afloat? How am I going to pay salaries?

An instant headache kicked my forehead. Why? Why did she destroy Jack's firm? Steely calmness lifted me up. *I'll find a way even if I have to go to hell and back!*

"What doesn't kill you makes you stronger," I reminded myself.

The Art Tower

Carter & Co conference room
August 20, afternoon

"Now you know everything I do," I said and looked around. Jamie's teary eyes didn't leave me for a second. Hannah was biting her nails. Charlie put on his poker face. I informed the team about Carter & Co's financial situation as realistically as I could, without sparing one gory detail. I wanted them to be fully aware of what they were getting into should they decide to participate in the rescue mission.

I had never been in more trouble in my life. A captain of a sinking ship trying to keep the ship afloat and her crew alive with her hands tied behind her back.

"So, now you know everything I do," I repeated. "If you do not wish to work for Carter & Co under these circumstances, you may resign immediately, and I'll assist you with finding a new job."

No one moved. The room became deadly quiet.

"I am staying," Jamie stood up.

"Me too," Charlie joined her. "Thanks for giving us a chance."

"And giving Carter & Co a chance," Hannah added.

She was right, I could have abandoned the ship. But it wasn't an option for me. I was hell-bent on bringing Carter & Co back to life. Yet, I couldn't do it alone. I needed the team.

Hannah came over and hugged me. "So sorry about Jack." Jamie was right behind her and the rest of the team followed. Their support both moved me and overwhelmed me. *Can I repay their trust in me?* I was determined to fight for their jobs and their pension fund as much as for Jack's legacy. I returned the hugs, thanked everyone, and slowly extracted myself from the meeting room.

3:28 p.m.

Time to go. I rushed to my office and grabbed my bag, checking that the two flash drives I had confiscated from Victor's office were in it. Securing the drives had been my first priority after landing in Dallas.

Perry had offered to drive me home, but I asked him to drop me off at Carter & Co. No one else was in and I went straight to Victor's office. I didn't expect to find the drives, but they had been in the second drawer I opened.

I left my office, entered the Sky Gondola, and descended to the parking garage. I took in the oily, rubbery smell and walked over to the Giulia. I opened the passenger door of the dark van parked to the left and stepped inside.

Collin was behind the wheel. We drove out of the garage and got on 35 North. In silence, as always.

The rest of the procedure was different.

Collin hugged me as soon as we reached his office.

"I am so sorry," he said simply.

"Thank you."

"Do you want to go on?" Collin went directly to the point.

"Absolutely," I said firmly.

"Are you sure? I'd let you out of the contract if you want to," Collin offered.

I leaned forward and looked directly into his deep, gray eyes. "Collin, finishing this project is my highest priority."

Collin cocked his head almost imperceptibly, his gaze never leaving me.

"And Carter & Co?"

I took a deep breath.

"There is a chance to save it. It will be an uphill battle, but we are going for it. I just had a heart-to-heart with my team. They are all staying."

"You are one tough cookie."

I chuckled. It was my first laugh since the crash.

"A tough cookie in a lot of trouble," I replied.

"Tell me," he commanded. "Tell me everything."

"I will. But before we start, can you recommend someone who can check these out?" I took out the flash drives.

Collin's eyebrows knitted. "What are we expecting?"

"Difficult to say. It could be absolutely nothing. And it could be a proof that someone hacked Carter & Co's computer system. The financial part, to be more specific."

"Let me take a quick look."

Collin inserted the first drive into the USB port on his computer, holding it in the sandwich bag I packed the drives in. He punched a few keys.

And whistled.

He studied the screen and punched a few more keys.

"Please tell me how you found this."

"Everything?" I asked.

"The whole story from the beginning to the end. Don't leave a word out."

"How much time do you have?"

"As much as it takes."

So I told him. The Jaipur event. Jack's call. Victor's story, Stan's story.

"Did anyone get in touch with Marty?"

"No one's been able to find him."

"Did you ask Vivien?"

"No."

"She probably knows."

"Yes, but would she tell me?"

Collin snorted.

"Does anyone know that you have the flash drives?"

"No. Not to my knowledge."

"Perfect. Keep it that way."

"You must have all computers at Carter & Co inspected and secured," Collin ordered. "Trey is the best guy for it."

I agreed. Collin was like an island of sanity in the sea of madness.

"OK. Let me call someone to work on the flash drives. You've hit the jackpot with these two babies."

We switched to the Wall. The plans were readjusted while I was gone, but we were ready to go full speed ahead.

"And last but not least." Collin took out a new phone and gave it to me. "Have this beauty with you at all times. Use it only to reach me. Don't use it for anything else. OK?"

"Yes. Thanks." I inspected the phone. It looked exactly like mine.

"And don't use names or any other identifiers. It's a safe phone, but the less is said the better."

"Got it."

I was still in a lot of trouble, but my outlook became much brighter.

Dallas

The Art Tower
September 12

"It's an absolute outrage." Vivien stood in front of the Art Tower, lecturing a local TV crew.

"The woman should never be in charge of my husband's company." Vivien looked directly into the camera.

"Why not?" a reporter asked.

"Well, let me give you the facts." Vivien lifted her hand and formed a fist leaving her thumb up. "One: she isn't qualified." Vivien's index finger shot up. "Two: she stole millions of dollars from the company and blames it on me. Three: she mislead my husband and sent him on the fatal flight to Lukla. Four: she is abusing Carter & Co's employees. Five: she is a foreigner who ran a fine Dallas firm down to the ground." Vivien ran out of fingers and out of breath.

"Do you have the evidence to support these claims, Miss Gibson?" the reporter asked.

"I'll present the evidence when the time is right." Vivien smirked. "But let me give you a tip: follow the money. And guess what, you will not find it in my account."

It was true. All Vivien's financial sources had dried out. Her Facebook accounts, her research assignments, and now Jack's account. She didn't expect that. She assumed that Jack would fix things as he always did, and she'd be able to draw her $7,000 per week. *Just a thousand per day*. But the account was blocked, and she couldn't get in.

She couldn't have known that Jack would get himself into a plane crash and leave her behind penniless. While Alex got everything. *It's not fair*, Vivien fumed, *I should be living in Alex's house*.

"How did Mrs. Carter mislead her husband to fly to Lukla?" The reporter tried another angle.

What is she talking about? Vivien was momentarily confused and then realized that the reporter called Alex Mrs. Carter. Vivien wasn't amused.

"I am not going to tell you anything more," Vivien responded coldly. The interview was over.

This isn't right. Alex playing the widow... *It's my role,* Vivien's fists tightened. A plan emerged from a deep crevice of Vivien's mind and she embraced it without hesitation.

Vivien defied reality.

Saint Crooks

September 14

Marty jumped out of bed and drove to the golf course, eager to work on his game. He took in the lushness of the course and once again congratulated himself on his achievements, not in the least suspecting that his carefree days in paradise were numbered.

In fact, he had less than two minutes left to live his dream. But Marty did not know that, still assuming that money and location were the principal ingredients of bliss. He focused on the ball, ready to tee off. Fragrant zephyr ruffled his salt and pepper curls. A last kiss of a dreamland.

Marty raised his golf club. And dropped it down.

A flash of clarity struck him. There was no point in hitting the ball. He'll never be a good golfer. In fact, he hated the game.

The purity of this sudden insight hit Marty right between his eyes. After decades of suppression, the authentic Marty pushed through the layers of pretenses and scared the living daylights out of the Master-of-the-Universe Marty.

For a brief sickening moment Marty intensely disliked himself. But the Master of the Universe tightened his jaw and regained control. *Do you want to be back in Dallas?* Drowning in the mess Jack left behind? No, thank you.

So he didn't feel like playing golf. So what? He was free to do whatever he wanted.

Unperturbed, Marty exchanged his golf gear for his beach gear and drove to the finest beach Saint Crooks had to offer. White sand. Tall, shady palms. Emerald waves. Paradise.

This is what I would've killed for. Marty eyed the beach approvingly.

"You killed for it," a little voice whispered, but drowned in the sound of breaking waves.

Marty settled under a gently swaying palm and opened one of the books he always wanted to read but never had the time for.

The first book failed to grab him. Marty tossed it in his beach bag and jumped into the waves.

Refreshed, he reached for the second book. It was boring and so was the marvelous beach. Marty broke camp and went to the Vic's for an early lunch.

The extra-large martini put him in a much better mood. For a fleeting moment he considered going home and doing some work. But why should he? He was free to do whatever he wanted to. His business thrived. Making Caitlin his assistant was a brilliant move. She made him more money on her worst days than he made on his best ones.

Caitlin's success sent an uncomfortable tremble through Marty's ego and opened a tiny crack for the authentic fool. The Master of the Universe nipped the mutinous thoughts in the bud: Caitlin wouldn't be earning any money if I hadn't taught her my ninja tricks.

Reassured of his supremacy, Marty ordered another martini.

But the damage was done. A little latent bug latched itself in the tiny crevice of Marty's ego: Caitlin made him redundant. Marty wasn't ready to admit it to himself yet, so he chatted up a group of new arrivals and partied with them until the wee hours.

The next day he woke up around noon, ready to enjoy a late lunch at the Vic's, the mini-crises forgotten.

The Vic's became Marty's headquarters. He established himself as a know-it-all guru and spent most of his days at the bar, "working" on his computer, drinking, entertaining tourists and educating them on "making it big."

The more he bragged about his success, the bigger it became. While the Master-of-the-Universe Marty edutained, the authentic Marty was exiled behind the thin but convincing veneer of good cheer and manly bravado. All was well.

Until a disaster struck.

Dallas

Alex's office in DD
September 17

I'd never seen anything like this.

The ice storm left as quickly as it came. It hit in the morning, trapped living plants in its deadly icy grip and set the stage for a spectacular photo shoot. By noon, a bright sun chased the ice queen away, exposing the ravage caused by her brief reign.

Several tree branches snapped under the weight of the ice and hung down like broken wings. The vibrant colors of my merry zinnias were reduced to a uniform brown. The proud, sparkly impatiens turned into a heap of unseemly goo. The regal cannas put their heads down, looking like widows shrouded in mourning.

A surge of sadness choked me up. The devastation resembled too closely the destruction Vivien unleashed on my life.

The garden will recover, I tried to boost myself. But will Carter & Co? The backlash of Vivien's latest media rant hit us where it hurt.

My lawyers filed a defamation suit and slapped Vivien with a gag order, too late to stop the damage. I thought no one would take Vivien's outbursts seriously, but thrilling lies are evidently much more convincing than the boring truth. And repetition defies reality.

Vivien's fabrications resonated and I felt it. Even people who used to trust me now wondered whether I had embezzled the money, destroyed Carter & Co, and tricked Jack to get on the flight to Lukla. I could see it in their eyes…and in their hesitance to work with me.

To top it all off, Hannah told me that Vivien was telling anyone who'd listen that Jack wanted to leave me and get back to her.

The latest casualty of this drama was Vincent Russo, Jack's ex-partner from the days when Carter & Co was Russo, Carter & Co. Vincent had cashed in his share in the firm several years ago and became a full-time horse breeder. I had asked him to temporarily come back and serve as a consultant, for Vincent's impeccable reputation would help assure clients

THE WALL

and creditors that even without Jack we had enough experience in house to deliver the goods.

Vincent had been thrilled to get on board, but had called me this morning and cancelled the deal.

"I'll be honest with you, Alex. I had a dinner with Vivien yesterday and she told me what's going on. I just can't work with a person who did so much damage to Jack and his firm and family."

Speechless, I'd sat behind my desk for a few minutes, paralyzed by self-pity, disbelief, and anger. And then moved on to strategizing how to survive. That's the roller coaster you are strapped to when your path crosses with the likes of Vivien Gibson.

The irony of Vivien's latest move was that Vincent was another piece of proof of her guilt in the defamation suit. He didn't know it yet, but Vincent would make a marvelous witness.

As for Carter & Co, we'd have to get through this without him. I was in awe of the team's resilience and determination to succeed against all odds. If we could pull this off, doing so without Vincent would make us even stronger.

Deeply in thought, I walked to the mailbox to pick up my mail. The load of junk obscured a package, which slid out on the kitchen counter. Curious, I turned the package around. And drew my breath in sharply. It came from Delhi. Not knowing what to expect, I carefully unwrapped it.

Inside was Jack's handmade, personalized notebook. I opened it and a little note fell out:

Dear Mr. Jack Carter,

It's my pleasure to mail back to you your notebook, which you forgot in our hotel. I hope you are well and will visit us again soon.

Respectfully,

J.J. Chatterjee,
General Manager, the Taj Garden hotel

I sat at the kitchen counter and leafed through the book, tears running down my cheeks, missing Jack terribly.

The last pages were filled with sketches I hadn't seen before. A children's hospital. It must be the design Jack had agreed to do pro bono.

I loved it. It was different from any other of Jack's designs. Brilliant. "A magic place where children can heal," Jack had scribbled between the sketches.

The last sketch had a small dedication penned in above the entrance to the hospital: "For Alex, the love of my life."

Would a man who wanted to go back to his ex-wife write this?

NO!

Oh, Jack…

I wanted to beam myself to the Taj Garden hotel and give Mr. Chatterjee a Canadian bear hug. He sent me a piece of Jack that connected directly to my heart. I took a picture of the sketch and made it the wallpaper on my phone. If this wouldn't give me the strengths to fight, I didn't know what else would.

Next, I studied Jack's notes:

Financing OK? Check - Howard, Perry.
If so, ask Alex to do the interior: Inside-Outside!!!
Set dates, be in Kathmandu for building - make up trip for Delhi <3

Oh Jack, darling Jack. Was this the surprise you had for me? I smiled and cried at the same time.

I'll build your hospital, I pledged. I didn't know when and how, but I was confident I'd find a way. To get the project going, I took a picture of the most detailed sketch and emailed it to Perry with a meeting request.

Dallas

Cafe Magnolia
September 21

Lexi was in the cafe already, seated at "their" table. The last time they had been here, Perry was going to point out to her that she didn't have to stay with Jack if she was unhappy with him, but the emergency caused by Vivien had cut their meeting short. Lexi was free now but more out of reach than when Jack was alive.

She was absorbed in some documents, not paying attention to anything else. Perry took in the dark circles under her eyes and the hollows under her cheeks. Her eyes looked huge, burning with resolve. His heart melted.

Perry would never forget the horrendous day in Kathmandu, seeing Lexi heartbroken after Jack had died in the crash. The pain consuming her face had carved deep valleys in his heart and filled him with despair he hadn't been able to quash since.

Perry had never loved anyone more than Lexi.

She can't be trusted. Chilling logic stepped in.

"Why did you send me the picture?" Perry went directly to business.

"I wanted to find out what's the status of the children's hospital in Nepal," she said. "I thought you would still want to use Jack's design."

"That's not the picture I am talking about," Perry jumped in. "Why did you send me the picture of the car crash?"

"Car crash?"

"And what's this?" Perry slid a printout of an email across the table to her, hearing his voice getting louder.

Her eyebrows shot up. "Ugh. I am sorry. It was a beautiful Jag. I used to love this model."

"This car killed my mom."

She gasped, right hand landing on her chest.

"I am so sorry Perry. I didn't know. I didn't mean to…" The huge eyes sent over loving kindness. "When did it happen?" she asked softly.

"When I was eighteen. It was a hit and run accident. Unsolved. I want to find out who did it. So please tell me what you know, Lexi."

"Nothing. This is the first time I've heard about it." She studied the email again.

Perry shifted impatiently.

"Got it!" Lexi looked relieved. "This is not my email address."

She slid the printout back to him, pointing to the top. "See, it's alex-at-carterco-dot-me. Mine is alex-at-carterco-dot-com."

"Hm. So why would the sender use your name?"

Lexi stared at the email, deeply in thoughts. He could almost see her brain running through options. He wished she would think out loud.

But she shook her head. "I do not know," she said firmly.

But you have a suspicion, Lexi. He almost took her hands into his and asked her to share her thoughts.

"I am really sorry I can't be of help, Perry," she said. "Now, I understand this is perhaps not your priority, but our meeting was about the children's hospital."

"This is not the right time to start. There's too much going on. Jack's estate isn't finalized yet. There are too many unknowns." Perry heard himself drowning in excuses.

He didn't have the heart to tell Lexi that Richard's office was advised not to give her any support because she, not Vivien, likely embezzled Carter & Co's money. Perry didn't quite believe it, but Lexi's not leveling with him didn't help.

She listened to him, head tilted to the side. She straightened up when he finished and looked directly into his eyes. Perry was overwhelmed by the resolve, sadness, and love flowing over to him. He loved her more than ever.

She can't be trusted.

"I understand Perry." Lexi held her head high, but the wetness in her eyes gave her away. "It makes no sense to waste time on people you don't trust."

Her words bounced of Perry, flipped in the air, landed on him again, and slowly permeated his defenses: p-e-o-p-l-e—y-o-u—d-o-n-t—t-r-u-s-t.

Stunned, Perry automatically fumbled with his phone. The screen woke up, but he didn't see a word. He blinked as a memory came to his mind. "She told me she loved me, but couldn't marry me, unless…" Dave never finished that sentence, Perry recalled. What was Mom waiting for?

She never told him. She put her connection with Dave on hold until it was too late.

Perry looked up, his mouth dry, a tight grip pressing his forehead. Lexi was gone.

The last time I felt this miserable was when Mom died, Perry realized, frustration getting the better of him.

Dallas

The Pure Potential Restaurant
October 12

"I hope we can build the hospital one day. It's possibly Jack's best work." I gave Jen and Victor copies of Jack's sketches. Except the last one with the dedication. That one was just between me and Jack for now.

"It's brilliant." Jen looked up, her eyes moist.

"It *is* his best," Victor added. "We've got to build it. I'll talk with Perry about it."

Ugh. "Perry wasn't open to it when I talked with him," I said, still smarting from the meeting. I had assumed that Perry was immune to Vivien's poison, given people still used her sexting fabrications to discredit Richard. But Perry distanced himself from me like a seasoned politician.

"What did he say?"

"That there are too many unknowns."

Jen rolled her eyes.

"Yeah. I know," I said quietly. "Although he might have a point. The guys at Carter & Co love the design and want to work on it pro bono as Jack promised, but we are terribly busy right now."

"But a project like this would do wonders for the firm." Victor wasn't ready to give up.

"Absolutely," I agreed.

"Maybe we can figure out something else," Jen thought out loud. "We could use the design to promote the firm while we work on securing the finances."

"That's an excellent idea, provided we can avoid a conflict with Richard. Senator Howard."

"I bet there isn't a contract," Victor said, "and if Richard isn't playing, someone else will."

"Love it," I said.

And I loved how easily the kids got involved in the project and wouldn't take no for answer.

"By the way, how is it going at Carter & Co?" Victor's seriousness made him look older than his years.

"We are making reasonable progress and keep the payroll going so far. But I'll be honest with you." I paused, searching for gentle words. "The latest allegations that I embezzled the money and so on cost us dearly. Some people are opting out of their contracts with us because of it."

Jen put her head down. "I am sorry," she said in a barely audible voice.

"It's not your fault, Jen."

"No, but still. That's why we are here. We want to help." Jen gave me a look filled with hope.

"We want to make our trust funds available for Carter & Co," Victor said firmly.

"Thank you. It means a lot to me." I was moved but couldn't accept their offer. I'd fought hard to secure the money for Jen and Victor and using it to offset Vivien's fraud was out of the question.

The trust funds had first come up when Vivien accused me of forcing her out of the house. I'd asked Jack what he knew about her moving, expecting he'll answer "nothing." But Jack told me that Vivien was willing to sell the house if Jack would buy her a condo downtown, which would be a great investment for the kids.

"Jack, if you want to invest for the kids, why don't you help them with their condos or open a trust fund for them?" I asked. Knowing Vivien, she'd mortgage the condo to the hilt, and the kids would never see the money. But it had taken weeks of endless discussions for Jack to finally make up his mind and open the funds.

"It's incredibly generous of you, but I'd like to put your offer on hold for now," I said. "Jack set up the trust funds as long-term investment and I'd like to keep it that way."

"But Carter & Co needs money," Jen countered.

"Yes. I've decided to use the credit line I have on DD."

Jen gasped. "You can't do that. That's exactly what she wants."

"Mother wanted to take DD from you ever since you bought it. She thinks it's hers, you know," Victor explained.

I knew...

"Alex, she wants to destroy you and will not stop until you are completely ruined," Jen pressed on.

"Another reason not to get your money involved," I said.

"She is after us too," Victor said. "After the trust funds."

"And she tried to get me fired from my job." Jen pursed her lips.

"Jeez."

A chill ran up my spine. The destruction had no limits.

I have to stop Vivien if it's the last thing I do.

Saint Crooks

The Vic's
November 23

Marty was chatting away with his man Tim when the tail end of another conversation caught his ear.

"Please ask the bartender to switch the channel to the game?"

Marty recognized the voice. Silvery singsong raising at the end of each sentence, making it sound like a question. Memories flooded Marty's mind. "Marty, here is your Rueben?", "Marty, I love your tie?", "Marty, Jack needs you right away?"

Jamie, Marty's secretary. Ex-secretary.

Delighted, Marty jumped off his stool, arms wide open, ready to give Jamie a hug.

"Jamie," Marty called out and stopped in mid-sentence as Jamie's cheerful face took on a cold disapproving mask.

"What are you doing here?"

"What's wrong, Jamie?"

"What's wrong? YOU ask me what's wrong?"

"What's going on, Jamie?" A stocky guy stepped to Jamie's side.

"Ugh... This is Marty Wilson. The asshole who bankrupted Carter & Co."

Several patrons turned around, enjoying the unexpected entertainment.

"I didn't bankrupt anyone."

"You didn't? Then who did?" Jamie's voice filled the Vic's. "The whole of Dallas knows that Carter & Co almost went bankrupt because YOU grossly mismanaged our finances." Jamie delivered the allegation with vehemence, jabbing her finger at Marty.

Marty had good four inches on her, but Jamie seemed to tower over him.

"Jamie, I merely executed Jack's orders," Marty responded meekly.

"Yeah. Blame it on the dead man." Jamie began to walk away but stopped after a few steps, turned around, and looked into Marty's eyes.

"You are a coward, Marty. You betrayed us all." Tears filled Jamie's eyes and spilled over her cheeks.

Loud applause broke through the atypical quietness that took over Vic's in the last few minutes. All eyes were on Jamie.

"Way to go Jamie!" "Well said!" "Jamie, drinks are on us!" Patrons shouted and returned to partying.

Life was back to normal.

No so for Marty.

"You killed him," a little voice whispered.

The little latent bug that latched itself onto Marty's ego and made Marty feel incompetent found a big sister: bad conscience.

Marty had never dealt with such a monster before.

The Art Tower

Carter & Co, Alex's office
April 10

"We'll get that amended," Emma Fitzgerald said. "No worries. You'd be surprised how often these mistakes happen."

Emma was exactly what I needed, as Liz predicted when she recommended her as my estate management attorney.

Still, I worried. After months of waiting, the Embassy finally sent Jack's Consular Report of Death, but the first thing I noticed was the wrong date of death. Emma's assurance that we can now proceed with finalizing Jack's estate didn't go far. Just the thought of having to postpone the execution of Jack's will until the report was corrected gave me a pounding headache.

I felt like I was walking a tightrope with a crushing load on my shoulders, moving forward step by step, but every time I was nearing the other side the ground slid away and the rope swayed, leaving me out of balance, one wrong move away from tumbling into the deadly abyss below.

I couldn't keep Carter & Co going much longer without establishing clear ownership. Vivien and other sharks were circling, and we needed to get on solid legal ground to keep them at bay. We had been holding our own so far, but meeting the payroll and paying our bills was a nerve-wracking struggle.

My alarm went off. Yikes. Going down and embarking on the silent ride was the last thing I wanted to do right now. The Wall was in trouble and a solution nowhere in sight.

Spears of pain lanced through the right side of my forehead when Collin explained the technical problems his people ran into. They were collecting a lot of data but the much-needed breakthrough eluded them. Collin tightened the grip on his chair, his eyes taking on a darker gray.

I was racking my brain for ideas but didn't get any. "By the way," I changed the subject, "I wanted to ask this many times but always forgot. Why did you name this project the Wall?"

"At first because it was on the wall. Literally." Collin relaxed a little bit. "But then we realized that we are dealing with an almost impenetrable wall."

"I see."

"You are our passage to the other side," Collin added.

I took a deep breath. If I was the passage, I wasn't functioning. I wanted a more active role. Watching from the sidelines drove me crazy. I said so to Collin.

"You have enough on your plate already," he said after a moment of pensive silence. "Anyhow, how are you holding up?"

I told him about the latest challenges. "You know, it's the craziest thing. I am responsible for running Carter & Co in Jack's absence. But I can't run it responsibly because of Jack's absence." I shook my head. "It's a catch 22. I wish there was an insurance policy or something."

I stopped in my tracks.

"Insurance!" we said in unison and jumped up from our chairs.

"Is it possible?" I looked at Collin expectantly. "Legally, I mean?"

Collin rubbed his chin.

"I think we might have a small window there."

Dallas

Alex's office in DD
May 6

The property was huge. I studied the pictures of a sprawling farmhouse in Frisco, letting my mind generate ideas. The clients wanted a seamless mix of old and new, streamlined and romantic, outside and inside. I was working on the design at DD, but Carter & Co occupied my mind.

One day to go.

One day until the probate court ruled on Jack's last will. I was jittery, although Emma told me it was just a formality. We were not out of the woods yet, but we'd survived and could start rebuilding Carter & Co on a solid ground as soon as the will was probated.

The team deserved it. In the last months we fought like lions for every opportunity we got. Charlie and I acquired a number of smaller jobs that paid the bills, and Hannah took over our older projects, emerging from underneath Jack's shadow like a bright star. She and her assistant tweaked the design of the Vancouver tower to enhance the tower's visual appeal, delighting the owner and making the tower their signature skyscraper.

I'd learned a lot about running the business since I had returned from Nepal. Design was still my forte, but there was something surprisingly gratifying about managing projects and making sure that everything added up and everyone had what they needed to be at their best. I loved working with the team. As time passed, my focus shifted from preserving Jack's legacy to creating a future for Carter & Co's people.

The guys still adored Jack. A few weeks after his notebook arrived, they surprised me with a maquette of the children's hospital, made to scale from Jack's sketches. It became our mascot and presided over all important meetings.

Yet, as I got more involved in running the firm, I discovered that Jack didn't always play straight. I had to admit to myself that the old rumors accusing Jack of taking advantage of his young associates were closer to truth than I'd originally believed. Working closely with Hannah convinced me that the applauded, prize winning designs Jack took the credit for were more her work than his.

That was one part of Jack's legacy I was not going to continue, and I had decided to make Hannah and Charlie full partners in the firm as soon as I could. I recalled Hannah's face flooding with surprise, joy, and well-deserved pride when I shared my plan with her. One more day!

Totally absorbed in the memories, I almost missed the phone vibrating on my desk.

"Alex, come immediately!" Hannah sobbed. "Vivien is here. She claims Carter & Co is hers. You've got to fix it. Oh my gosh… She smashed our maquette."

"Call security," I said. *Has Vivien gone mad?* We hadn't heard much from her lately. She kept spreading her rumors but didn't launch any new attacks.

"Give me the phone." I heard a struggle in the background.

"I am on my way," I yelled but got disconnected. I ran to the garage, dialing Forever Secure. Voicemail.

The tightrope swayed perilously once again and left me balancing above the deadly abyss.

Dallas

The Art Tower
May 6

I couldn't reach anyone at Carter & Co. Forever Secure called back and said that they were monitoring the situation but had no reason to interfere at the moment. I winced. The Sky Gondola stopped on almost every floor. By the time I got out on the fifty-third floor, a throbbing headache turned my forehead into a battle zone.

A security guard let me into Carter & Co and escorted me to the conference room.

"About time," Vivien said. She presided over our conference table, dressed all in black, another guard standing by her side. I took a better look at him. He didn't seem armed but looked familiar.

"Do you think I have all the time in the world? I have a business to run!" Vivien yelled.

"Please tell us why you are here, Vivien," I asked, keeping my voice low.

"Because I am the owner of Carter & Co."

She must be bluffing. Trying to trick me into doing something stupid before the probate hearing.

"The probate hearing is tomorrow," I said.

Vivien laughed. "No, it's not, you got it all wrong. The hearing was today. The judge appointed me the executor of Jack's last will. Jack's last last will. In which he left everything to me."

Vivien waved a piece of paper at me.

"Jack had come to his senses before your stupid trip and confided in me that marrying you was a huge mistake. He wanted to take care of me should something happen to him and wrote a new will."

Murderous rage pulsed through me, but I managed to stay calm on the outside. I was not going to give Vivien the pleasure of seeing how much she affected me.

"May I see the last will?" I asked.

She handed the paper to me. It was a copy of a page ripped from a notebook like Jack's. The will was written in Jack's handwriting. My heart skipped a beat. Then I saw the date on the top of the page. *Vivien is lying.*

I handed the paper back to Vivien, trying to meet her eyes, but she looked away.

"Do you have the order appointing you as executor?"

Vivien waved another piece of paper in front of me. I glimpsed the name of the judge who signed it. Helen D. Jefferson. Not our judge!

"My lawyer..."

"That's enough," Vivien said. She stood up, crashing her chair into her guard. "Get out," she screamed, turning crimson. "You are fired, and you are trespassing my property. Guard, escort her out of the premises."

I didn't move. The guard grabbed me by my shoulders and forced me out of the conference room.

"Stop!" I ordered him without effect. "Let go of me!" I screamed, but he dragged me towards the front door and pushed me out. I lost balance and fell on my knees, my humiliation complete.

A dark abyss swallowed me.

Dallas

The Art Tower

It's the same guy.

The marathon pusher. No doubt about it! The guy who pushed me down, kicked me, and nearly ruined my race. So Vivien *was* behind it! White-hot anger swirled up from my gut and annihilated my humiliation.

This. Is. Not. Right.

I'll not let you ruin my team's work.

I stood up and headed towards the stairwell. I needed to take action. Immediately.

Emma was the first person on my list.

"Miss Fitzgerald is in a conference."

"Please get her out. This is an emergency."

"But Miss…"

"Do it." The secretary put me on hold. I leaned against the wall.

"Alex, what's going on?" Emma sounded alarmed. She knew I'd never drag her out of a meeting unless it was absolutely necessary.

"I thought you'd tell me."

"What happened?"

I told her.

"That can't be true."

"It's just happened, Emma."

"I believe you, Alex, but our hearing is scheduled for tomorrow. I haven't received any notification of change."

"Well, can you find out what's going on? She waved an order signed by a judge in front of my nose."

"Judge Hobbs?"

"No. Jefferson, I think." I'd seen it for just a millisecond.

"Helen Jefferson. I know her personally. She is a really good person. I am terribly sorry, Alex. This is totally unprecedented."

"What can we do?"

"The court is closed now. I'll call some people and get back to you. Give me an hour or two."

I got out of the building and walked aimlessly, organizing my thoughts, strategizing. I wandered into Neiman Marcus and nearly bumped into Megs.

"What are you doing here?" she hissed.

"What do you mean?"

"What do I mean?" Megs raised her voice. "You've ruined Jack's firm and family. How could you? I trusted you. I gave you your first job in Dallas. And you…"

"What got into you, Megs? I've put everything I had on the line to save Carter & Co."

"Oh, have you? I hear that you gutted the company. And now have a nice nest egg offshore."

I looked at Megs, speechless. A small crowd gathered around us. Several women were taking pictures with their phones.

"Enjoy it because you will never work in Dallas again."

"Megs, do you really believe this?"

My response came too late. Megs turned on her heel and marched away. Her upbringing didn't allow her to spit on me, but I'd swear she wanted to do just that.

Dallas

DD
Half an hour later

"I've got some news, Alex. It's very strange." Emma phoned me just as I entered DD. "I got hold of Helen Jefferson. We've talked informally, I'll get the official pieces tomorrow. Our hearing was indeed rescheduled. We were supposedly informed about the change, but I have not received anything. Have you?"

"Of course not. I would have told you."

"OK. The story is that Judge Hobbs had some kind of emergency and asked Helen to fill in for him at the last minute. He told her it's a cut-and-dried case, she just had to close it."

"The next issue we weren't informed about is that Vivien Gibson's lawyer submitted a holographic will. That is a handwritten will, which revoked the last will you have."

"Can we contest the validity of the handwritten will?"

"The will looks technically valid. It satisfies the criteria for holographic wills. That's why the judge accepted it."

A chill ran up my spine, but I wouldn't give up.

"Hm. But the will is dated July twenty-eight. Jack didn't leave the house the whole day on that day. I have witnesses to prove it."

"Well, according to Vivien's statement, she'd met Jack on the twenty-eighth in the early evening. In the Pyramid Bar. Jack had told her that he was going on a trip and wanted to make sure Vivien was taken care of should something happen to him. He stated that marrying you was a huge mistake and he didn't want you to run away with their family money."

It was the second time I had heard this story today, but each word was just as devastating as the first time. A deadly stab in my heart.

"I am sorry. I am reading this from the document I got. Vivien stated that Jack wrote the last will in his notebook, ripped out the page and gave it to her."

This wasn't true. I checked and double checked.

"Emma, do you remember the day? The twenty-eighth of July last year?"

"No."

"But you probably remember the big storm we had at the end of July."

"The one with flooding and hail and a tornado hitting somewhere near Garland?"

"Yes. It happened on that day."

"Oh."

"I remember it exactly," I went on, "because Jack and I had a picnic for the grandkids. They ended up staying overnight because no one with half a brain would drive in that weather. Jack was with us the whole day."

I remembered how we ran in, shut the doors and watched the storm pummeling the backyard. How excited Bailey and Ian were about the unexpected adventure. The blueberry pancakes we made from scratch the next morning. The happiness. I wanted to scream. If Vivien were alone with me now, she wouldn't be safe.

"Oh my God." Emma gasped. "No one was on the road then."

"That's right. And there is more to it." I collected myself and told Emma about Jack's notebook.

"We'll appeal this and we'll win. With all this new evidence, we can probably ask Helen to reconsider. I'll look into it. She was very surprised that we didn't get any notification regarding the change of date. She assumed we just didn't show up."

We made an appointment to prepare for the appeal, but I'd been around Vivien long enough not to share Emma's optimism. Vivien will claim that she and Jack met on any other day, and that Jack made an honest mistake when he wrote down the date. And she'd probably find someone who would testify to seeing them together in the bar.

But what if Vivien met Jack at the end of July, he wrote the will and got the date wrong?

I froze.

No pages were missing from the notebook I gave to Jack, but he could have had another one. Had he been living a double life? Having two loves of a lifetime?

I looked around DD, seeking answers. Jack seemed to be everywhere. Every detail of the house replayed a video of us together. Jack fastening my necklace and kissing my neck. Jack bringing me a gorgeous bouquet of roses, smiling his boyish smile. Jack on the phone, fist in the air, being told that the he'd won the Vancouver tower contest…

Did you betray me? I asked. I'd never know. Doubts marred my memories.

Vivien was winning big.

Dallas

DD
May 7

All Carter & Co employees resigned.

It was poetic justice that Vivien lost my people, but the consequences of their brave act were close to catastrophic. With no one working, Carter & Co's projects were not being completed, which meant that our invoices would not get paid, and Carter & Co would default on paying me back the loan I took to keep the firm afloat.

Even if I won the last will fight, project delays and cancellations would leave us deeply in the red. If Vivien remained in charge, Carter & Co was finished. Any which way, Vivien had bankrupted Carter & Co for the second time in less than a year.

How did she get away with so much? She stole $2.7 million from us, and when the firm is rebuilt, with my money, she claims ownership. Because she is the owner, no one will sue her for the 2.7 million. All the work my team did was for nothing, I am out my money, and Vivien laughs all the way to the bank.

Furious, I quickly scrolled through my text messages. Perry's URGENT! text caught my attention. He wanted to meet for lunch. A ray of hope lifted my spirits.

Maybe Perry had some ideas how to get out of this. Even if he didn't, I could use a friendly ear. Although we were no longer as close as we used to be. Maybe Perry missed our friendship as much as I did and wanted to rekindle it.

It took me forever to get ready, my mind pulling me in thousands of different directions, my puffy eyes not helping either. I made it to the cafe just in time.

Perry was already seated, jaw tightly set. He didn't get up and kiss me as usual. My hope that he'd heard what happened and wanted to help melted away like the snow in spring.

"Why do you keep doing this?"

THE WALL

Perry demanded, agitated. I wasn't Lexi anymore. I was a no-name.

"Doing what?" I asked.

Perry got out a greenish envelope. A memory flashed in the back of my mind, but my overloaded brain swallowed it before I could grasp it. Perry took out a bunch of pictures and slid them towards me. It was the green Jag again. I was careful not to touch the pictures.

"I didn't do this, Perry." I looked squarely into Perry's eyes. Lots of anguish there.

"My people traced the IP address of the email from which one of the photos came to your home." His eyes darkened.

"Right. So now we know where the pics came from," I said more ironically than intended.

Watch it! I reined myself in. I was pretty sure where the pictures came from. But I couldn't share it with Perry. His anguished eyes played on my heartstrings. I wished I could take his pain away, but I couldn't. Too many other people were at risk. I took a deep breath.

"Perry, there is a lot happening in cyberspace. You would probably be surprised if you knew what's connected to your IP. Or Senator Howard's."

Perry shrugged. "Yeah. Just blame things on others. I didn't want to believe it, but maybe people are right about you." A bitter smile contorted Perry's face. "No one in Dallas trusts you anymore. The word is that you gutted Carter & Co and created a nice nest egg for yourself offshore. And let everyone believe you are the victim."

A slap in my face wouldn't have hurt as much as these words. I knew Perry had it all wrong, but I was drowning in shame nonetheless.

Vivien scored and scored and scored.

Perry used to be one of my most favorite people. No, he still was. I still liked him. A lot. *I love him.* I bit my lip. It took this horrendous moment to sort out the jumble of feelings I had for Perry. *I love him.* I allowed myself to take in his handsome face, angry now. Beyond reach. Another loss.

I wished I could clear my name and salvage what was left of our friendship. But I couldn't. I wished I had gone to Dubai first and never became involved with Jack and Vivien. But would I have allowed myself to love Perry then, without knowing what I knew now?

Perry was looking at me, his eyes two dark pools of disdain. Just as Megs...

"You too, Perry," I said quietly. Something shifted in his face. The disdain gave way to surprise.

I stood up and walked out of the restaurant before saying something I would regret later. I blended with the lunch crowd on the street, tears streaming out of my eyes, but my head was clear.

This whole thing went too far. It was costing me too much. The sooner it ended, the better.

I knew exactly what to do.

Dallas

DD
May 30

"Should I call you during the auction?" Joyce asked.

"No, please just let me know when it's over."

I was walking around in a haze, nothing feeling real. *I am selling DD. Lock, stock, and barrel. Cutting my losses and getting out of town.*

Since I had left the lunch with Perry, I operated like a robot. I didn't allow any space for lingering doubts. I worked with Joyce on assessing DD and preparing it for sale. I rented a storage unit and moved the few items I decided to keep into it. The Giullia was ready to be dropped off at CarMax after the auction. I worked with Emma on the appeal. I kept emailing with my team. I contacted all our clients and business partners and asked them to put their final decision regarding Carter & Co on hold for a month, by which time we would get more clarity about the last will issue. I didn't expect much from this but was moved by the support we received. Vancouver went on and several other clients hired our key people as consultants to keep their projects going.

Last but not least, I made a "DD guide" for the new owners. Strangely, describing who serviced the air-conditioning, who cleaned the windows, where the sprinkler controls were, how to feed the koi, when the gardening crew came in, et cetera, did me good. It showed me how much I had accomplished with DD and made me ready to move on.

The grand old lady stood proud, in perfect condition to be handed over to the new people and become part of their story.

Most importantly, I strategized with Collin. The Wall became my absolute priority. We were finally nearing the finish line and the tension was mounting. My stomach twisted into knots just thinking about it. Scenarios of the wrong kind started to play in front of my eyes. *It's only a warning that makes you sharper*, I calmed myself, but the only sure thing was that a gnawing worry would be my intimate companion in the coming weeks.

I walked through the house and checked once more that I hadn't forgotten to pack something important. My biggest worry besides the Wall was that no one would buy DD. Joyce lined up a group of selected buyers for the auction, but what if Vivien poisoned them all and no one would touch my property?

The auction went on for a long time. Not knowing what was going on unnerved me. In hindsight, I should have let Joyce keep me in the loop. But that would have been excruciating too. Feeling raw and edgy, I grabbed the fish pellets and went to feed the koi.

"Come on boys, I have an extra treat for you today." They nibbled out of my hand.

For a few blissful moments I forgot about everything else. The phone startled me. Joyce. I braced myself for another disaster.

"Alex, you are not going to believe this." Joyce was bubbling over with excitement. "We got almost five times the asking price. Five times! I've never seen anything like this."

"Wow." I didn't know what to say. Maybe I wasn't totally doomed. "Oh my. You've done a marvelous job, Joyce."

"Alex, let me tell you, I wish you didn't have to sell, but this is phenomenal."

Joyce told me how the bidding went up quickly until only two people remained, how they were chasing each other up up up, and then our buyer hesitated and the room went deadly quiet. But after a few minutes our buyer put in a very high bid and the second person stopped, and then such a ruckus broke out, you couldn't hear your own words.

"Who is the buyer, Joyce?"

"I don't know. The last two people were bidding anonymously over phone, via their agents. I spoke with the agent and she told me that the house couldn't go to a better person."

Relieved, I went back in and sat behind my desk for the last time. I called Emma and told her what happened at the auction. She and Joyce would finish all the paperwork when I was gone. I asked her to make an anonymous donation to Futures, Evelyn's orphanage charity.

"Are you sure?" Emma asked when I told her the sum.

"Absolutely." The donation was one of the few things I was sure about. It had been on my mind for a long time and auctioning DD made it possible.

"You know, you don't have to pay this immediately," Emma went on. "You could wait until the last will case is over. Make sure you really want to do this."

"I know, but I want to do it now." I'd thought about it long enough.

"OK. I'll prepare the paperwork. Have a good trip, Alex. And good luck. We'll stay in touch."

Next, I composed emails for Jen and Victor, carefully selecting every word. The message had to be crystal clear. I sent it and made a lunch appointment with Liz.

My new life was almost ready to begin.

Dallas

Deep Ellum's Rooftop Heaven
May 31

Liz was late.

Because Liz was never late, I assumed she gave up on me just like Megs and Perry. It hurt like hell, but it was her choice. My choice was to say goodbye to her as a friend. If she didn't show up in person, email will have to do. I started composing it right away to keep myself busy. It was almost finished when Liz floated in on a cloud of lily of the valley perfume.

My heart fluttered with joy. Not all was lost.

"So sorry. There was an accident on Woodall Rodgers. I thought I would *never* get out of there."

We hugged.

"Thank you for coming, Liz. I really appreciate it."

"Why wouldn't I come?"

"Lots of people wouldn't."

Liz threw me a look without saying a word.

"Because they believe I gutted Carter & Co and stashed the booty in an offshore account."

"The good ones don't believe this," Liz said confidently.

"They do. Megs, Perry. I am getting out of here, Liz. I am leaving Dallas."

"No."

"Yes. I've sold DD."

Liz's hand flew to her mouth.

"Oh my gosh. Honey, DD is..." Liz stopped and gave me a long look. "You did sell it, didn't you?"

I nodded. The pity oozing out of Liz's eyes was killing me.

"Why?"

I told her about Vivien's visit to Carter & Co, about the last will and the court mess up, about being thrown out of my office, and about running into Megs in Neiman Marcus.

"You've got to fight this." Liz's voice was raspier than usually.

"I am fighting it." And how. *If only you knew.* I wished I could share it all with Liz, but I couldn't.

"You can't fight it when you run away."

"My lawyers are fighting the legal stuff. I was rendered ineffective. My people were betrayed twice in less than one year. The second time, Vivien destroyed months of our work in one afternoon. I failed them."

"No. You didn't. But you will if you don't stay and fight back," Liz repeated.

"Yeah. That's exactly what I thought, Liz." I sighed. "I've spent nights thinking about this. But I am not a superwoman, I can't do it all on my own. Even if my team decided to stand behind me once more, I can't save a business in a place where people trust con artists more than me."

Liz looked down. She steepled her hands and put them to her lips. Neither of us said anything.

"Not all people fall for con artists," Liz said, breaking the silence.

"You are right," I agreed. "But strange things happen when Vivien gets involved. People let her get away with murder. I tried to fight it. I have fought like a lion since I married Jack, Liz. And I lost."

Liz took my hands in hers, sadness taking over her face.

"I am so sorry, honey," she said quietly. "So where are you going?"

"Dubai."

"When are you leaving?"

"This afternoon."

Dallas

Senator Howard's office
The same day

"This isn't right." Liz's voice thundered through the speakerphone.

Perry peeked into Richard's office, ready for their meeting on housing. The senator waved him in.

"We must do something, Richard. This just can't go on."

"What do you want to do, Liz?"

"I want to see justice done."

"Then you have to let it run its course."

"Yes. But Vivien's getting away with murder."

"Maybe. But it's not our problem."

"That's the problem, Richard. When people like us do nothing."

"Liz, I have a meeting now. Let's talk later."

"OK. But, this is not right!"

Richard shook his head. Perry looked at him quizzically.

"Jack Carter left a mess behind and his wives are fighting over it. They are both so enmeshed in accusations and counter accusations, I don't know what to believe anymore. The first wife claims that Jack left everything to her. Carter & Co is out of business again because the first wife kicked Alex out and all their employees resigned. Alex can't take it anymore and is moving to Dubai for good. And Liz is very upset about it."

Perry sucked his breath in, shocked by Richard's update. He knew that Alex had sold her house, but he didn't know about her moving to Dubai. He buried himself in work after their disastrous lunch, trying to shut down the roller coaster of guilt and grief he had been on since.

"Liz is right, Richard. This isn't right."

Perry put the report he was clutching in his hands on the senator's desk. It was his most important report so far. Perry spent weeks researching and analyzing the housing issues, but it all became irrelevant within the last minutes. He had to find Lexi.

Since Kathmandu he'd fought the urge to take her in his arms, comfort her, protect her. He held back, not wanting to intrude in her space, respecting her need to mourn Jack...although he could hardly endure watching her struggling alone, attacked from all sides, yet so determined. Just like Sylvia.

Lexi had seemed unreachable, but Perry waited, trusting that the right time would come. But then the devastatingly convincing allegation came that Lexi engineered the Carter & Co fraud. And the digital evidence appeared, probably fake, but looking real enough to trigger doubts and distrust nonetheless. *Exactly as it was intended,* Perry bit his lips, livid about falling into the trap and giving this hogwash serious consideration.

I have to act. Now!

"I need a leave of absence, Richard. The report is ready, you can reach me at any time, but I have to go now."

"Does it have something to do with Alex?" Richard asked, not looking in the least surprised.

"It has to do with all of us," Perry replied, running out of the senator's office.

I am not going to wait until it's too late. Perry took a deep breath. It was high time to let go of fears and follow his heart. He would give his life for Lexi, and now he had a chance.

Once in the corridor, Perry took out his safe phone and dialed.

"Yes," a deep, pleasant voice answered.

"I need to talk with you immediately."

Saint Crooks

Marty's villa
June 1

Marty was burning in his private hell. Since Jamie's visit, no matter how late he went to bed or how many martinis he consumed, he woke up every morning at 3:00 a.m. sharp, seeing her teary face and hearing her words:

"You are a coward, Marty. You betrayed us all."

The few locals who'd witnessed Jamie's tirade had forgotten all about it the next day. Marty couldn't.

He could handle Jamie's anger. He could live with her accusations. But her tears killed his sleep.

Night after night, Marty tossed and turned, unable to go back to sleep until the crack of dawn, when restless slumber knocked him out and left him dry-mouthed and exhausted. On some days Marty spent the whole day in bed. He had no reason to get up.

Often he caught himself longing for his old life in Dallas. He dreamed about going to a Mavs game, buying a round for the guys at Oceans, or strolling through the Klyde Warren and grabbing a beef tenderloin sandwich from a food truck.

Most of all he missed the tedium of the office. He would give anything to be back at Carter & Co, crunching numbers day in day out, participating in the pointless chat at the coffee machine, having the predictable Reuben Jamie got for him from the deli downstairs. Being one of them. It was the perfect life.

It took several months of being away from Carter & Co for Marty to realize how much he had lost. He had been a respected Chief Financial Officer, an important player on a winning team. He still would have this life had he not been seduced by the island lifestyle. And Vivien.

Marty knew for years that Vivien was bad news. He'd experienced more of her peccadilloes than he cared to admit. Yet, being Vivien's rescuer and protector filled him with ecstasy he would kill for.

"YOU KILLED FOR IT," the little voice that used to whisper shouted. No matter what Marty did, the voice wouldn't go away.

The only way to shut the voice up permanently and irreversibly was suicide.

Marty had it all planned out. When the first significant storm of the hurricane season hits the shores, he'd go to the beach at night, swim far out, and let the waves take him. Nobody would know what happened. Nobody would miss him.

A perfect end to an imperfect life, Marty chuckled.

That settled, the nagging voice had disappeared. Filled with peace, Marty read some of the books he had always wanted to read. He resumed his patronage of the Vic's, but instead of edutaining tourists, he read blogs, oblivious to what anyone thought about him. Knowing that he would soon put an end to his island hell, he enjoyed himself. He had nothing to lose.

The authentic Marty had finally come to life.

Reading other people's blogs inspired him to write his own. Unhampered by pretenses, Marty wrote whatever he wanted, whenever he wanted. His raw message attracted a rapidly expanding circle of followers. Marty could easily monetize his blog, but he wasn't interested in it. He wanted to keep things pure and simple.

He enjoyed himself so much that his carefully engineered exit plan slipped out of his mind. He let out a sigh of relief when the first tropical system of the season failed to become a storm. He secretly wished that it was the last hurricane of the season and his suicide plans would have to be put on hold for another year. But then the phone calls started.

The first call was from Vivien's brother Ted, who offered Marty a CFO position in Houston. Ted was as unreliable as Vivien, and Marty refused without thinking. Yet, as the day went on, fantasies of being back in Dallas filled his mind. Living in one of the new upscale high-rises downtown, in walking distance to his favorite hangouts. Maybe he could even walk to work. And he would be respected again.

Marty couldn't think about anything else. So when Ted had called two days later and mentioned that the job could be moved to Dallas, Marty had said he would think about it.

The third call came a few moments ago, a minute after 3 a.m., just when Marty woke up.

"The CFO job in Dallas would be perfect for you. A complete rehabilitation."

"Who am I speaking with?"

"You know."

Marty shivered. He knew.

"The job is much bigger than your Carter & Co shtick was. And it pays much better." The caller laughed. "And the company is going to take over Carter & Co." The caller laughed again.

"I am retired," Marty answered, sweating.

"Don't wait too long. You know how much I value loyalty."

The caller hung up.

An invisible hand hiked the temperature in Marty's hell. He was doomed if he did, and doomed if he didn't.

"Why don't you give it a try?" the Master of the Universe reinserted himself. "You'd have the perfect life."

"You killed for the perfect life!" The nagging voice was back.

A flight from Dubai to Pokhara

June 3

The restaurant shakes. The patio tilts to one side and I barely catch my water glass. Where is Jack? Ha! I know what's coming.

I woke up and almost laughed out loud. This nightmare could no longer scare me.

"Don't you understand that I have nothing to lose anymore?" I chased the nightmare from my mind. "Being dead is less scary than being alive, you silly monster."

I couldn't remember how many times I wished to be dead in the last few months. How many times I wished I had been on that plane with Jack. Holding hands to the end.

Being left behind, alone with all the unanswered questions was the worst nightmare ever. Did Jack betray me? Did Vivien trick him? Why did he change his flight and not tell me about it? Did he lead a double life? Is the holographic will real or fake?

Too many unknowns, too much hurt.

Too many losses.

I lost everything I loved. My husband, my house, Carter & Co, my Dallas friends. And pretty much my belief in humanity.

In spite of Vivien's intrusions, when Jack and I were together, our days were filled with love, joy, design, DD, dinners with friends, awards, glossy covers. That life is gone forever. My life made no sense anymore.

Except for one thing.

The Wall. TW.

I put my seat in the upright position for landing and took a deep breath. I'll never get my old life back, but I was determined to finish Collin's project with flying colors. We still had a chance.

All the delays, setbacks, and boulders crashing in our path notwithstanding, I wasn't giving up. There was an opportunity to crack the Wall, and I was going for it.

The first step had been easy. I'd stopped in "my" temporary apartment in Dubai and gave my laptop and phone to Collin's agent who took over my customary online activities, while I snuck out of there and caught a flight to Pokhara. I needed to get off the radar and let everyone believe that I gave up, ran away from everything and was hiding in Dubai.

No one knew I was flying to Pokhara, except Collin. Collin wasn't happy about Pokhara, but I insisted. I could have gone anywhere, but Pokhara called to me like the Sirens. I longed to go on the trekking tour Jack and I had wanted to take. Get into the mountains, climb, sweat, challenge myself and forget about everything else. Clear my head and prepare myself for the grand finale of TW.

The plane descended over the city and touched down near Lake Phewa. My heartbeat picked up. We were still taxiing, but I felt as raw and jittery as the last time I was here. I swallowed hard. All the emotions were flooding back.

"I have a great surprise for you, Alex." Jack's melodious baritone echoed in my ears.

Pokhara, Nepal

June 3

This is a colossal mistake.

Collin was right. Too much too soon. Instead of closure, I was going to re-live the pain all over again. Part of me wanted to turn around, catch the first flight back to Dubai, and bury myself in work.

Don't be such a chicken, I chided myself and caught a taxi to my hotel.

Escaping the grief won't do. Sixteen-hour workdays didn't work in Dallas. The more I wanted to get away from the grief, the more it latched onto me. I had to face it, embrace it, and let it run its course.

Easier said than done.

My fingers trembled when I counted the rupees for the taxi fare. The driver wished me a good stay. "You'll love Pokhara, miss."

I rolled my trolley to the reception desk and checked in. The young man behind the counter was reciting something about the spa and breakfast and checkout times, but I hardly listened. I was drowning in self-doubt.

That's exactly what Vivien was after. Vivien excelled in triggering self-doubt in anyone who crossed her path. Her lies ruthlessly exploited the smallest cracks in people's confidence in order to blast through and let her get her way. My self-doubt was Vivien's best friend.

I dropped the trolley in my room and rushed to the travel agency on Lake Side. My trekking cure couldn't start soon enough.

The agency was completely empty. Strange, they were bursting at the seams last year. I looked at the board with available tours. All tours were crossed out.

A banner announced that due to bad weather conditions, all trekking tours were cancelled until further notice.

"When will the tours start again?" I asked the clerk.

"We don't know."

"What's your guess?"

"Ten days. Two weeks maybe." My heart sank. I didn't have that much time.

"Can I get a private guide take me to a safer area?"

"No. You don't want to be up there. Lots of flooding."

"Mud everywhere," another clerk said.

I left the agency and walked down to the Phewa, feeling sorry for myself. Three gliders slowly circled above the far side of the lake. Free as birds. I envied them.

I mindlessly followed the path along the water, my losses weighing me down.

And then it hit me:

How come you feel so heavy when you lost so much?
I have nothing more to lose. I am free.

The jitters were gone. I walked on and ended up at the small teahouse I had visited before, totally at peace.

In a flash I saw myself from a bird's eye view. My whole life was like climbing a steep mountain wall. The only way to get off the wall was to reach the peak, which would set me free and earn me the right to be fully me. Assuming that my life would start after I made it to the top, I strived to achieve, give my best, climb higher and higher. And lost everything I cared about.

All I had left was me. The real deal. Rain or shine, peaks or valleys, climbing or not climbing. And it was *my* life all along. I didn't have to climb to the top for permission to be me. All it took was to *be* me.

Ahhh… It was a good thing to come here after all. I sat back, stretched my legs and took in the scenery.

Heavy clouds rolled over the horizon. The peak of Machapuchare stayed stubbornly hidden, making all uninitiated believe that it didn't exist, that all the bright pictures in the tourist shops were photoshopped.

Yet, it was a sunny, mild day down here in Pokhara. Boys played soccer near the lake. Birds were chirping. Incense wafted through the air. Nepali prayer flags fluttered on a string tied between "my" teahouse and a wobbly dock, a home to a fleet of rowboats painted in pastel pinks, blues, and greens.

I closed my eyes and pretended that Jack was sitting next to me, sketching in his leather-bound notebook. Our forearms touched and triggered a wave of delight. We rented one of the little boats, caught up with the kids on the other side of the lake and surprised them with tea and cookies.

Jack's face kept disappearing. I tried to hold on to it, but all I saw was Jack's notebook. His sketches, his notes, his doodles. The numbered pages, the inscription on the inside of the cover: Memoires, book number, handmade for Jack Carter. I tried to focus on the book number but couldn't grasp it. It didn't matter—Memoires, the company that made the book, would help me with it. I calculated the time difference between Nepal and Montreal. It was still too early to call them. I'd have to wait at least an hour.

I'll never know with certainty what Jack was up to, but I had a pretty good idea what Vivien did. *You'll not get away with it, Viv.* Not this time. I was ready to fight with everything I had to bring Vivien to justice. I opened my eyes.

And gasped.

Pokhara

Lake Phewa
June 3

"Perry?"

How did he find me? I froze. *Is TW compromised?* I braced myself for the worst, but Perry's eyes were telling me I had nothing to fear. They were transmitting a message filled with love, tenderness, concern.

Perry sat next to me and wrapped his arms around my shoulders. It felt like the most natural thing in the world. A wave of tingles opened a book I assumed shut. Tears streamed down my cheeks. The comfort of Perry's arms melted my defenses, and the grief I had held in check since the crash flooded Perry's shirt.

It would have been so easy to disappear into Perry's soothing embrace. But I had a job to do. TW would not wait. I allowed myself a few more luxurious seconds and asked, "Perry, why are you here?"

"Because I love you."

Our eyes locked. Time stopped. Our souls embraced.

See, you didn't lose it all. A message raised from a place I didn't know existed. *You longed for this. Enjoy it.*

"I love you too," I heard myself saying from the depth of my soul.

"Oh, Lexi."

I closed my eyes and felt Perry's lips on mine.

Everything would have been different had I gone to Dubai before going to Dallas, I thought. Perhaps, but who knows what would have happened? The past is the past. *Cherish now.*

"I fell in love with you when I saw your picture in the SKY Club. And I knew we were meant to be together since the moment we first touched." Perry gave me another kiss.

"I felt it too, but it was so unexpected. I didn't think it was possible and there was so much going on, it took me a long time to sort out my feelings," I admitted.

"I didn't know how to...and then I didn't trust you for a while," Perry's face crumbled. "I am so sorry about that. But when Liz said you were moving to Dubai, I knew I had to break through the doubts and trust in us. Lexi, please don't move to Dubai."

I swallowed hard. I couldn't share anything about TW with Perry.

"I have a job to do, Perry."

"In Dubai? What are you going to do?"

"Just keep doing what I do." That was as close to truth as I could get.

"Lexi, there are plenty of designers to equip bathrooms with golden faucets. It's a waste of your talent."

Perry gave me an earnest look. A bit angry, actually. But his words confirmed that my story worked: I had convinced Liz that I was moving to Dubai. Hopefully she was spreading the word around.

I hated misleading Liz and Perry, but compromising TW wasn't an option. There was no turning back. Now, what to do with Perry? *Ask for help*.

"Perry, can you give me two weeks to decide about the final move?"

"Why?"

I took a deep breath. I had to be honest with Perry without giving anything away. *If he truly loves you, he will give you the space.*

Perry watched me, waiting for my answer.

"Because of a job I must finish. It's very important to me."

Perry looked at me, surprised.

"Wait... So you haven't made a final decision yet?"

I slowly shook my head.

Shadows clouded Perry's eyes. I prayed Liz and Perry would forgive me when this was over. Perry was deep in thought. Then he looked up.

"Got it. I think." His face lit up in a huge smile.

"I am Plan B," he said. "And you must be Plan A."

Don't talk about TW with anyone! I gave Perry my best poker face. Yet, *he* was obviously not worried about sharing classified information. *What's going on?*

Perry grinned and reached into a pocket of his cargo pants.

I froze.

Pokhara

Lake Phewa

"We are on the same team, Lexi." Perry retrieved a phone. "Plans A and B came together. You are the personal angle and I the political one and now it's just one plan," he said and clicked on a contact.

"Yes." Deep, pleasant voice.

"Hey. I am talking with her. But you have to convince her that I am the legit B."

"Sure." Collin laughed. "I knew you would put one and one together."

"Here she is." Perry handed me the phone.

"Hi."

"Hi. There is a new development. Our Plan B man wanted to get in touch with you, and I've asked him to give you a lift to your next destination."

"Let me call you back." I wasn't taking any risks. I took out my phone and dialed.

"Yes." The same deep, pleasant voice.

"Please repeat what you've just told me."

"Hi. Our Plan B man wanted to get in touch with you, and I've asked him to give you a lift to your next destination because we have a new development."

It was Collin and not a tape. I could breathe again. "Oh man. Thank you. You've made my day."

"And you've made mine." Collin chuckled. "I want to hire you full time. Anyhow, how are you?"

"As good as new. Ready to go."

"That was quick."

"All it took was a bit of fresh air."

"Good. We are on a roll here. Things are happening quicker than anticipated. We need you to do the interview in three days. I'll give you the details in an hour or so."

"OK. Now, what's the deal? How much may A and B share?" I asked.

"Everything. You are a team now."

Perry and I melted in a heartfelt hug. We had a much better chance to defeat Vivien together than alone.

"So, let's get to know each other." Perry smiled and ordered Nepali lemon tea for us.

"Yes. And I have to make an urgent phone call. It's part of it." I clicked the number.

"Memoires. What can I do for you today?"

"Hi, I ordered one of your books for my husband some time ago, but I forgot the model. Could you help me with that?"

"Sure. What's his name?"

"Jack Carter." I heard fingers sprinting over the keys.

"Got it. It's the ML1, our medium leather-bound model. It was made for Mr. Carter almost two years ago."

"Thank you. I thought there was another book made for him later."

"Let me check."

I held my breath.

"Could it be under another name?"

"Yes, Vivien Carter or Vivien Gibson."

"Vivien Carter. MP2. That's the paper-bound model with somewhat thinner pages. Made in October of last year."

October! Two months after the crash. My fingers trembled.

"Thank you so much. I'll have to think about the model."

"No problem. Here are the serial numbers to speed up the reorder. The ML1 is 3439 and the MP2 is 9352."

Perry scribbled the numbers on a napkin.

"3439 and 9352," I repeated. "Great. Thanks again."

"She faked the will." Perry took my hands in his.

"Yes. And she convinced a judge to believe her. She's getting away with murder."

Perry shook his head.

"I bet she has something to do with the pics of the Jaguar, too," he said.

A memory flashed in my mind and disappeared before I could grasp it. Frustrated, I returned my attention to Perry.

"I know she does. The pictures resided on the same VPS as the SenHowdy21 sexting video."

Perry gasped. "How do you know?"

"Trey discovered it. I'll tell you about Trey in a sec. Anyhow, the alex-at-carterco-dot-me email, from which one of the pictures came, originated from that VPS as well. Vivien, or whoever has access to that VPS, rerouted the email and made it look like it came from my IP." It felt good to get this off my chest.

"Jeez. I can't tell you how sorry I am I ever considered..." Perry's eyes told volumes.

"You couldn't have known and I wasn't allowed to tell you. It feels good to share it now." We hugged. The pain melted away.

"By the way, how did you get involved with Collin?" I asked.

"After the sexting-gate. We detected a series of highly unusual attacks on Richard's computers around that time. That's when Collin came in. The attacks looked unrelated to Vivien's sexting tape, but we didn't find their source. A few weeks later Collin let me in on the full scope of his operation. I had no idea Vivien was part of it. Collin didn't use people's names and I would never associate her with such a high-tech scheme."

Perry's eyes darkened, just like when he showed me the pictures of the Jaguar the last time.

"Oh my God." I gasped. The memory came fully back to me.

"What, Lexi?" Perry looked alarmed.

"The envelope," I said. "Do you still have the envelope the pictures of the Jag came in?"

"Yes. In fact, I have two of them."

"Good. The memory of it just flashed back in my mind, but I couldn't place it."

"I hate when that happens."

"Yeah, but I've got this one. It's the envelope. Some time ago Vivien broke into my house. She was sitting at my kitchen counter when I came back from running."

"Ugh."

"Yeah. She claimed the reason for her visit was to bring some photos Jack forgot. The pics were in the same envelope as your pictures of the Jag. I remember it because the envelope had an unusual color."

"Pissy yellowish green." Perry nodded and grabbed his phone. "Do you still have your envelope Lexi?"

"You bet." I told Perry how I preserved that piece of evidence.

"Which means we have her DNA and fingerprints, if they still use that." Perry rubbed his chin. "If the envelopes match, she is careless."

"Yes. She is." I told him about the perfectly matching signatures on Vivien's invoices. "I count on her carelessness, but we shouldn't underestimate her."

We arranged for our envelopes to be compared and analyzed, and I texted Emma the information from Memoires.

"Now, to be practical, what's the destination I am taking you to?" Perry asked. "Collin never told me."

"At least he kept part of the confidentiality deal intact. We are going to Saint Crooks."

"The Caribbean?"

"Yes."

"I'll let the pilot know. Now, should we head somewhere for dinner and perfect our Saint Crooks strategy?"

"Yes, we have three days to become a team."

"Uh-uh." Perry shook his head and kissed me. "We have a lifetime to do that."

Pokhara

The Pokhara Lodge
June 3

"Lexi, why did you think it was impossible for us to be together?" Perry nuzzled me tenderly.

"Because I was married... And you are younger than I and have all these gorgeous models."

"The models were only for charity events. And I am not that much younger."

I didn't say anything. Perry interpreted my silence as an invitation to fortify his argument.

"Most men marry younger women, yet at least fifty percent of marriages end in divorce. It's not in the age."

Perry presided over the king-size bed, grinning.

Moonlight slid through the French doors and veiled our room in magic. I studied Perry's profile. Exquisite. Life surely takes unexpected twists and turns.

I ran my hand through Perry's sun-bleached hair and then traced his forehead, nose, and lips with my finger. He kissed the finger, the palm of my hand, and my forearm, pulling me closer to him. I loved feeling his strong body. This was the first time in my life I was in love but not taken over by it. Bliss...

Curiosity got the better of me and I propped myself up on my elbow.

"Perry, when did you *know* we could be together?"

"Deep down, since I saw your picture I believed we would be together. But when you told me 'You too, Perry' during our last lunch, I knew I couldn't wait for the right moment any longer. There was so much love in your eyes."

"That's when I realized for the first time how much I love you."

"I felt that. I loved you so much, but I wasn't sure I could trust you. I felt horrible. I ran after you, but you were gone. I didn't know what to do. I tried to buy your house, was bidding like crazy, imagining giving you

THE WALL

the keys back, but at the last moment I realized you probably wouldn't want that. If you wanted to stay in DD you would have found a way."

"Oh my...you were the mysterious second bidder." I looked at Perry, astonished. "And you were right. I couldn't live in the house anymore. It's just... I loved DD, but I can't." I bit my lip. "Well, someone wanted the house badly."

"My grandma."

"Your grandma?"

"Yeah. Gloria. I guess she doesn't know she is my grandma."

"Gloria Lowell?"

"You know her?"

"I know about her. But I didn't know she bought the house."

"I traced her to the company that bought it."

"A company?" I gasped. "The koi... Joyce said that a person bought DD, not a company. I hope they'll take care of the koi. Underwater Paradise will feed them to the end of the month." I was thinking out loud. "I didn't want to uproot them unnecessarily. The koi, I mean. But I should've."

Perry took me in his arms and held me tight.

"It will be OK, Lexi. From what I hear, Grandma likes animals more than people. And she is on the board of a charity that protects animals. I am sure the koi miss you, but they'll be fine."

I let out a deep breath.

"Did they eat out of your hand?" Perry asked.

"Yes."

Perry told me how he loved to feed the koi in his Dubai office. And then he shared his aha moment.

"All this time after the plane crash, I didn't trust you. There was so much BS floating around, I didn't know what to believe. It's tough to sort things out when good people repeat bad stories." Perry frowned. "But when you told me 'you too' and walked out on me, I realized I was focusing on the wrong person. I thought I couldn't trust you, but the truth was I didn't trust myself. I longed to be with you, I was dying to be there for you, but I didn't trust I could handle it if things didn't work between us."

Now it was my turn to hold Perry tight.

"I've struggled with this my whole life, Lexi. I wouldn't trust anyone, except in business. I can do deals with people because I believe I can handle it if they don't deliver. It took me forever to figure out that relationships weren't much different."

I told Perry about my struggles, the nightmare of not knowing what Jack truly did, about climbing a "mountain" my whole life and discovering only this afternoon that I didn't have to do that. That all I had to do was to be me.

"That's two sides of the same coin," Perry said, "being yourself and trusting yourself."

We lay in each other's arms, two ships used to rough seas resting in a safe haven.

"You know what's the strangest thing about encountering Vivien?" I asked.

"That it made us stronger."

"Yes." I nodded. "I can't stand her, I despise her behavior, yet, crossing her path made my life richer, more precious. It's difficult to describe."

"I know what you mean," Perry said. "These things derail you and you can never get back on your old path. Clearing a new path for yourself is tough but can be mightily rewarding." Perry took my hands and told me about his mom's accident and how afterwards he had only worked and didn't have a life until he went back to Houston and reconnected with Dave.

"That's why we missed each other in Dubai the first time, Lexi."

"I wondered many times about that. What would have happened."

"Maybe this is how it's supposed to be." Perry kissed me.

"Yes, maybe I had to go through this whole thing with Jack first." To let go of unrealistic dreams. To find myself.

"And maybe we had to learn how to overcome all the deception," Perry replied.

"Speaking of deception, it's not over yet." I shivered.

We switched to Saint Crooks and Marty. Speaking with Marty was high on my list for months, but Collin didn't want to alarm him until everything else was in place. Collin was right. All I wanted to know right after the crash was whether Marty was involved in the fraud and I could get Carter & Co's money back from him. The stakes had gone up since then: we were counting on Marty's relationship with Vivien to crack the Wall.

"She uses people," I said. "He must have done enough chores for her to learn a thing or two about her shady dealings. The question is, will he play?" The warm look in Marty's eyes at the end of our last meeting gave me hope.

"Oh, he definitely did a lot for her." Perry told me about Vivien's marketing scam.

"That's terrible. I never trusted Marty, but this…" I shook my head.

"The word is that he didn't know what he got himself into. She tricked him, used him, and dumped him."

"That could help us."

"Well, if he doesn't play, we'll play him to push the first domino."

Our goal was to provoke Marty to cause panic and push Vivien to careless digital transactions, which would allow Collin's techs to break through and collect crucial evidence.

Perry studied his phone. "The techs will get on board in Kingstown. It's just a short hop to Saint Crooks from there, but it will give them enough time to explain to us how everything works."

"Nice. We can get straight to business when we land."

"And avoid suspicious rendezvous on Saint Crooks."

Perry was right. This operation wasn't without risks. And it was about so much more than Vivien. I took a deep breath, taming fears.

"The second tech team will be waiting for us on Saint Crooks, but we will not have direct contact with them." Perry finished his briefing and looked at me. "Are you ready?"

"You bet."

Saint Crooks

The Vic's
June 6

The olive looked bigger than life. It was suspended on the Vic's see-through, trademarked cocktail spear that made the olive look as if it hovered in the center of the extra-large martini all on its own. Illuminated by sunrays passing through the sharply cut crystal glass, the olive reigned.

Mesmerized, Marty could not take his eyes off it.

This particular olive, the queen of all olives, marked Marty's fourth martini. He downed the first three cocktails like bitter medicine, their olives totally lost on him. But the fourth olive got his attention. He gazed down at this bright green, sparkling universe convinced that it was sending him signals.

For days he prayed for a sign that would show him the way. The olive answered his prayers. Marty wanted to take another sip of his martini but did not dare disturb the olive's vital broadcast. Yet, what was she saying?

"Is it time to go?" Marty asked expectantly, his eyes glued to the olive. The message was right in front of him, but he didn't understand it. He did not have the code!

The hope that filled him a few moments ago drained to the ground.

Marty took a gulp of the martini. And then another one. The olive was suspended in midair. Marty stared at it incredulously.

Did it laugh at him?

Why is this happening to me? Marty didn't understand. He did everything right, yet everything went wrong.

He would kill to feel again like he felt when he came to the Vic's after quitting Dallas. He had it all. Freedom, money, and a place in paradise. He had made it.

He had made it only to discover that he had lost it all.

A tropical storm was approaching the island.

"Is it time to go?" Marty asked, flustered.

The olive remained mum.

Saint Crooks

The Vic's patio
The same day

The Vic's was surprisingly busy for this time of day, which was the perfect cover for my mission. Most of the crowd were boaters who came ashore because of the hurricane warning. The patio was filled with people watching the dark clouds in the distance, taking pictures, speculating whether the tropical storm would turn into a hurricane and reach the Crooks Islands.

The locals didn't think so. They predicted the storm would stay to the north and land in the US Virgin Islands or Puerto Rico. Or turn even further north and head in the direction of the Bahamas and Miami.

The wind was picking up. The sky was getting darker by the minute. I had two hours max to get my job done and get out of here. I took a deep breath and stepped inside the Vic's.

Marty sat at the bar, staring intently into his drink. He looked different, and it wasn't just the absence of a business suit. His shoulders were slouched, his customary arrogance gone. The salt and pepper curls were more salt than pepper. I walked over to the bar, not sure what to expect.

"Hello, Marty," I said.

Marty jumped up. His foot caught in the base of the bar stool. He flailed his arms and sent his martini glass flying. The sparkling crystal tumbled in the air and slowly descended to the stone floor where it shattered into hundreds of pieces.

A giant olive hopped over the shards and stopped by my foot.

Marty stared at the olive, mesmerized.

"Shards bring luck," I said, assessing Marty.

"I certainly need some," Marty said, looking like he went from drunk to crystal-clear sober in two seconds.

"So do I. Let's sit down in one of the booths."

In the corner of my eye I saw Perry and two techs taking a booth next to us as we planned. Good. Marty's fingers were mindlessly sliding over the wooden table, giving me the shivers.

"So, what have you been up to?" I asked.

"Ugh…eh… I was just contemplating suicide." Marty lifted his head and gave a tiny smile.

"Well, the possibility of suicide has saved many lives," I said gently.

"Why didn't I think of that?" Marty straightened up, his eyes sparkling.

"Neither did I," I said, astonished to witness Marty's second transformation within minutes. He looked as if the weight of the universe slid off his shoulders.

"No, no, that's not what I mean, Alex. I studied Nietzsche. But I never understood this statement. Until now. Thank you."

This was definitely not the Marty I knew.

"I am not going to beat around the bush, Marty. I am here because I need your help."

"What can I do?"

"Tell me what you know about some financial transactions between Vivien and Carter & Co."

"Sure."

"OK. Do you remember this invoice?" I showed Marty the first $5K invoice.

"Yes. Vivien gave it to me."

"And you submitted it to Jack for authorization?"

"No." Marty looked straight at me. "It was already signed by Jack."

"How about these invoices?" I put Vivien's artwork in front of Marty.

His eyebrows knitted. "I haven't seen any of them before."

"They are signed by you."

"I didn't sign them."

I lined up all the invoices and held them against the light. Marty leaned forward to look. "Oh my God…she…"

"I take it you didn't make these transfers?"

Marty shook his head.

"Who could have?"

"Jamie was the only authorized person besides me."

"Jamie didn't. Could Jack have done it?"

"No way." Marty laughed. "I mean he had the authority, but Jack didn't make one payment in all the years I worked for Carter & Co. He wouldn't have known how to get into the system. Didn't even have a sign-on. Delegated all the financial stuff."

The same response as Stan's. Relieved, I leaned forward to ask Marty about the trickier issues, but he had his own story to tell.

"I am sorry, Alex," Marty said. "I should have caught this. To be honest, I noticed a couple of the recurring payments. I wanted to ask Jack about it, but I didn't want to pry. I thought Vivien talked Jack into paying her some extra money. At that time I believed her stories about you and thought she deserved more. I've learned the hard way…"

And Marty went on to tell me about his involvement with Vivien. His story was not much different than Victor's. Savior turned into slave and dumped as soon as she had no use for him. Another person brought down by Vivien. I wondered how many were there.

"I was really distracted at that time. Vivien always wanted something," Marty went on. "That's not an excuse. I will fully cooperate with any investigation. And take the consequences. But Alex, these invoices couldn't have bankrupted Carter & Co."

"No, it was the 2.4 million dollars Vivien transferred out of our account when Jack and I went to India."

"2.4?"

"Yeah, that's what nearly bankrupted us. And plundered our pension fund." I showed Marty a copy of the transaction. He sucked his breath in, speechless.

"What do you know about Vivien's offshore accounts?" I seized my moment.

"A lot. I set them up for her. I can probably still get into the account she has here." Marty took out his laptop and moved to my side of the booth so that I could see the screen.

We were getting somewhere.

"Let's jump in." Marty punched a few keys. A new screen popped up.

I suppressed a gasp.

The Vic's

"That's a unique background picture," I heard myself saying. My heart was thumping.

"That's Vivien's." Marty responded matter-of-factly. "She uses a special laptop to access her offshore accounts. She has it with her at all times. Calls it 'my Little Fella.' I bet she sleeps with it, too." Marty chuckled.

That explained why Vivien always carried that huge faux crocodile bag. But I had a much bigger question on my mind.

"Are you in that laptop now?"

"Yes. Vivien didn't want her home IP to be connected with Little Fella, so I made a shortcut for her that makes it look as if she signed on from somewhere in Arizona. I used the shortcut to get in now."

Collin's techs must be salivating. If all went as planned, their bots were tracing Marty's every move.

"I see. I've never seen a wallpaper made of a smashed Jaguar. Have you?" *This one is for you, Perry.*

"No. Vivien calls it her lifesaver. Said it motivates her. Reminds her that anything is possible."

Marty tried to sign into Vivien's bank account. The first attempt didn't go through. I held my breath.

"I probably misspelled it." Marty sighed. "I always misspell the first attempt."

Marty entered the login again, the screen changed and showed the account summary.

"Voila!" Marty triumphed. "This is unbelievable, you know." He shook his head. "She hacks everyone but never changes her own passwords."

"Vivien hacks everyone?"

"Man, and how. That's her passion. She lives for gossip. Read all your emails, you know."

I knew. But how did Marty? I asked him.

"Because Viv bragged about it. She used to read stuff from your emails to me. Like Jack calling you his DG."

I winced. Knowing that someone hacked my email was infuriating, hearing intimate details like the Dream Girl nickname from a third party was a whole new ballgame. *I'll get you, Viv.* I wanted to find out more about Vivien's hacking, but her account was the first priority.

"So, we've got a balance of more than two million. $2,321,869.45." Marty's eyes lit up.

He scrolled down and I saw a lot of deposits, but not the last transfer from Carter & Co.

"The $2.4 million didn't come to this account." I looked at the copy of the transfer. "In fact, this account has different number then the one on the invoices," I said.

"That's because the money goes first to the account in the Caymans, which is on the invoices, and then is rerouted through several untraceable accounts before it comes here."

"How long did it take you to set up these offshore accounts?"

"No more than fifteen minutes. Vivien had the instructions on her Little Fella. I just followed it step by step."

Did Vivien's friend provide the instructions?

"I'd like to take pictures of these deposits. Who knows, maybe we'll be able to recover some of the money."

"Sure."

"I wonder what Vivien did with the 2.4 million," I said while checking that my pics covered everything relevant.

"Are you sure she did it?"

"She admitted it to Jack," I gambled. "She said she needed the money to pay off a bad investment."

"Oh my God." Marty's eyes opened wide. "She said she'd make Jack pay for it, but I didn't think she meant it literally." Marty flipped through the invoices.

"See this one? That's the $150K for the original investment," Marty said, excited. "Vivien was pushing me to make the same investment, but I refused. That's what broke us up. I refused and told her not to do it and she got furious with me. And then all hell broke loose when the investment went bust."

"When was that?"

"About a week after I got here."

Just before we went to India. "Did she tell you how much money she owed?"

"Yes, it was more than two million. She sent me an email. I'll look for it. So, where should the money go?" Marty looked at me.

I didn't understand at first. Then I got it.

"Marty, if you are thinking what I am thinking, it's a no go."

"No, it's not. I am still authorized to manage this account to the best advantage of Ms. Gibson and her businesses."

"Marty."

"And the best for Carter & Co, which Ms. Gibson claims she owns now, is to put the money in the pension fund." Marty smiled. "And it's also the least I can do to correct my negligence."

The light blinked. I looked outside. It was dark and windy. The patio was almost empty, except for a few enthusiasts and the waiters who were taking down the large umbrellas.

"Let's do this quickly." Marty worked the keyboard in deep concentration.

"Do you have the current account number of the pension fund?" he asked.

"Yes." I retrieved it from a file on my phone, thanking Collin's techs for transferring it from my old phone, which was still in Dubai.

"How much money did she take from Carter & Co? In total."

"2.73 million."

"Let's transfer about 2.3 million and leave some change in the account, just in case." Marty set up the transfer, typed 'Loan installment payment, outstanding balance $408,200.00' in the memo section, double checked everything, and clicked on complete transaction.

"Done."

I could hardly believe what I had witnessed.

"Let's get something to drink. What would you like, Alex?"

"Just water, please."

Marty waved a waiter over to the booth. "Hey, bring us two sparkling waters, will ya?"

"Thanks for helping out, Marty."

Our waters arrived. Marty almost emptied his glass in one sitting.

"OK. I was going to look for the email from Vivien."

I sipped slowly while Marty scrolled through pages of emails, my hands shaking.

"What the… It must be here. Hm… Oh wait. Got it! Here you go, take a pic."

I read the email word by word.

Marty went through the papers on the table and took out the copy of the $2.4 million transfer. "Where is the account number? Here. Let's… It's a match." Marty gave me a fist bump.

The $2.4 million went to the Hugh Donaldson investment fund, which ordered Vivien Gibson to pay it in the email Marty just retrieved. This was a solid proof of Vivien's involvement in the fraud.

It's too good to be true. The skeptic in me couldn't believe the information was real. It all went too easy. But I took a picture of the email anyhow.

Marty and I sat in silence for a few moments.

"You know what puzzles me, Marty?"

"That she paid the money?"

"Yes. Vivien never paid a bill unless she absolutely had to."

"There you have it. I bet Donaldson scared the living daylights out of her. He is one of the biggest crooks around, as crooked as the Brazos."

A message popped on my phone.

UNKNOWN: *Bet on the right horse! Wrap it up*

An ominous wind gust leaped in from the patio. The storm joined the party. The lights blinked.

Startled "aaaahs" resonated through the Vic's.

The Vic's

Marty checked his connection with the Little Fella. It was still on. He took a deep breath, relieved. This was his opportunity to settle the score with Viv, and he was fired up to get on with it.

"I better get going." Alex stood up.

Marty slid out the booth and hugged her.

"Thank you, Marty."

"Anytime. Be careful, Vivien has some powerful connections and lots of favors to call in."

"What do you mean?"

"The hacking. You and Jack weren't her only targets. She's got lots of dirt on lots of people. Judges, politicians, you name it. She used to brag that she knows more about politicians than anyone in Texas. Especially about the two senators."

"You mean Senator Howard and Senator Lowell?"

"Yup, and their staff. Remember the sexting scandal? She was actually sexting with Lowell. He used the Howdy21 name. Vivien wanted something from him, but he wouldn't budge, so she made the sexting public. It was a warning for Lowell, letting him know that she could put him in a world of pain at her whim."

"But it was Senator Howard who ended in a world of pain." Alex looked puzzled.

"Vivien didn't care about that. I was there when she made the video. She giggled like crazy, thrilled that she got them both."

"But why?"

"She loves to have the upper hand on people."

"I see... Well, take good care of yourself too, Marty." Alex gave him a big smile. "And keep up the good work," she added with a wink.

Marty chuckled. "Do you need a ride?" he asked.

"No, thanks."

Marty watched her leave the Vic's and then returned to his laptop, happy smile on his face. His good work wasn't finished yet.

He checked once more that the bank transfer was in order, thinking about the many times he had urged Vivien to tighten the security on her account. Now he was thankful that she had adamantly refused to follow his advice.

"I want to get my money when I want it. I am not going to wait for some banker's approval. It's my money." Vivien had yelled at Marty, forbidding him to set up any transfer precautions. And now her money was on its way to Carter & Co.

"Gotcha!" Marty grinned.

The banking business out of his way, Marty composed a press release and scheduled it to be sent out from Vivien's account the next day.

Then he cleaned all evidence of being in the Little Fella. Nothing like using Vivien's own methods to undo her. *Hack the hacker*. Satisfied with his progress, Marty signaled Tim and ordered the hurricane special. A burger topped with a fried egg was what the doctor ordered.

Marty had a long evening ahead of him.

Dallas

The War Room
June 7

"We are ready to go." Not a muscle moved in Collin's face.

The War Room had been transformed to an ultramodern communication center. Only one branch of the TW flowchart was still on the wall. The rest was covered with large screens. One of them cycled through images of "my" apartment building in Dubai.

The island in the center of the room hummed with computers. Coffee cups, empty soda bottles and pizza boxes attested to the team's long hours. The War Room had operated 24/7 since the day I left for Dubai. And so had Collin...

Perry and I came here directly from the airport. We'd flown in from Miami in the morning, bringing back the two tech crews and a group of kids from an orphanage in Miami that had been evacuated in case the hurricane hit. The busy flight helped me keep my nerves in check but being in the War Room made the stress almost unbearable. I took a deep breath.

The tension had been escalating since we'd left the Vic's. Collin had ordered us to leave Saint Crooks immediately, not wanting to subject our operation to potential sabotage. The storm disagreed. A wind gust almost blew the door off my car when I got out at the airport. The pounding rain soaked me within seconds. The pilots and Collin went back and forth assessing the pros and cons of staying and leaving. Leaving won.

We outflew the storm's hellishness, but Perry and I had held hands all the way to Miami, our jubilation about cracking the Wall tempered by the events that were about to unravel. We had promised to each other that no matter what happened we would handle it. Together. As one.

Collin called us as soon as we landed in Miami. "Hit the jackpot, kiddos!" I detected traces of excitement in Collin's usually guarded voice. His techs had virtually taken control of Little Fella and intercepted a key communication, which had led to more intercepts.

The Wall was cracked, the target under siege. We were ready to go.
"All units: sign in!" Collin ordered.
"D1 in"
"D2 in"
"D3 in"
"D4 in"
"H1 in"
"H2 in"
Perry squeezed my hand.
The waiting began.

Dallas

The Obsidian
The same time

Vivien stirred her second margarita and inserted the smoky black straw in her mouth. Her suction power would put a Dyson to shame.

Soothed, she surveyed the bar. "Smoke and mirrors of the most delightful kind. And the biggest drinks in town," the Observer wrote about Dallas's newest and hottest *it* spot. Vivien agreed. The drinks were huge. As they should be.

True to its namesake, the Obsidian boasted all black interior. Its dark, shiny walls seemed fluid, thanks to the strips of tinted mirrors that reflected the slightest movement in the space. A rare obsidian specimen weighting 126.43 pounds dominated the bar top. It mesmerized guests and seduced them to touch its silky surface. The rock allegedly possessed the power to remove negativity, a feat many a happy toucher attested to. Vivien sneered.

She did not need the giant obsidian to cheer her up. No sir. Vivien was elated all on her own. She could not imagine a better ending to her crusade.

The slut was out of town, running for her life. Hiding in Dubai. Ruined.

What a glorious revenge for all the suffering Alex put Vivien through. But Vivien didn't give up. Vivien persisted and got her life back. With interest.

You have to think positive. Vivien nodded as if she were interviewed on a talk show. She considered herself a positive person. Vivien believed in her right to win and she won. It was that simple.

She gave herself another margarita boost. *God knows I deserve it.*

High on righteousness, Vivien sat back and flopped her backless high heel sandal against the bottom of her foot. She admired her shocking pink toe nails, filled with pride.

She was no longer the gray mouse eclipsed by her actress sister and richly married brother. She was rich, and she made the national media!

Inflated by her achievement, Vivien scanned the crowd but didn't recognize anybody. *Too bad.* She wanted to share her victory. You've got to share the good things. The more you give, the more you get back.

Vivien shifted in her chair, suddenly bored. With Jack dead and Alex out of town, all the excitement had faded out of her life.

Vivien scanned the crowd again. No one she knew. Only young people. Most of them younger than her children.

The thought of Victor and Jen clouded Vivien's jubilant mood. Vivien wanted to swipe the cloud away, but it was too large. Its darkness swallowed her and filled her with all-consuming rage. *How dare they!* After all her sacrifices, they failed to keep her and Jack together. And then accused her, their own mother, of cheating and stealing.

Vivien's fingers spasmed into killer fists.

It was all Alex's doing.

Alex befriended Victor and Jen and poisoned their minds. Fooled Jen, the ugly duckling, into believing that she became a swan. And even Victor barely answered Vivien's texts.

The injustice of it twisted Vivien's face into a hard grimace. But Vivien never gave up.

How foolish of Victor and Jen to assume they could abandon their own mother. They hadn't learned a thing from what happened to Jack.

Vivien took the last sip of her margarita and smirked. She imagined Victor and Jen's faces dropping when she walked in on their dinner later tonight. They'd crawl back to her after she announced her spectacular news. *They'll have no choice but do as I say.*

Vivien had a plan.

Dallas

The Art Tower
The same time

He, too, had a plan.

Revenge.

He parked his dark luxury sedan and scanned the terrain. Satisfied that nothing prevented him from executing his exercise, he strolled towards the Sky Gondolas. His perfectly fitting suit, crisp shirt, elaborately stitched cowboy boots and a fine leather briefcase put him on a par with the tower's regulars. Anyone seeing him would assume he was a banker, CEO, or a top-tier attorney.

His eyes told a different story. He was a man at war.

Those who sent him running would suffer as they never suffered before. Their days as prosperous Dallasites were numbered. There was no hiding from him.

Returning to the city fueled his resentment. Walking through the streets of Dallas and inhaling the smells he grew up with rubbed in how much had been taken away from him. All the good years he had been robbed of when he was forced to move from place to place, deep in hiding.

His fury swelled like a hot air balloon.

As always, fury made him bigger than life. It supercharged his faculties and let him soar above the pitiful worms. He sought revenge with a singleness of purpose unmatched by his opponents. Everyone, every single one, involved in this gruesome injustice would be destroyed. Slowly and surely. The hit list was long, but his thirst for avenging himself knew no bounds.

He'd hide no more. He was back, thanks to the fine Brazilian plastic surgeon, and he was here to stay. He came out of hiding earlier than planned, but he couldn't resist such an easy opportunity to annihilate his adversaries. Dead or alive.

He snorted.

The Art Tower hit was only a small job, but no job was too small for him. He craved the action. He craved feeling his own power.

No one entered the Gondola on its way to the fifty-third floor. He strolled out, confidently swiped his entry card and entered the dark, empty offices.

Outlived you, Jack, he sniggered. *And outsmarted you. Again. You should have never crossed me, you old fool.*

The office he was looking for was to the right from the reception desk, the fifth one down. He walked through the secretary's room without stopping and settled himself in the inner sanctum. The target computer was turned on. Careless.

He opened his briefcase and went to work. It took him only a few minutes to get into Carter & Co's bank account. He sneered.

There it was. Ten million dollars deposited this morning from OMG Mutual Insurance. OMG Mutual kept its word. He liked that.

Viv is surely salivating. He sneered again. The poor thing can't wait to get her little hands on this windfall but can't get into the account because the hack he had given her earlier was cut off. All Carter & Co's accounts were temporarily frozen, and no one could get in. Except him.

Vivien had no choice but beg him to create a new hack for her. But her greed had frozen her brains and she failed to tell him that this OMG bonus was on its way. He smirked. Did she think that he'd buy her story about wanting to monitor the account? Silly girl. So foolish to assume that she could cross him. HIM!

He smoothly transferred the ten million to his safe haven.

Outsmarted you Viv, you big bad girl.

He prepared a downloadable version of the hack for Vivien, enabling her to enter Carter & Co's account and witness the carnage with her very eyes. The few minutes it took him were worth the fun he'd have when she discovered what had happened.

It would be priceless to see her face when she found out the ten million was gone. He chuckled. *Hell, why not?* He didn't have any better plans for this afternoon. He zoomed in on Vivien's location: The Obsidian. The biggest drinks in town.

Why not? He was in a mood for celebration. He closed his briefcase. His work was done.

And then all hell broke loose.

Dallas

The War Room

It happened so quickly, I didn't know which screen to watch.

The arrest squad surrounded Carter & Co as soon as the perpetrator walked in. He settled behind Marty's computer and worked the keyboard like a piano. Then he closed his briefcase, Collin gave the signal, and agents armed to their teeth jumped down from the ceiling. More agents blocked the door to Marty's office.

Not even Houdini could escape from this.

The perp fought but had no chance. The D1 Unit easily overpowered him. They pushed him to the floor, face down, and handcuffed him.

"D1. Got him."

"Great job, wrap."

"Dallas 2, 3, GO!"

"Houston 1, 2 GO!"

I gave Collin the thumbs-up, but he and Perry were already focusing on the newly engaged teams. I followed the Carter & Co operation. The agents jerked the hacker to his feet and took him out of Marty's room.

Vivien's friend? His head was down, and I couldn't see his face. The techs moved in to secure his briefcase and Marty's computer. Another piece of equipment I'll have to replace. Strange what your mind focuses on during a crisis.

H1 was done, D3 got delayed, I heard in the background, but my eyes were glued to the Carter & Co screens. The hacker's head was still down.

H2 had to change plans.

"D4 get ready to move. Watch for any communication from H2 subject." Collin's voice resonated through the War Room.

D2 was done. I wondered if Vivien's security guards had been arrested.

Team D1 was taking the hacker out of Carter & Co. The cameras changed. He looked up.

"Aaaah... It's Dylan!"

Perry came over. "Jeez. That explains a lot. The chutzpa."

"This gives a new meaning to someone spying on you through your toaster," I said.

Perry gave a short laugh and stopped himself. But as soon as we looked at each other, the giggles took over, liberating us from the overpowering tension.

"Who is Dylan?" Collin asked.

"The caterer," Perry and I said, forcing our straight faces back in place.

D3 was finished and Collin congratulated them.

"The caterer? Who is he?" Collin asked.

I took out my phone and scrolled to Dylan's contact information. Collin looked over my shoulder and dispatched a unit to secure Dylan's place.

"He was underneath our nose all this time." Collin wanted to say something else but H2 came in.

Collin's face tightened. H2 was in trouble.

Dallas

The Obsidian

Vivien consulted her oversized watch. Almost ready to go. She scooped Little Fella from her bag.

She waved down the waiter and ordered another margarita. And her second portion of nachos and cheese with extra guacamole on the side.

She checked the time again. Vivien hated waiting.

The waiter brought her the nachos and guac.

"The margarita will be ready in a minute ma'am."

"Why is it taking so long?"

"Our margaritas are one hundred percent handmade. Our bartender prepares them from scratch. Let me tell ya, it's quite a process."

"Ah." Vivien dismissed him and concentrated on the nachos.

She was sporting 168 healthy pounds again, all Alex's fault. It couldn't be expected of her to go through all the legal battles on an empty stomach. My war pounds, Vivien called them and displayed them proudly.

After all, she was an established personality. She did not have to lose her sleep over a pound or two. She was going to make the social pages whether she was size six or sixteen, so why worry about a few extra inches around her waist?

The margarita arrived, and Vivien treated herself to a soothing mega-sip.

The waiting was killing her. He was twelve minutes late. Vivien wasn't the most punctual person, but he was. Vivien rechecked her connection. It was fine, but nothing was coming through. Fear seized her gut.

Maybe it's a mistake and I am an hour early. Vivien tried to calm herself. *It's a time zone error.*

To kill time, she signed in to her offshore account. Reviewing the balance always gave her solace and strength. With her eyes glued to the screen, she absentmindedly sucked on the smoky straw.

The tequila couldn't obliterate her shock. Vivien drew in a sharp breath.

Her prized account showed a balance of $69.45.

Vivien blinked. This can't be right. There must be a mistake. She signed off and signed on again. The account balance was still $69.45. Then she remembered the hurricane. They probably had a power failure.

Vivien fired a quick text to Marty. He'd let her know what was going on.

She expected his answer within a minute or two, but nothing arrived. Vivien's patience reached its limits. She was shaking inside out.

She scrolled down to the transaction section. $2,321,800.00 went to an account she didn't recognize. *Loan installment payment, outstanding balance $408,200.00*, the memo read.

Vivien stamped her feet.

They can't do this to me!!! She sucked on the smoky straw, but all she got was rattling ice cubes. The margarita was as empty as her account.

She looked up to wave the waiter over. Her face was staring down at her from the giant screen.

"Coming next. A Dallas architectural firm gets a much-needed bailout."

Vivien's image was replaced by the Art Tower. Confused, Vivien couldn't take her eyes off the TV.

"There is hope for Carter & Co, the prizewinning Dallas architectural firm that fell on hard times lately." The anchor smiled to the camera.

"The firm struggled since its founder, Jack Carter, tragically died in an airplane crash in Nepal. Speculations about financial fraud and a bitter fight over the firm's ownership kept Carter & Co balancing on the verge of bankruptcy for months."

Vivien's picture filled the screen again while the anchor continued.

"However, in a surprising turn of events, Ms. Vivien Gibson, Mr. Carter's ex-wife, announced today that she is withdrawing from contesting Mr. Carter's last will and will no longer pursue the ownership of the firm.

Moreover, Ms. Gibson announced that she will repay in full the money she had borrowed from the firm prior to Mr. Carter's accident. An initial payment of 2.3 million dollars was made yesterday and the remaining installments will follow shortly."

"NOOOOOOOOOOOOO!" Vivien jumped up and screamed like a wounded animal.

"I didn't repay anything. Carter & Co is MINE!"

A group of young people surrounded Vivien. She tried to reach for Little Fella, but someone yanked her arms behind her back.

"Vivien Gibson, you are under arrest. You have the right to remain silent…"

"NOOOOOOOOOOOOOO!" Vivien screamed again and tried to twist herself free. But two pairs of strong arms rendered her ineffective.

Reality defied Vivien.

Dallas

Perry's penthouse
June 8

My phone chimed nonstop. It was Saturday, but the news of Vivien's arrest spread like a wildfire. People who hadn't exchanged a word with me for months were telling me that they always knew Vivien was wicked. Vincent Russo wanted to buy back his share of Carter & Co and restore the firm to its old glory.

Too little too late. For now, I was responding only to people who'd stuck with me to the end.

Jen and Victor wanted to get together ASAP.

Liz and Rich wanted to have us over for dinner.

Hannah, Thomas and Jamie were organizing a restart meeting on Monday. I had to find out when we would be allowed to use Carter & Co's offices again.

The fiscal lawyers wanted an emergency meeting on Monday too.

Emma wanted to meet immediately, Monday at the latest.

Perry was juggling three phones, a laptop, and an iPad. Marty's news that Richard's staff had been compromised by Vivien hit hard, and Perry and Richard were working around the clock to minimize the damage.

Dave walked into the room with a platter of cherries and freshly baked croissants.

"You two have to eat something."

"You are an angel, Dave," I said. Perry barely looked up.

"That makes the two of us." Dave smiled and walked out as quietly as he came.

Dave and I liked each other since the first moment we met. Before, actually, as Perry told me a lot about Dave when we were sharing our life stories on our way to Saint Crooks.

When Perry and I had come in last night, Dave, Shaun and Lewis had been loudly debating the latest news they were following on TV and several computers.

"Hey, you sound like the talking heads." Perry laughed.

Seconds later we were all embracing in a group hug.

"Oh, so good you are back." Dave gave a relieved smile.

"We were going out of our minds not knowing where you were…"

"You have to tell us everything."

"…every detail…"

"Lexi, take your shoes off. You must be exhausted…" Dave inspected me and Perry. "Although you don't look tired at all."

"Winners are never tired," Shaun quipped.

"Oh man, well done…"

"Well…this is definitely a champagne moment," Dave concluded and went to the fridge to get it. Five champagne flutes were already waiting on the table.

"To love." Dave raised his glass. Perry wrapped his arm around me.

"To justice."

"To getting them."

"Phenomenal job."

"Can you imagine, she uses the Jag as her screensaver…"

"Calls it her lifesaver."

"And she hacked just about everyone in Texas."

"Richard is livid."

The networks were repeating their spiel, so we turned the sound down and talked about the real story until late into the night. When "the boys" went to bed, Perry and I retired to his terrace above Dallas, too wound up to sleep. A soft breeze sent lovely wafts of jasmine our way. Curious where they were coming from, I followed the fragrance and discovered two pots planted with jasmine bushes. Delighted, I put my nose in them.

Perry had laughed and hugged me. "I know you love them, Lexi. That's why I planted them here…" We'd kissed, TW temporarily forgotten.

Being with Perry and his guys felt so natural, so right, so soothing… I was grateful for that. Their kindness gave me the strength to handle the aftermath of TW. Last night we celebrated justice being done, this morning brought a sobering mix of victory and sadness.

Vivien's casualties were too heartbreaking. Someone shared a video of Vivien's arrest with the media who played it over and over, crushingly humiliating Jen and Victor. In my whole life I had never wished more intensely to eat my cake and have it too. I wanted Vivien and her criminal gang being taken out of commission but without destroying the lives of innocent family members. I wished I could somehow protect the kids from this misery, but it was as impossible as stopping the earth from turning. Once your path crossed with Vivien's, getting hurt was inevitable.

My Collin-phone rang. Perry's too.

"Good to have you both on. Are you ready for a briefing?" Collin sounded tense.

"Yes," we both answered. "Is everything OK?" I asked, doom scenarios racing through my mind. Did someone escape? Did they have to let them go because of some technicality?

"Yes. We need you to go through some evidence and wrap things up."

I wasn't convinced. Something in Collin's voice alarmed me. I looked at Perry. He heard it too. We hugged.

"You know, today is the first anniversary of our first touch," Perry whispered in my ear.

"I wanted to toast our first touch this evening, but you beat me to it," I said, delighted that Perry remembered.

"Close your eyes, Lexi."

Perry put something on my wrist. "Open."

A marvelous emerald bracelet. "Awww...exquisite."

"Just like you." Perry grinned. "I had it made after our terrible lunch and wanted to put it on your arm today because that's where I first touched you... You had your muddy gloves on, remember?"

"How could I forget?" I kissed Perry, deeply moved, wishing the moment would never end. We hugged, holding on to each other, collecting our strength.

"I wonder what the briefing is all about," I finally said.

"Whatever it is, we'll handle it Lexi. Together." Perry winked.

"Yes. As one," I said with conviction, but my heart broke into a wild gallop.

Dallas

The War Room
One hour later

The strategists were all present, but I didn't see any of the computer whizzes. Crunching the new data, I guessed. Everyone looked relaxed, including Collin. I must have misinterpreted the ominous tone in his voice. But Perry heard it too...

We hadn't said much since we left Perry's place. Just held hands, worried that something would go wrong at the last minute and the nightmare would start all over again.

"C'mon Collin. Give us the latest count."

"Hear, hear." The team demanded information.

"We've got them. Singing like birds." Collin gave a tiny smile, but the triumph in his eyes told it all. Mission accomplished. Everyone applauded.

"Let's take it from the time Alex and Perry left Saint Crooks." Collin looked at his notes. "Marty voluntarily turned himself in."

I wasn't surprised.

"He gave us an extensive statement, which included a couple of developments we weren't aware of." Collin looked at me. "Moreover, Marty feels that his negligence bankrupted Carter & Co and indirectly killed Jack. Nonetheless, we have no case against Marty. He helped Vivien set up her accounts, but that's not illegal in itself."

I felt relieved. Marty seemed to have been punished enough already.

"Marty wants to pay back the money Carter & Co lost because he didn't pay attention."

"How do we know he is going to pay us back with legal money?" I asked.

"He is on the Crooks Islands legally. Is not hiding accounts or evading taxes. Has a legitimate business."

Perry sighed.

"Our agency deals with crimes, Perry," Collin quipped. "We leave ethics to politicians."

Everyone laughed and chatted about the money transfer and the press release Marty sent in Vivien's name.

Collin tapped his water glass with a pen.

"As you all know, we arrested our three main suspects yesterday afternoon: Ralph Gibson, also known as Rough Ralph, in the Art Tower; Vivien Gibson in the Obsidian; and Ted Gibson in his office in Houston. Further, we got two more suspects in Dallas and one in Houston. All suspects are in custody, being interviewed by our teams."

Perry squeezed my hand.

"Our lawyers are confident we have enough evidence to put the Gibson trio away for a long time. They are talking multiple first degree felony charges." Collin turned towards me and Perry. "That's five to ninety-nine years in prison."

I gasped. I didn't expect Vivien to go to prison. I hoped to get solid proof of what Vivien had done to Carter & Co, evidence strong enough to clear me of any wrongdoing. I wanted a chance to rehabilitate Carter & Co and stop Vivien's assaults. I assumed her lawyers would get her off, but multiple five to ninety-nine? What would this do to Jen and Victor?

"All three of them?" I asked.

"Yes. Just the larceny would be sufficient, but we have much more on them. Racketeering, mail and wire fraud, you name it. And all three suspects are wanted regarding a felony hit and run in Houston."

I looked at Perry. Head down, biting his lips. I took his hand in both of mine.

"We thought that would be the most difficult crime to solve because it happened such a long time ago, and we didn't have any physical evidence," Collin said softly.

"The good news is that our detainees effectively narrowed the field of suspects to three people: themselves. Namely, Vivien blames the accident on Ralph, Ralph on Ted, and Ted on Vivien. All three of them admitted being in the Jaguar at the time of the accident."

Perry looked up.

"And Senator Lowell?"

"Senator Lowell is not a suspect in the hit and run. He never knew about the meeting."

Perry sat back and closed his eyes. Our fingers interlaced. This is what Perry prayed for: that his dad hadn't killed his mom.

"We will get to the bottom of this, Perry. The Gibsons are trying to incriminate one another now because each of them still believes they can get out of this scot-free. But as we present them with more evidence, at least one of them will break and tell the truth."

"I appreciate that." Perry nodded. "Justice must take its course. But personally I hold all three of them responsible. They were there, they knew what happened. They didn't do the right thing."

"And they went on with not doing the right thing."

Collin's phone rang.

"Let me take this."

He frowned and walked out of the room.

Dallas

The War Room

Collin walked back in the War Room, his face unreadable.

I took a deep breath and looked at Perry. Could the same thing happen again? Collin had almost got Ralph Gibson into custody several years ago, but someone on the inside had betrayed the operation, Ralph had slipped through and disappeared. Collin never discovered the traitor...

I lived with the fear of being betrayed since Trey and Carl's party, when Collin told me about Ralph and swore me to secrecy...

"Pay attention, y'all." Collin tapped the water glass again.

"We've got six new arrests. Two here in the Dallas area. Three in Austin and one in Houston. All thanks to the information we extracted from Vivien's Little Fella and her phone." Applause filled the room.

"One person from the Houston faction escaped. We are investigating what happened." Collin's face tightened. I wondered how dangerous this person was.

"Now, back to the leader of this tight little unit." Collin switched subjects. "We've confirmed that Ralph Gibson is indeed the same person as Dylan the caterer. Which verified our information that Ralph underwent substantial plastic surgery to alter his looks. The work was done by a Brazilian surgeon who died in a suspicious boating accident shortly afterwards. That's not all. Ralph is also Hugh Donaldson. We expect more personas to emerge."

"Hugh Donaldson?" Perry asked. "The same..."

"Yes, the same Hugh who scammed Vivien. With Ted's help," Collin answered. "They are one happy family."

"In any event, we got Ralph in flagrante delicto, red-handed, caught with his pants down." A tiny smile played around Collin's mouth.

This is what I was hired for. To help Collin and his team trap Ralph Gibson, Vivien's beloved uncle. Swindler, scammer, cheater, hacker, possibly a killer, and a guy who wanted to hack voting machines in Texas and take over the state.

I became a candidate for the job because Trey found Ralph's unique code in my computer and told Collin about it. Collin's team had been after Ralph for years, without much success. Vivien's hacking expeditions to my accounts helped them latch on to her and get closer to Ralph, but he was as slippery as an eel, retreating behind his impenetrable firewall before they could catch him. Until Vivien's greed trapped him. With the help of OMG Insurance.

"Ralph didn't anticipate being caught," Collin continued. "We found the blueprint of his coup in "Dylan's" apartment, out in the open. Places, dates, strategies, you name it. His contacts read like who's who in the world of international crime and terrorism."

I shivered, hoping that Ralph would never get out of prison. "You helped get him there," a tiny voice comforted me.

"We also found Ralph's blacklist. It looks like nobody who ever crossed him was spared. It's a very long list of people, their 'crimes' and 'punishment.' Our psychologists will be busy for years studying this stuff. He didn't want to kill these people. Just torture them."

My stomach turned.

"Ralph gave only one person on his list a death sentence." Collin took a dramatic pause. "Vivien Gibson."

I gasped.

"Thus arresting her saved her life," I said.

"Yes."

That made me feel better.

"And speaking of Vivien Gibson. Yesterday she kept repeating that she has done nothing wrong, that we should go after you, Alex, because you framed her."

"I guess all of Dallas knows that," I said. The guys laughed. I didn't. I wanted to clear my name.

"In that case, all of Dallas must reconsider because Vivien changed her story this morning, after we convinced her that it's Ralph who framed her. She lost it when it dawned on her that she paid 2.4 million dollars to Ralph posing as Hugh Donaldson. Now she blames everything on him."

"She'll lie her way from here to hell," Perry said. "But, besides stealing the money from Carter & Co, is there enough conclusive evidence against her?"

"We are not through it all yet, but the answer is yes already. The evidence on Little Fella shows that she originated many of their activities and demanded that Ralph provide her with hacking programs."

Collin checked his phone.

"And we've just got more evidence." Collin nodded at Perry. "Just like Rough Ralph, Vivien didn't expect our visit. There was evidence in plain view all over her bedroom. It's a developing story, so I'll mention just two pieces now. We've found the notebook she presumably used for faking Jack's last will. The lab is analyzing it. The second piece is this phone." Collin projected a picture of it on one of the screens.

The image knocked the air out of me.

Change of venue. Had to fly to Lukla urgently.
Will meet you there at 12:15 p.m. Richard

Will be in Lukla at 11:30 on SW 122

The second text was from Jack.

My hands were shaking. Did Vivien send Jack to Lukla?

Perry took my hand. "One," he mouthed. "One," I mouthed back.

"The phone belongs to Lauren Gibson." I heard Collin's voice from a great distance. "She had reported it lost on the day this message was sent. *Before* the message was sent. Lauren remembers the day clearly because losing the phone almost cost her a role in a miniseries. Vivien had paid Lauren an unexpected visit that day, and the phone was missing after she'd left."

It was difficult to imagine that the sun was shining outside, people were having fun, went about their business, loved one another. Can I ever be part of it again?

"As you know, Lauren Gibson cooperated with the police on the trespassing charge." Collin looked at me. "But at that time she didn't elaborate on the 'you are a killer' accusation. I've just learned that she said a few words about it after we questioned her about the phone."

Perry drew his breath in.

Collin consulted his phone.

"Here it is: 'My sister Vivien told me that she hit a woman in front of the Houston Regent hotel and drove away.'" Collin looked up. "Lauren didn't bring this up earlier because Vivien was intoxicated when she told

THE WALL

her the story and Lauren couldn't believe it was true. But all the details Lauren mentioned are consistent with the hit and run."

Perry closed his eyes. I held his hand gently, my heart crying for him and his mom.

Vivien! All these years, Vivien got away with murder. Literally. I swallowed hard. This was too much.

"We have one more piece of key evidence," Collin said before I had a chance to absorb the enormity of Lauren's revelation.

"It's a video recorded one day after the plane crash in Nepal." The ominous undertone was back in Collin's voice. My heart took off as if racing for the Triple Crown. Collin stepped closer to me.

"This material is very sensitive, Alex. You may choose to view it alone." This must be bad. The pity in Collin's eyes told volumes.

I am not a victim! "No, thank you. I'll view it here."

Perry looked up and squeezed my hand.

Collin pointed to a screen on the wall. The video started. A man was sitting on a rattan couch, next to a bamboo plant in a large Nepali pot. A Casablanca fan slowly turned above his head.

The man was Jack.

Dallas

The War Room
June 8

"My name is Jack Carter. I am here to report a crime." Jack's melodious baritone resonated through the silent War Room. Perry tensed. Our eyes met.

Is Jack still alive?

The camera zoomed in on Jack's face. Exhausted eyes eclipsed by dark bags, hollow cheeks, bitter mouth taken hostage by deep grooves, lackluster hair. A broken man.

Looking down, Jack told how he found out about the financial irregularities and tried to undo what Vivien had done. Every now and then he picked up his phone, looked at the screen, and put the phone down.

I took in Jack's every word, but all I could think of was that when the kids I and were in Pokhara and Kathmandu, heartbroken, raw, frantically piecing together what had happened to Jack, he was alive. Just one text away. I couldn't get out of my mind that he must have seen all our texts, messages, emails. Our despair.

My heart cringed.

"Vivien, my first wife, admitted to me that she took money from Carter & Co, but I can't believe she could have done it on her own. She was never computer savvy." Jack paused for a second and took a deep breath. "At first I suspected Marty Watson, my CFO. Ex-CFO. But Marty had no access to the system when the bulk of the money was stolen," Jack explained.

Collin stopped the video.

"To make a long story short, Jack concluded that Rough Ralph must have been helping Vivien. Moreover, he also noticed that the text about moving the meeting to Lukla came from an unknown number, and neither Perry nor Senator Howard confirmed Jack's reply. So, at the last moment he hadn't boarded the flight to Lukla but called his old contact in our agency instead."

"Jack had...has a contact..." My voice broke before I could finish my question.

"Had. The man's retired. But he came back to talk with Jack because Jack wouldn't trust anyone else. You see, Jack had worked with us to trap Ralph years ago. Jack reported Ralph because he thought that Ralph was using Vivien to trick people into signing up for one of his financial scams. We found out that Ralph wasn't Vivien's uncle. He was adopted. And was Vivien's lover for years. Ralph and Vivien had plans to leave Dallas together, but Ralph ran away and left Vivien behind. Vivien didn't seem to have any contact with Ralph after the failed operation, and Jack believed that Ralph was gone for good. Jack even used the evidence of Vivien's affair with Ralph to divorce her. But in the spring of last year he began to suspect that Ralph was back."

And never told me anything. I could understand that Jack didn't want to talk about Ralph. After all, I didn't share TW with him either. Yet, Jack knew what Vivien was all about and protected her anyhow. Let me struggle, called me paranoid, even blamed me for some of the troubles.

Something snapped in my heart. I felt Jack floating away, as if the thread that connected us gave up, unable to withstand the tension. I'd been overwhelmed by the finality of the plane crash, the abrupt and absolute end of the life Jack and I had together. But that finality was nothing compared to what I felt now. Part of me will always be fond of Jack, but he and I could never be together again. My heart gave up on us.

"Jack thought that he would contact his guy, get the investigation started and go back to his business," Collin said. "But then the plane crashed and Jack's contact proposed they could use that to get to Ralph quicker. They were negotiating with Jack about protective custody, but he hesitated." Collin restarted the video.

"I want to go back to my family, I want to fix my business," Jack said, despair taking over his face. "But as long as Ralph is on the loose, we will not have a life. He'll go after us one by one."

I shivered. Snippets of bigger and smaller events flew through my mind, lining up and forming a coherent picture. A lot of it made sense now, except one thing: why didn't Jack share what was going on? And why didn't he contact his man at the agency earlier?

At least Jack wanted to protect us from Ralph. I was thankful for that. But by disappearing and leaving such a mess behind, he left us exposed to Vivien and Ralph. Without warning. Without protection.

Perry shifted in his chair.

"Where is Jack now?" I asked.

"In Nepal." Collin took a deep breath. "We didn't learn that Jack was alive until almost two weeks after the crash because his contact worked for another branch of the agency and didn't know about TW. When we found out, one of our people immediately flew to Kathmandu to talk with him." Collin looked at me gently. "But found Jack dead in his room."

I gasped. "How?" I managed to ask.

"Abdominal aortic aneurysm."

A shiver ran through me. Just like Nicole's dad. Excruciatingly painful but fast death.

"I am sorry, Alex. Nothing could have been done." Collin's voice caught.

"I know," I said. "It wasn't to be."

Perry gently put his arm around my shoulders.

I knew Perry and I would talk about all this later, in the peace of Perry's terrace. Dallas sparkling in front of us, lovely jasmine wafting in the air, we would go through all the events that couldn't be mended and put them to rest.

For now, I took solace in the fact that my and Jack's actions in the months leading to the crash hadn't led to Jack's death. It hadn't mattered that we didn't get the financial audit done, that Jack hadn't contacted his man at the agency earlier, that I hadn't gone to Delhi with Jack. Jack's aneurysm was a ticking bomb ready to blow us apart.

Jack and I weren't meant to be, but, for better or for worse, our short union had real consequences.

I took a deep breath, momentarily overcome by a glimpse into the eternal game of chances and choices, at times playfully attracting one another without much ado, at times colliding like billiard balls and causing turns of fate. Never stopping, never redoing a play.

I'll never know what would have happened had I gone to Dubai first.

Would Vivien and Ralph be brought to justice if I hadn't married Jack and Vivien hadn't left traces of Ralph's programs in my computer?

Would Hannah have become a rising star in the architectural world if we hadn't had to fight for Carter & Co?

Would I still be climbing my "mountain," hoping that the perfect life awaited me on the top?

Would Perry and I have found the courage to embrace our love?

I'd never know.

Life rolls on in one take, we can't go back and reshoot the alternate paths. Every second counts.

And every second is a marvelous opportunity to be.

Epilogue

Washington DC
Walter E. Washington Convention Center
January 20 (nineteen months later)

Perry looked at Lexi and gently squeezed her hand. She smiled and gave him the loving look reserved only for him. Not that long ago, Perry would have killed for one of these looks. He softly kissed the side of her cheek and caught a whiff of her perfume. She pressed herself lightly against him and squeezed his hand back. As always, his body responded with a wave of love.

Perry's mind slipped back to the first time he touched Lexi. It seemed like ages ago, but Perry still felt the heat of that particularly sweltering Dallas day. He had run into his college friend Victor, and they had ended up visiting Victor's dad to put an old disagreement to rest. Victor was mixing Mint Juleps for them but got sidetracked by an urgent phone call. Not wanting to intrude, Perry wandered out to the lovely garden. A lithe woman in cut-off jeans was digging a hole for a giant Texas hibiscus, her perfectly oval face framed by unruly dark auburn curls. She looked up and lifted her muddied hands.

Hands he had many times since released from their gardening gloves, to retrieve perfectly manicured fingers waiting to be kissed. But at that moment he had been limited to watching this exquisite creature swipe sweat from her forehead. A narrow smudge of dirt appeared near her hairline. His fingers itched to remove it.

"Perry… What a surprise! Glad to meet you. Finally."

Her French r's rolled languidly over her tongue. He longed to put his lips on hers. Their eyes locked, silent messages running back and forth with the speed of light.

"I will not shake your hand now. Sorry…too muddy." She smiled apologetically and lifted her hands again to prove her point. Dimples played next to her lips. Perry laughed and spontaneously squeezed her naked forearms.

A wave of tingles swept through him. Perry held Lexi's widened eyes, smitten. He knew right there and then that they were meant for each other.

"Oh, you two have met already." Victor came out and set their drinks on a large garden table.

"Alex, this is Perry. You know, the guy who makes rooms talk and fridges walk. Perry, meet my stepmom Alex, as delectable and sweaty as she can be."

Golden bells of laughter flew from her lips, resonated in Perry's ears, and sent waves of yearning through him.

Now, less than three years later, Perry still felt the intensity of that moment. He looked at Lexi again. Resplendent in a deeply cut, midnight blue gown, dark auburn curls regally tied up. Triple drop emerald earrings followed the exquisite line of her neck, exactly as Perry designed them.

"Get ready, please." The steward ushered them closer to the stage where Richard and Liz danced their first solo waltz as President and First Lady.

Lexi squeezed Perry's hand and sent him one of her irresistible radiant smiles. Her necklace fired a salvo of sparks. Perry followed the knotted diamond chain to Lexi's cleavage, where two large emeralds dangled on the chain's loose ends. Naughty emeralds, she nicknamed them.

Perry allowed himself to rejoice in the moment. He had flown over oceans and crossed continents to be with Lexi. Now she was his wife, for the whole world to see.

"Go!" The steward sent them on the stage to join Richard and Liz.

"Ladies and gentlemen, Vice President and Mrs. Lowell!"

Note to Readers

Thank you for reading *The Wall*. If you enjoyed it, would you be willing to spare a few minutes and give me a review on Amazon? I learn a lot from reviews, and it's wonderful to connect with readers after so many hours of solitary writing… The review doesn't have to be fancy or long, just a few words, one or two sentences… It would mean the world to me. Thank you!

Acknowledgments

My heartfelt thanks to:

Alina, for generously editing the first draft. Your kindness and encouragement mean the world to me.

Lynn, Terry, and Carl, for reading the first draft. Your insightful remarks gave me valuable and much appreciated feedback.

Charlie, for sharing with me writing strategies and your sixth sense for spotting superfluous text.

Steve (GFX-1), for pouring your creativity into the cover design.

Robin Samuels (the Artful Editor), for being a magnificent proofreader. Your detail-obsessed heart is just what the doctor ordered. Needless to say, any blemishes in the text are solely my responsibility.

And last but not least, C, my husband, best friend, and wonderful partner. Thank you for your faith in my ability to write a novel. And for the most delightful and inspiring breakfasts…

About the Author

I.C. Cosmos loves storytelling and dreamed of being a writer since as far back as she can remember. Before turning to writing fiction, she was a business consultant, a director of an expertise center for forensic psychiatry, and (co-)authored numerous scientific and non-fiction publications. Her debut novel, The Wall, is the first book in a series of thrillers featuring Alex Demarchelier.

I.C. and her husband live in Texas.

https://iccosmos.com/

https://iccosmos.com/

Facebook: https://bit.ly/2IpLXkN